MASTER OF WAR
VIPER'S
✝
BLOOD

DAVID GILMAN

HEAD
ZEUS

First published in the UK in 2017 by Head of Zeus Ltd

This paperback edition first published in 2017 by Head of Zeus Ltd

9 7 5 3 1 2 4 6 8

A CIP catalogue record for this book is available from
the British Library.

ISBN (PB) 9781784974480
ISBN (E) 9781784974459

Typeset by Ben Cracknell Studios, Norwich

Head of Zeus Ltd
First Floor East
4–8 Hardwick Street
London EC1R 4RG
WWW.HEADOFZEUS.COM

VIPER'S
+
BLOOD

DAVID GILMAN enjoyed many careers
– including firefighter, soldier and photographer –
before turning to writing full-time. He is an
award-winning author and screenwriter.

www.davidgilman.com
www.facebook.com/davidgilman.author

For Suzy

Everywhere was grief, destruction and desolation, uncultivated fields filled with weeds, ruined and abandoned houses… In short wherever I looked were the scars of defeat. The ruins go right up to the gates of Paris.

The Italian poet Petrarch travelling through
France after the English army's passage

CHARACTER LIST

*Sir Thomas Blackstone
*Henry: Blackstone's son
*William de Sainteny, child born from Christiana Blackstone's
    rape

THOMAS BLACKSTONE'S MEN
*Sir Gilbert Killbere
*Gaillard: Norman captain
*Meulon: Norman captain
*John Jacob: captain
*Perinne: wall builder and soldier
*Renfred: German man-at-arms and captain
*Will Longdon: centenar and veteran archer
*Jack Halfpenny: ventenar and archer
*Robert Thurgood: archer
*Collard: man-at-arms
*Elfred: master of archers who commands Blackstone's men in
    Italy

FRENCH NOBLEMEN AND MEN-AT-ARMS
*Bernard de Chauliac: captain of the French royal guard
Gaucher de Châtillon: Lord of Troissy, Captain of Rheims
*Philippe Bonnet: brigand
*Grimo the Breton: brigand leader
*Sir Louis de Joigny: commander of Cormiers
Robert de Fiennes: Constable of France

Simon Bucy: Counsellor to the Price Regent
Jean de Neuville: nobleman who led invasion of England
*Paul de Venette: brigand and citizen of Paris
Count of Tancarville: French hostage in England
Jean de Dormans: French Chancellor

ENGLISH NOBLEMEN, KNIGHTS AND SQUIRES
Henry of Grosmont, Duke of Lancaster
Earls of Northampton, Warwick and Suffolk
Sir Reginald Cobham
Bartholomew Burghesh: King Edward's Chamberlain
Sir Walter Mauny
Sir John Chandos
Sir Richard Baskerville
*Sir Oswald de Chambres
*Sir Walter Pegyn: Duke of Lancaster's knight

ENGLISH ROYAL FAMILY
King Edward III of England
Edward of Woodstock, Prince of Wales

FRENCH ROYAL FAMILY
King John II (the Good) of France
The Dauphin Charles: King John's son and heir
Princess Isabelle de Valois: King John's daughter

ITALIAN AND TRANSALPINE NOBLEMEN, KNIGHTS, CLERICS AND SERVANTS
Galeazzo Visconti: ruler of Milan
Bernabò Visconti: ruler of Milan
*Antonio Lorenz: Bernabò Visconti's illegitimate son
Count Amadeus VI of Savoy
*Girard Goncenin: feral child
Marquis de Montferrat: Piedmontese nobleman, enemy of the Visconti and Amadeus

*Niccolò Torellini: Florentine priest
*Fra Pietro Foresti: Knight of the Tau

FRENCH CLERICS, OFFICIALS AND SERVANTS:
Abbot of Cluny: Pope Innocent VI's delegate to King Edward
    and the Dauphin
Simon of Langres: Dominican monk and papal delegate
Hugh of Geneva: papal delegate
*Clarimonde: lady-in-waiting to Princess Isabelle de Valois
*Cataline: Clarimonde's daughter

CITIZENS OF BALON:
*Malatrait: mayor
*Aelis de Travaux: healer
*Jean Agillot: barber
*Madeleine Agillot: the barber's wife
*Etienne Chardon: blacksmith
*Petrus Gavray: furrier
*Charles Pyvain: cobbler
*Stephanus Louchart: pardoner

* Indicates fictional characters

1360

FROM RHEIMS TO MILAN

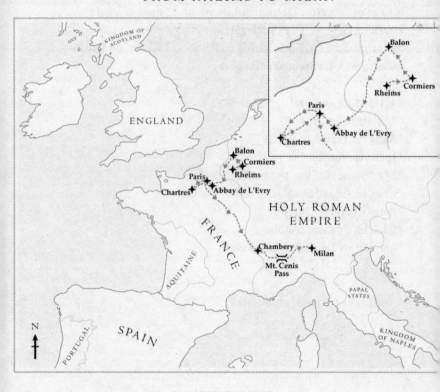

BLACKSTONE'S ROUTE --▸--

PART ONE

TO SEIZE A CROWN

France 1360

CHAPTER ONE

Thomas Blackstone spat blood.

The axe-wielding Frenchman's blow missed his open helm but the fist clutching the axe slammed into his face. Blackstone's height and strength carried him past the assault into the hacking mêlée as John Jacob, a pace behind, rammed his blade beneath the man's armpit. The snarling roar of close-quarter battle mingled with the screams of mutilated men. Blood and entrails squelched underfoot as the city's defenders fell beneath English violence. Step by step Blackstone and his men fought their way through the defensive ditches that had been dug around the city of Rheims. The walls were higher than heaven. Men died in their shadow, cast down into bloodstained mud. Some who fought cursed the cold and the rain, and some the King of England, who had brought his host of ten thousand men to this place of death. Sweat stung Blackstone's eyes as he carved a path towards the Prince of Wales, the man he was sworn to protect and who was in the vanguard of the battle. Two of Blackstone's captains, Gaillard and Meulon, huge bears of men who matched Blackstone's size and strength, flanked the Englishman they had served these past fourteen years. Their spears thrust into the terrified French, some of whom were city militia who had never experienced the surging terror that now befell them.

Blackstone saw the Prince wheel, his shield slamming down a French knight. The man raised his visor and cried out, but his voice was swept away in the bellowing cacophony. His gesture was one of surrender. The Prince hesitated, but the weight of men around him forced him across the fallen man as Meulon leaned forward and pushed his spear into the man's face. The Frenchman's hands desperately snatched at the steel; his body bucked. Meulon wrenched the blade free; the man was already dead. Blackstone trod on his chest, unconcerned at the spume of blood that splattered his legs. He reached the Prince who, despite being flanked by his retinue, cleaved a path towards the city gates. For the past thirty-three days of the siege no one had expected such resistance from the walled city's defenders; no one had believed that the winter rain could be so persistent; and only Blackstone believed that King Edward III in his pursuit of the French crown had made a foolish mistake in trying to take the city whose guardian, the nobleman Gaucher de Châtillon, had fortified the walls, blocked the drawbridges and dug defensive ditches. Ditches that Blackstone and his men had fought through for the past two days, and whose quagmire sucked men's legs and sapped strength. Two days of half-starved fighting so that the English King could seize the city that traditionally crowned every King of France. New Year had passed but Edward wanted that crown.

'My Prince!' Blackstone yelled as the King's son slipped. He leapt forward, slamming his shield into mail-clad footsoldiers, forcing himself between fighters who had poured from the city gates wild with fear and determination to stop the vile English horde from advancing and thinking that they might seize Edward's son. The sight of the Prince falling to his knees gave them renewed courage but then they saw the shield bearing Blackstone's blazon: the mailed fist clasping the sword blade. Its cruciform and declaration, *Défiant à la mort*, heralded death and made them falter. To stand against the renowned Englishman whose very name was enough to make men surrender before his violence was unleashed was an invitation few would accept. But the weight of those behind pushed them forward. Frenzy ruled the day; blood-lust defeated fear. They fell on Blackstone. His shield took the blows of mace and sword as he half bent his body, turning their blows away and thrusting with killing jabs of Wolf Sword's hardened steel. As he spun around he caught sight of the Prince of Wales vomiting. He spewed across his own men and those who lay dead and dying at

4

his feet. A banner dipped as willing hands reached for him. Rich food and plenty of it! Blackstone thought derisively. A king's table groaning with succulent cuts and rich sauces. A sight he and his men would never see, let alone share. Most of the troops were starving. Man and horse had been deprived of supplies as the French burned food stores ahead of the English advance and the flooded rivers ran with waste, poisoned by slaughtered carcasses. Deny the English invaders supplies and they will be defeated had been the Dauphin's command. A worthless son of a worthless French King in a worthless land in a worthless war. For Christ's sake! What were they dying for in this country? In this ditch?

Blackstone backhanded Wolf Sword's pommel into a French-man's face contorted with hatred and purpose; then he rammed the rim of his shield beneath the chin of another. He shifted his weight, allowed a strike against him, saw the man stumble past, left him to die beneath John Jacob's sword and then surrendered to the blood haze that filled his mind and softened the roar of the battle. He was cocooned in the place he knew well. Now the killing rage was with him again; his instinct to kill and maim enveloped him like a rising tide and swept him along, a warring demon blessed by the angels. Beneath the rolling clouds that brought the swirling curtains of rain, a darker storm swept across the battlements. English archers laid a deluge of arrows onto the city walls. Blackstone saw the bowmen in his mind's eye, felt their effort in his heart. *Nock, draw, loose!* Sheaves of arrows carried by pages and anyone else ordered to feed the greatest weapon in the King's army would be borne relentlessly to the thousands of archers. Will Longdon would be in the sawtooth line with his men, Jack Halfpenny, Robert Thurgood: men who had fought and suffered with Thomas Blackstone. All of them had swept across France during the years of war, back and forth to Italy where Blackstone and his men defended the road to Florence until finally returning to France a year before last. It was there an Italian assassin had ripped away Blackstone's heart by slaying his wife and child.

Blackstone led the assault as the English swarmed forward under cover of the arrows that kept the wall's defenders' heads down. Two wooden assault towers were pushed and pulled towards the battlements as carpenters and engineers dragged cut trees and building timber forward across the defences, using them to breach the earthworks and get closer to the five city gates that had not yet been boarded up. Three divisions had assaulted the city, swarming around its walls like wolves bearing down on a beast of prey. The Duke of Lancaster had attacked from the north, the Earl of March from the east, Richmond and Northampton from the north-west, but it was Blackstone's men fighting with the Prince of Wales's division from the south-west who had made the most progress. The defenders, however, had taken their toll. Frenchmen had made sorties to block the ditches and fight viciously while others on the walls defied the arrows and used machines behind the city walls to rain down rocks on the attackers. Apart from the Prince's division, the English were being held, dying where they stood: only Edward's men were making ground, forcing a wedge through the enemy ground troops in a thirty-foot causeway across the ditch on the western side of the city. They fought shoulder to shoulder, spit and blood and men's waste staining the ground and the stench of death and shit fouling the cold air.

Despite the rain, choking smoke swirled down the narrow confines of the ditches as the French fighters set the timber fillings alight. Men struggled from one smothering cloud to another, eyes stinging from the smoke as sudden death loomed unexpectedly from the miasma. Blackstone and his men slithered down into another ditch; he glanced up and saw the man who had first taken him to war, who had rallied the English at Crécy against overwhelming odds and who, with Blackstone at his side, had held the gap in the hedgerow at Poitiers years later when the French cavalry tried to crush them. Sir Gilbert Killbere liked nothing better than killing Frenchmen. He yearned for it. Grieved for its loss when fighting in Italy and relished the skill it took to defeat a blood enemy. Now he led a determined group of men against

6

those who had set fire to the timbers, raising his shield above his head as another shower of rocks fell from the sky. Blackstone, Meulon and Gaillard brought their shields together and rammed back half a dozen militia, behind whom were the noblemen who urged their men on, but the city soldiers were no match for the savagery that was being inflicted on them. The Prince's men, now led by Blackstone, edged forward yard by yard, sword and spear length at a time. If those burning timbers could be dragged to the closed gate Blackstone knew they would have a fighting chance of entering the city.

He turned away from the raised swords and axes of those who opposed him and changed direction, taking them by surprise. Forty men or more turned with him; there were still enough behind them to hold the ditch.

'Gilbert! The fire! We use it!'

Killbere looked as fatigued as every other man. His raised visor exposed a soot-streaked face. Sweat, rain and blood trickled down his forehead from an earlier wound. He turned his back, shouted a command and the soldiers with him formed a phalanx ready to cut a wound into the Frenchmen. Blackstone, Meulon and Gaillard took the weight of one of the long timbers onto their shoulders. It was burning at one end from pitch that billowed black smoke. With the fire behind them they dragged the wooden beam forward. Blackstone would burn the bastards out, provided he and the others survived long enough to stack burning timbers and beams at those gates. The wind changed; flames threatened to lick their backs. Meulon cursed and Blackstone shifted his shield further onto his back. He altered course and tried to get the wind at an angle. For a moment it worked. The flames were subdued into acrid smoke that screened them from the Frenchmen who were now swarming forward from the ditches into the dense smoke to assault Killbere and his men.

Killbere strode forward. Two, three long strides, shield up, the blood knot from his sword biting beneath his gauntlet. An indistinct bellowing roar rose above the clash of steel and flesh as his men vented their determination to kill. They would protect Thomas Blackstone – or die rather than face the shame of life should they fail.

The gods of war favour the bold, but the King of England favoured their lives even more. As Blackstone got within 150 paces of the gate trumpets heralded the retreat. Their bright notes soared across the battlefield, their command distinct and unquestionable.

Blackstone half turned and saw the look of disbelief and disgust on Killbere's face as the repeated demands made him falter. It gave the French the chance to retreat.

'A pig's arse!' shouted Killbere and waved his sword, urging Blackstone on. The three men hauled the timber up the slope; Blackstone fell to his knees in the mud, cursed and let his anger give strength to his muscles. He was defying his King. Again. The last time – when he tried to kill the French King at Poitiers – he had suffered exile, but on this occasion he would claim that the noise of battle had deafened him to King Edward's command. Others broke rank and tried to help Blackstone heave the rain-sodden timber forward. The pitch would flare again with a good strike of a flint and something dry to kindle the flames. But there was nothing dry. Man and ground were soaked, their breath billowing, steam rising from their bodies as the heat of sweat met the cold air. The men's extra strength gave Blackstone and the others the power to move forward as Killbere fought on one flank and John Jacob rallied men on the other. Blackstone watched his hardened captain methodically strike down those who stood in his path, cutting a way open for Blackstone to get the timber in place. Blackstone glanced back. Others had followed their example, dragging and heaving burning tree trunks and dismantled bridge supports towards the one gate that might yield them the city. Then Edward could have his crown and they could all go home.

Closer now. Eighty paces. Eighty strides of muscle-tearing effort. The trumpets blared again. Signal flags punctuated the King's demand. *Retreat!* The French would not yield a damned yard and the mud slowed the attackers. More Englishmen fell. Crossbow bolts and stones continued to rain down. The English bowmen had stopped releasing their yard-long shafts: the bodkin points no longer tore through French flesh. The King had commanded it and now Blackstone's men were exposed and abandoned. They were too few. Blackstone saw at once that even if they reached the high gate they would die beneath the walls. He swung his shield around and let the timber go. Killbere knew it as well. They had tried and failed. Had more men stayed at their back they might have had a chance. Killbere spat and let his sword dangle from its blood knot around his wrist as he put a finger to each nostril and blew clear the snot. And then in an act of sheer disdain he turned his back on his enemy and trudged back towards the English lines.

Blackstone laughed. The battle-hardened Killbere was the same age as the King. His forty-seven years had made him despise death more than he hated the French.

'All right,' Blackstone said. 'We've done enough here.'

The men hesitated, and then they too dropped their burdens. The French had not come forward, perhaps grateful that they did not have to face the ferocious assault any longer. Blackstone gazed up at the high walls shrouded in mist and smoke. King Edward might pursue the siege again but not today. He looked at his exhausted and wounded men. Some leaned on their weapons, others spat out the foul taste of death, most grinned. There was no shame. No one else had got as close.

CHAPTER TWO

Blackstone's meagre shelter offered little comfort from the cold and wet. The canvas dripped and the fire smouldered. There was no dry kindling. Blackstone watched men going among the badly wounded and killing them. Bodies were being dragged into a ditch so that their stench would soon be covered in a mass grave. The French did the same with their fallen. The King's retreat had become a truce to despatch the maimed and dying. It would not be long before peasants, wraiths from the forests, crept from cover and went among the dead to strip what they could from the corpses. English archers might kill them if they had enough arrows, but on a great expedition such as this would not waste missiles on grave robbers. The killing ground became a dream-like scene. The breeze swirled the grey drizzle around the peasants who bent like crows pecking at the dead; archers went forward to pluck arrows from the slain; and screams and moans rose and fell as knives were used to end men's agony.

Killbere stripped off his mail and undershirt and, ignoring the chilling drizzle, bathed a wound on his ribs. It was barely a hand's width in length and his sodden shirt had clung to it and stopped it from bleeding further, but once the fighting started again his efforts would open it. He smeared a thick pungent wax-like cream across his flank and allowed a grimace as the astringent ointment stung the raw flesh.

'I swear by a whore's tits that the monks are poisoning me. I gave them good coin for this after we were ambushed at Laon, and it stings like a flail. They said it was good for horses' wounds.'

Blackstone had pulled his mail free and let the sweat-soaked undershirt cling to him in the rain. The cold prickled his skin but his mind dismissed it. Best to embrace the weather rather than fight it. He reached into his saddle pannier and took out a roll of torn linen. 'You should have confessed your sins first and asked for absolution,' he said. 'Then they would have given you honey and herbs to dress your wounds and a cask of their best brandy to ease your pain.'

Killbere gave a nod towards the silver goddess that dangled from a cord around Blackstone's neck. Arianrhod. The Celtic goddess of the silver wheel was a pagan symbol pressed into Blackstone's hand by a dying Welsh archer when the young Englishman first went to war and fought at Caen. She protected a fighting man in this life and then carried him across to the next. 'Sweet Jesus, Thomas, when have you ever loved scab-arsed monks or priests? And when have I ever had the time to confess my sins? There's a war to be fought. You'll bind the damned thing for me?'

'If you sit still long enough.'

Killbere grunted with impatience and raised his arm so that Blackstone could wrap the linen around his ribs. 'Cold, wet and not a decent meal in days. The supply wagons stretch back God knows how many leagues, the horses are dying, the men are starving while the King is warm and fed, and all because the...' He winced. 'Jesus, Thomas, you're not swaddling a child, not so tight... all because King John has not paid his ransom. Why did we shed our blood at Poitiers for a captured King not to pay his debts? Am I a money-lender to royalty now? If he paid up we wouldn't be in this godforsaken mess. What good is it for Edward to take the French crown? Eh? Answer me that. A country laid bare, a bankrupt nation, as useful as a eunuch in a whorehouse.' He waved Blackstone away. 'All right, all right. That will do well enough.' He straightened his back and drew in breath. 'You crush my lungs. I'll cut it free when we go back to the walls.'

'I doubt the King will send us back soon. We lost too many men. Gilbert, you should take yourself off to the nearest nunnery and have them attend you. Only they would have the forbearance to put up with you.'

Killbere tugged his wet shirt back on and then a leather jerkin. 'Did I ever tell you about the nun I fell in love with?'

'Often,' said Blackstone and draped his own shirt over three sticks that had held the cooking pot above the flames when there had been fire. It would help ease the stench of sweat from the cloth but he would stink of woodsmoke like a cured ham.

Killbere found a piece of dried meat in a sack and squatted beneath the dripping canvas to eat it. 'Where's the boy?'

'He'll be here,' said Blackstone and let his eyes scan the hundreds of men huddled around their makeshift shelters, sitting in the smudge smoke of meagre fires. Further still, along the treeline and beyond, were thousands more. The King and his three sons had brought the might of England to teach the Dauphin a lesson in war and politics. An agreement had been made between Edward and King John, who had been captured at Poitiers just over three years before, who still sat in London as his prisoner. Lands were to be ceded; a massive ransom was to be paid. Neither had been forthcoming and the Dauphin and the Estates General had refused to acknowledge the treaty the two Kings had made. The world would have been a better place had Blackstone managed to kill the French King at Poitiers as he had sworn to do. The world, he thought, would have been better had death not then wielded its scythe against his family.

'He'll be here,' he said again, dismissing the horror that had befallen his wife and child from his mind.

Killbere grunted as he chewed the meat, and probed a maggot free with a fingernail. 'I have not mentioned it often. Of that I am certain.'

'What?'

'The nun!'

'You told me more than a year ago as we made our way down to Meaux.'

'Ah. As recently as that. Well, I apologize. I'm starting to chatter like a damned washerwoman.'

'There he is,' said Blackstone as he caught sight of his son, making his way through the encampment, a small sack slung over his shoulder that was seeping blood. Henry Blackstone served as John Jacob's page, the intention being that he would one day rise to squire under the man-at-arms's tutelage and the watchful eye of his father. Had Blackstone's wife lived she would have argued the case for the boy to continue his studies, not learn the art of war. But she had not lived and Blackstone now had his son at his side, but he honoured her memory and ensured the boy continued with his schooling too.

'Henry. Where's John Jacob?' said Blackstone. His son and his squire had been sent to check on Blackstone's men as had Meulon and Gaillard to check on theirs.

'My lord, he was summoned to the Prince,' the boy answered.

Killbere looked at Blackstone and pulled a face. No words were needed. Blackstone would hear bad news soon enough. Killbere stretched around. 'Boy, I hope you're not carrying French heads in that sack. I've sliced enough of those today.'

Henry dropped the sack and knelt down, reaching inside it. 'No, Sir Gilbert, they don't cook so well.' He lifted a piece of venison and smiled in triumph. 'Will Longdon shot a deer.'

'They'll flog him for poaching the King's game,' said Killbere. 'This is Edward's realm now.'

'No, Sir Gilbert. The sergeant-at-arms said that to Master Longdon but I told him he was wrong,' said Henry.

'By the dog's bollocks, you did not,' said Killbere.

'Son, what happened?' said Blackstone.

'Father, I hope I did not shame you but the sergeant was going to arrest Master Longdon until I told him that our sovereign lord had yet to be crowned. It's only the French King's deer,' said Henry.

Blackstone and Killbere were dumbfounded and then Killbere guffawed and laughed until a coughing fit and the pain in his side stopped him. 'Sweet Merciful God, Thomas, you've a wolf pup here who knows the law of the forest.' He grinned with pleasure. 'Henry, you are a credit to your father.'

The boy beamed but soon lowered his eyes at the stern glance from Blackstone. 'You challenged a sergeant-at-arms, Henry. You're a page not a squire. And you should bear your learning lightly. You risked shaming the man in front of the archers.'

'Yes, Father.'

'Will Longdon spoke up for you?'

'He did. He knew the man so they parted on good terms.' He raised his eyes and dared a grin. 'And I parted with this.' Henry wiped the blood from his hands on the sacking. 'Will said it ran in fear from the forest when the King's bombard went off. Said it ran right across the line of archers. Said it was a French deer showing disrespect for English archers.'

'And the rest of its carcass?' said Blackstone.

'Will's sharing it with as many of his archers as he can.'

'My mouth waters, boy,' said Killbere, 'but raw venison is hard to chew with my old teeth.'

Henry smiled and pulled out a wad of wood shavings. 'The carpenters were cutting timber.'

'Good lad!' said Killbere. He reached for his aketon and picked away a couple of stitches of the padded jacket with his knife. He tugged free some of the wool and gave it to the boy. 'Fire and food.'

'You checked my horse? He's fed?' said Blackstone.

'Yes, Father. They have him roped in a glade. They did as you instructed and kept him well away from the other horses.'

'No injuries?'

'Not to your horse, Father. One of the boys in the baggage train got too close and he kicked his leg. They say he won't walk again without a staff.'

'Serve him right. Everyone knows to keep clear of him.' Blackstone looked up at the clouds. 'It will blow clear for a while. Make haste, Henry. We'll save some for John for when he comes back.'

'You spoil your men, Thomas, I've always said it. Though I grant you John Jacob deserves to be treated well.'

'And Will Longdon, and Meulon and Gaillard and Jack Halfpenny, and Robert Thurgood and –'

'God's tears, Thomas. You cannot feed the five thousand… Yes, yes… them as well. Come on, Henry, do as your lord and father commands. All that killing has worked up my appetite.'

As the boy set about his task Blackstone's gaze ranged beyond the temptation of the venison and the promise of warmth that even a meagre fire would offer. John Jacob was making his way towards them through the scattered men and with him was one of the Prince's messengers.

More censure from the man he had sworn to protect? Blackstone wondered. Perhaps the sergeant-at-arms had not been so accommodating after all. The fire crackled into life; Henry laid the skillet on top. Whatever the messenger wanted, Blackstone could see by the scowling frown on John Jacob's face that it was not good news. Blackstone doubted he would get to enjoy the only fresh meat they had seen in days.

CHAPTER THREE

The Prince's encampment lay in Villedommange, a few miles from the city walls. From its rising ground the hamlet afforded the Prince a view of the plain before him. Blackstone strode ahead of the Prince's messenger; the only words he had uttered were that Sir Thomas Blackstone had been summoned. John Jacob had turned to accompany Blackstone as he picked his way through the resting troops, but his sworn lord insisted he stay with Killbere and Henry and eat the fresh meat that Will Longdon had supplied. Through the grey drizzle and mist Blackstone saw the pavilions of the Prince's retinue. A forest of pennons declared there were several bannerets and more than a hundred knights who fought close to the King's son. Their squires would number in the hundreds, and the fighting men would be reinforced by nearly a thousand mounted archers. The Prince's pavilion sat beneath his barely fluttering banner of Drago, the Welsh dragon that had rallied men at Crécy and Poitiers. The soaked material proclaimed the presence of one of the greatest fighting princes that England had produced. King Edward's three other younger sons, Lionel, John and Edmund, had embarked with him to earn their spurs as their father came to seize the French crown. Blackstone doubted whether any of them could ever match the fighting skills and bravery of their older brother. Edward of Woodstock was a great knight who relished the rigour of battle as much as his warrior father. Blackstone and Prince Edward had been both blessed and cursed at the battle of Crécy when, as a sixteen-year-old archer, Blackstone had thrown himself into the fray in a vain attempt to rescue his own brother from a German knight who had struck the mute boy down. Blackstone's action had failed to save his brother but stopped the young Prince being slain. Since then an uneasy and often embittered relationship had formed between the two men. The Prince's sharp-edged anger at Blackstone's defiance was tempered only by respect and a grudging gratitude.

Men-at-arms barred Blackstone's way. He stood without protest as a steward went ahead of him into the pavilion. The rain became heavier, tapping out a staccato rhythm on the taut wet canvas. Rain dribbled down Blackstone's neck but he stood unwavering as the men-at-arms hunched their shoulders. The tent flap was raised and the steward beckoned him forward. Blackstone entered into the half-light of the sumptuous lodgings of a prince at war. The flap was tied back and the burning candles made the damp air heavy with their sweet smell of beeswax. To one side a trestle table draped in a white linen cloth was covered with an assortment of silver and gold plate that bore the evidence of what must have been a feast. Some cold meats and a hank of bone, bowls half filled with bread. Fresh bread, his nose told him. The Prince sat on a bow-armed backless stool, a fresh shirt visible beneath his half-buttoned doublet embroidered with a curving vine and a bird about to take flight. He looked as though he had spent the day hunting, not fighting for his life.

'Thomas,' said the Prince.

'Sire.' Blackstone went down on one knee.

The Prince beckoned him forward. 'A good day's sport, Thomas.'

'Aye, your grace,' said Blackstone, remembering the slaughter and the stench of it, all less than three hours before. The fair-haired Prince made light of the battle, thriving as he did on the desire to fight, knowing perhaps, Blackstone thought ungraciously, that there were men around him who would throw themselves against the enemy so that no harm would befall him. Good sport providing you weren't killed or maimed.

Edward waggled a finger and from the near-darkness at the back of the tent a servant stepped forward with a silver tray and a goblet of wine and offered it to Blackstone. He accepted it with a curt nod of his head and the servant faded away as quickly as he had appeared. Blackstone hoped the Prince did not want a drinking companion for the night; without food in his belly his head would soon be reeling – and then his tongue would loosen and he would be on more dangerous ground than facing a French cavalry charge.

The Prince nodded again, meaning Blackstone to sit on a nearby stool – one without the comfort of cushions or embroidered arms.

'You stink, Thomas. Have you no water to bathe?'

'No water and no fire even if we had, my lord. Nor is there food for my men or sufficient fodder for the horses,' he went on, unable to stop himself. He quickly tried to cover his accusation by bringing the goblet to his mouth.

'We are aware of their discomfort,' said the Prince, 'and our gratitude to our men will not be forgotten when we take the city.'

Blackstone lowered his eyes to avoid confrontation.

'You may speak freely, Thomas. We are not always in agreement, but over the years we have learnt to tolerate some of your more outspoken thoughts. We see no purpose in denying you the right to speak freely here.'

'I did not come here to offer my thoughts. I came at your command.'

The Prince nodded. He would draw out Blackstone one way or another either by threat or promise. The scarred Englishman was too valuable to his father's cause. 'We have food here for you,' he said and once again beckoned the servant forward. 'Fill a plate for Sir Thomas,' he commanded.

Blackstone's mouth filled with spittle at the thought of the tender cuts of meat. He raised a hand. 'My lord, with respect I would rather not. I eat when my men eat,' he said, wondering if behind the offer of food a stern rebuke for Henry's impertinence with the sergeant-at-arms lay in ambush.

The Prince of Wales gazed at him for a moment, tugging his fingers through his beard. It was not matted with filth and blood like most of his men, and harboured no lice. Since retiring from the field he had bathed and washed with honey and rosemary soap. Blackstone's gesture was in its own small way an act of defiance. A gesture to tell a royal prince that Thomas Blackstone could not be bribed or bought. He would rather suffer the pangs of hunger than yield to enticement.

'And if we command you to eat?'

'Then I would obey,' answered Blackstone.

For a moment it looked as though the Prince would do just that but he waved aside the servant. 'So be it. We can hear your stomach rumble from here.'

'It rumbles louder than the bombards that fail to break the walls or smash the city gates,' he answered, again unable to contain the criticism that he had promised himself to keep locked firmly behind clenched teeth. 'We had a chance to reach that gate. Enough men were with me: we could have burned it down.'

The Prince bristled. It usually took longer for Blackstone to irritate him. But today he was tired from the fighting and its lack of success. 'You were recalled because we were losing too many men. You defied that command.'

'I did not hear the trumpets, my lord,' Blackstone lied, 'and I was concerned that... that you were given sufficient time to leave the field when I saw you were stricken.' He gave his response simply without any hint of derision that the Prince had eaten too well too soon before undertaking the rigours of combat.

'And that you shielded us is why we summoned you. To give our thanks,' said the Prince.

'No thanks are ever needed, my prince. I am honouring a pledge.'

The Prince's temper almost bubbled over the rim of his patience. 'We are not to be wet-nursed, Thomas. We are not obliged to have you at our shoulder at every waking moment.'

'That would make the royal bedchamber too crowded, my lord,' Blackstone said and smiled.

The Prince was gracious enough to allow his knight's boldness. 'And the royal bed, Thomas. We would not share our women with you so it would be a long and lonely night that you would endure.' He sighed. 'Thomas, you vex us,' he said finally.

Blackstone remained silent.

'You were lured to England by our grandmother, Thomas, and then ensnared. Our father knew her political skills and the influence she had before her death.' The ghost of Isabella the Fair, once Queen of England, still haunted those who knew her and had fallen under her influence.

'I was at the command of a woman who could scare a French cavalry charge better than English archers, even when she was ill and dying. She took my arm for support once and I could not deny her anything. I doubt any man could. She told me where my wife and children were in exchange for my promise to protect you. Would you dishonour me by insisting I abandon that promise?'

Edward lowered his chin to his chest. He gazed at the brazier's flames. No one could demand Blackstone's pledge be relinquished. The Prince's life was entwined with Thomas Blackstone's as surely as a woodbine wraps itself around a tree trunk. It was a cause of frustration engineered by his grandmother, the woman who had embroiled the English Crown in intrigue and political manipulation until the day she died. She was still honoured by his father despite rumours spread by those who believed he had banished her from court. Her cleverness had been such that the boy archer, Blackstone, knighted by the young Prince those years before, was now obliged to ensure that he, Edward of Woodstock, heir to the throne of England, would survive as long as Blackstone drew breath. The mother of the greatest of English kings had even made Blackstone fight him in the St George's Day tournament the year before last. Blackstone had fought without colours as an unknown knight and would have beaten him, had he not allowed his Prince to win. It had not been obvious to the onlookers but Edward had known. He let the memory fade.

'We were grieved when your wife and child were slain, Thomas. We offered our prayers.'

Blackstone bowed his head. The Prince would not have demanded his presence simply to thank him for his guardianship in the ditch, nor to express sympathy, nor to offer chastisement for refusing to answer the trumpets' call. There was yet more to come but only when the Prince was good and ready.

'Can you see a way into the city, Thomas? Is there a weakness in its structure? Does your stonemason's eye tell you how the walls can be breached?'

'The bombards are useless. They are not powerful enough. Our chance was to get fire beneath the gates. That chance has gone now, my lord, and the French will expect it. They will stop us even getting close. We cannot mine beneath the walls: the rock is granite that would take years to tunnel through. And even if we did breach the outer walls Gaucher de Châtillon will have chains across the streets to slow us down, burning pitch and oil on the rooftops and men at every alleyway to harass and kill us. Have you forgotten Caen? The bloodiest street fighting I have ever seen – but Rheims will be worse.' He paused his litany of bad news and gave his final verdict. 'We have the greatest army: one that can defeat anyone brought against us in the field. But we do not have the means to defeat this city. The King should abandon the siege.'

'He will not,' the Prince said.

Blackstone got to his feet as the Prince, distracted by his thoughts, tore at a piece of bread and then changed his mind before it reached his lips. 'My lord, I beg you. Talk to him. Get Lords Lancaster and Northampton with you. They'll see the truth. There's no crown to be had in Rheims. To lay siege here will take a year to starve them out and in that time the French will raise an army greater than anything we saw at Crécy or Poitiers. We are ninety miles from Paris and we will have to fight for every walled town. Our supply wagons are leagues to the rear. Blacksmiths and forges, carpenters, building supplies, ovens, corn mills, boats: they cannot move quickly enough. You have ten thousand troops to feed but you have almost no food left. Half of them are mounted archers who will soon have no arrows. No matter how many sheaves the King has brought, they will be wasted here. You cannot lose your archers to starvation and lack of arrow shafts. Not so soon after we have invaded.'

His comments agitated the Prince, who began to pace back and forth in the tent. He tossed the crust aside. He knew Blackstone was telling the truth. He also knew that Blackstone wanted to convince him because he was the only person likely to sway the King's mind.

'We left England too late. October committed us to a winter campaign and now we are paying for it,' said Blackstone.

'Our King is paying for it!' the Prince bellowed, his patience exhausted. 'The cost of this war is not coming from the Treasury, it is borne by our father. He is paying for this war and he decided when he should invade. It is not for you to criticize your King! You were lying a sodden drunk in a rat-infested cellar when we called for you. Were it not for the loyalty of your men who found you, and the desire of our father to bring you to war, you would be lying dead, choked on your own vomit.'

Blackstone lowered his head: to remain facing the enraged Prince would have been foolish. Let his blood settle and allow him to wipe the spittle from his face. Blackstone waited until the Prince calmed.

'It was no cellar, my lord. I was lying senseless with grief and drink in the back room of a rat-infested inn.'

The Prince gazed at him. Blackstone stood slightly taller. His scar had faded but it still cut a path through his weather-beaten face. The scar had been etched in battle, on the day they were both plunged into the violent hell of Crécy, but the deeper scars that Blackstone bore now were from a more savage beast than war. They were wounds that had brought a great fighter to his knees. That he was here now, before him, and had thrown his life once again into the fray to act as the Prince's shield, was most likely the act of a benevolent God.

'Very well. We will tell our father that his son's wet-nurse

22

believes this great quest should be abandoned. We will not face his anger. We shall use you as the whipping boy.'

Blackstone lowered his eyes. Once again his name would be brought to the King's attention, embroiling him in court politics.

The Prince continued: 'When you fought as an independent captain you seized towns by escalade. Your men have the skill to go over a town's walls and seize it.'

'That can't be done here. The walls are too high, the ditches too deep. Escalade can come at a high cost in lives. Even your assault towers cannot breach those walls. Ladders would not do it.'

Waving aside the servant the Prince poured himself a drink. He hesitated for a moment and then poured another, which he handed to Blackstone, who knew the real reason for being summoned was about to be revealed.

He took the drink from the Prince's hand.

'Not here, Thomas. There's another prize to be had.'

CHAPTER FOUR

'God's tears, Thomas, I'm in no mood to be dragged on a wild goose chase. I am happy here,' said Killbere. 'There's a chance the King will assault the city again.'

Blackstone led the way through the soldiers huddling beneath soaking wet blankets, red-eyed from their smudge fires. He could see Meulon and Gaillard in the distance gathering his men. Some needed a kick to roll them from their blankets, but not the archers: he glimpsed Will Longdon quietly leading them from the field. Their paths would cross at the treeline. John Jacob and Henry trudged behind Killbere, a couple of levies carrying the men's armour and weapons. It was another half-mile to where their horses were tethered behind the lines.

'Gilbert, the King has released me for now from my duties with the Prince. We have work to do for him.'

'Ah,' Killbere grunted, and then spat out the acrid taste of smoke, 'but I am already doing my work for him. I kill dog-breath Frenchmen who shit their braies when they see our blazon. I take no surrender. I leave the bodies of our King's enemies as a bridge of tears for their wailing widows and orphans. I cannot do any more than I do already. I am happy here.'

'In the cold and wet without food in your belly and rough wine on your tongue,' said Blackstone. 'And no plunder on our pack horses, or women straddling your thighs. Christ, man, you can't sit in this mud and yearn for it.'

'Women, you say?' said Killbere, opening his stride to catch up with Blackstone. 'There are women where we're going? Don't tell Will Longdon, he'll run to this place of mystery you're taking us. The last time I saw him he was starting to look at the baggage boys. Lads younger than Henry here. He's an irritating turd when he's not dipped his shaft for a while.' Having made his plea he waited for an answer but Blackstone was giving nothing away. 'Where are these women, did you say?'

'All in good time, Gilbert. Henry, run ahead and warn them to have our horses saddled. The archers need good mounts. I don't want any horses with saddle sores. Tell them I have the Prince's command. Run, boy.'

Henry loped forward.

'He obeys without question, Sir Thomas,' said John Jacob.

'So does a beast of burden if you thrash it hard enough,' said Blackstone. If John Jacob had any problems with Henry Blackstone then it would be he who would cuff the boy.

'He's no dull-witted page, he's got learning and he knows what's what,' said John Jacob, and then, in answer to the unspoken question. 'I've never had to raise a hand to him.'

'He's twelve years old. He needs discipline. All boys do,' said Killbere. 'A good thrashing once a week is to be expected. A boy needs to feel the switch on his back. Never did me any harm.'

'Aye, Sir Gilbert, but he's got something of Sir Thomas in him. He's stubborn and he'll make your balls ache with some of his questions. He craves knowledge and he wants to please his father.'

Killbere's grunt passed for a laugh. 'Thomas makes your balls ache because he doesn't answer any questions. And he's been stubborn since I hauled his arse ashore at Normandy back in '46. Christ, Thomas, where are we going?'

Blackstone smiled and nodded ahead to where Meulon and Gaillard waited at the forest's edge. 'I'll tell you when the captains are gathered, Gilbert.'

Meulon the throat-cutter grinned. 'The men are ready, Sir Thomas. They're happy to be rid of this siege.'

'Sitting on our arse with only two days of killing gives a man no hope of plunder,' said Gaillard.

'We could have breached that gate, Sir Thomas,' said Meulon. 'Damned if we couldn't. It was wrong to blow the recall. Another hour and the bastards would've been under our swords.'

Blackstone placed a hand on Meulon's shoulder in commiseration. 'At least now we won't be sitting on our arses in the rain.'

The small troop of men followed Blackstone through the trees into the clearing where the rear echelon was encamped. Will Longdon waited for his sworn lord. He should be in command of a hundred archers, but Blackstone's centenar had only half that number standing behind him. Cock-sure, arrogant, tough bastards, thought Blackstone as his gaze fell on them. There was no one like them in the army. Christ, he thought, if they were let loose in the streets of Rheims they would run faster than their arrows and be twice as lethal. A part of him was thankful that the city walls would not be breached because he knew some of the men would disobey his order not to rape. Enough wine and blood-lust would countermand any commander's order. And then he would have to hang the rapists.

A few of the archers wore the half-green and -white coats of Cheshire and Flint bowmen. The others wore jupons bearing the cross of St George and Blackstone's blazon. Jack Halfpenny and Robert Thurgood stood at Will Longdon's side. Under the guise of tugging free his steel skullcap Halfpenny gently nudged Longdon, who reluctantly took a step forward. The clumsy gesture did not go unnoticed.

'Sweet Jesus,' muttered Killbere, 'here we go. There'll be a complaint about something I'll wager.'

'Will?' said Blackstone.

'Sir Thomas,' Longdon said loudly enough for all to hear the mark of respect despite his being one of the knight's long-serving friends. His head twitched slightly, as if not wanting the men behind him to hear what he had to say. He stepped closer and lowered his voice. 'It's these Cheshire and Welsh archers,' he said, and by way of emphasizing his predicament shrugged his shoulders.

'What am I to do with them? They've been sent by their captains. I can't understand a damned word the Flint men say and the Cheshire men think they are the Virgin Mary's gift to fighting men. Can I send them back?'

'We need them, Will,' said Blackstone. 'We've twenty-six men-at-arms and only thirty-four of our own bowmen. The Prince boosted our ranks with the additional men.'

Longdon winced. 'These Cheshire men hate the Welsh because they refused to embark on the invasion unless they were paid up front. It's a matter of aggravation. They'll be at each other's throats.'

He glanced hopefully at Blackstone, who looked past him to the scowling green-and-white-clad archers. 'It's good to hear that your centenar speaks so highly of you!' he proclaimed to the new men as Will Longdon groaned quietly. 'Your King and Prince have placed you under my command and Will Longdon speaks for me when the time comes to fight.'

Killbere meanwhile lowered his head and voice and glared at the centenar. 'Do your damned job. You're not a mewling infant at the tit. There's killing to be done. Our sweet merciful Christ suffering on the cross died for your sins, you heathen bastard, so get to your duties before the damned resurrection.'

Will Longdon gritted his teeth and turned back to his men. 'Find your mounts!' he ordered.

Blackstone turned to Killbere. 'You'd make a fine priest, Gilbert. Perhaps that nun of yours has affected your soul.'

'She infected my cock is what she did. Every damned monk in the convent had had her, not that I knew it at the time. Don't mock. I might have left a broken heart behind but I left a damned sight more broken heads.'

'You told us before that you had not bedded her because she was too good for you,' said Blackstone. 'Or that you were not good enough for her.'

'Ah...' said Killbere. 'That was a different nun.' He grinned.

Blackstone gathered his captains around him. Meulon and Gaillard stood like granite gateposts each side of the half-circle of squatting men. Jack Halfpenny had been made ventenar of twenty archers and was included in the group along with Robert Thurgood, who, like Halfpenny, had joined Blackstone's men in Italy and had proved loyal when the men fought their way back to England the year before last. A year that was a lost lifetime for Blackstone, when desolation had wreaked havoc with his heart and mind more viciously than any army that swept across the landscape bringing it to its knees. Perinne squatted with the captains. He was one of the few who had survived the years fighting at Blackstone's side. John Jacob and Killbere sat on half-barrels gazing down at the sticks and stones that Blackstone had laid out on the ground as a map. There were a half-dozen Germans who now rode with Blackstone's men and he had made one of them, Renfred, a captain. They had proved to be good fighters and loyal to Blackstone.

'Until the King defeats the Dauphin and wins France he is hard pressed on this war. He needs money,' said Blackstone.

'May God grace our sovereign lord,' said Longdon, 'but he should try and live on sixpence a day like any mounted archer.'

Killbere gave the veteran a gentle kick. 'Be grateful he does not take payment for every arrow you let loose.'

'There would be no victory then,' said Meulon, 'not one shaft would fly with Will's tight grip on his purse strings. It would be left to us fighting men to win the King's wars.'

The men jeered at Will Longdon, but Thurgood and Halfpenny were careful not to be too vocal. Longdon was their captain.

'Routiers have seized on our King's invasion and follow behind us,' said Blackstone.

'Skinners?' said Jack Halfpenny. 'Are we to fight them as well as the French? With these few men, Sir Thomas?'

'We travel light and with the numbers we have,' said Blackstone. 'Too large a force would be quickly noticed on the route we must take. The routiers strip what little remains of food and money from village and town, supplies that we need. One of the Dauphin's noblemen has taken over the regional mint at a town called Cormiers. He sends the money to the Dauphin but he has enough silver and gold coin to buy off some of the routier captains and pay them to attack us. The Prince gave me these.' He spilled out a few gold coins from his purse. Willing hands snatched at them.

Will Longdon turned a coin in his fingers. '*Mouton d'or.* The Lamb of God,' he grinned. Halfpenny looked nonplussed. 'I'll wager even silver pennies are strangers to your purse, Jack.' Will held the coin between thumb and forefinger. 'See? The etching on the coin. A sheep with a halo and a banner? Eh? That's supposed to be Our Lord Jesus.'

'How can a sheep be Our Lord?' said Halfpenny, squinting at the markings.

'Because... because it is...' said Longdon, lost for explanation.

'The sheep is the lamb,' said Gaillard. 'It is Old Testament. The lamb was sacrificed as was Our Lord. That is its meaning.'

Longdon nodded in agreement. 'There, y'see. Gaillard only looks like a wild man. He might be as big and stupid as a tree but he knows his scripture, does Gaillard. Probably buggered by a priest when he was a lad to drive the lessons home.'

'My spear will drive its lesson home through your arse,' the Norman answered, used to their ongoing taunts.

Robert Thurgood licked his coin. 'Gold, Sir Thomas. Nothing tastes as good.'

Killbere had not demeaned himself by reaching for the tumbled coins. He took Thurgood's. 'How much are they paying the skinners?'

'One was given twenty thousand,' said Blackstone.

Killbere was as impressed as the others. 'The Lamb of God has fallen into wolves' jaws,' he said. 'Independent captains can retire in comfort and buy themselves a walled town for protection. Better that we have it.'

'The King,' Blackstone corrected.

'So that we may give it to the King,' Killbere recanted but with a glance to Blackstone that intimated there might be enough to share with the royal purse.

Blackstone ignored him. 'The more we take from the French the quicker they weaken and the sooner Edward seizes his crown. To win we must draw the Dauphin from behind the walls of Paris. Scour his land, raid his towns and villages and seize whatever money he has to buy troops and bribe routiers.' He opened his palm for the return of the coins and, once they were secure in his purse, pointed with a stick to the landscape on the ground. 'We travel south-east. There are towns and villages scattered across the whole area but across the river are two walled towns, one of which has the money.'

'How do we know this? Deserters?' said Meulon. 'They could be sent by the French to draw us into a trap – these rivers can be deep with swamps and ponds beyond them.'

Will Longdon said, 'Meulon's right. Think back how often we failed to find river crossings when we fought before Crécy. We'll need luck to find a ford.'

'I have one in mind. This information came from prisoners not deserters,' Blackstone said. 'This town is called Cormiers. Do any of us know it?'

The men shook their heads. No one had passed through that part of France before.

'There are two hundred or more men inside the walls, according to the prisoners that were taken,' Blackstone said.

'Halfpenny is right,' said Killbere. 'We are too few to seize walled towns, especially when outnumbered.'

'Chandos has been sent by the King. He has near enough three hundred men. He will attack once we've scaled the walls at night.'

Every man in the English army was aware of Sir John Chandos. The veteran fighter was known for his courage and his ability to plan and execute strategy but it would be Blackstone and his men who would go and penetrate into the heart of the enemy.

'Then we take the greater risk,' said Perrine.

'When have we not?' said Killbere. 'How do we know where this town is?' he asked Blackstone.

'Information from the prisoners.' He pointed with a stick the route they would take, where he thought a ford might exist across the River Aisne and where there was danger from the French and routiers. The mercenaries roamed freely and most of the bands were several hundred strong, some as great as two thousand. With luck they would sight them before the skinners became aware of the small band of Englishmen.

'Perinne, you and Jack find the way forward along this route I've shown you. Take a dozen archers in case you need to fall back and defend yourselves. We will be an hour behind you.' Blackstone looked at each man, giving them the opportunity to raise any questions. All stared at the ground plan, seeing the reality in their mind's eye. No one spoke.

'All right,' said Blackstone. 'We do not ride hard. We edge our way through the French. We meet Chandos in four days' time.'

Blackstone went beyond the trees where the horses were tethered. His horse was further back in the forest, its huge bulk an almost invisible shadow in the woodland. It was tethered and hobbled. Its head drooped, its eyes were closed but its ears swivelled at the sound of his approach even though Blackstone trod quietly across the wet grass. It feigned sleep.

Blackstone stepped closer. And waited. Experience had taught him not to get too near the bastard horse without care. It might have been hobbled, but its yellow grindstone teeth would snap and bite. He took another step. It was an ugly beast. Sired, said the stable-hands, repeating the legend, by the devil, unyielding in its belligerence. Its black hide was dappled as if singed by the cinders of hell. Its neck, as thick as a man's waist, supported an oversized and misshapen head. A battering ram in battle. Its hooves the breadth of a man's hand bore iron shoes that tore the ground and smashed limbs. Bulging shoulder muscles encased a tireless heart. Battle-scarred, it was a horse that Blackstone loved more than any other. It had the fiery soul of a fighting warrior.

Blackstone made a small sound with his lips. It shook its head, its eyes still closed.

'Damn you,' he said quietly. 'I'll not be ignored by a dumb beast.' He reached out, palm forward towards its muzzle, letting it get his scent, even though it knew his voice. It suddenly lunged, eyes wide, lips curled, teeth snapping; then it snorted, held by the restraining ropes. He slapped its muzzle. It was less than a fly swat to the war horse. Its ears and eyes were on him. 'Bastard,' he muttered and carefully eased the saddle blanket across its back. A shudder went down its spine as he settled the curved saddle. Its head lifted; he knew that, like him, it was eager to be free of its constraints. He pulled the opposite rein tight to stop the beast from swivelling its head and biting him as he eased up into the saddle. Its ears pricked; its head rose. It trotted without command to where the other riders waited. The bastard horse whinnied and took its rightful place at the front of the column.

A fickle breeze shifted the mist from the skeletal leaf-bare trees clearing a path across the undulating landscape. Blackstone urged the horse forward. Like the dark spirits of the forest, demons lurked within him. The sooner he could pursue and confront them the sooner they could be vanquished.

CHAPTER FIVE

Blackstone and his men rode east through the English lines following the shallow contour of land between Rheims and the rising ground to their right where King Edward was encamped at Verzy ten miles from the city walls. Soldiers raised their eyes from their preparations to continue the siege as the renowned knight passed among them. They raised an arm and cheered. Cries of Crécy. Poiters. Blanchetaque. Men who had been in the ranks fighting the same vicious battles and who knew of the scarred knight's prowess. None of Blackstone's men acknowledged the greetings, riding as they did hunched from the wet and cold. Once they left the lines fifty miles of uncertainty lay ahead at the end of which would be a fight to secure a worthless town where men would die and others would share their plunder. Blackstone heeled the bastard horse into a trot. Better to ride with hope than sit and waste away in a futile siege.

The following day's meagre sun gave barely any warmth in the early morning hours but it served to lift the men's spirits as they rolled free from their damp blankets. Men cleared their throats and spat out the stale taste of night. By the time they ate their pottage from the small iron pots nestled into their fire's embers the sky became sullen again, smothered by the creeping low cloud.

Blackstone and his men gave the pockets of woodland a wide berth in case of sudden attack. They had passed three abandoned villages and seen no sign of the people who lived there and by midday rested on the outskirts of another. The wattle-and-stone hovels were in ruins, a few dead dogs lay bludgeoned or slashed from spear or sword, but once again there were no villagers. The charred thatch was already cold and crisp; the black timbers of a ruined barn bore witness to the fact that the attackers had not passed recently. A dozen men dismounted to search the tumbledown buildings as Will Longdon set his archers in a protective shield in case those responsible for the destruction were hiding in the woodland two hundred paces away.

Meulon squelched his way back down the track that served as the highway through the hovels. 'Nothing, Sir Thomas,' he said and gestured with his spear in an arc. 'There's no sign of anyone. They must have run before the attack. Fences are broken, livestock taken. These dogs stayed too long.'

'The people have run for the nearest walled town,' said Blackstone.

Killbere eased his horse alongside Blackstone's. 'I rode down to that stream; there's a bloated cow's carcass poisoning the water. There's nothing here for us, Thomas, but I'll wager we are following in the skinners' path. There'll be more of this and sooner or later we'll catch up with them.'

Blackstone looked across the horizon. 'It might not be routiers. Edward had his scavenging parties out far and wide. Whoever took this village did it days or even weeks ago.' He looked at Killbere, who guzzled from his wineskin. There was a sheen of sweat on the veteran knight's face. 'You're sweating even though the air is cold.'

Killbere belched. 'It's a chill, nothing more. A lifetime of soldiering and lying on wet ground does a man no good. You wait till you're my age. Your knees hurt, your back aches, your teeth come loose and your piss takes longer to come. It's reward for serving the King.'

Blackstone eased his knee into the horse. No need to tug the rein: it knew it was meant to turn. 'I'll find a convent for you and have them take you into the infirmary. They'll clothe you in a habit and feed you gruel so you don't have to chew. A pisspot by your side and a hot stone on your mattress for your aching bones. I'll sell your armour and weapons to pay for it.'

Killbere followed him. 'A true friend, Thomas. I'm grateful. And when you try and take me from my horse you'd best have Wolf Sword honed because I will gut you and any man who thinks I am unable to fight another day.' He spat red wine spittle. 'I'll die with a damned sword in my hand like God intended or I'll not die at all!'

The two men laughed. 'Then I'd best find you a decent fight, Gilbert. We cannot have you inflicted on the world for eternity.'

'Sir Thomas!' Perinne called. Blackstone and the others looked to where he pointed. The low cloud hovered over the land and seemed to rest above the heads of the dozen horsemen who watched them from the gentle rising land a mile away.

'Chandos's scouting party from the north?' said Killbere.

Blackstone squinted in the flat light. 'Perhaps. It's the direction he'd travel. I don't know... Will? Jack?'

The archers tented hands around their faces, their keen eyesight searching for any telltale clue.

'No pennons or banner, no colour on their clothing, Sir Thomas,' said Longdon.

'And no helms. There's not a knight among them,' added Jack Halfpenny.

'Chandos would have his men-at-arms scouting,' said Blackstone without taking his eyes off the distant men. They had not moved. 'Besides, if it were Chandos's men they would have seen who we are and come down.'

'Routiers, then,' said Killbere. 'As I said.'

The horsemen on the skyline disappeared down the reverse slope of the hill.

'Shadowing us, do you think?' said John Jacob as he climbed back onto his horse after searching the village.

'Perhaps. Brigands, outlaws and the dispossessed. France is in tatters and our King wishes to seize it and hoist it like a battle flag,' said Blackstone. 'It seems a worthless place to me – and there's no honour in slaughtering unarmed villagers. Whoever's up there will kill for what they need.'

'The countryside is crawling with vermin,' said Killbere.

'It might be the French,' said John Jacob. 'There are still castles and strongholds with their troops.'

'Vermin are vermin, John,' said Killbere. 'Best we kill them all.' He glanced at Blackstone. 'But not today, eh, Thomas? Bastards are probably trying to draw us in. We outnumber them until we get over that hill and there's a goddamned army waiting.'

'As you say, Gilbert, not today. It's good to see that your ailments have not affected your brain.'

'You should only concern yourself when I cannot raise my sword arm, Thomas, because who will look after you then?'

Blackstone smiled and lifted the silver goddess to his lips.

The daylight grew short. As they edged southwards, Blackstone kept his men in the open ground. He also placed a rider between them and Perinne and his scouting party so that those acting as Blackstone's eyes remained in sight, and would not fall foul of any ambush from the dense forests that pockmarked the landscape and could hide an army. The wet ground gave no indication of horsemen travelling in the same direction, but the preceding days' rain could have hidden any tracks. His own men's horses made distinct indentations in the soft winter grass. If an enemy were in front of them then they would not have travelled recently. Blackstone turned his face to the breeze that came from woodland three hundred paces away. There was no odour of fire or men. Soldiers, be they brigands or otherwise, relieved themselves in a communal area. The stench of excrement would drift on the wind but there was no such smell, only the scent of wet ground and pine resin mingling with the clean taste of rain. Half the forest had its branches covered in needles; they would make a soft bed on the ground beneath them, drier than the exposed ground. The other trees were bare on the men's opposite flank, so no one would be hidden there.

'We need to camp,' said Blackstone. 'But there's no cover out here and if we are being followed we need to get into those trees.

John, ride forward and have Perinne look at that forest over there.' He pointed to the small woodland. 'It's big enough for cover and small enough not to hide any large body of men.'

John Jacob spurred his horse, followed without hesitation by his page Henry Blackstone. Blackstone watched his son lean into the horse's rhythm. He quietly acknowledged the satisfaction it gave him. The boy's upbringing in Normandy and the fight to the death at his mother and sister's side had matured him. The years since the boy's birth were as clear as a bright spring morning in Blackstone's memory.

Killbere noticed Blackstone's intent stare at the distant horsemen. 'He's a natural horseman, Thomas. Better than you at his age, eh?'

'I didn't have a horse at his age, Gilbert. I had been cutting and carrying stone in a quarry since I was a child.' Blackstone quickly dismissed any sentimentality. 'I'd whip him if he didn't ride that well. He had the best of horses when we lived in Normandy and Christiana had him serve with a God-fearing knight. A good man savagely slaughtered by peasants but who taught the boy well. Henry must prove himself. I'll not tolerate any favour shown to him. He'll have no special privileges because of who he is.'

'Sweet Jesus, Thomas, your heart has become even harder since Christiana died. The boy worships you. He's a reason to live.'

'The reason I had to live was taken from me. I serve my King now, that's enough.'

The two men watched as Henry and John Jacob reached the outrider. Killbere sighed. 'Ah, Thomas, you're an honest man who lies badly. You've always served the King even when his son treated you badly and banished you.'

'I deserved it,' admitted Blackstone. 'I tried to kill the King of France.'

'A pity you failed. We would be lying with our favourite whores these days instead of sitting with our arses in mud.' Killbere settled his arms across his pommel and nodded towards the boy. 'Another three or four years and that lad will grow into a fighting man who'll bring tears to your eyes at the sight of his courage.' He fixed Blackstone with a querulous look that asked his friend to prove him wrong.

Blackstone remained silent. Watching his son already brought the taste of salt to his lips and those feelings were best kept to himself. He did not want the man who had first taken him to war to think less of him because he was now weakened with sentiment and love for the boy. And fear. To lose Henry would be to suffer a wound so grievous it might finally kill him.

'Light a dozen fires. They'll smoke. If they come we'll be ready.'

CHAPTER SIX

The killers came at first light. They rode slowly, their horses at the walk, bridles bound with leather and cloth to stop them jangling. The muted creak of their saddles could have been mistaken for the easing of tree trunks against the morning breeze that had freshened enough to blow clear the rolling low cloud. They rode four abreast, 128 men, bunched knee to knee as if they were preparing a cavalry charge. But they carried no lances, only sword, axe and mace. Their plan was to swoop down on the Englishmen, trample them underfoot and slaughter the dazed survivors before they could shake themselves free of the half-sleep that plagued men sleeping rough.

They followed the tracks made by Blackstone's horsemen that skirted the woodland to their left and led on towards the hollow ground that would afford the men some cover from a biting wind. The smell of woodsmoke lingered and here and there a wisp of it hovered in the still air. Their leader raised a hand. His eyes scanned the bare landscape. There was no smell of food being cooked and no sign of the men camping where the scouts had reported. He turned in the saddle and snarled at the men behind him: 'Where are they? You said you saw them settle before dark. Out there. In the open.'

'Aye. We did. They hobbled their horses and lay down their blankets and lit their fires,' answered one of the men, knowing that the brigands' leader would as soon cut his throat as tolerate failure.

'Then where the fuck are they?' he snarled.

The routiers on the left of the column raised their eyes. The wind carried a different sound, like a flock of birds rising from the forest. As they squinted into the half-light the source of the fluttering sound became obvious. The riders cried out a warning as their horses panicked. Too late. The dark storm of arrows falling from the sky already had a second wave of shadows following behind. Those routiers who wore breastplates escaped the glancing strike of the bodkin-tipped arrows on their chests, but the hurtling missiles pierced thigh, neck and arm. Steel tips caught those who gazed up stupidly at the sky in the face, punctured horses' necks and haunches. The whinnying beasts and screaming men formed an uncontrolled mass of fear. Men fell; horses landed on top of them. Their leader was already dead, pinned through the throat.

Amid the panic the routiers saw the surge of mounted men-at-arms swarm from the treeline behind the hailstorm of arrows. The skinners cursed, screaming at each other to face the attack, realizing that the English had fooled them by laying down tracks into the open meadow and then moving into the forest at night. And now those who had fallen into the trap were being slain. Most of the routiers tried to flee – they were now too few to fight a pitched battle – but the confusion prevented any easy escape. Fallen horses kicked and screamed and suddenly the three hundred paces from the forest were not enough and the Englishmen were on them. Some, moments before they died, saw the Englishman's blazon and knew who it was that had tricked them and who would show no mercy.

Blackstone's horse barged into the routiers' flank, Meulon, Gaillard and Killbere led their own charge either side, and John Jacob had already ridden past Blackstone. Steel struck bone and shields thudded on impact. A hacking, desperate defence was no use against the impetus of the charging horses whose hooves smashed men on the ground and reared over dead horses. The English slashed their way through; unhorsed routiers tried to turn and run but were clubbed or speared to the ground. Within minutes, fewer than twenty men were left amid the carnage. Back to back they stood their ground, shields raised, swords ready; those who wore stolen armour lowered their visors. The English horsemen barely took breath as they carried their killing forward. The bare-faced knight who spurred his great beast of a horse towards them showed no hesitation, no glimmer of mercy. If nothing else, the routiers knew they were going to die. They had been soldiers, Hainaulters and Germans, Englishmen and French, deserters and pillagers who had formed bands of thirty men or more and then joined others until they numbered in their hundreds and were strong enough to take towns and seize plunder after slaughter. The mercenaries, screaming curses, broke ranks, hurling themselves at the English horsemen. Killbere was tumbled from his horse. They fell on him, raining blows, but he smothered himself with his shield. A cry was heard: 'Sir Gilbert!' and others came to his defence; men who were clothed no differently than the attackers cut the routiers down. They were bludgeoned to death and one huge man dismounted and quickly cut their throats.

One routier fought better than the rest and, as the companion at his shoulder went down wounded onto one knee, he stepped in front of him to protect him. The scarred-face Englishman shouted a command and those who were about to attack him stayed their hand and turned their horses. The lone man stood amid the fallen, lungs heaving.

'Are these all the men in your band?' Blackstone demanded.

'There are more, Sir Thomas. They roam the hills and plains. They are everywhere. You English will meet more of them,' the man answered, raising his visor. His sweat-streaked face was that of an older man. Older than Sir Gilbert Killbere, it seemed to Blackstone.

'You know me?'

'Aye. Your blazon and your reputation. I was at Poitiers when you tried to kill the French King.'

'Which side?'

'The French. I'm Philippe Bonnet. I'm no knight, Sir Thomas, but my family were not low-born. They held land but lost everything to the English.'

'And you ride with brigands.'

'I do. My King's army had no need for many of us after Poitiers. And I hate you English for the plague of violence you brought on us.'

'You're a routier. Don't preach to me of violence.'

'Hate can carry a man on a long and desolate road and I have travelled it willingly. But I have need of plunder. How else are we to live?'

'By not killing your own.'

'Peasants have no souls to return to God. They're like beasts of the field. I'm tired. Let's be done with it.'

'Where else are the skinners?'

'Everywhere. They'll catch you soon enough.'

'Me?'

'You're worth money, Sir Thomas. Dead or alive.'

It was not unusual for those with a thirst for glory and reward to try and kill Thomas Blackstone. The Savage Priest had tried years before and now his body hung on a mountain pass, his skin shrivelled to his bones, blackened by the bitter winds.

'Your wounded friend?' Blackstone said, nodding towards the man Bonnet protected.

'Just that. A friend.'

It seemed to Bonnet that the Englishman understood sacrifice for friendship.

'It is as it is,' said the Frenchman.

'It is as it is,' said Blackstone.

Blackstone heeled the bastard horse around and the horsemen next to him spurred theirs forward. It took only seconds for Bonnet to be slain and his friend dispatched.

Killbere was carried back to the forest. It took an hour for him to recover his senses after the blow to his helm, whereupon he cursed and slaked his dry throat from a wineskin. Blackstone had never seen him so unsteady on his feet, but Killbere demanded that he be left alone, and the others finally succumbed to his threats and backed away. Henry Blackstone returned with John Jacob and Jack Halfpenny. A dozen men-at-arms and half a dozen archers had backtracked the mercenaries' route. They returned with a small hay cart pulled by a pair of donkeys and laden with food and wine. There had been a small rearguard with the victuals but John Jacob and his men had not even had to draw their weapons. Halfpenny and his archers killed them from a hundred paces. It had been a successful morning's killing and the men now needed food – and sleep too, for Blackstone had kept them alert throughout the night in case the routiers had dared to strike in darkness. It would have been uncommon for such men to do so but in the past Blackstone himself had used skittering clouds and temperamental moonlight to assault sleeping troops. Vigilance and the loss of a night's sleep was a small price to pay to avoid a surprise attack.

The dead were left in the open; what horses survived were hobbled and taken as spare mounts. Anything of value was taken from the dead mercenaries. A good knife, a purse of coins, a fine leather jerkin that would fit well once the blood was wiped from it: all manner of plunder was chosen or discarded as befitted its use or value. Will Longdon took the contingent of Welsh and Cheshire archers among the dead to salvage what arrows they could. Blackstone would let his men rest for the day and night and then take up the ride to meet Sir John Chandos.

Blackstone posted sentries and had fires lit and food cooked. His men ignored the contorted bodies nearby as they ate hungrily.

'Ah, Sir Thomas,' said Jack Halfpenny, his mouth gorged with meat, 'we should declare this a feast day, the Feast of the Dead!'

'Aye, Jack, perhaps we should. Let's not forget there are more of them out there and their swords might well feast on us if we don't keep one eye on the horizon.'

'Only need one eye, my lord.' Halfpenny grinned. 'An archer's eye!' Those around him cheered as Blackstone smiled too, and shared their laughter.

There was a town to be attacked and it was Blackstone's men who would take the brunt of its assault, and that meant some of those he walked among and who nodded their respect at his presence would soon be carrion for the rooks and crows who now descended on the slain mercenaries. He spoke to those he had seen fight well that day, praised the archers for their skill, shared with the Welshmen the story of how he came by Arianrhod, and then made his way through the slender saplings into the deeper forest seeking a place of quiet and solitude and the stream he knew meandered at the far edge of the forest. He needed to wash the bloodstains from him and try to rid himself of the stench of death.

Intuition guided him through the rising shrouds of morning mist that burned free from the forest floor. A small pond shimmered, its surface disturbed by the air from the fluttering wings of small woodland birds, scared into flight by his approach. A crow crawked its rasping annoyance as the tall creature ventured into its domain. Avoiding brambles, Blackstone stepped carefully over tufted grass as the breeze rattled the bare claws of the high canopy. Forests were where spirits dwelt that could draw a man into their dark embrace. Where once he might have been fearful of legends and folklore, he now ignored his own instinctive warning. He had vowed nothing would ever make him fearful again. Not after seeing the mutilation and murder of his wife and daughter. That fear could never be surpassed.

Chain mail of light freckled through the branches and as he walked deeper sunlight speared the trees until he stepped onto the edge of a small glade. A movement, barely noticeable, caught his eye. He stopped and used a tree trunk to help obscure his position. A fawn raised its head and snuffled the air and then a gentle whimper reached its ears. Its wide-eyed mother edged carefully into the sunlight, alert to danger but not yet aware of the man's scent. The fawn delicately stepped up to its mother and then the two were gone. There was a brief haunting of colour as the mottled and dead foliage still clinging to the bushes shimmered. Dry amber leaves took the form of a woman's hair and a splash of sunlight created a face in the hollows. For a brief, stomach-churning moment Blackstone saw Christiana as he had first seen her when he was a young archer. Her copper hair the colour of autumnal leaves and the light on her face. A sixteen-year-old boy falling in love with the woodland image of the girl he would rescue and marry. The breeze turned, the sunbeam shifted and she was gone, vanished like the deer. In the instant he saw her his hand had been outstretched towards her. The illusion had snared him. He rested his face against the weathered tree trunk; it was covered in florets of moss and the lichen clinging to the bark was rough against his cheek. He cursed the grief that still held him, but the memory was quickly put aside as a sudden movement out of the corner of his eye alerted him to danger.

A sparrowhawk swooped at waist height. Despite its eye-blinking speed Blackstone's gaze followed it. Suddenly its wings rose, stalling its arrow-fast flight, its talons unfurled and it struck down into the grass. There was a writhing struggle as the hawk gripped a viper. The hawk's beak opened as it tried to tear at the snake, but the viper curled itself so quickly the sparrowhawk suddenly became the victim. Despite the talons piercing its flesh, the snake's coils wrapped themselves beneath the bird's wings and around its chest. No matter how it tried to free itself the snake had a firm grip. Blackstone moved quickly but the struggle had ceased: the hawk was motionless, its yellow-ringed eyes staring at him, its tongue moving in silent alarm in its gaping beak. The raptor's beauty would soon be crushed and without another thought Blackstone put his hands beneath the snake's coils in an attempt to deliver the hawk. The snake's head struck at his hand; he pulled back quickly, just in time: a viper's poison could kill a man or at the very least incapacitate him for days. He tried again; found the place behind the snake's head, used his free hand to unwind the coils and release the bird. The serpent fought his grip and tried to wrap its yard-long body around his arm. He flicked his wrist, pulled it free and then threw it into the grass. Defeated, it slithered away beneath the brambles.

The sparrowhawk's wings were still unfurled, its beak, like its eyes, open, but then they closed in an almost silent whisper of breath. It appeared dead. Blackstone turned the hawk curled-talons down, spread the wings in his hand and placed a palm beneath its softly feathered chest. It lay unmoving. Blackstone realized he was holding his breath. He'd now seen that no matter how swift a killer might be, its victim could turn and strike back with equal speed.

The wings suddenly beat as quickly as had his heart in the glade. The sparrowhawk took rapid flight and the woodland hunter was gone. The glade's light shifted; the pond's surface remained unblemished. Blackstone waited a moment longer, letting the silence settle over him. Then he turned his back on the forest's heartbeat, suddenly craving the open landscape and the chance to see the distant horizon.

CHAPTER SEVEN

The following day, after four hours' ride, Perinne led a dozen men across a shallow ford on the River Aisne. He had chosen the crossing well for the shallows and sparse grasses on either bank offered no cover for an enemy ambush and the way ahead was open countryside. The advance party spread out, searched the ground for half a mile in a great semi-circle and then signalled it was safe for Blackstone and the others to cross. Another hour saw Blackstone's force riding across undulating plains where pockets of forests blotted the landscape but where there was still no sign of Sir John Chandos. Perinne, riding ahead of the others, raised his arm, beckoning Blackstone to him.

'Hear that?' said Perinne.

As they drew closer they heard the steady thud of axe against wood and the murmur of men cursing from the forest that lay four hundred paces ahead.

'Sounds as though they couldn't wait to start,' said Killbere. 'The more work they do the less there is for us.' His body trembled. Blackstone looked at him with concern.

'You're sick,' he said.

'I'm not,' he insisted irritably. 'I'm cold. I'm wet and cold. This damned weather is worse than home. Christmas has come and gone and all we've had is rain and cold. Cold and rain. Whichever way you say it it's misery. A man fights no matter what the weather but this time of year there should be snow underfoot. Snow softens the world, brings with it its own warmth, settles like an angel's wing feathers and cloaks a man in its mantle. My undershirt is soaked in sweat and the wind bites like fleas on an inn's mattress.' He drank thirstily from his wineskin. 'And we should talk less and get on with the King's business.'

'I'm pleased to hear you're in a good mood,' said Blackstone. There was little point in arguing with Killbere. He had the strength of a bull and despite chills seemed as willing to fight as ever. Men died on campaign from the sweating sickness, others coughed blood from ruined lungs, but Killbere would not be one of them.

As they approached the forest they saw a knight sitting on a tree trunk. His head was bare, his squire standing ten feet away holding his horse and helm. The shield that was hooked across the saddle bore a weathered blazon with a stark red inverted triangle against a dull yellow background. There appeared to be no other soldiers but those who laboured in the forest and the exalted knight Sir John Chandos who casually watched over them.

His teeth tugged at a piece of smoked meat. His beard, cut square a hand's breadth beneath his chin, broadened his face; a white line was etched across his forehead from where his helm usually sat above his weather-beaten features. Chandos was not born of the nobility but this had not hampered his success as a knight. He was continually rewarded for not only his skill as a fighter but also as a negotiator, a man who could parlay a peace treaty on behalf of the Prince or act as envoy for the King.

'Sir Thomas,' he said without standing. 'I thought I would let my men make a start on your scaling ladders. You'll not object, I hope?'

Blackstone dismounted and, without looking at the working men, strode towards the seated knight. 'You can make them and use them if you so choose, Sir John,' he answered.

Chandos grinned. 'Ah, no. That's the risk you must take.' He stood and gripped Blackstone's hand. 'Good to see you again, Thomas.'

Blackstone tried to remember whether he had ever shared the knight's company. He looked to be at least ten years older than Blackstone, a sturdy man, muscles bunched on his shoulders from

48

the years of fighting, his grey-blue eyes unflinching in their gaze. Chandos saw the crease in Blackstone's forehead.

'We nudged each other at Poitiers. You were busy killing. I was at the Prince's side.'

'Then forgive me. I had other things on my mind. Am I late?'

'No. I am early. My men are half a mile back. We raided for four days up country and all we came away with was food. No plunder to be had, but that will soon change when we breach the town walls. If we don't the day will soon come when I'll have to pay the men myself and that's something I would prefer to avoid.'

The knights who recruited troops were paid a *regard* of a hundred marks a quarter for every thirty men-at-arms they raised. Chandos was held in such esteem by the Crown that he earned twice that. He gave Blackstone an enquiring look; it would always be good to know what others might be paid in the service of their King. Chandos's face broke into a grin, teeth uneven through the unruly beard. 'I heard the King paid for your men at Calais when you were pissed and disappeared for all those months. You were honoured.' Chandos's blunt approach was both a query and a challenge. Was Thomas Blackstone still such a common man that he would be subservient to the renowned Knight of the Garter or would he take umbrage at being taunted as a drunk? If his pride was offended then Thomas Blackstone's reputation was ill founded. Chandos needed the legend to be intact if they were to prevail against a well-defended town. Anything less meant that Chandos had a weakened man as part of the assault.

'A drunk does not know honour. He knows self-indulgent misery and violence. I have benefited from the King and the Prince; both have honoured me in their own way. Both have chosen to ignore my time in purgatory,' said Blackstone.

Chandos grunted. It was a good answer. 'I can see why you have such a loyal following from your men and the favour of our sovereign lords. None of us know when we might slip into the darkness of the abyss and fewer still know whether we have the strength to admit the affliction and haul ourselves back into the light.'

They had reached the group of men who bent over the felled trees and were tapping wedges into their length to split them. An adze was skilfully employed to fashion the logs into long planks for side rails, and then holes were drilled ready for the hewn rungs to be hammered into place. The men had cut a mortise into each end of the two rails and then tapped in the holding bars for rigidity. The scaling ladders were built for strength, able to bear the weight of fighting men as they clambered up onto the walls. Iron spikes were driven into the feet to stop the ladders slipping. Chandos's men knew what they were doing.

'You've how many fighting men? Twenty or so?' said Chandos. 'You'll not take your archers over?'

Blackstone shook his head. 'Men-at-arms first. My centenar will bring some of his men up onto the wall once it's breached; they can help cover us so we can reach the gate.' Blackstone looked at the length of the three ladders nearing completion and guessed they were going to be thirty feet long. That was a high climb and gave the defenders plenty of time to inflict injury and death on his men.

'Show me the walls,' he said.

Sir John Chandos picked a piece of meat from his teeth and gazed out across the terrain that lay between his troops' position in the forest and the well-defended town a few hundred yards away. A ringlet of shallow ditches had been dug in front of and behind the remains of ancient walls that lay crumbling, barely chest high in some places. An orchard had survived the town commander's cutting down of the forest that once grew closer to the town's walls.

'There's one gate in across that row of ditches,' said Chandos, pointing towards the heavily built gate at the far side of a fixed wooden bridge that straddled the nearest ditch to the wall. 'I cannot assault Cormiers in daylight because the crossbowmen would slaughter us. By the time we try and clamber up and down those ditches we would have no cover. And those tree stumps will slow us down even more.'

Blackstone studied the walls. They had been well built and there was no sign of weakness, no postern gate to assault and none that had been walled up. No battering ram would get close enough to take down that gate. 'Those walls are higher than thirty feet,' he said, turning to face the man who lay next to him, each of them shielded from the watchful eyes of the sentries on the walls by low branches.

Chandos shrugged. 'Not by much. A couple of feet perhaps. You will breach the walls with a bit of effort,' he said, smiling, and continued to peel an apple until the skin formed an unbroken ribbon. He cut a slice and handed it to Blackstone, who accepted. There was little point in chastising Sir John for his miscalculation. It would not have been his mistake; it was likely one of his captains.

'I was told there were two hundred troops inside,' said Blackstone.

'I had scouts here watching for three days. We cannot be sure how many there are but the knight who holds the town had at least a hundred men under his command and the Dauphin sent another hundred more to secure the mint. The commander's name is Louis de Joigny. He is by all accounts a harsh man, like so many of these French noblemen. I find them more amenable when they lie dead on a battlefield.'

Blackstone shrugged. The regional lord's name meant nothing. It was unimportant, though what he protected was. 'Only soldiers? How loyal are the people?'

'We've seen townsmen on the walls and villagers have taken refuge inside the town, so there might be militia as well. The villagers took in food. We think the town has grain and wine and we saw enough hay carts carrying fodder.'

'They've cavalry?' Blackstone asked. 'If they ride through the streets we won't have much chance of living through it.'

'No, the fodder was for cattle and sheep the peasants herded inside. But we could use it for our horses once we've taken the place. The Dauphin has played a good hand. The villagers desert their homes and go into the towns taking what they can, burning everything left behind. They leave us nothing.' He teased fingers through his beard. 'But if we seize the gold and silver in there at least the Dauphin can't buy routiers to attack us. They swarm everywhere and in strength. If they sniff there's gold here they won't wait for the Dauphin to offer it. They'll come to take it for themselves and we don't have the strength to fight both.' He nodded, pointing with the chewed twig he had used to pick his teeth. 'The keep. That's where the money will be.'

Blackstone could just make out the squat roof of the town's keep rising above the walls. The French commander's banner showed three broad black stripes and a ram's head.

'It's an ancient town. That's more like an old three-storey hall,' said Blackstone. 'I can see they had good stonemasons for rebuilding the town's walls but that's older; I'll wager we could tear that down with our hands if we had to. What we don't want is for them to barricade themselves inside because then...' He let the words hang. To fight inside an enclosed space meant too many men would die.

Blackstone and Chandos fell silent. Both were at a disadvantage in trying to take the town.

'The orchard,' said Blackstone. 'I'll use it as far as those ditches and low walls. You'll have to keep your men back in the trees until you see we're inside.'

'I agree. I'll hold them in the forest but the moment I see you go over the walls we will make for the gate. I doubt we will get closer than a hundred... perhaps a hundred and fifty yards... There... that second row of ditches in front of the gate. We're exposed until you raise it. I cannot risk getting any closer in case you fail.'

Blackstone had seen enough. 'Be ready, Sir John. We won't fail.'

CHAPTER EIGHT

Darkness and rain smothered any movement or sound as Blackstone's men inched their way forward. Daylight had imprinted the town's fortifications in Blackstone's mind and by nightfall he had advanced with his men from the woodland five hundred yards from the town's eastern wall. The men-at-arms sweated and cursed as they carried the cumbersome ladders, the weight slowing their advance, splinters snagging their callused hands, although the men ignored the stings. The fighters slithered their way forward, bent double and then crawling, using the orchard for cover.

Will Longdon hunched down with twenty archers behind him, the remainder of the bowmen kept as a rearguard with the horses. Jack Halfpenny was at the end of the line of men lying flat on the wet ground. Blackstone, Killbere, Meulon and Gaillard sat with the twenty-six men-at-arms below the broken walls that had been built by Roman legionaries but had crumbled centuries before. Beyond the shallow ditch and ruined fortifications the town's walls rose up forty feet, rebuilt by a royal captain a dozen years earlier. They were a further one hundred yard-long strides across two four-foot-deep ditches.

'Bollocks,' said Will Longdon quietly, having crawled forward to peer through the darkness at the looming shadow of the walls. 'The damned ladders are too short.'

'Did you expect Chandos's men to ease your journey?' said Meulon. 'Your arse is even shorter. We'll have to throw you over.'

There was a glint of teeth in the darkness. Someone blew snot from his nose. Another broke wind.

'Merciful God,' whispered Killbere, 'that stench could alert the night watch on the walls.'

'It will slay the night watch,' said Gaillard and those close to him felt him half turn in the darkness as he hissed an order to the waiting men. 'Tighten your arses. No man under my command will shit himself. You've enough brandy in you for warmth and courage.'

Blackstone had made sure that every man had been given enough of the brandy seized from the routiers to deaden the fear that faced them all. The town was well defended by men who outnumbered them. If Chandos's captain couldn't get the length of the ladders right then his estimate of the garrison's strength might well be inaccurate too.

A figure moved in the darkness in front of them and the men's breathing quietened in anticipation. A voice whispered warning: 'Sir Thomas.' It was John Jacob and Perinne returning from their reconnaissance of the walls. They clambered over the low parapet and slumped into the ditch. Perinne pulled off his steel skullcap helmet and sucked in his breath. A reluctant moon gave brief illumination as the rainclouds scuttled away and exposed a patch of sky. Both men were soaking wet and John Jacob's legs and chest showed that he had slithered through mud.

'I think I found where to go over,' said John Jacob quietly, gratefully accepting the flask of brandy from Killbere's outstretched hand. He took a mouthful and let the sharp liquid catch his breath. He handed the flask to Perinne without any complaint from Killbere. 'Thirty yards down on the right. Perinne saw that the ditch's bank rises beneath the walls. When they dug the defences they piled the dirt too high. The ladders will reach.' He grinned.

Blackstone grunted in satisfaction. He turned to Will Longdon. The archers' bow cords were not yet fastened, protected from the rain beneath the men's helmets and caps. So too the arrows' goose-feather fletchings in their waxed linen bags. The sheaf of arrows each man carried was not enough for a sustained fight but once they were over the walls and Chandos's men were through the gates there would be little need for the archers in the confines of the narrow streets. They would fight with knife and sword. By the time the invaders reached the keep and the town's final defence the archers would be resupplied.

'Will,' said Blackstone. 'Keep half a dozen men fifty paces from the walls. Use the ditches for cover. As soon as we are on the wall, kill the night watch, especially anyone in that watchtower.'

Will Longdon screwed up his eyes at the walls. The darkness gave them little chance of seeing the night watch let alone anyone in the dim watchtower. 'We'll need some light, Thomas. Pray the moon breaks through.'

'The night watch will silhouette against this sky. You'll see them move even in darkness – there's enough light behind the clouds', said Blackstone. 'Once you've killed them bring the others inside and flank us on the walls. Cover the yard below until we get across the town square to the gates. Then be at our backs.'

Longdon nodded. 'God be with you, Thomas,' he whispered.

'And with your aim, Will,' he answered.

Longdon grinned and crawled back to his men.

'Gaillard, you take the middle ladder. Meulon the right. I'll go left with John and Sir Gilbert.' The two Normans grunted their understanding and crouched through the orchard to where their men waited. Each man leading the assault would have only his share of the twenty-six men-at-arms. It was Blackstone's job to open the town's gate and bring in Chandos's men for the assault through the town.

'I'll take a dozen men for the gates,' said Killbere.

'No, I want you at my back, Gilbert.'

'Standing in the dark with my cock in my hand? Thomas, I'll fight for the gate.'

Blackstone edged closer to the veteran knight. He whispered, 'You've the chills and you tremble. Were you any other man I would have kept you back with the horses. You're my rearguard once I'm in that yard. They'll come from the streets and alleys, Gilbert. You can stand firm with half a dozen men and Will's archers.'

'Thomas, I –'

'No argument, Gilbert. Cover my back or join Henry with the horses.'

He heard Killbere suck his teeth in subdued protest. 'Then let's get on with it,' he complained and grabbed one of the ladder's rails. It would take three men to manoeuvre the heavy ladders across the undulating ground and then heave them up the bank of the ditch. His anger gave him the strength to show the men he was no weakling despite the aching that had begun to seize his muscles.

John Jacob grabbed the middle of the ladder as Perinne took the end. Blackstone ran forward crouching. Men slipped and cursed, recovered and then managed to follow the towering shadow towards the wall. Within minutes the half-light showed them the rising bank identified by John Jacob. They slithered up, kept their curses to themselves and once there hugged the walls. Much depended on Will Longdon's skill and timing in killing the night watch on the wall. At each end of the wall a man stood guard with two more in the watchtower. There was little doubt that even when the sentries were slain the action would alert those in the guardhouse, who could quickly break the winding devices for the gate, and then a defence would be rallied and Blackstone's men caught like rats in the town square. Chandos's men would be forced to make their way around the walls under attack from above. Casualties would be high and the survivors would then have to clamber up the ladders. Everything depended on those arrows finding their marks.

'All right,' said Blackstone. Men eased the ladders up, ramming the spiked ends into the ground. No sooner were they planted than Blackstone was already climbing hand over hand, shield across his back, Wolf Sword held in the ring at his belt, its naked blade free of its scabbard, unhindered when drawn. A lesson learnt more than a dozen lifetimes ago at the battle for the great city of Caen. A lesson given by the man who grunted his way behind him. Sir Gilbert Killbere.

The gods of war laughed at the Englishman and sent a gust of wind to push the clouds from the moon. Rain swept across the rooftops and with snare-drum urgency on slate roofs declared its retreat into the forest beyond. Caught in the glare of the moon Blackstone reached the top of the wall and clambered over. Neither sentry left or right had looked around, but as Blackstone drew Wolf Sword the scrape of hardened steel against the holding ring made one man turn. Blackstone was upwind. In an instant the man had twisted around, face contorted, his mouth widening into a call to arms. Blackstone knew he would never reach him in time, but strode towards him as his men breached the parapet behind him. Before the man's scream echoed across the cobbled square an ash shaft whispered through the air and took him through the jaw. Barely a breath later two more arrows thudded into him. The man crumpled, his spear clattering. The sound would have been heard by the other sentry behind Blackstone on the far end of the wall, but he was already dead, struck down by the deadly skill of the archers. There were distinct sounds of steel-tipped arrows tearing bone and flesh as the night-watch sentries went down at their posts. Had they survived moments longer those on the far walls would have seen Blackstone's men. Somewhere in the darkness a dog barked. And then another. The barking increased as if each dog were calling its warning to its neighbour.

The watchtower sentry was the more difficult target, but Blackstone knew he had to ignore him; he was Will Longdon's mark. Blackstone raced along the walkway towards the gate and those he hoped still slept in the guardhouse. The sentry cried out when he saw the invading shadows. His shout of alarm was dulled by the wind but it would have been heard. Blackstone saw the man's hand reaching for the bell rope. Arrows thudded into the wooden structure, the archers' aim thrown off by the shadows in the watchtower. Another cry of alarm, its urgency stifled by the wooden roof and the wind. Blackstone's eyes locked on the man. There were seventy paces to the steps that led down into the square, another 140 or more to the gates. *Kill him!* his mind yelled. *Goddammit, Will. Kill him!* The shadow that was the watchtower sentry suddenly bucked, head whipping back, arms splayed. An arrow had taken him through the eye and pierced his skull. The shaft pinned the man's head to one of the wooden posts and for a few seconds made his arms flap in a macabre simulacrum of flight. The man's death throes tore his body free and one flailing arm caught the bell's rope.

Blackstone went down the steps into the square two at a time. The cobbles glistened from the night's rain, moonlight glinting, its sheen soon to be tainted with blood. Across the open space another set of steps rose up to the opposite parapet where a windlass was positioned above the gate entrance. A chain descended to the base of the heavy, iron-studded top-hung gate so that it could be raised horizontally.

No commands were given and none were needed. Footfalls chased after him. He turned and saw his men streaming down the steps and as Perinne and John Jacob followed him Killbere and the others ran into the square.

'Thomas,' yelled Killbere. 'Be quick!'

Hundreds of fireflies shimmered from the dark alleys. Burning torches. And what had been silence a few heartbeats before was now overtaken by a rising roar of men's voices as from the streets and alleys men and women advanced in a surging line, torches held high. Fear and anger mingled in their throats. They carried pitchforks and scythes, falchions and iron bars. Women held kitchen knives ready to stab, their voices an eerie pitch that could raise the dead. Anger and fear drove them against the English invaders. And the French troops who pushed their swords into their backs. The garrison were using them as shields against the Englishmen.

Blackstone saw the threat. They would be overwhelmed. A greater fear needed to be inflicted. He raised his sword arm towards Longdon and his archers on the walls. 'Kill them!'

Without hesitation Will Longdon's archers turned their bows towards the snarling faces in the shimmering torchlight and as Blackstone raced for the steps screams echoed against the walls.

The bowmen were slaughtering the townspeople, but, shields held high against the arrows, the French soldiers came on, trampling their bodies underfoot. To French eyes, this was to be an easy victory. Fewer than fifty men appeared to have breached the walls. They looked to be routiers and they were now trapped in the confines of the square. Crossbowmen sheltered behind the advancing soldiers and four of Longdon's archers died on the walls.

Blackstone reached the windlass. He jammed in the turning pole. Normally it took two men to turn the drum but, letting Wolf Sword dangle from its blood knot, he grasped the handle and heaved his weight against it. The chain bit and the great door creaked. Meulon was suddenly at his side and lent his weight. The door was barely halfway up. 'Enough!' Blackstone said and Meulon jammed the holding rod into position.

They turned for the square. A hay cart blazed; shadows loomed high on the walls. They hurled themselves into the fray. Renfred, Perinne and John Jacob were shoulder to shoulder holding ground; Killbere was to one side and it looked as though he had been separated by a mixed group of troops and townsmen. The townsmen's fury and terror made a heady mix as the torches illuminated a scene from the underworld. Dogs howled and barked; some driven mad by the smell of blood panicked, snapping and snarling at both attackers and defenders. Both sides slew them. Will Longdon ordered some of his men to keep shooting at the surging crowd as Jack Halfpenny and Thurgood ran further along the wall with three other bowmen and loosed arrows into the Frenchmen's flanks.

Blackstone glanced over his shoulder. Where was Chandos? He turned around and saw the flames illuminating the throng of men and women who were still surging forward. Their weight of numbers might push Blackstone's few men back through the very gate they had raised. Killbere had cut down four of the attackers but he was overwhelmed and fell beneath repeated blows. Blackstone turned again, Meulon at his shoulder.

'John! Perinne!' Blackstone yelled. They saw him move

towards Killbere and within a few strides joined him. Thirty paces away Gaillard and his men had raised a shield wall and that had slowed the French advance; his men were thrusting beneath the wall into those who pressed against them, making no distinction between those they struck, turning the square into a charnel house more terrifying than any priest's threat of purgatory. Women writhed, screaming from their wounds; soldiers fell to their knees, hands grasping at entrails spilling from pierced bellies.

'Get him back,' Blackstone shouted to the men-at-arms who had manoeuvred themselves to join him. Two men grabbed Killbere and dragged him into an abandoned building. 'Stay with him!'

Several men were now at Blackstone's shoulder and with a skill born from years of efficient killing they moved forward in a wedge like a broadhead arrow, forcing the French back yard by yard in a grunting, sweating trial of arms that few could match. Blackstone reached Gaillard, saw the arrows still cutting into the French. Panic was claiming the enemy.

As John Chandos and his men stormed through the half-raised gate the looming shadows of Blackstone's men methodically killing anyone who challenged them almost made the veteran knight falter. He had never seen so many being slaughtered by so few.

And then he brought his men to bear and the surge forced the French to turn and run.

CHAPTER NINE

Blackstone and his men drew breath and allowed Chandos's men to relieve them. They had done what had been asked of them. They gathered in the corner of the town square and let the sounds of the killing recede down the alleyways. Will Longdon accepted the resupply of arrows from Sir John's levies and distributed two sheaves to each man. They had lost four archers; one of the Cheshire men and three of the Welsh had been brought down by crossbow bolts and their bodies now lay against the wall alongside the four men-at-arms killed in the fighting. Meulon and Gaillard set a defensive screen around the men who rested and guzzled water, sluicing the smeared blood from their faces. Blackstone was inside the room where John Jacob and Perinne attended Killbere. The space looked to have been used by guards. A couple of old stained straw mattresses lay abandoned, one of which now gave some comfort to Killbere, who was still unconscious.

'I see no sign of injury, Sir Thomas,' said Perinne as he unbuckled Killbere's breastplate while Jacob eased off the veteran knight's helm.

'I saw him go down under the blows,' said Jacob. 'There's no blood on his scalp but he took some hard strikes.'

Blackstone knelt and raised Killbere's head, and using a wet cloth wiped away the splattered evidence of the close-quarter fighting. Killbere, as always, had stood firm in the attack; he could sustain wounds better than other men. His lips moved as the cool water soothed him. Blackstone dribbled brandy onto them from the flask. Killbere spluttered, his eyes half opened, and he gazed at the man leaning over him. Shadows cast from the burning torches shimmering across his face. A scarred face, hair matted with sweat, features caked with dirt and blood.

'Mother of God, Thomas, you look like a devil's imp. Don't grin so. You would scare a child from the womb,' he said weakly. 'I was clubbed is all, leave me be,' he protested, trying to rise and push Perinne away, his fist curling in the stocky man's leather jerkin, but he had no strength and lay back, sighing with the effort. 'A few moments' rest and I shall be ready,' he said. He grunted, allowing Blackstone to half raise him and put a ragged blanket behind his head as a pillow. His eyes closed again. Blackstone took a swig of the brandy and passed it to the others. The three knelt for a few moments, unwilling to leave Killbere's side. Blackstone looked over his shoulder into the night.

'They'll take the keep without us,' he said, 'and that means they'll seize the gold. Chandos will take the glory for it and the King will reward him.'

Killbere's eyes opened. 'Gold…?' he muttered. 'Thomas… do we not have it? The fight goes on…?' He tried to raise himself but Blackstone placed a hand on his chest, gently restraining him. 'Keep your hands… to yourself…' Killbere complained, resisting the pressure. Then: 'Do your work, man!' he hissed, his fierce countenance startling all those around him. 'Get off your arse and find the damned gold,' he demanded. The effort proved too much and he slipped back onto the pillow, but his eyes glared at Blackstone and the others as if asking what it was they were waiting for.

Without another word Blackstone obeyed the man who had first taken him to war and who in Blackstone's eyes was the bravest of men on the battlefield. Pulling on his helm he stepped back out into the night. His men raised their eyes.

'We go back to the fight,' he said. 'We'll not let Sir John's fingers alone caress the Lamb of God.'

The men grinned and got to their feet.

Blackstone turned to Will Longdon. 'Choose six archers to stay. Jack will be in command, Robert with him.'

Halfpenny and Thurgood stood eagerly awaiting Blackstone's orders. 'You'll take position and shield Perinne and six men-at-arms,' said Blackstone. 'You are to defend Sir Gilbert who is in Perinne's care until we return.'

'Aye, lord,' said Halfpenny as Perinne and Longdon quickly chose the men to stay. There was no need for Blackstone to linger; each man knew his duty, and all would die before anyone breached their defence of the veteran knight now lying unconscious.

Blackstone led his men across the square, stepping across the torn bodies, which lay three deep from the earlier assault. They moved cautiously into the darkened alleys narrow enough to allow only four men abreast through them. It was unlikely any of the townsmen would strike out at them now that the initial defence of the town had failed and Chandos's men had forced their way towards the keep. Here and there bodies lay in doorways, blood smears showing they had been caught outside and had tried to beat down the doors that those inside would not open. Some of the wounded moaned and squirmed but Blackstone's men ignored them; there was no need to give them a quick death, they had tried to kill the English and now they had to suffer. Suffering was good for the soul.

Villagers' livestock wandered through the town, some panicked by the scent of blood and the cries of fighting. Backlit by the flames from a burning stall a cow stood in the street gazing forlornly at Blackstone's men; sheep the size of dogs flocked in groups of ten or more, running and stopping and running again, unsure where to seek safety. The fighting must have broken down or burnt their pens. Blackstone's men ignored the bizarre sight. If they survived the night they would feast on mutton. Somewhere a pig squealed. It had fallen under a blade.

Other than the animal pens the town had not been torched; it was to be kept intact because Chandos wanted to claim it in the name of King Edward and leave sufficient troops to hold it. It could serve as a defence in the east once Edward had seized

Paris. A chain of encircling towns clawed back from the French would form a belt of steel to help protect the city. The men trudged through the streets, senses alert, eyes straining in case anyone threw missiles from the upper floors. Rain came and went, flurries dashing against man and beast as the cold, hard drops danced on the cobbles yet Blackstone's men still sweated from their previous efforts, their undershirts stiff with it, and breath and perspiration steamed from their bodies in the biting cold.

The clamour of the fighting ahead – together with screams of agony from man, woman and beast, and the plaintive howling of an infant – guided Blackstone to where the streets grew wider until they flared into another broad open square in the middle of which stood the squat three-storey keep. There were enough bodies lying at its gates to show that the French troops had retreated inside and Chandos and his men had pursued them. The stench from the killing would soon be foul and Blackstone was in no doubt that the devil would be dancing with joy.

Blackstone halted the men. Some of Chandos's soldiers were killing the wounded in the square and from the darkness of the streets howls from women told their own story. The French knight's banner still flew from the top of the keep – he had not yielded the last of his defences but was fighting to the bitter end. Such fierce resistance meant the defenders retained their honour in their attempt to protect the Dauphin's gold. Blackstone knew he would have to get inside and force his way to the strong rooms or cellars, wherever the defence was the heaviest, because that was where the prize would be held. Narrow corridors and tight stairwells were hard places to fight in. A man could barely wield a sword and the ground favoured the defenders. His archers would be useless. He spat. There was no other way. Get inside and rout the bastards out and pray to God there would be no conflict between his men and Chandos's over the plunder.

He was about to stride across the square when he saw movement in the shadows beyond the keep. Had it not been for the shifting clouds and the moonglow, which momentarily made the shadow become a man, he would not have seen the priest who scurried with half a dozen soldiers at his back. They carried no torches and their stooped figures moved furtively but rapidly into the church door that was only just visible down the length of the dark street. The soldiers' shields did not bear the three black stripes and ram's head that was the town commander's blazon. The glint of light showed a silver lion on a black background, claws unfurled, its hungry red tongue protruding from the gaping jaws: a savage beast whose silent roar was known to the fighting men in Normandy and Picardy – and Englishmen had faced it at the battle of Poitiers. The blazon belonged to an old warrior, Robert de Fiennes, now Constable of France. As the first officer of the Crown he commanded the army, and his authority was second only to the King. But now he served the Dauphin.

Darkness swallowed the men. The noise of fighting increased from the keep; those of Chandos's men who had been killing in the square ran into the building. Blackstone turned for the dark passageway leading to the church. Let the devil have his fun: an angel had just touched Blackstone's shoulder. Sir John Chandos was fighting in the wrong place. The French commander's defence was a ruse. If the Constable's men were in the town they were there for only one reason. The gold.

CHAPTER TEN

They reached the church door and squatted by the walls, letting their breathing settle as they listened for any movement that might warn of approaching danger. Longdon's archers would struggle using the long bows in the narrow street but he positioned them so that they could cover the square surrounding the keep. Should any French defenders try to escape they would run into English arrows.

Blackstone laid the palm of his hand against the iron-studded church door and pressed it gently with his shoulder as John Jacob took hold of the iron ring to raise the latch. Together they eased open the door. The smell of damp from the cold church wafted across their faces and somewhere beyond the vast stone floors echoed the scrape of metal on metal. Blackstone crouched and ran quietly towards one of the great stone pillars that supported the vaulted roof. A few windows offered scant moonlight and as his men filtered in and waited, bent at the knee, swords in hand, they listened, heads turning slightly trying to locate where the soldiers had gone with the priest. They heard another door close somewhere near the altar, and after a quick look to see that there were no men waiting in ambush, Blackstone strode towards the sound. Their boots creaked and the jangle of belt and mail seemed deafening in the stillness. Blackstone raised a hand to slow those following. There was barely enough light for the dark forms behind him to see his command, but their senses were sharpened and they obeyed.

Muffled voices murmured somewhere close by.

John Jacob, at his shoulder, whispered, 'The crypt.'

Blackstone nodded and went forward, feeling his way past the altar towards a gaping black hole whose steps led downward. The palm of his hand against the rough stone wall guided him for he was soon in pitch darkness and fearful of stumbling and alerting those who were somewhere ahead. He widened his eyes, desperate for any mote of light to reach them, and then he saw a flicker some indeterminate distance ahead. Torchlight glimmered behind the door frame. He told John Jacob what he had seen and each man in turn passed back the information. Blackstone edged forward along the passage – like the street, too narrow to swing a sword. As they got closer to the light the voices became more distinct and they heard what sounded like a metal rod or blade sliding against a metal ring with a high-pitched screech. Blackstone blindly felt around the door frame until his fingers touched an iron sliding bolt, its worn handle big enough for a man's fist to curl around. He reached back to touch John Jacob and moved his face close to his ear.

'There's no room to fight here,' he whispered. 'The crypt must be behind this door. Ease past me; there's a bolt halfway down the right-hand side. The hinges are inside so it will open inwards. Heave it open, John, and we'll go in. Wait for my command.'

He felt rather than saw John Jacob nod his understanding as his squire eased past him. The next man in line was Meulon and Blackstone pressed his hands against the big man's chest. 'Step back. Be ready. We go through the door,' he whispered, needing to give themselves room to rush the crypt once the door was opened.

Blackstone's right hand curled around Wolf Sword's grip, his gloved left hand held its blade halfway down. He would thrust and stab the moment he was inside.

'Now,' he hissed.

The door slammed open into a broad, low-ceilinged room. Stacked four-high on each side were stone coffins that bore the chiselled blazon of the ram's head. The final resting place of the lord's ancestors. In the middle of the room a priest bent over two chests. One was closed with an iron bar fitted through steel rings at each end that would enable men to bear its weight. The half-dozen soldiers were bending to the task of lifting one chest and readying the other. None held a weapon in their hands and their sudden cries of alarm were deadened by the crypt's confines and the coffins. Blackstone's men attacked silently. The priest cried out and was pushed to the ground as the soldiers dropped the chest and attempted to draw their swords. Blackstone went for the farthest men, barging aside the two nearest. The force of his charge allowed Meulon time to kill one and for John Jacob, who was a pace behind him, to thrust his knife into the other's neck. Blackstone rammed Wolf Sword's tip into the open-face helmet of one of the men on the far side of the chest and slammed his elbow into the other, who collapsed. Blackstone leaned against Wolf Sword's hilt as the blade pierced the fallen soldier's chest. He writhed but Blackstone's boot pressed hard into his stomach as Blackstone withdrew the blade and pushed it into the man's throat.

The other two soldiers of the half-dozen men had been behind the open door, which caught one in the face when it was slammed open. Gaillard struck him with his fighting axe, which gave the other Frenchman time to draw his dagger and lift his shield. He was ready to fight but John Jacob's momentum carried him forward and he wrapped his arms around the shield, smothering the Frenchman's efforts.

'Kill him!' Jacob yelled as the knife's blade skidded off his shoulder guards. He might not be as lucky with the next strike. There was no room for spear or sword in the corner where Jacob grappled with the man. Meulon half turned and lunged bare-handed past Jacob's face at the soldier's throat. Bones cracked. The man gasped and then Jacob's thumbs were in his eyes as the man tumbled with Jacob on top. His knife hand wavered but the Englishman tore the dagger away and pushed its blade hard and fast beneath the rim of the man's helmet.

Meulon grabbed Jacob's belt and, despite his weight, hauled him free from the sprawled man and then, in case the twitching body was not dead enough, snapped the man's neck with the heel of his boot.

The priest cowered as Blackstone stood over him. The crypt was suddenly crowded with men who barely had room to move.

'Outside!' Blackstone ordered. 'Tell Will to keep his men in the street. Everyone else in the church. Stay silent. Wait for me.'

The men turned and shuffled their way out. 'Captains stay here,' he said. 'Gaillard, there's air enough down here for these torches to burn. Go forward and see where this crow was sending the soldiers with these chests. Take one of the men with you.'

Gaillard ordered Renfred to join him from the other side of the door and picked up one of the fallen torches, then went on down the narrow, dark passage with the man-at-arms at his heels. The priest pushed himself back against the wall, knees drawn up, a hand clutching the silver crucifix at his chest, lips silently moving in prayer. Blackstone nodded to Meulon, who threw open the chests. The church's silver plate was in one, gold and silver coin in the other.

John Jacob sighed. 'This would buy a town, Sir Thomas. We could all retire with this.'

'Priest,' Blackstone snarled, 'how much is here?'

The priest's desperation to find the right answer was obvious. He stuttered. 'I don't know, thousands... Spare me... Twenty, thirty thousand...'

Meulon's eyebrows rose. It was a fortune.

The priest barely drew breath. 'We had yet to finish counting... I beg you, do not kill me...'

'Do you not have enough faith in your saviour to meet him in the afterlife?' said Blackstone. The tip of his blade hovered beneath the man's chin. 'What good are you to the people that were forced at sword point to fight us?'

'I could not stop Sir Louis... He... he is fiercely loyal to the King and to the Dauphin... We were ordered on pain of death to secure the coin.'

'How long have the Constable's men been here?'

'Yesterday. They came yesterday for the coin.'

'But English troops have been watching the town. They saw no sign of them.'

'The passage... it runs two hundred yards; there's a barred entrance behind bushes and trees and then open ground to the forest,' said the priest.

'Their horses must be back in the trees,' Meulon said, poking one of the bodies with his boot.

The priest nodded. 'Yes, yes. That's true.'

Gaillard and Renfred returned from the passageway.

'Does it go beneath the walls?' said Blackstone.

The Norman nodded. 'And then there's open ground to the woodland beyond.'

Blackstone looked down at the priest and pressed the sword point into flesh. A trickle of blood ran from the slight cut. It was enough to frighten him more. 'Lucky you told the truth. Why shouldn't I kill you? You serve no purpose.'

'There's more,' the priest gasped. 'Another five thousand... please... I'll show you where.'

They dragged the priest to his feet and he winced as his sandalled foot stepped in blood. He was bundled back into the stairwell and up to the nave where Blackstone's men waited.

'Across the street,' the priest whispered.

Once outside they could hear that the fighting continued in the keep. Blackstone called in the darkness to Will Longdon, who quickly shuffled past his archers.

'Have the French broken out of the keep?'

'No. They're being butchered where they stand. I reckon they must be holding every room and passage. Sir John's men have a fight on their hands.'

'Will, stay here. We're going across the street. No one must get into the church.'

Blackstone quickly followed the priest and as they went into the building opposite they could taste the sharpness of a furnace that was long since cold.

70

'Light them, my lord,' said the priest, gesturing to the cresset lamps on the walls. Meulon and Jacob touched flames to the oil lamps and the glow filled the room, revealing the blackened coals of the furnace and four stout wooden workbenches where roughly hewn stools showed that five or six men would have worked at each bench. Leather buckets sat at the foot of each stool. Blackstone ran his hand across the work surfaces, scarred with the signs of men striking iron-tipped dies to mint coins. He picked up the broken pieces of a die and rubbed his thumb across the iron cast on the end of the stub of wood. It was not difficult to picture the gold and silver being smelted and, when cold, hammered into coins. Each die would have a life of a few thousand strikes before becoming unusable. These dies were not that old: the ends of the punches not sufficiently flattened by repeated blows from a mallet.

'The soldiers made sure the dies were destroyed so my lord Sir Louis could not mint more coin.'

'And the gold and silver?' said Blackstone.

'Stolen plate. I salvaged what I could for the church but the Constable's men insisted they take that as well. We are all helpless when men desire gold and silver.'

Blackstone tossed the broken pieces aside. 'And the five thousand?'

The priest went to a corner of the room and took a metal spike from a workbench. He levered up a floor plank, went down on his knees, reached inside and strained to lift a sack out of the hole. Gaillard quickly smashed his heel down and broke another plank and then bent to lift the weight clear. He dumped the sack on a bench and untied the cord that held the opening. He dipped a hand inside and came out with a fistful of minted gold and silver coins. He grinned in the flickering light. 'The Lamb of God has been saved.'

'So you too were helpless when it came to gold and silver,' said Blackstone to the priest.

'It can buy food for the people.'

'It can buy escape and a life of comfort in a convent,' Blackstone said.

'Sir Thomas, we could rest through the winter without more effort,' said Gaillard.

'We'll all benefit from it,' said Blackstone, 'but we stay silent about this until I say otherwise,' he told the men. He pulled the priest to him. 'What's your name, priest?'

'I am Robinet Corneille.'

The men laughed. The priest shrugged. There were times he wished his name did not mean what it did. There was always fun to be had with the sobriquet. Especially with the English.

'So... Corneille the "crow" priest, what is this?' Blackstone asked, touching the small pewter emblem of a flask stitched to the priest's cloak. 'This is from Canterbury. You've travelled in England as a pilgrim?' The flask was supposed to contain drops of water from a miraculous well.

'Years ago, my lord.'

Blackstone grunted. Perhaps this crow priest knew the ways of the English, which might make him less troublesome than another rural French cleric. 'Do you have medicine here? Can you administer to the wounded?' he said.

'I have little skill, lord, but I have stitched and treated wounds and I have some knowledge of how to bleed veins and administer potions.'

'Then you have some use after all,' said Blackstone. 'Your miserable life might still be spared.' He pushed him into Meulon's arms. 'Bring this thieving crow and see where else he's feathered his nest.'

CHAPTER ELEVEN

As Blackstone withdrew his men from the church and the area around the keep, the bodies of the citadel's defenders were being tossed from the windows into the street below. The search was going on inside for the money but Blackstone had already ordered the chests removed from the crypt. He and his men made their way back to the town square where Jack Halfpenny still held a defensive cordon around Killbere. Blackstone hauled the priest into the building where his friend lay unconscious.

Perinne looked worried. 'He's taken a turn for the worse.'

'Use your skills on this man,' said Blackstone to the priest. 'If he dies you die with him.'

The priest sank to his knees and pulled open the bag of medicines that had been retrieved from the church. 'If he dies it is God's will.'

'Then pray it is not His will that you die with him,' said Blackstone. 'Perinne, stay with him and watch the priest. If he does anything that you think causes Sir Gilbert harm, kill him.'

He went outside to where the men were gathered and saw his son lead two donkeys into the square through the gate.

'That's the third time your boy has come inside the walls,' said Jack Halfpenny. 'Once Sir John's men had stormed through the gate and we held this position he came looking for you. And then he saw the hay carts and brought in the donkeys, said our horses could do with the fodder before Sir John's men took it.' Halfpenny grinned. 'Did it all on his own, Sir Thomas. I offered him no help because we were protecting Sir Gilbert.'

Blackstone watched a moment longer as Henry whipped the

donkeys and guided the remaining hay cart towards the gate. The boy was soaked from the night's rain and his efforts must have made him sweat as much as any of the fighting men, but he looked neither left nor right as he went about his task. He gave no glance towards the men-at-arms or archers who now gathered around his father as Sir Gilbert was being attended to. The boy sought no acknowledgement or sign of approval.

'He left his post and the horses,' said Blackstone and Halfpenny's smile faltered.

'But, Sir Thomas, the lad –'

'Left his post. I'll deal with him later.' He pointed to the chests that had been brought from the church. 'Secure them in one of the rooms. Post a guard.'

Halfpenny pointed to several men and did as he was ordered. Will Longdon waited for his orders but stood close enough to Blackstone so that only he could hear what he had to say.

'Henry used his noggin, Thomas. Thought it through, saw the opportunity to help us all. A punishment would be unkind.' He pulled his helmet from his head and rubbed his sweat-soaked hair. 'And, dare I say, unjust,' he added.

'You sound like Sir Gilbert. Why does everyone think I am an ogre to my son?'

Will Longdon shrugged. 'He's a boy who yearns for your approval. It doesn't matter that he's your son; he knows he won't get special treatment. Thomas, I remember waiting with the Shropshire men at Portsmouth before the invasion in '46 and Sir Gilbert arrived with a sixteen-year-old archer in tow. Him and his brother were wet behind the ears. Neither had known the fear of battle but Sir Gilbert spoke up for you. I remember him telling us veterans your name, said none of us could pull the draw weight of your father's war bow that you carried, and said that you protected your brother and that you were both his sworn men. I remember them words from all them years back because he said any act against you and your brother was an act against him. You was given protection and if that's not special treatment then I don't know what is.' Longdon pulled his helmet back on. 'Begging your pardon, Thomas.' He turned back to his men.

'Will,' Blackstone said, halting Longdon. 'Well said. Have one of the men fetch my saddlebags.' Longdon nodded and walked away.

Blackstone remembered the trepidation he had felt when first taken to war and the uncertainty at being placed with the veteran archers. Will Longdon was right. Blackstone and his brother had been given a chance to prove themselves under Killbere's protection. And there was no harm in one of those archers who had shared his journey through the war years reminding him.

'Sir Thomas!' a voice called from across the square. Blackstone turned to see Sir John Chandos leading his bloodied men. Behind him twenty or so Frenchmen, some wounded, were being herded forward. One of them had the bearing of a nobleman. Chandos grabbed the proffered flask from Blackstone and guzzled water. He slurped, spat water into his hand and sluiced the sweat and blood from his face. His men settled in the town square and availed themselves of the water troughs. 'God was merciful, Thomas. We killed more of them than they us. We will have a mass said for our fallen and get about burying our dead.'

'There must be close to a hundred townspeople slain, Sir John.'

'Aye, I know.' He took another drink and looked back to where the bodies still lay three deep across the cobbles. 'We'll drag them into one of the houses and burn them.' He cleared his throat and spat phlegm. 'We were hard pressed. The bastards had courage. And him,' he said, nodding towards the knight who stood, unbowed by the possibility of imminent death or the wound that trickled blood on his bare head. 'De Joigny fought well but refuses to tell us where the gold is. There was nothing in the keep.'

Blackstone was no stranger to fighting in the narrow streets of city and town and knew that those citizens who had been slain would be fewer than those who remained hidden. 'You still want to hold this town for the King?'

'I do. I'll leave two-thirds of my men here; that's a strong enough garrison. I brought only a small contingent with me. I'll not be short-handed for the war. We found food and wine stored in the cellars. It will be enough until spring.'

'Then bury their dead,' Blackstone said. 'Give them a Christian funeral. Ease their resentment at us killing them and at them losing the town. Share the food; leave them with a fair-minded captain. There's less chance of them coming out their hovels and alleyways to cut your men's throats at night.'

'Good reasoning, but it was de Joigny and his men who pushed these people at sword point onto our blades. And I have promised to ransom him.'

'You give your word of honour to men of honour, Sir John, not a man who uses the people he is sworn to protect as shields for his men. Spare the Frenchman and you'll lose the town in weeks. Hang his men and behead de Joigny as his rank demands and hold the town for Edward.'

'Christ, Thomas, you've a ruthless heart.' Chandos sighed. 'Aye. I understand what you're saying. But although they've stripped the dead there's little plunder to be had for my men; I can at least ransom him.'

'Your men will be honoured and rewarded by the King. The mint here is no more. The dies are broken. The silver and gold was hidden in the church's crypt. The Constable's men were already here to take the coin back to Paris or to pay routiers to attack us day and night.'

Sir John's jaw hung open. He blinked. 'What?'

'I have the gold. Probably thirty thousand *moutons* and a chest of silver plate that I want as reward for my men. We scaled the walls and found the gold for the King. It's a small enough payment.'

'It's yours!' said Chandos, slapping Blackstone on the shoulder. 'The coin. It's safe?'

'Over there. Guarded by my archers.'

'I'll be damned. Any other surprises you have for me?'

'There are probably a handful of the Constable's men beyond the south wall in the woods. Nothing more than a rearguard with their horses.' He glanced up at the clearing sky. 'It'll be light soon. Can your men flush them out and kill them?'

Chandos nodded. 'We didn't see them when we kept watch on the town so, yes, we'll sweep the shit from our own stable.' He glanced back at Sir Louis de Joigny. 'But... I gave him my word that he would be ransomed.'

'He has lost everything. The town, the gold, the trust of the Dauphin. He'll pay the ransom and then he will come back and take the town to regain his honour. You need the people here to declare for Edward. Peasants need to be shown that those sworn to protect them will do so. No matter how poor they are and how desperate their lives, they need to see justice done. Kill him.'

Chandos hesitated and then shook his head. 'I cannot.'

Blackstone's voice took on an edge. 'You are not seeing this clearly, Sir John. Your honour is not in question but your King has asked you to secure this town. When this Frenchman comes back with five times as many men he will slaughter Englishmen, hard fighting men who were prepared to follow you in battle. You risk their lives over your word to a vicious lord and, worse, they will have died for nothing when the town is retaken. The King must need this town and others like it to protect his flank. We serve the King, Sir John; we should do what is in our power to give him what he needs from us.'

Chandos studied the man who stood head and shoulders above him. The eyes bore down on him and were he a lesser man he would have buckled to the demand – because that's what it was, a demand to execute the town's commander.

'You confuse me, Thomas. Your own honour forbids rape and the murder of women and children, and yet you expect me to break my word no matter what the cost.'

'Hang his men and take the gold,' Blackstone advised and turned away. There was no point pursuing an argument that could not be won. He left Sir John striding across to where the gold and plate was being guarded. Blackstone had secured enough treasure without betraying his King. Let Chandos think he had his due by allowing Blackstone to keep the plate. The King was expecting twenty thousand *moutons*; he was going to receive more. The sack containing five thousand would reward Blackstone's men and be enough money to keep them for a year if needed.

'How is he?' he asked the priest. A fire had been lit in the hearth, Killbere had been undressed down to his undershirt and the priest looked more concerned than before.

'My skills are limited, Sir Thomas,' he said, having learnt Blackstone's name from the men who served him. 'His fever comes and goes. I have given him drops of hemlock in wine to ease the pain and I have cleaned his wound.'

'Wound?' said Blackstone. 'I saw no wound. He took a blow to the head.'

'Not that,' said the priest and gestured for Perinne to help him turn Killbere. Perinne eased Killbere over onto his side and the priest lifted his shirt to expose the hand-sized wound Blackstone had seen at the siege at Rheims days before. The ointment Killbere had smeared on after the fight had been cleaned away but the puckered and raw skin was inflamed and full of pus; the stench of rotting flesh could not be ignored.

'There is poison inside him. A barber surgeon would cut away the rotten flesh but I do not think it will save him. How long has he been sick?'

'Days,' said Blackstone. 'We thought he was weakened by the chills.'

The priest helped ease Killbere onto his back and covered him with a blanket. 'I suspect the wound has festered on its own or what was put on the wound was... poisoned.'

French monks had sold Killbere the balm. Perhaps they wrought their own vengeance on the English invaders.

'You must save him,' said Blackstone.

'I cannot,' said the priest.

CHAPTER TWELVE

Despite the priest's insistence that he did not have the skills to save the veteran knight, Blackstone demanded that he try. The priest crossed himself for the twentieth time; perhaps God might bless him with a miracle. He watched as Blackstone bent his height below the door frame and went out to attend to his duties. Any moment alone with the dying man was miracle enough.

Blackstone ordered his men to find bloated carcasses of any beast slain before their attack. They were to search kitchens and butchers for hung game or meat or for any dead dog in the street, and for the maggots to be scraped from the rotting flesh.

'Henry,' Blackstone called. 'Not you. Come here.'

'My lord?'

John Jacob and Will Longdon watched the boy being summoned to accompany his father out onto the battlements.

'The lad does not deserve chastisement,' said John Jacob. 'He might have left his post but he got fodder for the horses. You'll keep my thoughts to yourself, Will.'

'They're no longer thoughts when you open your mouth, John. Who knows what Thomas will do to the lad? He's changed.'

'Henry?'

'Aye, him as well. He's not a child any longer. Not after what he went through with his mother. But I was thinking of Thomas,' he said.

'Christ, can we wonder at it? What he witnessed when his wife and child were slain? He's always been a hard man when need be, but I wager he's harder still now. We've both seen him fight but there's a fury to him now greater than I've witnessed before.'

John Jacob paused and chewed his lip, keeping his eyes on father and son as they walked along the walls.

Longdon looked at Blackstone's squire. Clearly there was more to be said once the words were considered.

'Almost', said Jacob reluctantly, 'as if he had a death wish.'

Longdon unsheathed his archer's knife ready to scoop the maggots from a dead cow that lay belly up. He turned his face from the smell, hawked and spat. 'I've seen him spit in the devil's face many a time. But I think you're right. We'd best make sure we're shriven. It will be the end for us all one day because where Thomas goes we follow.' His face crumpled in disgust. 'John, your cap is bigger than mine. Pass it to me – there are handfuls of these wrigglers.'

Blackstone and Henry looked down at the town square as the men went about their duties. Then Blackstone turned to gaze out across the battlements. The wind bit his face. 'Do you think the rain will spare us for a few more days?' he said.

Henry looked at the horizon across the forest and then around the surrounding countryside. 'I don't think so, my lord. In a day or two perhaps it might break. You can see the weather veers from the east. You can smell it, can't you?'

Blackstone grinned. 'You remember your childhood lessons well,' he said.

'Thank you, my lord.'

'When we are together you must call me Father.'

The boy beamed. 'I will, gladly.'

'You were instructed to stay with the horses in the forest and yet you left your post and came into the town when we were fighting.'

The seriousness of his father's question snatched away the smile. 'I did. The archers in the rearguard were complaining about not being in the fight. I said I would go forward and see if Will or Jack needed them. When I came into the square there had already been much killing and then I saw the hay carts. I knew we needed fodder... so I... took them. Were they not mine to take?'

'They were there to be seized. You did well. It was a good decision and a brave one.'

'There was no fighting in the square, Father, and Jack and Robert were there. I was in no danger.'

'I meant it was a brave decision disobeying my orders.'

Henry realized he had not understood quickly enough that there was an element of censure in his father's praise. 'Yes, sir, I disobeyed you because –'

'Don't explain again, Henry. You made your claim for your actions: stand by them. There is no need to defend yourself. We let our actions speak for themselves.'

They watched as the trees rustled from the veering wind.

'Will Sir Gilbert die?' said Henry.

'He might.'

'He is a great man. He and John Jacob cared for me when you... when you went away. They all did. All the men.'

Blackstone's disappearance for the better part of a year after the death of Christiana and Agnes at the hands of an assassin had never been broached. 'Henry, I was taken from you by grief. It was something I did not understand and an enemy I did not know how to fight. It will not happen again, I promise you.'

The boy nodded and smiled bravely. 'I hope not. I miss them too. But I... I remember when you killed the man who did it. I... I did not take pleasure in it... like you and the men. I could not. And I don't know why.'

'Don't question it. Killing comes differently to us all. Live with who you are. We are blessed with the men at our side. And you have known them all for some years now. You're satisfied serving as page to John?'

'I hope I serve him well and that he is satisfied with my duties.'

It was a good answer from a boy who might see his service as demeaning given his father's status.

'John Jacob thinks highly of you and is well pleased with your work. He tells me your swordsmanship is coming on, but what of your studies?'

Henry fell silent for a moment as he considered his answer. 'May I speak freely?' He looked up at his father. 'I remember telling you when we buried Mother and Agnes that I could not be a fighter like you even though I had killed to save them from the Jacques. I had promised Mother that I would study and when you were gone Sir Gilbert made me attend to my studies. He instructed my tutors to beat me if I did not apply myself. I was not punished very often. I learnt quickly and it came as easily, as when you taught me to read the wind and understand the animals in the forest. But Sir Gilbert said that I was to understand what was not written in books.'

'And what was that?' said Blackstone.

'Loyalty, Father. He said that was the greatest treasure a man could possess. And that is why he brought me to you that day when grief claimed you at that London inn. And that is why I will serve you as the others do. But I have no books with me so I cannot read when my duties allow me. I have tried to fulfil my promise to both you and Mother.'

Blackstone felt the wind sting his eyes. He almost reached for the boy to hold him close, but then the tears could not be blamed on the cold.

'I am proud of you, as was your mother. I am blessed that you are my son.' He felt the stricture in his throat and feared the love for his son and the talk of Christiana would defeat him. He pushed the emotion away and took a small leather-bound book from beneath his jupon. 'I know you have no books with you.' He handed the volume to his son, who held it as if it were a block of gold. 'It was your mother's. It stays safe in my saddlebags and I kept it by my side all the years we were apart. It is all I have of her joy, so cherish it. Now, go and attend to your duties. See that my horse is groomed and fed, and be careful of him. It seems you're the only one he doesn't try to kick and bite.'

'Oh, he does! But I give him apples and make sure he has the sweetest hay. He's getting to know me.' Henry grinned and went down the steps. Blackstone watched him. The boy turned back and lifted the book. 'Thank you, Father. Thank you.'

CHAPTER THIRTEEN

Blackstone administered the squirming larvae himself into Killbere's suppurating wound. He had given orders that fresh linen be boiled and dried over the fires, no matter if smoke clung to the bandages: it might help heal the wound.

'I have not seen this done,' said the crow priest. 'To take maggots feeding on death is to put death into the wound.'

'I've had it done to my own wounds,' Blackstone told him. 'They eat the rotting flesh better than any barber surgeon can cut. It cleans the wound. We use your potions once they have done their work and you bleed him.'

'Bloodletting is better served when done on a saint's day.'

'Then find a damned saint and draw his blood.'

Robinet scratched his head. 'What day is it today?'

Blackstone looked blankly at him. Then called to the men outside. 'Perinne? Will? What day is it?'

There was a murmur from the men and Perinne stepped into the doorway. 'We don't know, Sir Thomas. We left Rheims what... six days ago? Eight? Why would we need to know?'

'The priest needs it.'

'My lord,' said Henry, who appeared at Perinne's side. 'I believe it is the seventeenth day of January. I might be wrong by a day or two but... I believe that is close.'

Blackstone smiled at his son, thankful that he had taken Will Longdon's advice. 'Well remembered, son.'

When Henry turned away Blackstone looked at the priest. 'Well?'

'A day or so here or there should not make much difference...

Saint Andrew the Confessor of Peschiera is remembered... on the nineteenth. We will invoke his goodness to help your friend.'

'Do everything in your power to save him. Your life has not yet been spared.'

Robinet the Crow, as the men now called him, shook his head. 'I have told you, Sir Thomas, nothing I have can heal him. We can only pray.'

'You think Our Lord will listen to words spilling from your lying mouth?'

'I think it is the only chance your friend has.'

As the night closed in and his men slept he allowed the priest to question why the veteran knight was so important to him. Blackstone's disdain for the thieving cleric was tempered when he shared his own story of serving the French royal captain, Sir Louis de Joigny. There had been a time when the local villagers, as ignorant and superstitious as any peasant, attended Robinet's services in the town's church. But de Joigny had demanded payment to be made: a tribute, no matter how modest, be it a handful of goose eggs, or a clutch of fish from the river. The villeins were poor enough and they soon preferred to be without God's grace than the food in their bellies. And the royal captain's demands were not restricted to the villagers. Even though the towns-people were dependent on the villagers to grow crops and slaughter beasts in winter to help feed them, they too were squeezed by the nobleman's demands. Louis de Joigny saw to it that food was always rationed and that the city cellars were well stocked in case of siege but those were supplies held to feed the soldiers not the people. Being the Champagne region's mint was the town's staple means of income from the French Crown. Payment was made for casting the coin and then distributing it to the French troops in the area. The town's craftsmen, skilled in leather and carpentry, earned money from selling their wares in larger towns but Sir Louis exacted his own tax on everything they sold. When the English invaded, Cormiers was the only place of safety for those within and without the town walls. The priest had challenged Sir Louis on a number of occasions on the people's behalf but the tyrant had ignored him, secure in his position as a favourite of the Dauphin who could do no wrong in the eyes of his court. When the priest complained too often Sir Louis threatened to tear down the ancient church and use the stone for outer defences. Robinet Corneille decided to hoard what he could and when the Constable's men had arrived that night to seize the last of the minted coin he quickly hid the sack of contraband. If the English or routiers came he would pay for the lives of those unable to pay ransom.

'And for yourself,' said Blackstone. He eased another handful of twigs into the fire's embers to build up the warmth in the room whose stone walls were only now beginning to hold the heat against the cold outside.

'Of course. I would speak up for others but if it was them or me I would choose the person I know and love the best.' He grinned. 'I have no wish to die because a routier or an English soldier sees no worth in my life. I will pay to live. What man would not? You spared me once you knew about the gold.'

'I spared you to heal my friend.'

'And you still intend to kill me? What good would that serve?'

'None,' Blackstone admitted. 'I can see that he is beyond help. You can keep your church and pray for those who survived the fight, but if your people rise up against the soldiers who stay here, then I promise the English King will not be as merciful as me. It's up to you to convince them to obey.'

The priest wrung out a cloth in a bowl of water and laid it across Killbere's forehead. 'The truth is I was going to run, Sir Thomas. Oh, I would have left some of the money for the poor, but I was going to take to the road and make my way to Avignon. It's warmer there and the Pope has his own wealth; it's a city of –'

'Greed,' Blackstone interrupted. 'I've been there.'

Robinet shrugged. 'I think I would like Avignon,' he said. 'And now that you're not going to kill me perhaps my... let's call it desire... my desire might serve us both.'

'How does your... let's call it greed serve?'

'The fact that Sir Louis de Joigny is a prisoner will not hinder his authority among the French once his ransom is paid. He will find power elsewhere. He will cast the same shadow of fear on us all. I may be a contradictory priest but I could take my tale of misery to the Pope and with sufficient embellishment I could have de Joigny excommunicated. I could cause his family shame. It could serve as a fitting revenge on behalf of us all.'

'Then you should start walking. Avignon is a long way.'

'He would hear of it and have me hunted down and flogged, or more likely stripped and mutilated; a victim of brigands is the story that would be told.'

Blackstone waited. There was more to come.

'If Sir Louis de Joigny were to be killed then much could be achieved,' he said. 'I would be safe to do as I wish and the people of Cormiers would be free of a tyrant and the English could stay here until hell freezes over.'

'And who would do the killing?'

'I would expect it to be you.'

'And why would I kill him?'

'Because if you agreed then I believe your friend here might have a chance to live. A slim one, but a chance.'

Blackstone grabbed the priest's cloak and yanked his face close to his own. 'Bastard priests don't bargain with my friend's life.'

'It's all I have,' said Robinet confidently without any hint of begging.

Blackstone thrust him away. 'How do I save him?'

'Two days' ride away is a man who conjures healing magic. He uses herbs and incantations.'

'Sorcery is condemned by the Church and herbalists by the French King's decree,' said Blackstone.

'Ah yes, condemnation and a King's ignorance. Medicine and healing, prayer and incantation. Are the latter so different?'

'You're a corrupt priest.'

'I do my best,' he said, grinning through blackened teeth.

* * *

Sir John Chandos did as Blackstone suggested. He allowed the townspeople to dig a communal grave and the priest to pray for the souls of the dead, and then he had the surviving French soldiers hanged from the elm trees beyond the walls. Chandos and his men were ready to return to Rheims. Blackstone would stay to keep a watchful eye on Killbere. The veteran slipped in and out of consciousness but when he was awake he ate well enough of the mutton broth and drank enough wine to kill the pain without needing the careful administration of hemlock. He snarled when the fever clouded his mind and cursed those caring for him, insisting he was not injured sufficiently to need fussing over. The tirades came and went and Blackstone and the men were grateful whenever Killbere fell into peaceful sleep. It was a mystery to them why such an ill man should eat and drink so well. It was because his dying body demanded it, the priest told them. It was a bad sign, not a good one. There were probably only days left before Killbere died.

Chandos commiserated with Blackstone. Killbere's death would be a loss. He promised that a mass would be said for such a loyal servant of the King once the news was taken back to Rheims. 'And we shall tell the Prince of what you did,' he said as he prepared to leave. 'And your good advice. A Christian burial offered them solace.'

'Some. But not enough,' said Blackstone.

Chandos grimaced. The noise from the streets beyond the square was proof enough that the town would never declare itself for the English King. Soldiers blocked the streets as townsmen and -women hurled abuse at Sir Louis de Joigny who rode between two men-at-arms at the front of the column behind Sir John.

'They would tear him apart like a pack of dogs now that his soldiers are dead,' said Blackstone. 'Give him to them.'

De Joigny stared down his beaked nose at the scar-faced knight who had placed a hand on his horse's bridle. He wrenched the reins free and addressed Chandos. 'Sir John, I am not to be insulted by a common mercenary.'

'He is more than that, my lord, he serves my King and my Prince,' said Chandos. 'He is held in high regard.'

'Not by me,' said de Joigny. 'I know of his reputation. A paid killer without honour. A man who once tried to slay my King. You heard what he said: he would throw me to those vermin. I am a royal captain. Respect is my right.'

Blackstone smiled. 'Your shit does not smell sweeter than any other man's. I have slain better and braver men than you and were it in my hands you would be hanged, drawn and quartered and your guts fed to the dogs while you were still alive.'

De Joigny leaned forward in the saddle, his sneering face closer to Blackstone's. 'I am under the protection of a gentleman and a Knight of the Garter. You are a barbarian. A peasant who should have been kept in the fields.' He hawked and spat at Blackstone.

Blackstone did not flinch but his hand snatched de Joigny's belt and hauled him to the ground. The horses spooked and Chandos cursed as his own horse veered away. The Frenchman gasped with shock but his hand went to his belt to draw a dagger. Before it could be eased from the sheath Blackstone slapped him hard with his open hand. The man's knees went from beneath him but Blackstone's strength hauled him free of the nervous horses and then flung him down onto the cobbles for all the town to see. The crowd fell silent, their gasp of disbelief heard at the gates.

Chandos was no fool. 'Thomas! No!'

Blackstone ignored him and as Chandos's men's hands went for their swords Will Longdon's men already gripped their bows with arrows nocked. Chandos yelled orders for his men to sheathe swords. What was about to happen could not be stopped.

'I killed French peasants when they rose up because they slaughtered the innocent, and you are no better than those Jacques. It is you who are the scum. You whip men's bodies and murder their souls,' Blackstone said.

His taunt wounded French pride. De Joigny scrambled to his feet, sword drawn, and attacked. Blackstone sidestepped. The Frenchman slashed left and right but Blackstone parried the blows

88

and forced him further back to where the townspeople gathered. Their moment of silent awe at what was happening was soon replaced by baying for Sir Louis's blood. The Frenchman did not lack courage; his heritage and years of fighting were as much a part of him as the air he breathed. He would not be defeated by a man of low birth no matter how formidable his reputation. Legends were just that. Myths. Embellished stories to create fear. Louis de Joigny was not afraid. He did not have time. Wolf Sword's blade severed his head in a single blow.

The corpse shuddered. Blackstone bent and picked up the head by the hair. He stepped to the cart that Chandos had loaded with the French soldiers' weapons. He pulled a spear free and jammed its point into the soft torn flesh and then hoisted Louis de Joigny's arrogant head for the townspeople to see. They cheered.

Chandos wheeled his horse, anger clouding his face. 'Damn you, Thomas. The King will hear of this.'

'Tell him the town and the gold *moutons* are his. Tell him I am riding north to seek help for my wounded friend. Tell him what you like, Sir John. This needed to be done.'

Blackstone rammed the spear shaft into the dirt. De Joigny's sightless eyes gazed on the town and the people who raised their fists and their voices. The town had been bought for the English crown; Blackstone had secured, too, a slim chance of survival for Sir Gilbert Killbere.

PART TWO

THE WITCH OF BALON

CHAPTER FOURTEEN

Mist and rain crept along the Seine, smothering Paris, but the grey blanket of weather failed to deaden the noise of the largest and most populated city in northern Europe. Street traders shouted and cajoled; carts rumbled; cattle were driven through the streets, their bells clanging, to be slaughtered in the butchers' and tanners' quarter near the Châtelet by the river. The beasts' pitiful bleating at the scent of blood was lost in the clamour of a city alive with commerce; the stench of the killing mingled with that of human waste that ran down open sewers. Depending where you were in the city, relief from this noxious odour could be found in the sweet aroma of baked wheat sprinkled with sugar and angelica and freshly baked, stacked tiers of loaves. A miasma of laundry women's steaming cauldrons failed to rise above the damp air.

Counsellor to the Prince Regent Simon Bucy looked out from the Île de la Cité across the river to the bustling streets. Who would be foolish enough to lay siege to and attack Paris? Only the English and their ravening King, who had slain the greatest army in Christendom years before and captured King Jean le Bon at Poitiers. Part of him wished they would try. Let them come, he thought, let them storm the gates and fall into the maze of narrow traffic-clogged streets and alleyways below the tall wooden buildings. It was his city, a place that had given him wealth and status, a walled fortress that protected thousands. His indignation at the thought of the English threatened to overtake his rational mind. There was news from Rheims and business to attend with the Dauphin. At times he wished he did not carry the burden of office, but he always dismissed that thought quickly. Not for him the slabs of cooked meat on open fires in the streets, the sizzling fat scraped onto slices of rye bread to be gorged without manners, the squatting in doorways playing dice as mendicant monks rattled their begging bowls and chanted prayers. Better to be cocooned by the finery of wealth and privilege.

The city's noise abated only after curfew, but during daylight hours Bucy had always welcomed its cacophony. Paris was the heart of the nation; it pumped life into France. At times its bedlam and smell seemed tame compared to the stench of cheap perfume and bustling insincerity of courtiers who jammed the inner chambers seeking favour with the court. He had lived long enough to recognize the smell of fear and treachery that being a close adviser to King Jean le Bon had brought. And he knew the threat that was England would never leave France; it would forever recur, as did the plague. The English – he sighed with distaste at their very name – had captured his King four years before and his absence was an additional problem for the adviser. How to fulfil the absent monarch's wishes and talk sense into his son, the Dauphin Charles?

As he climbed the steps towards the royal chambers he felt old and tired. Every damned joint seemed to ache from the perpetual damp that the Seine inflicted on him. Yet endurance was an essential attribute for those who desired to wield power, and Bucy knew in his heart that he of all people would endure. He had been the First President of the Parlement; he had witnessed and survived the plague; he had withstood the Paris uprising, which almost cost him his life when he had been deposed by the peasants' revolt a year and a half before. He grunted at the memory. That time had almost finished him. Those ignorant scum had not only deprived him of a great swathe of his wealth but also his role in government when the leader of the Paris merchants had briefly taken control, depriving him and the other advisers of their influence over the young Dauphin. The marauding Jacquerie had looted and burned his three suburban mansions at Vaugirard, Issy and Viroflay, but by the grace of God his magnificent urban estate close to the Abbey of Saint-Germain-des-Prés had been spared. Bucy sighed with satisfaction. The scum had been slain and Etienne Marcel, the leader of the merchants, executed. Now Bucy was back in power at the side of the Dauphin. Sooner or later the French would have to sue for peace and Bucy would do all he could to achieve the settlement.

He was ushered into the Dauphin's presence. Hardly the kingly type, Bucy thought as he bowed to the sickly, pale boy. The Dauphin had no reputation as a warrior; in fact years before he had been ushered from the field at Poitiers, his father's last great battle, by the mercenary creature the Savage Priest. Despite that humiliation, he now ruled as regent, to the anger and despair of many Frenchmen. He lacked any prestige in the eyes of either the citizens of Paris or the fawning noblemen. But, Bucy admitted to himself, the boy did have backbone. Indeed, his father might have been proud of that fact, had the Dauphin not rejected the peace treaty his father had signed with Edward. Stubbornness was one thing – was it born from a feeling of inferiority? – but taunting the English lion was sheer stupidity. And now the English had stormed ashore with the greatest army they had ever mustered.

The Dauphin raised a lace handkerchief to his nose. He seemed to have a perpetually runny nose and watery eyes, thought Bucy, watching the contradictory twenty-two-year-old who appeared more determined to keep as much of France out of the English lion's claws than his father the King. The treaty had ceded half the country, which was why Charles refused to honour it and the French monarch's ransom had yet to be raised and paid.

'It still rains,' said the Dauphin.

'Incessantly,' replied Bucy.

'Four months! Nearly five. It has not stopped! We tire of it. It has caused havoc with the crops, the wine harvest has failed, everything is becoming expensive. There will soon be shortages, refugees flood into the city, our coin is devalued and the price of grain has more than doubled.'

Bucy swallowed his despair. It was going to be one of those meetings fraught with misery. How he dreaded them. 'It might be wet,' he said, his voice rising with attempted enthusiasm and assurance, 'but we are safe behind the walls. The English are in the open. Their supplies dwindle; their army is bogged down in mud.'

'But for how much longer can we endure? We do not desire another revolt from the people,' sniffed the Dauphin.

'Should such a time come they would rather starve than bend their knee to an English king,' said Bucy.

'Don't pander. You and the King were close for many years, you are still his trusted friend, but when you come into our presence it must be with the truth not fantasy.'

'It is the truth, your grace. Can you imagine that mob out there being told what to do by the English?' The very thought made Bucy laugh. 'The butchers and tanners would have blood running down the streets and it wouldn't be from cattle.'

The thought of English blood being spilled in his city lightened the Dauphin's mood. He smiled. 'Yes. So they would. They are rough and uncouth, but they are Parisians and they would draw blood before yielding. They are a troublesome people but they are *our* troublesome people.' He gazed out across the city he was sworn to hold. His eyes sought out the landmarks that proclaimed the city's greatness. The twin towers of that magnificent homage to God, Notre-Dame, which would soon break through the shroud that had covered them these past several days. The university of Paris on the left bank that was, despite its often violent students, acknowledged as the intellectual seat of theological learning. The Grand'Rue, the paved thoroughfare that was the great artery running through the heart of the city, a city whose mighty gates and miles of extra walls built by his father kept enemies at bay. All of these must be denied the English. Perhaps the English King's avarice for the French crown would rouse God's displeasure – this interminable mist and rain might be cloaking a mighty storm waiting to hurl him back across la Manche, the sea that had borne him to these shores.

He turned back to Bucy, who was waiting patiently. 'Now, Simon, what news?'

Bucy straightened his shoulders and raised his head. It was good to look as confident as possible given the nation's dire situation. 'Rheims has not yielded. The English cannot break them. Gaucher de Châtillon stands firm as a symbol of the honour of France.'

'Edward has not broken through?' said the Dauphin, hope rising in his voice.

'And de Châtillon sends out raiding sorties. He is a hard taskmaster, sire, he even has the Archbishop in mail and on the walls.'

'The good Archbishop will make sure we never hear the end of it. How do we know this?' The Dauphin gestured for the ageing man to sit on one of the plumped silk cushions that adorned an ornate chair near to him. Bucy nodded gratefully.

'He sent a messenger through the English ranks. The man is English himself, married to a local woman. He talked his way through the lines. De Châtillon desires that you be told that Rheims will never fall. Rheims is well stocked with food. They could withhold another year, and Edward does not have the resources to lay siege for that long.'

The Dauphin smiled. The English could still be defeated without him ever going into the field to do battle. Not that that could ever be a possibility. Other than the Constable with his cavalry, who were riding from town to town trying to bolster defences and raise what money they could, the Dauphin had no army. Had no money to raise one. A eunuch prince regent. Well, the lack of finances may have castrated him but he could outwait the enemy; if he could hold on long enough the day would come when Edward would relinquish his claims to the French crown.

'Providing we pay the ransom,' he said aloud, letting his thoughts take voice.

'Your grace?' said Bucy.

'We have still not raised the ransom for our father and the English will not go home until they have the crown or the ransom. Or both.'

'The Pope has sent his legates to parlay for peace. Your father is prepared –'

'To sell France!' the Dauphin interrupted. 'To give Edward vast swathes of territory. Which we will not do!'

'No, highness,' said Bucy with sufficient humility in his voice. 'But, highness, the English King had agreed the treaty with King John. That treaty has not been... fulfilled. Edward's honour demanded he invade.'

'His greed demanded it.'

'As you say. Greed is certainly a compelling reason, sire, as is having the biggest army the English have ever mustered.'

The Dauphin glared at his most senior adviser. With ten thousand Englishmen on the rampage and the bands of routiers who raped and pillaged unhindered, France might buckle.

'France will not die,' said the Dauphin quietly. 'We saved Paris from the mob and we will stand firm against Edward. God will grant us the strength and He will sustain our people.' He blew his nose into the handkerchief and for a moment Bucy thought there were tears in his eyes from the emotions that drove the boy. He quickly dismissed the thought. The Dauphin fought for France but also had a shrewd eye on the future. When his father eventually died Charles would inherit the crown and the kingdom, and the more Edward gained now the more the Dauphin would become a pauper in his own land.

'Our plans are being implemented?' said the Dauphin.

Bucy managed to conceal his discomfort with a brief smile. 'As we speak, highness.'

The Dauphin nodded. He might be trapped behind the city walls but there were men enough outside to cause some havoc to the English. Especially the most daring. 'When they land they must strike quickly. They understand that?'

Bucy's mind raced. The Dauphin had sent two thousand men to England to seize his father from the English and restore him to the throne. It was a bold, daring plan under the command of the nobleman Jean de Neuville. It had not been the Dauphin's idea but he had claimed it as his own. De Neuville had seized upon the opportunity and the Dauphin had seen the glory of it. The attack would strike fear into the English. It might even make Edward deplete his army and send them home. It was, Bucy knew, madness.

The fleet had been hemmed in by onshore winds against the Normandy coast and had been delayed by a week. 'They will cause great havoc. And their courage will see them victorious, of that we must remain confident,' said Bucy. It served no purpose to tell the Dauphin otherwise. And as the Prince Regent wallowed in the prospect of a victory that would never happen Bucy was trying to find a way to bring about a peace treaty. If, though, the raid *was* successful, then he would claim his part in its planning.

'And the other matter?' said the Dauphin.

Simon Bucy had sent raiding parties out into the countryside to kill the English wherever they could be found. The English scavenged and patrolled far and wide in small groups and a hundred Frenchmen eager to kill their enemy could prove a valuable way of striking fear into Edward's men. The cold and wet reduced soldiers' alertness. They could be ambushed where they slept. And if nothing else the French raiders were a welcome boost to the Dauphin's morale.

'Who knows, highness, they might even penetrate the English lines and reach Edward himself.' The words had tumbled too quickly off his tongue. His mind had formed a picture of French troops wearing English uniforms taken from the dead and getting close enough to the English King to kill him. But the Dauphin's sudden glare showed his displeasure.

'We do not slay kings!' said the Dauphin.

'Of course,' Bucy said, quickly backtracking. 'I meant only that they could seize him and then it is we who would control events.' A knife to the rapacious English King's throat would have been preferable. 'But, highness, that is not what they have been ordered to do.'

That seemed to mollify the impatient Prince. 'Very well,' said the Dauphin. 'Now, what news from Milan?'

'Your delegation has not yet returned with terms from the Visconti,' said Bucy.

The Dauphin nodded. This was a strategy he had quietly put into operation, first spoken of by his father more than a year earlier. It was a plan to sell the Dauphin's eleven-year-old sister to the ruler of Milan to be betrothed to Galeazzo Visconti's eight-year-old son. If the raid into England did not secure King John's release there was still the matter of the outrageous ransom demanded by Edward.

'The Visconti are awash with money. More than enough for a king's ransom,' said the Dauphin.

Bucy could not disguise his distaste. 'They're a brash, violent family. Over the years they have murdered their way to power. They're debauched.'

The Dauphin shrugged. Everyone knew the one brother, Bernabò, was as mad as a caged beast tormented with hot irons, but Galeazzo was the more intelligent and had visions of grandeur. 'Galeazzo spends money on art and music; he creates places of learning,' said the Dauphin.

'That does not excuse them.'

'Excuses are not needed, Simon, money is. At least this betrothal keeps our sister on the right side of that family and out of the mad bastard's reach. It's a straightforward business arrangement. The King of France needs to pay the English King's extortionate ransom; the ruler of Milan craves respectability among Europe's houses of nobility.' The Dauphin sniffed and hawked into his handkerchief and then threw the fouled lace aside to be quickly picked up by a servant. 'He'll pay,' said the Dauphin. 'He's no fool. But we must hold out until a new treaty is discussed and we can send Edward home with his coffers groaning under the weight of Italian gold.' He smiled grimly. 'We'll buy off Edward.'

Simon Bucy grimaced. They were bartering the glory that was France for a child's life as if they were common street traders.

'You disapprove?' snapped the Dauphin. 'Your counsel is valued, not your disgust!'

Bucy quickly recovered his composure. The King had always been intemperate but the trust and friendship between them had allowed his senior counsellor some flexibility to express opposing opinions. The Dauphin's nature was more of a spoiled child who did not wish to be admonished. Too much criticism and Bucy might find himself cast out from the inner sanctum. He bowed his head. He had saved the bad news until last.

'I apologize, sire. My expression was not one of disapproval,' he lied, 'but was, as you so rightly observed, one of disgust. Disgust and dismay at another matter that has been reported to me. Something that I can scarcely believe.'

Bucy paused and drew breath. The old trick. Show deep concern and imply careful thought by waiting a few heartbeats; thus convincing the listener that his wisdom and considered opinion as a long-serving lawyer were invaluable – and, more than that, giving the impression that imparting such bad news caused him personal grievous pain.

The Dauphin's eyebrows raised. Bucy's timing was perfect. Before the young man's impatience overflowed the veteran politician's words struck him as hard as a steel gauntlet.

'Thomas Blackstone is at Rheims.'

The Dauphin's jaw dropped as he sagged into his chair.

'The Englishman who came through the lines saw his blazon and then the man himself,' said Bucy.

'No. He's dead,' said the Dauphin. 'He drowned more than a year ago.'

'Then perhaps it is his ghost.'

The Dauphin unconsciously crossed himself. Perhaps the scarred knight *had* returned from the dead.

'Before Poitiers I tried to kill him with your father's blessing. We unleashed the Savage Priest on him, but de Marcy paid with his life and his skeleton serves as a warning on an alpine pass.'

'Blackstone,' said the Dauphin in barely a whisper.

'The enemy of France sworn to kill your father.' Bucy let the reminder settle a moment. 'Now is not the time to discuss it, my lord, but I believe I have information that may give us the means to finally rid ourselves of him.' He smiled. Information was a tool that could be used like an iron rod to stoke a fire. Ram it hard and watch the sparks fly. He gazed out of the window. 'Ah, look, highness, the clouds part. A sunbeam breaks through.'

CHAPTER FIFTEEN

They rode slowly with Killbere tied onto a canvas litter between two horses. For three days and nights they made their way north towards the town where the crow priest had told them was a man with healing powers. The priest was allowed to ride without his ankles tied to the stirrups but a rope was around his waist at the other end of which was Meulon. There would be no escape for Robinet Corneille who had neither the physical strength to pull the huge Norman from his horse nor the courage to even try.

Will Longdon was, as he told everyone, well versed in folk medicine. 'If he coughs blood then we must find a wet-nurse,' he informed those who would listen.

'He's no babe in arms, you short-arsed fool,' said Gaillard.

'You're a Norman oaf who has no knowledge of the English peasant,' Longdon said. 'We have cures for such ills. A man coughs blood: he needs the milk tit. Suckle the milk tit and the lungs clear.'

John Jacob gave a despairing glance to Blackstone and then turned in the saddle. 'Will, you'd take the cure yourself then?'

'Only for the healing it offered,' he said and grinned.

'Then you would know', Jacob continued, 'that the cure is not only the milk from the breast but also the teat of a goat. If there was no wet-nurse to aid your cure then you would suckle a goat, would you?'

'He belongs in a goat pen,' said Meulon. 'It was where he was born!'

Longdon had no time to reply. The men's laughter drowned out any chance of complaint.

103

On the afternoon of the fourth day the men awoke to a clear sky and the sight of thin trails of smoke on the horizon several miles away.

'Food and warmth,' said Perinne. 'That smoke's from a town's hearths.'

'Aye and the chance for some ale and a hot bath,' said Will Longdon.

Meulon spat. The Norman seemed impervious to the weather but not the men's stench. 'The bath before the ale, Will. You stink like a wet dog that's rolled in shit.'

'Were it warm enough the flies would be around you like a heaped dollop of cow dung,' he answered.

'Me, stink? No, you bow-legged fool, I smell as sweet as a whore's fart. Your nose is too close to your arse.'

The banter lightened the men's mood.

John Jacob rode at Blackstone's side. 'Is that Balon?'

'So the crow priest says,' Blackstone answered. He was worried. The ride to the town, which was still out of sight, would be across a vast undulating plain. The pockets of forests that lay behind them had so far afforded them cover and shelter, once Perinne and the scouts had established they were free of the enemy. The woodlands ahead were far to their left and right. To use the forests again meant losing more time. A two-day journey had already taken four because of the need to keep Killbere from being jolted but now the veteran knight's condition had grown worse. They had to risk riding out across the open ground, but if any French troops or marauding mercenaries were close by they could be overwhelmed.

Blackstone turned in the saddle and beckoned Meulon, who spurred his horse and dragged the priest with him.

'You're certain that's Balon?' Blackstone asked.

'I believe it is, lord,' said the priest.

'Believe or know?'

'There are a dozen small towns within twenty miles of Balon,' he said. 'Some are held by English routiers who raid and take what they can but Balon proclaimed for your King weeks ago.'

'So what?' said John Jacob. 'If the skinners are after plunder then Balon might have fallen to them.'

'No,' said Blackstone. 'If they're English routiers they won't attack a town held for Edward. We'll risk riding straight across. I want Sir Gilbert to have a chance.' He nodded to Perinne, who needed no further command. He and Robert Thurgood with a dozen others urged their horses forward. Perinne and Thurgood rode straight ahead; the rest separated and took up position half a mile or more on each flank as outriders to protect the others.

Up until now Blackstone and the men had barely made ten miles a day and it took another three hours before they reached the rising ground that allowed them to gaze down on the walled town. The breeze had freshened and a thick pall of smoke billowed, its dark, thick plume rising until the wind tore it apart.

'Smell that! Pork!' said Will Longdon. 'They've a pig or a boar on a spit roast. Hot food, warm ale and *then* the bath!'

Blackstone rose up in his stirrups so he could see above the town's walls below. 'Meulon! Gaillard! You and your men with me. Everyone else stay here with Sir Gilbert until you're called. That's no pig on a stick, Will. They're burning someone at the stake.'

He spurred the bastard horse forward.

The sentries refused to bow to John Jacob's demand that the gates be opened to his sworn lord who rode for King Edward and the host that now besieged Rheims. After a few minutes a burgher peered over the low wall and shouted down to the men on horseback outside his town's gate.

'What dialect is that?' Blackstone asked those around him.

'Champenois,' said the crow priest. 'He's the mayor.'

'Tell him to speak French before my patience gives way,' Blackstone demanded.

The crow did as he was told and the burgher repeated the question.

'You mean us harm?' said the town's mayor.

'If I wanted your town I would jump my horse over these broken walls,' said Blackstone. 'Open the damned gate before I do just that!' he demanded.

The mayor was cowed but his courage was bolstered by his authority. 'There is nothing here for you. We have declared for Edward. His name protects us. There is no place here for acts of violence, rape or looting.'

'Open the fucking gate!' yelled Meulon.

The mayor's eyes widened at the bear of a man whose bellowing voice threatened to shake the walls.

'Do as they ask,' said the crow priest in the man's own dialect in an effort to reassure him and his sentries. 'I have brought these men here because they are in need of the old hermit's administrations.'

The mayor looked as though he had been slapped with a wet fish. Hands flew to his face.

'What is going on?' said Blackstone to the crow priest. 'Speak to him again. Make sure he understands what it is we want.'

'I have already done that. And that is when he... did what he did.'

The mayor opened the palms of his hands. 'You will not punish us?' he asked in French.

'Not if you open the gate,' Blackstone demanded again.

The mayor's head bobbed as he looked down to those on the ground behind the gates, which began to open.

Blackstone urged his horse forward, flanked by the others, each man scanning the walls for any sign of ambush. Townspeople gathered in the muddy square backed away from the advancing horsemen and as they did they exposed the funeral pyre. The charred body was bent double in the chains that held it around the waist; fat dripped sizzling into the heat of the embers from the raw, red flesh still clinging to the bones. It was impossible to tell whether the victim was man or woman.

'Leave the gates open!' Blackstone commanded the sentries, his nose wrinkling as a waft of the burning flesh reached his nostrils. The mayor scuttled down the steps from the walls. 'Signal the others to come in,' Blackstone ordered Gaillard. The mayor stood close to Blackstone's horse, hands open in supplication. The bastard horse took advantage of the loose rein and snapped at him. The man leapt away, his heel catching his cloak, and fell on his back. He quickly got to his feet again.

'Who is that?' said Blackstone, pointing to the remains on the stake.

'Sorcery was performed here. Ill fortune was brought down on us because the devil was enticed here. Witnesses saw the demon being fed at night; there are those who watched as incantations were delivered to the dark lord.'

There was palpable unease among the men. The line between heaven and hell was a narrow one.

John Jacob crossed himself and glanced nervously at Blackstone. 'We can kill flesh and blood, Sir Thomas,' he said quietly so no one else could hear, 'but demons? We should leave this place. Sir Gilbert lies unconscious; his soul is vulnerable. They could possess him.'

Demons were the offspring of men and fallen angels, creatures of a middle nature who inhabited the place between earth and sky. If they had been conjured in this place through necromancy then they were all in danger.

'Keep those thoughts to yourself,' Blackstone said, handing him his reins. 'Watch the others get inside safely then close the gates and put men on the walls.'

'Do we disarm their militia?' said John Jacob.

'Yes. It would only take a single idiot to strike at one of us and we'd have another massacre on our hands. Quietly but firmly, John,' said Blackstone as he dismounted. The mayor took another few steps back. Blackstone grabbed him. 'Answer my question,' he demanded, although in his heart he already knew the answer. 'Who was burnt?'

'It is the man you seek. The hermit. The soothsayer,' said the mayor, his Adam's apple bobbing as he swallowed his fear. 'The sorcerer!' he added finally in an attempt to justify the man's death.

Blackstone pushed him away and gazed at the smouldering, blackened mass of the hermit's carcass and his bubbling innards.

'Open your town to us. Make no attempt to hinder my men. We have a wounded knight with us. We need food, beds and shelter, and fodder for our horses. And I need your house for my dying friend.'

'My...' The mayor quickly decided not to argue and clasped his hands together, his head bowing obediently.

Blackstone looked at the skeleton with its peeling flesh. 'Do you still have his potions and herbs? The priest with us might be able to use them.'

The mayor's eyes suddenly gleamed with hope. 'Your priest is proficient?'

'No, he's as useful as a tit on a monk's arse,' said Will Longdon, who had dismounted and moved closer to examine the funeral pyre.

'He is not proficient in the healing arts but he's all we have,' confirmed Blackstone.

The mayor looked undecided and then, tapping grubby fingernails against his teeth, made up his mind. 'There is someone who might help, my lord. But it is a great risk. She was going to be burned tomorrow.'

'Who?

The mayor glanced at the dead man. 'The sorcerer's daughter.'

Blackstone followed the cowed mayor through the town's streets. Despite the closeness of the hulking Englishman the mayor squared his shoulders and raised his chin, displaying an air of authority that shooed away the crowds, who needed little encouragement to go back to their homes and trades. Men and women quickly dispersed, dragging their dirty-faced children with them, crossing themselves at the sight of the tall, scar-face knight.

Mud squelched beneath their feet and rain dripped from the soaked roofs. Thomas followed Balon's mayor until they turned a corner and faced a large stone-built structure. It was obviously a more important building than the timber and clay-plastered houses everywhere else. It had once been fortified, but like the town its walls had fallen into disrepair and as Blackstone was led through the heavy oak door he saw that the roof had burned down.

'Our church,' said the mayor. 'A lightning strike, weeks ago. It was conjured by the sorcerer.' The mayor beckoned him to follow as he turned a key, which was the length of a man's hand and as thick as a thumb, into the lock of a side door. It opened onto a stair leading down. Cresset lamps flickered and burned dully, just enough to show the stone steps curving away into darkness. Blackstone turned sideways to accommodate his feet on the narrow treads. As they reached the bottom the confines of the stairwell opened out to a broad square room. It looked to be at least thirty paces wide and long. A brazier smouldered; the acrid smell of the coals tainted his tongue.

A latticed pattern of shadows stretched across the floor from the light behind an iron cage. It stretched ten paces by six and had a bucket in one corner and a half-naked woman manacled to the wall. The mayor held back, his wavering hand pointing to the caged girl.

'I warn you not to go too close to her. They say she has the gift of second sight. She will look into your future and see your very soul.'

Blackstone brushed past him and went to the cage. The woman's dress was torn to her waist and her breasts hung freely. He reckoned she was about twenty, or perhaps a couple of years older. She was strong, her hips wide and her breasts full. Her hair had been hacked short; its matted strands had pieces of straw in it from where she had slept on the cold stone floor and its miserly covering. A horse would have had more straw in its stall than this girl had in her cage. The chain that held her was long enough for her to move about the cell and enable her to lie

109

down. The bucket in the corner was her latrine. Her dark eyes followed him like a frightened beast as he paced the length of her cage, trying to see her more clearly.

'Lord, she spits, and if the chains give way from their fastenings her nails can still claw a man's face,' said the mayor.

Blackstone turned and faced the timorous man. 'My face has already been clawed by hardened steel. I don't fear a chained and beaten girl. Those marks on her tits and belly. You tortured her?'

'We used hot irons on her to make her talk.'

'Did she confess?'

'Of course.'

'Of course,' said Blackstone. 'Who would not? You did this to her?'

'Me? No, no. Our priest ordered men to bind her and apply the irons.'

'Where is this priest?'

'Dead, lord. Died in a convulsion. She cursed him and he died. Witches can summon fire from the sky and spirits from the night to seize a man's soul.'

Blackstone looked at the frightened girl. Her skin was covered in gooseflesh from the cold in the cellar; her shivering made her breasts quiver.

'You think her a witch?'

'As I said, lord, she confessed.'

'Did you find any sign on her? A third teat for her to suckle the demon?'

'There was none, but that does not mean that her powers are diminished. We all heard the incantations she used when she healed by magic; what we did not realize was that they were words that summoned forces from beyond this world.'

'And why cut her hair?'

'It was raven black, lord. Long and sensuous. It enticed men.'

Blackstone looked at the bedraggled girl. 'You've fed her?' he said.

'Why would we do such a thing? She's to be burnt.'

'Not yet she's not.'

The mayor gasped, his tongue licking dry lips, fingers laid nervously to his face. 'My lord, we must rid ourselves of this witch. We have paid a heavy price having her and her father here. Our pardoner has claimed that penance must be done and –'

'There's a pardoner here?' said Blackstone.

'Yes. Once our priest was dead he heard of it and came to help us. We must unburden our sins and cast out devils. Don't you see we must cleanse ourselves?'

Blackstone looked at the girl, who now crouched in the corner, arms across herself in an attempt to keep warm. Pardoners were the scourge of common men: they took money and goods in exchange for absolution of sin in the name of the Church. It was not difficult for such men to instil fear of witchcraft. Fear increased their payment.

'The pardoner is still in town?'

'Yes, lord.'

'What's your name?'

'I am Malatrait.'

'All right, Mayor Malatrait, go and fetch the big man who has a rope around my priest and bring him here. Do it yourself. And give me your cloak.'

'It's my best cloak,' complained the mayor.

'Then go and get your second-best cloak to wear.'

'Lord, this is too small for you,' he argued plaintively.

Blackstone's look needed no words. Malatrait loosened his cloak and gave it to him and then quickly moved to the stairs, pleased to be away from the witch and the man who seemed not to fear her.

Blackstone went to the bars and reached his arm through, tossing the cloak to the girl. She looked surprised but grabbed it and wrapped herself in its warmth. Blackstone remained silent. The girl's eyes widened. Perhaps she *was* possessed, he thought, and brought Arianrhod to his lips. Suddenly the girl chuckled.

'You are frightened of me?'

111

'No.'

'She's a goddess?'

'Yes.'

'You are a pagan?'

'I am careful. I'll seek protection where I can find it.'

The girl was emboldened by his fearlessness and moved closer to the bars. Blackstone stayed where he was and allowed her to study him. The chains restricted her but she reached out a hand as if she could touch the Celtic goddess on the silver wheel at Blackstone's neck.

'If you want me you'd better take me now because they are going to burn me tomorrow.'

'The men who tortured you, did they rape you?'

She smiled and then frowned. 'Are you stupid? Of course they did.'

'Even though they thought you a witch?'

'Even though. Perhaps they thought I would empower their cocks.'

He smiled. 'Did you?'

'Even a witch cannot perform miracles. Acorns are not oaks.' She retreated back to the corner and squatted down against the wall. 'If you want me then you will have to step inside my cage.'

The way she said it made Blackstone's skin crawl. The enticement tested his courage, for it was a threat too.

'I'm not here to rape you,' said Blackstone and was grateful to hear the scrape of boots on the stone steps. He heard the priest mutter and Meulon swear beneath his breath. 'Bring him closer,' said Blackstone.

Meulon pushed the nervous crow priest forward as the mayor stayed behind the men, putting as much distance between himself and the caged girl as possible. With a priest in the room there was hope that she could not inflict her spells on them.

Blackstone glanced at Meulon. The throat-cutter's eyes were nervously watching the girl.

'Priest,' said Blackstone. 'This girl is accused of necromancy.

She's been tortured and raped. Doesn't a witch bear a mark that shows she's a witch?'

'Yes.'

'They found none on her.'

'Then she must have used magic to perform her rituals.'

'Fairground fools use magic. Priests use magic when they use a relic to cure the sick. Incantations are what physicians use when they implore God to aid their healing.' Blackstone beckoned the girl to the bars. 'Come here, girl.'

The priest backed away but Blackstone held him. 'What else makes this girl a witch?'

'Heretical magic... I... I cannot say... without questioning her.'

'Then ask. She has nowhere to go except into the square and the stake.'

The priest stammered but then found his authority. 'Child, have you conjured demons?'

'They say I have,' the girl answered. 'They made me confess through torture to such things.'

'The demon was witnessed!' blurted the mayor.

'It was a stray cat that escaped from the market-day games. The boys kick them to death for sport, but I stopped them and rescued it. The creature never left my side after that.'

'And you have made charms?' said the priest.

'I have. I soaked a piece of wool in bat's blood and gave it to a man who wished his wife fucked him more. He put it under her pillow.'

'And... and the charm worked?' stuttered the priest.

'It stained her linen. She beat him with a stave.'

Blackstone grinned, the priest looked uncertainly at him. 'Keep going,' Blackstone insisted.

'Do you heal with magic?'

'With potions and herbs and prayer. But that is not witchcraft. I was taught by my father.'

'Then you perform religious magic?'

113

'Miracles are not my doing; they are God's. It is He who changes the natural order of life and death.'

'And what of prophecy and divination? Do you have that gift?'

'Sometimes.'

The Mayor hid behind Meulon but pointed an accusing finger. 'You sacrificed chickens and boiled their guts for the devil to slurp! You infused herbs to attract the devil's snout!'

Meulon pushed the mayor back with his elbow.

'I killed chickens for their broth. And I use herbs for healing. As did my father. An innocent man who healed your sick! And you burned him alive for such kindness!'

'Well?' said Blackstone to the priest.

The crow priest chewed his lip. 'Mother Church's view is that religious magic is God's gift but all else is perversion. How are we to know what else she has done?'

'We don't.' He turned to the mayor. 'Malatrait. Release her.'

CHAPTER SIXTEEN

Flanked by Meulon and the priest Blackstone took the girl to her father's house. At the sight of the girl those few still on the streets crossed themselves and slammed closed their doors. The living quarters were up a set of turned stairs over a workshop. As Blackstone pushed open the door a rat scurried across the reed floor. It was obvious that her father had been taken from this room. The single chair and trestle table were overturned; there was a spray of blood staining the wooden boarded wall. Quills, ink and sheets of parchment had been scattered. The small window gave barely any light but there were no signs of candles or oil lamps; they had probably been stolen, thought Blackstone. There was little else in the room worth taking. A half-dozen bound manuscripts had been flung onto the floor and the shelf they had once been on lay broken and hanging from its bracket. The bed's mattress, if there had ever been one, was missing.

'Priest, you look in this room and determine whether anything indicates the girl's father was enticing the devil.'

The priest nodded obediently and began to gather the fallen papers.

The girl showed no sign of shock at the room's destruction or the blood splatters evident on wall and scattered parchments. After a moment's hesitation she stepped forward and picked up the broken-legged chair. The cloak came apart, exposing her breasts, and as she turned with the spindle chair in hand and balanced it carefully against the wall she glanced at Blackstone and made no effort to fasten the garment. It was not a brazen attempt to attract him, he reasoned; her nakedness merely bore testimony that she had had everything taken from her. A low, narrow door of solid oak on iron hinges was set into the stone wall to one side. There was a keyhole in the plate below the latch. She bent down, brushed aside the reeds on the floor, eased up a floorboard and took out an iron key. The small oak door opened and she bent to enter the room beyond. Blackstone followed her and saw that her father's attackers had not been inside. There was a workbench of chestnut, its rich dark hue smooth from many years of the man's hands travelling across its surface. Along one wall there were shelves of glass bottles containing tinctures and liquids of various colours and behind the door was a single bedstead. Next to it was a nail in the wall that held a threadbare cloak, a dress and an apron. The girl unhooked the cloak and draped it across the bed, and then spilled water from a jug into a bowl and wrung out a piece of linen that she used to dab on her breasts and stomach. She dried herself carefully with a bolt of cloth and then reached up for one of the coloured glass bottles. She pulled free the stopper and he saw her pour a thick, clear, slow-running liquid onto the cloth, which she then dabbed onto the tortured skin. As she applied the healing ointment she told Blackstone who had come for her father and then taken her to the cellars and raped and tortured her. How one of her persecutor's wives had stolen her clothes, charms and potions, taunting her that she would now be the one who could charge money for their healing properties.

Blackstone had not taken his eyes from her. She turned. 'Who is it that has saved me?'

'I am Thomas Blackstone.'

'A knight or a brigand?'

'Some say both. Who are you?'

'I am Aelis de Travaux. Now that we have been introduced, will you put this on where they burned my back?'

She held out the cloth, he took it and she turned around. He dabbed her inflamed skin, which quivered as he touched each wound, but she made no sound.

'It's done,' he said.

'Thank you. Now, look in the other room and see if they have left one of my father's undershirts. I need to cover my wounds.'

Blackstone did as she asked and rummaged through the upturned room. He found a shirt beneath the spindle bed. He turned back. She had already pulled the dress from the hook and was pulling it up to her waist.

'They've taken anything of value. There's this, though it's covered in dust from the floor and no doubt fleas,' he said, shaking the material. 'I have a clean shirt in my saddlebags.'

'This is enough,' she said, and eased the shirt across her wounds and then tied up her dress. She pulled a wooden-toothed comb through what was left of her hair and plucked out the detritus that had lodged there from her cell.

She pointed to a satchel. 'Will you carry that for me? My burns are too raw for its weight.'

Blackstone peered around the door and saw a leather satchel, bigger than his saddlebag. He lifted it and heard the clink of bottles.

'We will start with what we have there. Where is your friend who needs me?'

Blackstone almost replied but the shock of realization stopped him. He had not mentioned the wounded Killbere.

She smiled at his uncertainty. 'It is not magic, Sir Thomas. It is reason. Why would a man who does not wish to rape me have me released? Why would you and your priest question me about healing? Someone is injured. Now, take me to him.'

Henry Blackstone had swept away the soiled reeds on the mayor's floor. They contained a winter's worth of fleas and lice, dog shit trodden underfoot and spilled food and wine.

'We lay new reeds in spring,' moaned the mayor's wife, hands clutching the crucifix that dangled from her neck.

'Get fresh covering now,' John Jacob had ordered the frightened woman. 'Light fires. Get warmth in here.'

'Lord, there is little dry wood. We eke it out as best we can.'

'You had enough to burn a man to death. Light the fires,' Jacob

117

snarled. The mayor's wife scuttled from the room, bleating for a housemaid's help.

Will Longdon had pulled the rope-corded bed frame over to the window. 'Bring that mattress, Jack,' he called as Halfpenny manhandled a straw mattress taken from one of the other rooms. 'On here. Sir Gilbert will need warmth and air.'

By the time Blackstone and the rescued woman arrived, Killbere was lying on the mattress covered with blankets near a fire that burned in the hearth. Those men who lingered in the passageway stepped back and made the sign of the cross as Aelis swept past them. The fresh reeds underfoot crackled as she approached the wounded knight. Men crowded in the doorway watching the sorceress as she quickly peeled back the blankets.

'The wound?' she asked.

'On his side,' said Blackstone.

'Turn him,' she commanded.

Blackstone knelt and eased his friend over. She lifted off the dressing put there by the crow priest and the smell of rotting flesh was unmistakable.

'Who put the maggots in the wound?'

'I did,' said Blackstone.

'It is likely your action has so far saved his life.' She turned her face to Blackstone. 'If he lives until dawn tomorrow then he will likely survive. What will you pay me?'

'You bargain for a man's life?'

'Why should I not? I don't know what it is you plan for me. A woman must use whatever bargaining skills she has. Every healer must be paid.'

'If he lives I will grant what you ask for,' said Blackstone.

She smiled and delved into the satchel and began taking out pouches and small bottles. Then she turned to the men, held out a pouch to no one in particular, and said, 'Boil water, soak these herbs and then bring the water to me.'

The men gaped, their nervousness plain to see. None would accept her instruction. A moment before Blackstone was about to order Will Longdon to obey, Henry stepped forward and took the pouch.

'Bring it in an earthenware jug, boy,' she instructed. She stood and took a step towards the men in the doorway, who all shuffled back. She smiled at their fear of her and tossed a handful of powder into the flames: a mixture of sulphur, arsenic and antimony, used for its aroma and effectiveness against rat fleas. The sudden burst of sparks made the men even more nervous.

'The air is foul and a wounded man will suffer more from it. As foul almost as your stench,' she said to the men.

'We've fought and ridden for days,' said Will Longdon defensively. 'I'll wager that close up you smell as ripe as a cowpat.'

She took another step and once again the men stepped back, pressing against those behind them. 'You would like to get closer?' she taunted.

'Sweet Jesus on the Cross, you're Satan's gate if ever there was one,' said Gaillard, pointing an accusing finger.

Aelis made a swift feint forward and this time the men nearly fell over themselves as they shuffled backwards. She laughed. 'Stay away from me and let me get on with what I have to do. Go!'

'My lord?' John Jacob said. 'We cannot leave this woman alone with Sir Gilbert.'

'I'll stay,' Blackstone told him. 'See to the men and horses and have the women heat water for us all so we may bathe. Gaillard, search out their provisions. We need food cooked for us. No man walks alone out there, always two at a time. They may have declared for Edward but they have not for us.'

The men nodded, accepting their orders. The passageway was soon empty.

'You do not trust me to be alone with him?' Aelis asked.

'I trust only those who have stood at my side over the years. You do not frighten me, no matter what incantation you chant or spell you cast.' As he spoke he knew the words to be a lie. Serpent-like fear crawled inside him. Perhaps the townspeople were right. Aelis de Travaux and her father may have been dabbling in the dark arts. It would take little imagination to see her as a witch. 'And if I see any action that I believe will cause my friend further harm I'll cut your throat.'

She studied him for a moment. 'Then before you put a blade to my neck make yourself useful. Order a chicken broth to be made for him and tell the mayor I need a candle, one that adorned the altar from the church.'

'A church candle has power to heal?' he asked, uncertain of what ritual might follow.

'It has the quality and thickness to burn slowly. It holds no other significance than that,' she answered. 'Then get more firewood. Put a blanket on the floor so I can lay out what I need. You're ignorant of what I do so do not attempt to interfere. I will attend your friend but I do not have the power of life and death. Get us food and drink and be prepared to stay through the hours of darkness because that is when he will either be taken by the angels or cast back into this world.'

Blackstone looked down at her and she met his gaze fearlessly. 'Bring the devil into this room and I'll make you scream loud enough for him to turn tail and run back to hell,' he threatened.

'Perhaps the devil's agent is already here and standing in front of me,' she said and bent to the task of preparing the herbs and potions she needed for the dying man. She placed a smooth-edged crystal, the size of a small rock, about the size that could fit comfortably into the palm of her hand, on the blanket. Once again he saw the swell of her breasts and felt the urge for her settle on his tongue. He had not been with a woman since Christiana's murder.

He turned on his heel and dismissed the thought. Lying with a woman like Aelis could do more than bewitch a man: it might snare his soul. He felt the cool touch of silver at his throat. Perhaps it needed a Celtic goddess to ward off such charms.

CHAPTER SEVENTEEN

Meulon had brought cheese, bread, smoked fish and a jug of wine for Aelis and Blackstone. The woman ate hungrily and when she was satisfied pushed aside the plate and wiped her hands on the mayor's cloak. She knelt next to Killbere and raised his head, ready to trickle the herbal liquid that Henry brought between the wounded knight's lips.

Blackstone gripped her wrist. 'What is it you give him?' he said, and took the jug, sniffing its contents.

'It is rye steeped in hot water. It breaks down the humours,' she said.

Blackstone held her a moment longer and then released her.

'Have the bowl ready,' Aelis ordered Henry.

The boy did as instructed without seeking permission from his father. Blackstone saw that the boy's courage had not deserted him. The young page seemed not to care that some thought the woman employed black arts. After a few moments Killbere convulsed and spewed black bile.

'You purge him?' said Blackstone as he bent to restrain the shuddering knight.

'I prepare him,' she answered. She nodded for Henry to remove the bowl and its foul contents. 'I have a preparation of sage that will soothe his nerves and help put strength into his paralysis.' She spoke without looking at Blackstone, taking oil from one of the bottles in the satchel and trickling it into the palms of her hands. Her voice lowered as she rubbed the oil onto Killbere's chest, murmuring as if treating a sick infant. 'Almond oil is good for his chest and will ease any cough.' She turned her face to Blackstone. 'He must be able to breathe freely.'

'When will you bleed him?' Blackstone asked. 'The priest said it was best done on a saint's day.'

'What happens when a man is wounded in battle? Is he not weakened by loss of blood? I can see he has already been bled. He needs no more.' She looked at Henry, who stood in the doorway. 'Boy, you know what plantain is?'

'I do,' said Henry. It was a common enough weed Old Hugh, his father's overseer, had ordered cleared from his mother's potager when they lived in Normandy.

'Go and collect two handfuls and then bring it to me.' Henry nodded and turned. 'Wait,' she ordered. 'I also need a cooking pot and water for this fire. Bring it all before nightfall.'

Aelis wiped Killbere's face. 'Now, we must treat the wound. First one thing and then tomorrow at first light another. Turn him,' she ordered.

Blackstone eased Killbere onto his uninjured side as she opened a clay jar of astringent-smelling ointment. 'Comfrey and thyme,' she told Blackstone. 'This will stay on his wound tonight, and then tomorrow if he is still alive we will use the plantain. Each has its own healing qualities.'

Blackstone nodded. He had seen such balms and poultices used before.

Aelis smeared balm on the wound and laid a clean piece of cut linen across it. 'You will stay awake tonight, Sir Thomas, and give him six spoons of this throughout the night,' she said, reaching for the clay pot of broth that nestled in the embers of the fire. She lifted its lid. Wisps of steam escaped. 'Do not scald him; warm broth is what he needs. I have put herbs in it.' She gave Blackstone the church candle. 'Make equal marks down its length. Feed him whenever the flame reaches the mark.'

Blackstone scored the candle equally down its length with his knife and replaced it on the three-legged stool near Killbere's mattress.

'And what will you do?' Blackstone asked. 'Do you pray or cast spells? What powers do you invoke to save my friend?'

She moved away from Killbere into the corner. 'I invoke sleep,' she said and pulled the cloak over her. 'I hurt and I must rest.' She curled up. 'If he dies then I can do no more for him so kill me or let me sleep.'

As the night wore on there was little sound to be heard over the roofs of Balon. The breeze had shifted, but the rain held off. It would benefit the night watch on the walls. Blackstone knew there was no need for any high degree of vigilance: unlike his own men night attack was a skill few had. The town's granges were well stocked with food and wine and by the time the town fell into darkness every man had bathed and fed. Blackstone's captains organized their men into pickets that alternated throughout the night.

As the long hours dragged by attending to feeding Killbere, Blackstone kept himself awake remembering the dozen years and more that had brought him to this place. Each memory was etched on his heart like a nick on a sword's blade. And the man who lay close to death on the mattress in front of him featured strongly, at first a guardian and then a friend. The candle flickered as the flame touched the last mark. As Blackstone's mind ranged across landscapes and places yearning for his loved ones overtook him. He turned his face away from the spectres that filtered through the shrouds of darkness. His mind told him that he must be asleep but he could not force open his eyes. His mind's eye saw the walls cast looming shadows and, like a ghost hovering in the room, a black-cloaked hooded figure leaning across Killbere. A stab of fear pierced him. Was this the angel of death come to take the knight? A slow, hypnotic chant emanated from the figure. A chant that seemed to be Latin but was not; it sounded like an old language that might summon ancient spirits. The cloaked figure took the form of a woman rocking slowly back and forth across the wounded man. Blackstone could not see the dark angel's face but saw that her breasts moved rhythmically. He willed himself to break free from the dream but could not.

123

He heard Killbere grunt. The woman turned her head; the cloak fell back exposing her thighs that straddled his friend. And then as Blackstone fought like a drowning man for the surface the woman was gone.

Blackstone dragged himself awake. He lurched forward, cursing himself for succumbing to sleep, and saw and heard the candle wax spluttering. He raised his friend's head ready to spoon the broth between his lips. Killbere's eyes fluttered and his lips parted, uttering a whisper. Blackstone lowered his face to hear what his friend said.

'She was here,' Killbere murmured.

'Who?' said Blackstone, relieved that his friend had finally regained consciousness.

Killbere smiled. 'My nun. She came and lay with me.' He coughed from the effort of talking. His lips relaxed into a smile and his eyes closed as he slipped into a fever-free slumber.

Blackstone eased Killbere's head down onto the pillow. The room suddenly turned cold. It had been no dream. He could not have shared his friend's illusion. It was not possible. His spine tingled. He turned and looked to where Aelis lay in the corner of the room. She was gone. Her dress lay crumpled. He got to his feet and, holding the candle before him, stepped into the darkened passage. Aelis was facing him, eyes bright in the dull candlelight, her nakedness obvious beneath the cloak. Blackstone pressed his back to the wall. It was as if an apparition had appeared.

'Sir Thomas?' she said quietly, her eyes questioning.

'Where have you been?' he said, forcing the uncertainty from his voice.

'I needed to relieve myself,' she said.

'You've discarded your dress.'

'I was hot. The fire gave enough warmth.'

'How long have you been out of the room?'

She reached out and took the candle from his hand. The hot wax dripped onto his skin but he ignored it.

'Not long,' she answered. And then brushed past him.

There could be no explanation other than Aelis had been the woman he had seen with Killbere. He turned after her, an inexplicable desire to take her surging through him. He snatched at her arm, forcing the candle to fall and extinguish. The glow from the firelight caught her face. She showed no sign of fear. His mouth went to hers and his hand cupped her breast. And then he hesitated.

'You are no different than the others,' she said, as if his attempt had been no surprise.

He pushed her away, his fist gripping her cloak. 'You lay with him.'

'I drew the poison from inside him. He has already been bled. His vomit, his seed. All must be taken. And to do that I use whatever skills I have been given. Condemn me or pay me. There is a price for what I do.'

'You're a common whore,' he said, unable to disguise the lust for her in his voice. 'Get dressed.'

'I am Aelis de Travaux. The daughter of a man who healed the sick and never caused harm. My mother nurtured my skills and my father gave me his knowledge. Your friend has benefited from this. You promised payment if he lived through the night. See for yourself,' she said without turning to face the small window.

Blackstone looked past her and saw the light seeping into the grey sky. The town's night watchman's cries declared the town to be safe and that the good citizens of Balon should be out of their beds.

'How much to save a good man?' Blackstone said derisively.

'I give you his life freely. The price I want is for those who injured me and my father to pay for the hurt.'

125

CHAPTER EIGHTEEN

The town went about its business, avoiding the macabre twisted figure of the man they had burnt to death. Blackstone ordered the mayor to bring before him the four men who had raped and tortured Aelis.

'My lord...' the mayor began. He was barely able to keep the stammer from his voice, yet was trying to assert his authority in front of the scarred Englishman. 'These men have families and are tradesmen and as such are vital to our town's welfare. I beg you not to cause them harm.'

Blackstone looked up to where Aelis stood at a window. 'I made a bargain with the dead man's daughter.'

The mayor shuffled nervously, wringing his hands. 'Then you made a bargain with the devil's daughter,' he said vehemently. 'I will not deliver these men to you.'

Blackstone considered the man's defiance. 'You have no manorial lord. The French knights who once lived here have deserted their land or been killed by the English or routiers. You have declared for King Edward of England as protection, and I serve the King. Are the men who raped and tortured her in the same tithing?' He saw the look of concern on the mayor's face. Each town's population was divided into tithings and each of those units swore to uphold the law. If one of its members committed a crime the others were obliged to bring him to justice. If they did not then they suffered a collective punishment.

'Lord,' said the mayor, swallowing two or three times in panic. 'The tithing seized the old man at the behest of our priest.'

'Who has already gone to hell most likely,' Blackstone answered. 'Bring all those men to me.'

'We were forgiven our actions because they were done in the name of our Lord Christ.'

'And de Travaux's goods? Who took them? Who stole a dead man's few possessions and a condemned girl's clothing and potions? Was that done in His name?'

'We were pardoned!' insisted the mayor, jaw set firm. Blackstone sensed the man felt himself to be on firmer ground. His chin tilted. 'We would have done penance before God; we would have fasted and prayed for doing what was necessary to rid ourselves of evil.'

'And I want him as well,' said Blackstone. And then to dismiss any doubt in the man's mind: 'The pardoner.'

The mayor realized he had no more bargaining power, no further means of protecting the town's citizens. He seemed dazed, as if struck.

Blackstone nodded to Meulon and the big man stepped up to the mayor and handed him a piece of parchment. 'Don't try and bring us villeins who have come here for safety from their villages,' Meulon growled. 'We know peasants can be bought to take another man's punishment. Not this time.' He shoved the scrap into the mayor's tunic. 'We know who they are. Jean Agillot, Etienne Chardon, Petrus Gavray and Charles Pyvain.'

Meulon's big hands turned the nervous mayor around and pushed him with enough force for him to take a few stumbling steps.

'Bring them now,' said Blackstone, 'or lose our protection and have your gates burnt and your walls pulled down and then see how quickly the mercenary wolves find you.'

The mayor nodded and walked away. Across the square some of the townspeople had started to cluster, unsure of why their mayor had been summoned by the English knight. Their worst fears were confirmed when they saw the bowed head of the usually arrogant Malatrait, a man used to enforcing his authority over others, and his voice calling for the town's constable. Heads turned, mouths uttered rumour and whispers spread like smoke through the alleyways.

'We might be poking a stick into a wasps' 'nest,' said John Jacob.

'They won't resist,' said Blackstone.

'Still,' said Will Longdon, 'we should have the men on the walls, don't you think?'

Blackstone nodded. 'Nothing too aggressive, Will. No arrows nocked and ready. Have the bows strung and the men warned. What we're going to do to these four men will put the fear of Christ into these people. John, Meulon, have half the men-at-arms around the square. Renfred and the others at the stables. If the town rises up I don't want the horses hamstrung.'

Blackstone stepped back and sat on a water trough. His captains waited with him.

Jack Halfpenny took Robert Thurgood onto the walls.

'Christ, Jack, what do you think Sir Thomas has planned?'

Halfpenny directed his archers to where he wanted them. 'You can be sure it's going to cause pain,' he said, nodding towards the two Norman captains, Meulon and Gaillard, who were sharpening their knives.

The four men appeared one by one over the next hour. Blackstone made them stand in the square. Drizzling rain began to fall and a chill wind blew flurries across the open space, but as each man was brought the crowd increased. Yet they kept their distance. Three of the men looked to be in their later years, men of forty; the fourth was younger, probably early thirties. The biggest of the men, Etienne Chardon, wore a black-streaked leather apron, his face behind the thick beard smudged with smoke, his hands blackened by coal. The town's blacksmith stood fearlessly before Blackstone, his muscled arms at his side. Each man looked like the tradesman he was: the barber slightly built; stooped shoulders for the cobbler; and barrel chest for the furrier. Behind them stood the constable, the mayor and several other men bonded by the same tithing as those who had been brought before Blackstone.

Blackstone walked along the line of men, gauging their level of fear. He stopped in front of the blacksmith. 'You heated the irons to burn the woman,' he said. He looked at the furrier. 'You burned her,' he said, and then stood in front of the cobbler. 'You waited your turn while our blacksmith friend clubbed her down and raped her and you,' he said to the barber, 'what did you do?'

'I... I... lord? I did nothing.'

'Nothing to save her. You raped her,' said Blackstone, 'after you hacked off her hair.'

'She enticed us, my lord. She flaunted herself. She taunted us. She cursed us all and we did what any man would do. We were afraid of her.'

'She was the devil's whore,' said Petrus Gavray, the furrier.

'And so you dipped your cocks into the well of darkness. If you were that afraid how did you know she didn't have teeth in her cunny that would tear your cocks to shreds? If she was the devil's whore weren't you afraid of that? Or did you feel inflamed by torturing her? Was it her tits that made you lust after her?'

They were interrupted by John Jacob and two other men-at-arms. Jacob had with him a man dressed in a cloak of fine cloth and a beaver-skin hat on his greying head. His boots looked new. The two men-at-arms led a mule with a small chest and two large bags tied across its saddle.

'He was at the inn,' said John Jacob. 'But his mule was packed and ready to leave.' He released his grip and pushed the pardoner closer towards the accused men and Blackstone.

'When your mayor sends word for you to attend you should obey,' said Blackstone.

'I am not of this town. I obey only Mother Church. I carry the safe conduct of the Lord of Avignon, His Holiness Pope Innocent.'

Blackstone raised his face to the drizzle, content for its coolness to keep him refreshed after the disturbed night's lack of sleep. 'I know the old Pope. I was at Avignon in '56. He's a lawyer who sides with whatever will profit him the most. Back then he yielded to the mercenary forces of Gilles de Marcy. Heard of him?'

'The Savage Priest?' said the pardoner. 'Yes. Who has not?'

'Then you know who slew that vile corruption of the Church,' said Blackstone, giving the pardoner a questioning glance.

The pardoner looked at the scarred-faced Englishman and crossed himself, realizing that of all men who could instil fear in a Frenchman's heart it was the Savage Priest's killer who stood before him.

'You're no messenger of the Pope,' said Blackstone. 'You trade indulgences. Are those boots payment for releasing this man from the crime of rape and torture?' He pointed to the cobbler.

'The merits of Christ are infinite!' the pardoner insisted. 'I offer a particle of the heavenly wealth bequeathed to us by St Peter. In my reliquary I carry a feather fallen from the wing of Archangel Michael.' He stood his ground and faced Blackstone. 'The Church cares for those sick in body and spirit! Those who give alms are assured a foothold in heaven. You claim to know the Holy Father – if you spoke with him then you would know Latin. Do you? Does any man here among you?' he said, raising his voice and gazing at the gathered soldiers.

'No,' said Blackstone. 'Latin is for educated men.'

'No! Of course you do not because your trade is killing.' He turned to the gathered crowd, who had edged closer. He began spouting Latin, making the sign of the cross in a gesture of forgiveness and benevolence. Some of the women knelt; men crossed themselves.

Meulon spoke quietly. 'Shall I fetch our crow priest, Sir Thomas? I still have him locked in a room.'

'We don't need him,' said Blackstone. He turned and sought out Henry, who stood back with the men. He caught the boy's eye. Henry moved quickly to his father's side. 'What's he saying?' he asked his son.

Henry listened to what sounded like a tirade against the soldiers. 'It's not Latin, Father. I think he is making up a language of his own. It sounds like Latin. But... no, it is not.'

'What's your name?' Blackstone bellowed, forcing the pardoner to halt mid sentence.

The pardoner turned back to face him. 'Stephanus Louchart.'

'Well, Stephanus Louchart, we welcome a man of learning in our midst.' He touched Henry's shoulder. 'Speak to him in Latin, boy. Make certain you say the words correctly.'

Blackstone and the men stood quietly as Henry spoke quickly and clearly. None had any idea what the boy said and it was soon obvious that neither did the pardoner. His face fell.

'You snare the fearful with lies and benefit from them,' said Blackstone. 'I should throw you from the walls and let your bones break on the rocks below.'

'Harm me and you will hang by your tongue over the fires of hell when death comes for you, as surely it will.'

'As surely it will,' said Blackstone and signalled John Jacob.

John Jacob and the men tipped out the contents of the small chest and saddle panniers. Clothing, jewellery, the tinkling of coins in leather pouches and the smashing of clay wine flasks quickly took everyone's attention.

Blackstone stepped forward, grabbed him and threw him to the ground. The expensive beaver hat fell off his head and the rain began to drape strands of hair across his terrified features.

'This man, Stephanus Louchart, will reclaim the charred body of the man you burned. He will dig his grave and the priest I brought will pray for the dead man's soul. By way of penance for his sins this pardoner will relinquish what he's taken from you in payment. He will forsake his fine clothing, which will be distributed to the poor, and he will be flogged in his undershirt and driven from this town riding backwards on a donkey. There are wolves in the forest. If he is an emissary of the Pope then God's grace might protect him.'

Blackstone turned to face the six men of the tithing who stood behind the four accused. 'You'll be hanged.' The men's shock allowed Blackstone's men to quickly bind them. He faced the accused. 'You'll also die at the end of the rope but before the rope tightens you'll be gelded.'

131

The blacksmith darted forward, bellowing defiance, but Blackstone sidestepped him and brought his fist down behind his ear. The dull thud of the man's body sprawling face down sounded as if an ox had been felled.

The accused men cried out for their wives and children. They begged Blackstone for their lives. Blackstone ignored them as his men-at-arms held them.

'And where is the woman known as Madeleine Agillot? The barber's wife. Where is she?' Blackstone's voice carried across the square.

The barber turned, wide-eyed, and then fell to his knees. 'Lord! No! I beg you!'

The crowd parted revealing a tearful woman dressed in the clothes that Aelis had described to Blackstone, taken by this woman, who had also seized charms and potions when accompanying the men who assaulted the healer's daughter. She looked terrified.

'You stole from a woman your husband mutilated and raped. Women thieves are punished by drowning.'

The woman screamed. Her legs gave way and she fell to the ground. 'Lord! We have children! They will be orphaned! Mercy, my lord. *Mercy!*'

Blackstone faced the townspeople. 'I am Sir Thomas Blackstone and I have no mercy to give.'

CHAPTER NINETEEN

The ten men of the tithing were hanged on the elm trees beyond the town's walls. Their bodies were spaced along the track that led from the open countryside as a stark warning to anyone who considered Balon undefended. Blackstone had denied Aelis the right to castrate her attackers. Allowing her to wield the knife would have been a punishment too far in the eyes of the townspeople. A devil's whore being given such a right would have inflamed the town and risked insurrection and greater slaughter. The four men who raped and tortured Aelis screamed as Meulon emasculated them, then they quickly fell silent as the noose tightened around their necks. The barber's wife was bound and carried, shrieking the names of her children, to the river where a basket of stones was tied around her waist and she was pushed into the deep water.

Thomas Blackstone had widowed nine women and made orphans of twenty-eight children. And he had instilled fear and respect into the town's population. No sooner had he inflicted punishment on the town than he made a proclamation. The town's men would cut timber from the nearby woodland and reinforce the town's walls under the guidance of Blackstone's men. And Blackstone would pay the mayor and the burghers of Balon in gold *moutons* to have the church roof restored and a new altar built. The gesture softened the town's anger. Some began to say that justice had been served and that the Englishman had inflicted God's punishment on those who deserved it, ignoring their own culpability and enjoyment in watching the old man burn at the stake. Eighty-seven people had paid the pardoner for indulgences.

Ten of them had been hanged so Blackstone gave each of the seventy-seven men and women the opportunity to lay one strike of the whip against the pardoner's back. Blackstone gave the crow priest the responsibility of overseeing the beating, a task he relished. False pardoners stripped the Church of penance, payment and prayer.

'It serves a purpose,' said Will Longdon in answer to Henry's question as to why his father had allowed such punishments. 'We hang rapists and make a town afraid. Now they see that we don't tolerate any wrongdoing. Makes 'em good Christians. Forces them onto their knees at night begging the Lord to keep them safe from indiscretions and an Englishman's retributions. Your father allows some of them to vent their anger on a man who lied to them. It's like clearing the bowels when you've been blocked. Makes you feel better.'

The bloodied pardoner was untied from the stake and carried away. The crow priest stood hunched in the early morning chill next to Blackstone as the town buzzed with the excitement of being allowed to inflict their own punishment. 'You'll conduct Mass for these people,' Blackstone ordered him. 'I gift you to the town of Balon.'

'Stay here?' the priest said as if being handed a punishment.

'Aye. A new church and altar to give them hope and a stipend to keep your greed under control. You'll no doubt find a way to grease your palm further. I won't be here to see it, but if you corrupt your congregation I will give the mayor and his burghers the right to have you stripped and flogged and sent out to the forest and the wolves like the pardoner. Know a generous offer when you see it, priest. It won't be given again.'

Blackstone could almost hear the thoughts that scuttled through the crow priest's mind. Blackstone had given him the opportunity of status and authority in a town badly in need of a priest. Market days would bring in villagers with their wares and an even bigger congregation. And, if he employed patience, he would soon become known as a good priest who offered salvation to those in need.

Then he could send a letter to the Pope begging the right to legally sell indulgences on behalf of Mother Church and that would put a few extra sous in his pocket.

'I accept wholeheartedly,' said the crow priest.

'I thought you might,' said Blackstone.

Aelis de Travaux had stayed out of sight on Blackstone's orders while the town was gripped by his punishment and then soothed with his generosity. By the end of the week, when Blackstone's judgments had been carried out, Killbere was conscious.

'I am as weak as a damned kitten,' he complained as Blackstone spooned broth between his frail lips.

'Then you'll do as you're told,' Blackstone said.

'I have a choice? My guts churn and I can barely make the pisspot.'

'We thought you dead on more than one occasion and your stench nearly finished us all. At times I didn't know who would be better served by your death: you or me.'

'Ah, selfish bastard that you are.'

'I've a gift for you when you're up and on your feet. A beaver-pelt hat. It's from a pardoner who doesn't need it any more.'

'Ah. Good. Those bastards wear quality.' He glanced at the foot of his bed and the empty bench where a wounded man's armour might lie. 'You haven't sold my sword and armour, I suppose?'

'No. Henry cleans it and keeps the blade sharp.'

'Good. I can't remember much of the fight but I remember the gold. You got it?'

'We did. But we are no longer at Cormiers.' Blackstone related their journey and what had happened at Balon. 'The woman who saved you tells me it'll be another two months before you'll be fit to ride.'

'Bollocks. A month. No more. We must get back to Edward, we've already been away too long.' He lapsed into silence for a moment. 'How long *have* we been gone?'

Blackstone shook his head. 'I don't know. It must be February.'

Killbere grunted. 'I must have slept the sleep of the dead. Tomorrow, you get me on my feet. I want to be on a horse in a week and then... well... then...' Killbere drifted away.

Blackstone turned to where Aelis sat on a chair in the corner of the room.

'The draught I give him makes him sleep. He needs it to heal and recover,' she said.

'Can he be left alone?'

'Yes. I will still need to attend the wound but the danger has passed.'

'Then it's time you went into the town.'

'I cannot,' she said. 'They will blame me for the revenge I took on them.'

'The town's fear and anger has been thrown into the task of cutting trees and dragging them across the fields to be laid against the walls. I gave these people comfort with a new church and a priest who will bear testimony that you are no witch. He will say what I tell him to say. You do not use heretic magic, you heal with God's grace and the skill your mother and father passed to you. You won't be harmed.'

'Can you be sure?'

'If you are at my side no one will –'

'No,' she interrupted. 'Can you be sure I do not use magical powers?'

He remembered the false dream he had had of her. He had been trapped, unable to move, knowing now that he had witnessed her lying with Killbere. She must have drugged him.

'Was it a potion I drank, or a narcotic powder thrown onto the flames? What did you do to me? I know it was no dream and I know what I saw that night.'

The vision of her nakedness had remained in his memory but now she sat before him fully clothed. She had been found suitable garments the morning after Killbere had survived the night. She was dressed simply with no adornments and wore a working woman's linen cap that covered her tufts of hair.

Her dress, tucked at the ankle, was overlaid with an apron.

'I am an enchantress,' she said. She smiled when she spoke, but Blackstone was still unable to settle the unease he felt when she said it. For all he knew she had brought spirits of the night into the room to heal Killbere. She had thrown a veil over his own mind as surely as a fish was caught in a net, yet she had allowed him to witness her lying with the veteran knight.

Blackstone stood up, anger flashing across his face. 'Don't play foolish games with me. I have had men mutilated and slain as payment for my friend's life. I could throw you to the crowd now and let them tear you apart. I will not be enchanted, I will not be drugged and I will not remain ignorant of what happened.'

She appeared to be unafraid of his anger. 'You were vigilant and protective. But you were tired and needed sleep. I burned herbs in the fire and you breathed their fragrance. Herbs that I am immune to because I have used them for many years. I put a few drops of a potion in your drink. Had I not held you in a stupor I could not have done what I did and your friend could have died. And so would I because you had threatened to kill me. You would not leave me alone with him so I did what I was forced to do.' She paused and then said, 'What you forced me to do.' Her eyes widened, questioning whether he believed her.

'All right,' he said. 'You walk with me through the town so everyone knows you are protected.'

'Even you cannot protect me, Sir Thomas. If a townswoman sought revenge for the death of her husband she would find the opportunity to slip a knife in my ribs. You would never find my murderer. She would become a shadow and no one would expose her.'

'Shadows cannot hide if the town is in flames,' he said. 'You're safe with me.'

CHAPTER TWENTY

The dead men's carcasses rotted slowly, the crows pecked away their soft flesh but the north wind that chilled ordinary men's bones caused no such hardship to the corpses. It swayed them gently on the gibbets beyond the walls. They also served as a warning to brigands: on more than one occasion those on watch sighted groups of riders on the low hills, but the brigands came within a half-mile of Balon and then turned their horses. At night the sentries heard creatures snuffling at the bodies. They were strung too high for wolves to reach them but that did not stop the smell of decay enticing them out of the forests. Sooner or later the ropes would fray and the men's carcasses would be dragged away and devoured.

It was the wrong season to replace the church roof with thatch but the people of Balon had been inspired by the promise of a new priest and a place of worship, and that Thomas Blackstone would pay them in gold *moutons* for their labour and materials. Despite the persistent rain and sleet the townspeople busied themselves both inside and outside the walls.

Perinne was given the responsibility of using the cut timber to reinforce the town's crumbling walls and over the days that passed it was not uncommon for Blackstone to be seen cutting and laying stone. Aelis had awakened desire in him that he wished to be rid of and the physical effort demanded by the rebuilding of the walls helped him push that lust away.

'Have you bedded her yet?' said Killbere one day as Blackstone helped him down the steps into the courtyard below the mayor's house.

'I have not and I will not,' he answered.

'Sweet Jesus, Thomas, she is ripe for it and you will forgive me for saying that you need to shed whatever burden you still carry for Christiana.'

Blackstone had not yet told the veteran knight that it was he who had already enjoyed the mysterious woman's carnal attentions. He was not sure why, but he sensed the time was not yet right and that it was best to let Killbere think that he had enjoyed his long-lost nun in his dream.

'That's not easy for me, Gilbert. Sometimes I catch a glimpse of her. She's still with me.'

'Bid her farewell, my friend. Carry her in your heart if you must, I can understand that, but your life is in front of you now. You and the boy. You need a woman and this Aelis girl owes you her life. Nothing like gratitude for a good hump. Blow the cobwebs away, man. Bed her.'

'I cannot,' said Blackstone, the tone of his voice telling his friend that the matter would not be discussed further.

Killbere had remained silent. It was unnatural for a man not to lust after a woman and this witch they had saved from the stake put the spittle of desire on a man's tongue. He allowed his friend's strength to help him down the steps and sit him on a stool as the sun broke through the low clouds. Its warmth for a few hours would do more good than days in bed.

'Go and lift those damned rocks for the walls. I'm glad I'm wounded otherwise you'd have me laden like a donkey.'

'The men need work and they need to keep up their strength.'

'And I need to get off my arse and back on a horse. Leave me my sword so I can feel its comfort, Thomas. But at least think on what I've said.'

'I have already. She's not the kind of woman a man should cleave to, Gilbert. She has a mystery about her that troubles me.'

'Be troubled between the blankets. You don't have to marry her! God's blood, if I were more agile I'd have her myself.'

Blackstone grinned and said no more.

Each day carts went out under escort to the abandoned manorial lord's house a few miles away. It had already been stripped by brigands and English scavengers months before Blackstone had arrived at Balon, but none had needed the slates on its roof. The tiles were hoisted up scaffolding to repair the town's church. Will Longdon, Jack Halfpenny and Thurgood hunted for fresh meat while Killbere went from being nursed at the fireside to walking unaided. Within days he was seen taking further steps to recovery as he swung his sword in the courtyard, practising the skills that had kept him alive through countless battles.

'See here,' said Will Longdon to Henry, 'this is what's needed to bring a man back to full strength when he's been wounded and lies helpless.' He took the boy into a cow byre and tied a rope around one of the beasts' neck. 'Winter's a hard time for everyone. You might not remember that growing up because your mother and father kept you fed and nourished. Hobble her,' he said, handing the length of rope to Henry, who took it and clambered below the stall and secured the cow's front hooves.

'I do remember,' he said. 'Father always made sure that his villagers had enough firewood and food.'

'But did he show you how to bleed a cow?'

Henry shook his head.

'Well, no man in his right mind will slaughter all his beasts in winter. All right to wring a chicken's neck for the pot when it's stopped laying, but eggs will keep a family alive for weeks on end. If he's any sense he gathers in his fodder and keeps the beasts alive. There's wool to be had for warmth from goats and ewes, as well as their milk, just like Madam Cow here. That gives a man cheese. No need for a man to starve if he has his noggin working proper. Put that pail just there,' he said.

'Are we to kill her?' said Henry.

'Didn't I just tell you that a man does not kill that which he needs?'

'You have the knife ready.'

'Watch what I do,' he said. 'Hold her leg, to help keep her steady.'

Henry reached forward and gripped the cow's leg above the hobbling rope.

'Find the vein... here... see it?' said Will. Henry nodded. 'Then... you slip the point of your blade in and release the blood. She don't feel nothing. She quivers is all. There... now we catch the blood in the pail.'

Henry's father had always said that his friend and archer could provide the men with food wherever they fought. He could hunt and cook and now Henry watched as Will Longdon's skill bled the cow.

'Right,' he said. 'That's enough. Pack a bit of mud and straw on the cut and then release her.'

Longdon took the boy back to where the men cooked and slept. The fire was always lit and the smell of pottage steamed in the room.

'Fetch that pot, Henry, and a few handfuls of oats from that sack. Good lad. Now we mix the blood and the oats and...' He rummaged for a smaller sack, tied off at its neck. '... herbs. Always need some herbs if you can get them.' He offered the open neck to Henry. 'Fingers in, take a healthy pinch.'

Henry did as he was told. 'That enough, Will?'

'Perfect. In the pot with them. And then...' He copied Henry's actions and dipped his fingers into an earthen jar. 'Salt,' he said. 'We stir and then we set the pot in the embers. Needs a slow cook and needs watching. When it gets thick we scoop it out and let it cool. Blood cake. Gives a sick man strength. You remember that because one day when I'm not around you can help save a man's life with it.'

'I will,' said Henry, gazing at the oats absorbing the blood.

'Good lad,' said Longdon and ruffled the boy's hair. He had a great deal of affection for the boy. It was not that many years ago that the archer had scaled a castle's wall with John Jacob and helped release Henry, his sister and mother. He had seen Henry's courage when he and his sister had been held captive by the Savage Priest. The lad had offered himself up for death, prepared to sacrifice himself to save his sister. That kind of courage earned respect. Will Longdon had never had any bond of fondness for woman or child, but the loyalty he felt towards Blackstone and the warmth towards Henry told him that such feelings were somehow precious.

He mumbled quietly to himself. He must be getting old to let such feelings stir inside him.

'Don't let it burn,' he said. 'It's for Sir Gilbert. We need him at your father's side. The fighting's not over yet.'

The month soon passed without incident or recrimination and the town began to breathe more easily. Under Blackstone's protection it settled into a sense of security and wellbeing. The tavern welcomed the archers and men-at-arms, none were short-changed for their drink, and some of the women became even more inviting.

Aelis did not venture far from the mayor's house, where she kept a vigilant eye on Killbere and administered to his wound, but neither did she fear being seen in the square once Blackstone had accompanied her. The distrust and resentment would never be fully cleansed from the town. The women averted their eyes from her; the men did not. Lust was not easily concealed.

Blackstone heaved a piece of cut stone into place on the parapet and turned to see the flutter of a banner rise over the crest of the hill.

'Riders!' the sentries on the walls called.

'I see them,' said Blackstone and calculated the number of distant figures. Forty men. Armed and heading straight for the town gates. 'Bring everyone inside,' Blackstone shouted down to Perinne. 'John! Get Will and Jack on the walls with the archers. I can't make out their banners.'

Blackstone pulled on his jupon and fastened Wolf Sword. The approaching horsemen were coming at the canter, ignoring the dead men's warning. Blackstone ran to the parapet above the town gates. The dull, grey light finally allowed him to recognize the gold lions on the bright red banner.

'It's Lancaster's men!' he called to those around him.

'Shall we open the gates?' John Jacob asked.

Blackstone shook his head. 'No. Just because they're the King's men doesn't mean they're friendly.' He grinned at John Jacob. 'Maybe they've heard we took some of that gold for ourselves.'

The men pulled up their horses three hundred yard-long paces from the walls. The horses were flecked with sweat, their snorting breath billowing in the cold air.

'Well, they know we have archers,' said John Jacob. 'They're wary and keeping on the edge of our range.'

'They haven't seen how Will and the lads can get another fifty yards,' said Blackstone. 'My lord!' he called to the knight who was at the head of his troops. 'You serve Henry of Grosmont, Duke of Lancaster. How may we serve you?'

The knight took off his helm and pulled back his mail coif. 'I am Walter Pegyn. I am charged with securing supplies for my lord's division. We protect the army's flanks.'

'Ah, we can't help you with that, Sir Walter. We barely have enough ourselves. Is there anything else?'

The knight looked dumbfounded for a moment. 'Sir John Chandos said Blackstone had ridden here. Fetch him now! This town has declared for Edward and it must levy supplies on demand.'

'I have already confirmed privilege on this town, my lord. I have assured them they will not be stripped of what little they have.'

'You're Sir Thomas?'

'I am.'

The knight said something to his men, who waited as he spurred his horse forward at the trot. When he was fifty paces from the gates he drew the horse to a halt.

'Did Chandos return with the gold for the King?' said Blackstone. He could see the man's face clearly now, and knew that he had offered his welfare into Blackstone's care.

'He did.'

'Then we have served loyally and may God grant our liege lord pleasure in spending it. Where is Chandos now?'

'South. With the King. The Duke of Burgundy has paid him to cause no harm in return for supplies. Then we will strike west and attack Paris.'

'Did we take Rheims?' Blackstone asked.

'You've not heard? The siege was lifted in January.'

'Ah,' said Blackstone. 'The Prince listened to my advice then.'

'Your...?' Sir Walter was momentarily lost for words but quickly recovered his authority. 'I need supplies for the division's raiding parties. I've two hundred men a few miles behind me. Open the gates so we might take what is required.'

'You would assault our walls?' said Blackstone.

'You defy your King?'

'I defy you. Go elsewhere for your supplies, Sir Walter.'

'I am commanded to –'

'And I command,' said Blackstone quickly. 'This is my town and I protect these people from assault and hunger.'

Blackstone was suddenly aware of Killbere at his side. The veteran knight had pulled on a boiled leather jerkin over his undershirt. 'Walter!' he shouted to the horseman. 'It's Gilbert!'

'Killbere?' Sir Walter called back. 'We were told you were dead.'

'Aye, and how many times have you heard that? I'd have Sir Thomas here invite you in for a drink but you're making us all nervous. The town's declared like he said and it's under our protection.'

'Merciful Christ, Gilbert. Aye, all right. I can see by this crow bait hanging here that you've inflicted punishment already. I've no taste for forcing my hand. I'll leave my men outside the walls.'

Killbere nudged Blackstone and lowered his voice. 'He's a belligerent old bastard but he'll cause us no harm and we need to know what's going on.' Then he coughed and wheezed from the effort of clambering onto the town walls.

'Get yourself back to the warmth, I'll bring him to you,' Blackstone said.

'And brandy. And some cuts of meat. If we're to soften his misery we must coddle him.'

Sir Walter Pegyn looked to be as old as Killbere, Blackstone thought when he accompanied the knight into Killbere's room. An unruly beard and hair badly cut gave him the air of a vagabond, but his scarred knuckles and evidence of old wounds stitched on his scalp told a different story. The chair that Killbere sat on was draped with a fur-trimmed cloak and blanket that offered some comfort as he sat in front of the fire. The mayor's servants laid food and drink on side stools.

'You look as though you have not yet cheated death,' said Sir Walter as he washed his hands in the bowl provided by one of the women.

'It's a wound I got before Rheims that went bad. I've had a woman nurse me these past weeks. I linger so I might enjoy the sight of her tits a while longer.'

Sir Walter had not yet availed himself of the fire's warmth or the food and drink offered. He loosened his cape and draped it over the bench, casting a sour glance towards Blackstone. 'Your reputation for impertinence does not disappoint, Sir Thomas.'

'Now, now, Walter,' said Killbere, 'let's not squeeze a man's balls till his eyes water. Thomas is who he is, no more, no less than the rest of us.' He grinned and pointed a finger at the aggrieved knight. 'Once I'd recovered from going down beneath that horse at Crécy, Walter and I fought together. We made some money, spent it on women and drink, and came close to organizing our own band of routiers. Not so, Walter? Good days. He's prized by Lancaster and the King.'

'No more than you and Sir Thomas here,' Pegyn said, lifting the beaker of brandy to his lips. 'Aye, truth is, the Prince values Blackstone more than he lets on, so don't spin your flattery on me, Gilbert, I'm not one of your whores.'

Blackstone sat slightly behind them, wanting the two friends to ease into their conversation, knowing it was better for Killbere to find out what was happening in the war.

'Have we drawn out the Dauphin yet?' Killbere said.

'No. He hides behind the walls of Paris. I and other knights skirmish and claim what small victory we can against the few troops he has, but it's mostly routiers we chase and kill. The King sits in warmer climes now and Burgundy has fallen from grace with the French King for making the arrangement with Edward.'

Killbere grunted in sympathy. 'We left Rheims on the King's business. Chandos helped but Thomas here was obliged to kill the French royal captain. Chandos was pissed off. He saw a ransom slip away. But it got me here and saved me.'

Blackstone knew Killbere was wasting time, drawing in his old fighting friend, wanting to get to the nub of what action had taken place in their absence.

'We control this area,' said Killbere. 'What few villagers there were around here are now within these walls. It's a stronghold for Edward. We've given him two towns now. It covers his flank when he attacks Paris.'

'And the militia here?'

'Trained by our lads. I keep a watery eye on them from up here. You saw our defences.'

Pegyn nodded. There could be no denying that for attacking men to try and clamber across the wooden palisades and the cut timber and brush that lay before them would cause many casualties.

'And Burgundy?' Blackstone asked, eager to know how far south the English had rampaged.

'As far as Guillon. The Burgundians could not take the onslaught, not after they had been fighting the routiers these past years. Edward agreed a three-year truce for two hundred thousand *moutons* paid over a year and a half.'

'Then he's content to sit a while,' said Blackstone, realizing that Edward would replenish his food stocks for his men and fodder for the horses. Two hundred thousand was not a great deal of money for the Queen of Burgundy and the duchy council to pay. It was a rich land worth protecting.

'How long before he strikes out for Paris?'

Pegyn shrugged and chewed the cut of meat from his eating knife.

Blackstone sensed the time was getting close. Once Edward's troops had been fattened they would scorch their way to the Paris gates and assault the city, and that, Blackstone thought, might spell disaster for the English. He guessed it would be three weeks, perhaps another week more before the King attacked. By the end of March the army would be on the move. The weather should be clearing by then. He glanced at Killbere. The veteran chewed meat and grinned. Both knew there was little time left to have the men fighting fit again. The banners of war would soon be unfurled once more as the English lions clawed the French crown from its master.

CHAPTER TWENTY-ONE

Killbere grunted with effort, sword raised, eyes focused as he attacked Blackstone.

He struck hard and fast. The sword's blood knot tightened on his wrist as he parried a blow with the mace he wielded in his left hand. His body half turned, shifting his weight, and as Blackstone retaliated he twisted Blackstone's Wolf Sword blade away and struck him across the side of his helmet. Blackstone whipped back his head. The hefty blow had been well aimed: had it not, it would have torn away Blackstone's face. Without hesitation Blackstone struck the flat of his blade against the coat of mail beneath Killbere's leather jerkin directly against his friend's wound. Killbere snarled but ignored the pain from the blow and pressed his attack once again. The fervour with which Killbere advanced against the bigger man was the same kind of assault Blackstone had witnessed across the battlefields of France. Blackstone closed quickly and threw his weight against the smaller man, pushing him off balance. Killbere fell heavily into the mud and gazed at Wolf Sword's blade that hovered at his throat. They had fought for an hour.

'All right, Thomas. Enough is enough.'

Blackstone offered his hand and heaved up his friend.

Killbere grinned. 'That felt good.' He spat phlegm from the exertion. 'You made a few mistakes, Thomas. I could have had you,' he said, shaking free the mud from his hands.

'I let you think that. I was drawing you in.'

'You're a terrible liar. Just as well you're a better swordsman. You believe me now when I say I'm ready?'

Blackstone grinned and nodded. He was finally satisfied that Killbere had regained his strength and was fit enough to return to the war. They had sparred every day with and without shield, using sword and mace, until the weakened man regained his strength and proved it by at times almost beating Blackstone. He was barely tall enough to meet Blackstone's shoulder but had the sinew and muscle of a man who had spent a lifetime fighting, which made him a dangerous opponent. On more than one occasion he had closed on Blackstone and with guile and unexpected strength tripped or unbalanced the bigger man. Only when Blackstone bore down on him and struck him time and again with the flat of his blade and saw no weakness despite the pain that Killbere must have been feeling did he finally relent and agree that his friend could sustain himself in battle.

In the fourth week after Sir Walter Pegyn had eaten his fill and taken his leave, Blackstone and his men prepared to leave the town under the command of its mayor and his constable. The time spent at Balon had healed their saddle sores and brought Killbere back to health as he had proved sparring with Blackstone the day before. Now Blackstone bristled with impatience, keen to get back to the fighting. The two men approached the square where Mayor Malatrait and the town's burghers waited.

'It's bad luck to take her with us, Thomas.'

Blackstone glanced to where Aelis stood. He had deliberately placed her between Meulon and Gaillard for protection in case of any final foolish act of retribution against her. 'She has her uses, Gilbert, you're testament to that.'

'I grant you she's healed me, and I swear I feel stronger than I did at Rheims. She's rid me of the poison and has given me back my strength, and for that I thank her. But we're talking about a woman who would have held men's vitals in her hand and sliced them off. That's no ordinary woman. Did you ask yourself how many women you've known would do that? And I wager she would have cut them slowly like carving a leg of goose. Think on it. She could hold your cock and balls and then start cutting. Mother of God, does that thought not make your blood run cold?'

'She had been raped and tortured. She had just cause.'

'Of course and you gave her justice. But a woman who's handy with a knife has a dark past, Thomas. What if she uses the dark arts and uses men's parts to conjure forces from beyond the grave?'

'I saw no sign of that.'

'Of course not. Witches and sorcerers hide in plain sight. They charm and entice. Listen, who would want to wake up in the morning and find their private parts frying in the fire as she chanted a heretical spell?'

'There's no choice, Gilbert. And I saw her with you and...' Blackstone hesitated, still thinking it was better that Killbere was not told of the sex he had unknowingly enjoyed that night. Again he questioned his reasoning and once more concluded it to be the correct decision. Lust could turn a man's mind and his friend was no stranger to it. If Killbere enjoyed the memory of the girl straddling him he might be drawn to her now. Blackstone's mind ran on to the consequences of the veteran knight desiring the girl, of her perhaps rejecting him, of Killbere's anger. Of the violence that might follow.

'And what?' said Killbere.

'She cared for you like a sister to a brother.'

'I squeezed her tits and she did not behave like a sister.'

'She allowed it?' said Blackstone. A woman behaving like a common whore among his men could soon wreak havoc.

'No,' confessed Killbere. He winced at his failure. 'She kept well clear of me after that and I had to content myself with a serving girl, but she has the look of a temptress and what good will that do to these horny men? Christ, given the chance every one of them would bed her.'

'You know as well as I do no man will go near her.'

'Aye, but only because they think you have claimed her yourself. Time will soon show that you have not.'

150

Blackstone stopped walking and turned his back so that the gathered townspeople would not hear what he said. 'Gilbert, I cannot leave her here. They still think she is a witch. She would be dead the moment the gates close behind us.'

Killbere subdued his irritation. His voice lowered. 'Thomas, what if she *is* a witch and we bring her into our midst? There, with us, day in day out, would any of us sleep easy in our blankets at night? I'm telling you it's bad luck to have a woman riding with us, let alone someone like her.'

The previous weeks had seen Aelis keep her distance from Blackstone day to day once she had walked with him through the town. His protection for her had been established and everyone knew that if one person attacked her then the town would be sacrificed. It kept their primal fear and hatred in check. She had slipped into near silence when attending Killbere, even when his hand strayed to her breast as she checked his wound. She had glanced at him with a reproachful look that made little impression on the veteran fighter, but thereafter she simply dispensed the ointments and herbs and insisted that one of the servants dress his wound. It mattered not to Killbere. The girl servant was willing enough to attend to more than his injury.

Blackstone said nothing in reply to Killbere's request, but his gaze was enough of an answer. Killbere shrugged and sighed. 'All right, all right. I tried. Don't say I didn't warn you. God's blood, I swear you become more pig-headed every passing day.' He spat and looked past Blackstone at the expectant crowd. 'Now, Thomas, don't go making long speeches. We've a few days' ride to catch up with the King,' he urged quietly. 'The weather has turned for the better; we can make good time.'

Blackstone glanced at him. 'They expect a speech. So I'm obliged to give them one. It'll be as long as it takes.'

Killbere sighed and nodded in resignation; then he followed Blackstone as he strode towards the crowd. Blackstone stopped ten paces from the mayor and the crow priest, both of whom bowed their heads respectfully, as did the townspeople. Killbere stood a pace behind his friend's shoulder, hands resting on his sword's pommel. Like Blackstone, he was uncertain whether someone might still harbour enough resentment to strike at them, especially now that they had trained the town's militia. He glanced towards Aelis. It would be suicide for anyone to try and harm her, flanked by those two mountain bears, but what about here, closer to the crowd? A sudden lunge by a few determined men? It was a fanciful thought and he knew it. Blackstone had given the town back its life. Still, he reasoned, it paid to be suspicious.

Malatrait stepped forward. 'You have taken grain from our stores. We have little enough for ourselves.'

'Fighting men need barley. That's all we have taken.'

'And now you leave us, Sir Thomas,' the mayor said, hands outstretched imploringly.

'The militia have been sufficiently trained to withstand an assault on the town's walls,' Blackstone said, addressing the crowd. 'If routiers come in numbers you know what your fate will be. If you don't fight they will kill you, if you show resistance you have a chance. Take consolation in the knowledge that King Edward's raiding parties have swept many of the mercenaries away.'

'Can we bury the men you hanged?' asked Malatrait.

'What remains of them will be left as the warning that I intended.'

There was a murmur of disapproval from the dead men's family members in the crowd.

'A Christian burial!' an anonymous voice cried out.

Killbere's eyes scanned the crowd but there were too many to identify who had called out.

Before Blackstone could answer the crow priest stepped forward and then turned to face the townspeople. 'Lord Blackstone is right! Their bodies remain where they are. They serve as a warning. I will pray for them and ask God to forgive their acts of rape and brutality. Their bodies will rot, but Our Saviour the Lord will receive their souls unblemished by the corruption of their flesh. Only He will judge them.'

152

Killbere glanced at Blackstone. Corneille, the crow priest, was playing his part. Mayor Malatrait raised his hand to quieten the murmurs of uncertainty. 'Our new priest speaks honestly. Their deaths might save our lives should routiers approach Balon. Let God embrace their souls as he said. These men acted in lust and their actions took them beyond that which they were ordered to do.' He looked over his shoulder at Aelis and then his eyes settled on Blackstone. 'It is just,' he murmured reluctantly. The purse of silver *moutons* Blackstone had pressed into his hand the day before had been an added guarantee of his loyalty. He faced the crowd again and raised his voice so those at the back could hear. 'It is just!'

Malatrait's words calmed the crowd. Blackstone nodded his approval to the crow priest and the mayor – both men bought off in their own way; both sufficiently venal not to want to risk losing what they had gained.

John Jacob and Henry brought Blackstone's war horse forward as one of the men-at-arms handed Killbere the reins to his mount. Blackstone climbed onto the bastard horse, the opposite rein gathered tight as always, stopping its cumbersome head from swinging around and biting.

'You feared us coming to Balon,' he said, 'but despite the punishment inflicted you have benefited. No woman was raped or harmed; no man suffered loss of trade. Your church is restored, your altar rebuilt. You have a new priest to care for your spiritual welfare and a wise mayor to guide you in the years to come.' He looked down at the two men. 'If they do not execute their duties wisely then I will hear of it.'

He eased the brute horse forward. 'My banner flies over your walls. My name will protect you.'

The crow priest suddenly reached up to Blackstone's pommel. 'Sir Thomas,' he whispered. 'Be careful. She is the devil's whore. I know it!' He quickly made the sign of the cross and stepped back.

Blackstone made no reply but the look in the priest's eyes reflected the genuine fear he felt. For a moment the priest's outburst caused a shudder down his spine. He shrugged it off and led his men towards the gates. The crowd parted.

'What was that about?' said Killbere as he rode alongside.

'He was begging me,' said Blackstone.

'Ah. He knows when he's well off. I'll wager he was pleading with us to stay?'

'No. He was begging me to look after the old man who rides at my side,' said Blackstone and before Killbere's curses reached his ears he spurred his horse forward.

As the gates closed behind the last horseman a great sigh could almost be heard from the citizens of Balon.

CHAPTER TWENTY-TWO

'The weather won't hold,' said John Jacob some days after Blackstone and his men rode out of Balon. 'Look at that horizon, Sir Thomas, we'll be drenched again sooner rather than later.'

They had already crossed the River Aisne at the same place they used months before. The bend in the river and the narrow banks had been difficult but caused no hardship. Now they were camped in the lee of a forest, the land sloping away from them, a place where if attacked their enemies would have to labour uphill before being able to strike. On the reverse slope another river, wide and treacherous, offered protection to their rear. The view was clear and the distant sky forewarned them that the weather would be an ally to the French. They could hear the rushing sound of water tumbling across the ford they had found on the river they believed to be the Yonne.

'We're still too far north,' said Blackstone. 'Perinne! Do you know this place?'

The barrel-chested fighter scratched his close-cropped head. 'We're nowhere near Auxerre and the King,' said Perinne. 'I'm sure of that. There's a Benedictine abbey on the river and we've seen no sign of it.'

'Then we're lost,' said Killbere as he gazed across the unfamiliar landscape. 'God forbid there would be a battle raging somewhere so we might hear drum and trumpet to guide us.'

'We need to get across onto the other bank,' said John Jacob. 'The King is to the west. Somewhere.'

Will Longdon trudged around the forest's edge. He was sweating despite the cold air brought by the easterly breeze. 'Our arses will

155

be soaked if we do, no matter how high you sit in the saddle. Me and the lads have been trying to find a better way across. There isn't one. I'm fearful the horses won't keep their footing, Thomas. The rains have swollen what shallows there are here.' He removed his cloth coif and wiped the sweat from his face. 'I reckon we'll lose men and horses.'

'And there's no other crossing place?' said Blackstone.

'We've gone downriver near enough another two miles. There are no villages in sight. So no one's built a ford to get cattle or wagons across and if the King crossed anywhere around here we'd see the signs. Ten thousand men leave a trail of shit that you'd smell before you step in it.'

Killbere chewed a piece of grass and pointed with it in the direction Will Longdon had come from. 'Walter Pegyn said the King would make for Paris. He'd have a hundred miles to get to the outskirts; odds are he's already there by now. We're better off being this far north. Save ourselves a long ride. Let's get ourselves across the damned ditch and if we're still in Burgundy hope it proves as friendly to us as it was to Edward. I don't want to be caught midstream by any French raiding parties.'

Blackstone considered the risk. He nodded at Killbere. 'See to it, Gilbert. I'll join you at the river.'

As the men stripped off their mail and armour and made their way down to the river Blackstone went to where he had made a place for Aelis. When they camped at night he had kept her on the edge of the men and placed a guard over her. As he approached he saw that she was standing gazing in the direction of their travel. Her eyes looked past him into the distance.

'Aelis,' he said softly.

She showed no sign of recognition or of hearing him and, uncertain, he faltered to a halt a few paces from her.

After a few moments she looked at him. 'Sir Thomas?' she said, as if seeing him for the first time.

'We need to cross the river here,' he said, ignoring her dream-like expression. She appeared to be still deep in thought.

'I see,' she said. 'And it's more dangerous than the other crossing we made.' She had not asked a question but had stated a fact.

'Yes,' he answered, wondering if she had foreseen the difficulty or whether she had heard the men who had returned from their reconnaissance speak of it. 'Get rid of your cloak. Wear the jerkin and breeches I gave you. Bundle your clothing and tie them on the saddle. The current is strong. Can you swim?'

'No.'

'We'll have a rope across to help horse and rider.'

'And if I fall into the arms of the river goddess then you will see whether I sink or swim. Perhaps then you will have the answer to the question that has been troubling you.'

Blackstone was in no mood to discuss the doubts he held about her. 'Get ready,' he told her and turned back to where the men had started to make their way down to the riverbank.

'Sir Thomas,' she called after him. 'You don't know what lies across the river.'

He turned. 'My King and his enemies are there. And once we are with him then you will be found a place to stay.'

'There's more,' she said. 'Your past is there.'

'I lived in Normandy for many years. That's no secret.'

'More than that. You'll see,' she said and then ignored him as she unhooked her cloak and began to undo the ties on her dress. He felt tempted to watch her strip off her clothing but, as a pious priest would whip his own flesh to rid himself of impure thoughts, Blackstone punished himself with self-denial and turned away. He was uncertain whether it was through fear of this mysterious woman or the clinging memory of his dead wife. Whatever the reason, he craved the distraction and sanctuary of battle.

Perinne struggled against the fast-flowing river. Occasionally his feet stumbled across the boulders below the surface, which afforded him a brief moment of purchase. If the current took him there were roots and half-submerged tree trunks to snare him. He gasped and floundered as his arms beat steadily against cold gushing water. Few of Blackstone's men could swim but Perinne had proved himself on other campaigns. Now he had offered to take the slender line across the other side of the river that would allow a rope to be hauled across and secured. He swallowed water, lost his footing, but then forced his head above the surface, gulping air, trying to control his choking. He saw through blurred vision the men and horses on the bank. They were shouting encouragement to him but the roar of water and its chill in his ears deafened him. He had plunged in a hundred yards upstream, fought the churning current and was now almost at the far bank directly across from the men. He had used the swirling water to bring him down to where the shallowest part of the river appeared to be. The leather sack strapped to his back contained shirt and breeches, which would be the only warmth available to him once he made the riverbank. For now he was naked, pinched and stiff with cold, and battling aching muscles. His feet found purchase in mud and gravel and he was suddenly only waist-deep. Throwing himself forward he grasped handfuls of grass on the bank and hauled his shivering body ashore. He ran to the treeline and began hauling the heavy rope across. It took only minutes and then he hoisted the rope around a stout tree trunk and tied it off so that its height would be that of a man's waist in the saddle.

Jack Halfpenny and Robert Thurgood stood shivering on the near bank with the other archers. Everyone had stripped down to jupon, undershirt and breeches. No man was to risk drowning because he was laden with weapons, mail and armour. Shields and swords were fastened securely to saddle straps and pommels. The war bows were nestled in waterproof linen bags. The water would cause less harm to their arrows, which nestled in their waxed arrow bags.

'I stay till the end and see if we can get the wagon across,' said Blackstone, nodding towards the hay cart that carried supplies.

'The mules are strong enough but if a wheel goes then we'll abandon it. I'll not have any men drowning to salvage smoked meat and wine.'

'We should feast on it first,' said Killbere. 'If a man's to drown better to have a full stomach and a confused mind from an over-indulgence in wine.'

'And if we cross without incident? You'll thirst and starve for the next week.'

'You give a man hard choices, Thomas. I'll stay back with you and help with the supplies. Let's get to it then.'

'Across you go,' Blackstone said to John Jacob. 'And then you, Henry.' His own squire and son would brave the water first.

John Jacob made no complaint and eased his horse into the water. For a moment it seemed the horse would panic before it found its footing, but the taut rope did its job as it pressed against the horse's flank and Jacob's leg, and bolstered man and horse's confidence.

'You'll pull me out,' said Halfpenny to Thurgood. 'I'll not drown like a gasping fish.'

'Fish don't gasp, you fool,' said Thurgood. The two men had grown up together in the same village and it had always been Thurgood who waded into lake and river to bring in their fish snares.

'If they're on land they do,' said Halfpenny. 'And so will I if I go under.'

'Hold your breath and you'll bob to the surface.'

'Aye, but what do I do then?' said Halfpenny. 'I'll be going downstream like a bobbing apple.'

'No you won't,' said Thurgood as he tied off his pannier and tested its security. 'The horse will probably kick you to death before that happens, or those half-submerged tree trunks will gut you like a Frenchman's halberd. It'll be slow and cruel but the cold will kill you soon enough.'

Halfpenny hunched against the cold. 'Bastard,' he said to his friend.

Will Longdon's firm grip held Thurgood's shoulder. 'Jack's a ventenar. There are twenty archers who need him. He's important. He goes in, you go in after him.'

'Aye, of course, Will. I was joking is all.'

'This is no joke. I hate rivers. When we waded across Blanchetaque I was up to my chest while bastard Genoese crossbowmen were loosing their bolts but at least I had Sir Thomas at my side and he swims like a bloody pike. I've damned near another fifteen years on my aching bones since then, so you'll ride between Jack and me,' said Will Longdon, poking a finger into the archer's chest. 'I'm a centenar. So if Jack *and* me go in you remember I'm more important than him. I'm the one you rescue first.'

Blackstone watched as his son followed John Jacob into the water. The boy balanced his weight as his horse found its footing. Its gait rolled and swayed but the young page instinctively allowed his body to anticipate its uncertainty. John Jacob rode ahead of him and when necessary raised his right hand to indicate where the best path would be across the uneven riverbed for the horses. Once half the men had followed, Blackstone nudged the bastard horse next to Aelis.

'Go next. The horses ahead are easing the current so your horse can follow in their wake. Grip his mane if you feel unsteady.'

The sorcerer's daughter barely acknowledged him. 'I know how to ride. I've as much skill as any man here.'

Blackstone refrained from challenging her. There were enough horses crossing to give her own mount a sense of certainty, but he knew that if she did not control the animal it could shy and she would be swept away.

'Who will carry my satchels of medicine?'

'They'll come across with the supplies.'

'And if the cart cannot get across?'

'Then they'll be strapped to the mule. And if the mule can't get across I will bring them. Get ready and do as you are instructed. Your river goddess seems to be a mean-spirited bitch.'

Halfpenny waited as she urged her horse down the shallow bank. He half turned to Thurgood and, keeping his voice low, said to him, 'I will let her swaying arse blank out my fear of drowning.'

'If the horses splash enough water I'll wager the ties on that jupon won't hold. I want to see her tits burst free from it. I swear, Jack, they could push their way through the gates at Rheims.'

'Hey!' Will Longdon urged. 'Enough chatter. You're as bad as washerwomen. Go.'

Halfpenny and Thurgood eased their horses into the river after Aelis. The cold water crept up their legs and thighs and the skittish horses needed a firm rein. Further ahead amidst the groups of riders some mounts threw their heads back as the water bubbled noisily beneath them. In midstream one of the men nearly fell when his horse lunged, trying to pass another. He cursed and brought it back under control but the beast's actions caused a ripple effect down the line. Men sawed their reins in an attempt to stop their horses from clamping their teeth onto the bit and forcing their heads forward. Riders' seats were precarious no matter how skilful they were.

As the horse in front of Aelis shied, its back legs slipped, then righted. The stumble alarmed Aelis's horse and its iron-shod hooves slid over the rocks. It fell. She threw herself clear of the stirrups and as she pitched into the water she tried to grab the safety rope. She plunged below the surface into a deeper pool, and then surfaced, choking, the current snatching her quickly away. She floundered, her feet trying to find purchase as she went over shallower ground, but the eddies below the surface clutched at her legs. Through the gushing water in her ears and mouth she heard vague, distorted cries from the men. Her blurred vision saw men trying to control their horses as her own clambered to its feet. One of the men on the bank spurred his horse downriver. A mottled beast, cinder-burnt, the men had told her. Scorched by the devil. The man who leaned forward in the saddle had raised an arm and shouted something.

Then she was under again. Darkness engulfed her mind. She was dying. She knew there was little she could do. No matter what goddess she implored for mercy, the one who lay waiting on the riverbed was about to claim her. She burst through the surface. Someone was close to her. She couldn't make him out. His face snarled with effort and spat water, but a callused fist reached for her. Beyond him the scorched beast was forcing its way into the current, its strength overcoming the torrent. The man's fist clutched at her. She felt its strength grab the front of her jupon, the ties tore but like a dog with a rat he shook her free of the drowning and shoved her face clear of the water. He was shouting at her. '*Don't fight! Don't fight!*' She tried to make sense of what he was saying. She had to fight. The river goddess was enfolding her into her arms. And then she understood. She tried to tell him but her breath was trapped in her lungs. Her eyes stung in a confused vision of rolling clouds and tumbling water. The man in the water had wrapped an arm around her. She felt her breast squeezed under his strength but the power in the man's embrace made her cough and splutter. '*You're all right! Stay calm! You're safe!*' The voices shouted in her ear. Pain pressed into her back. The man who had rescued her pushed his body against her. She realized he had pinned her against one of the half-submerged tree trunks. She could barely make out his features. One of the younger men. An archer, she thought. The man's grip loosened as the current nearly pulled him away. She slipped below the surface again and felt the water consume her. Once again he struggled with her and wrenched her upright. She forced her eyes open wider. A horse's black sinewed leg was close to her and then Blackstone leaned down, arm outstretched. The man in the water grunted with effort and hauled her into the horseman's waiting grasp. Then she smelled leather and sweat and felt the rough cloth of Blackstone's jupon on her face.

'*The stirrup! Robert, seize the stirrup!*' A voice, she thought it Blackstone's, called out. '*Robert! Strike out, man!*'

Then the horse lunged, its strength powering it back towards the riverbank.

* * *

Will Longdon and Halfpenny nearly went into the water when Aelis's horse lost its footing. As they steadied their mounts they saw her tugged rapidly away by the current. The water was not deep but the pools were and river goblins could snatch ankles as well as submerged branches. A foot caught between two river stones would quickly drown anyone caught below the water. They were traps set by the river spirits. As Halfpenny yanked his horse's reins he saw Robert Thurgood throw himself from the saddle. For a moment he thought that he too had fallen but seconds later saw his lifelong friend was striking out towards the flailing woman. Halfpenny urged his horse forward; no one could stay midstream without causing problems for those who followed.

The momentum of the other horses carried the men across the river. Jack Halfpenny could only watch Thurgood splashing towards the helpless woman. Every once in a while his friend disappeared from view and visions of boyhood jabbed away at his memory like an archer's knife. They had fought at Poitiers together and been in Blackstone's ranks since soon after. Killing an enemy and whoring with friends was a life well lived, but to die in a river was to fall victim to fate's foul claw. Unjust and cruel, it threatened to take his friend. For a brief moment he almost jumped into the water to help but knew that would have caused his own death. As water sluiced from his horse's shoulders and its hooves dug into the opposite shore's muddy bank, he was raised high enough to see Thurgood pressing the girl's body against a tree stump midstream. Its slimy trunk offered no purchase but somehow his friend pinned her above the water. 'Hold on!' he shouted as he urged the horse forward along the riverbank in a futile gesture of help. If he could find some shallows he could ride the horse into the river in the hope of his friend reaching him. *Let her go!* his thoughts urged. *No woman's worth dying for!* His progress was stopped by the trees further downstream. He could go no further. He saw Blackstone had already spurred his horse along the far shore and then fearlessly ridden it into the river. If any horse could withstand the current it would be that beast of battle. And then Blackstone had hauled her onto his saddle leaving Thurgood clinging to the half-submerged tree. Halfpenny laughed. *Cursed fool did it! He saved her.*

'Come on! Robert! Swim, man. Here! Come on!'

Blackstone had kicked free his foot from the stirrup and Thurgood stretched for it. But the current took him. Halfpenny saw the gaunt look of exhaustion on his friend's face. Perhaps he had heard his shouts of encouragement because he turned towards Halfpenny. It looked as though he raised an arm. *Yes, yes, Robert. I see you.* 'Strike out!' he yelled, cupping his hand to carry his voice.

Thurgood threw his arms into the water, thrashing, head down, turning for the bank. But he made no progress. For every stroke forward he went back five. He was caught in an eddy. He seemed to kick and half raise himself. Then the dark brown water swept him away. Halfpenny saw the agony of defeat on his face and then suddenly he was gone.

All that remained was the bend in the river, echoing with the gurgling laughter of the river spirits.

Aelis had no sense of how long it took Blackstone to reach the shore. She slipped in and out of consciousness and then felt the soggy ground beneath her back. A man's hands pressed below her breasts; she tried to fight him off, but then she vomited and spewed water and bile, her body curling like a child into a protective fold.

'*Bad luck. I told you, Thomas. She brings bad luck with her,*' a voice said from somewhere behind her head. '*She lives?*'

She opened her eyes as Blackstone covered her with a blanket. 'She lives,' he said.

CHAPTER TWENTY-THREE

Blackstone and his men pushed through the forest in an attempt to follow the river and find Robert Thurgood. The archer was a strong swimmer but Halfpenny had seen him swept away. His friend forged ahead of the others but after an hour it was obvious the river, and Thurgood, were lost to them. They were being slowly defeated by the tangled growth of the ancient forest and impenetrable thorn and bramble. They could smell wild boar and knew it was unsafe for a man to be more than a few yards from his companions. The deeper they went, the darker the forest became, even though the leaves had not yet fully formed on the branches. But the heavy sky and the interlacing canopy began to make the search dangerous. Beasts of the night would soon come out to follow the hunting paths.

Blackstone pulled the men out of the forest and returned to the camp where he had left Aelis, wrapped in blankets next to a roaring fire, one of a dozen Blackstone ordered lit: dry tinder and wood were plentiful in the forest. He knew that warmth and food were now more important than a fruitless and dangerous search in the approaching night.

Jack Halfpenny was riven with despair and no words of comfort from Blackstone would have eased his pain – so none was offered.

'Jack, you will stand first watch. Keep the fires burning,' Will Longdon told him. It was best to keep a man occupied when a grievous loss was his night's companion. 'I don't want to wake and see you or your men slumped. Pick three others from your twenty and make sure they patrol back and forth. Push two out on each flank within sight of the fires. Rotate the watch every three hours.'

Halfpenny obeyed, determined not to show his grief. Men died at your shoulder in battle; there was no good or bad way to die. Lance, fire, sword, mace, beneath the iron-shod hooves of a war horse: no difference at all. Dead was dead. Carrion for the crows. Better to die with friends, though, he reasoned to himself. The last cry for help given to the man you had lived and fought with over the years. Not like this! Not swept away like a helpless beast caught in a torrent. Yet a beast had no thought. Knew nothing about death. Robert Thurgood would have known every second of his final, desperate gasp for life.

Thurgood had felt as if he had wrestled with Meulon or Gaillard. These men, as tall and strong as Blackstone, could crush men with their bare hands. The weight and strength of the fast-flowing river twisted and bent his body and slammed it hard against some unseen obstruction in the river. The sight of Jack Halfpenny racing down the riverbank in a vain attempt to reach him roused a strange sensation within him. He knew he was moments from being pulled under but he tried to raise his arm in farewell to his lifelong friend. He saw that Blackstone had forged his way clear of the water on his war horse and that the woman had been saved. Bewilderment ran through him: why had he plunged in to save her? He had no feelings for the woman; she meant nothing to him. He had lusted after her as much as any other man, but knew she was untouchable. His thoughts mocked him. Perhaps she had been a lure dragged through the water and he, like a fish, had been entranced by her. Then he had choked and managed to push himself momentarily above the surface. The roar of water in his ears conjured images of battles he had fought in which men's voices rose up and became part of the very air they breathed. He remembered himself and Halfpenny bending into their war bows as one, loosing the arrows and knowing they were slaying a common enemy. They had challenged each other all their lives. Halfpenny was the better bowman, Thurgood had always known it, but never resented it – though regret scorched him now in these last moments of his life. He wished he had pillaged more, wished he had taken more women against their will when he had had the chance. Blackstone's threat of punishment for such crimes seemed of little importance now.

Thurgood felt the change in the current as he was swept around the bend and lost sight of his friend and companions. It carried him out into the middle of the stream where some power below twisted his legs as the current above fought it in the opposite direction. The shoreline forest deepened, casting its gloom onto the water. Perhaps this was the portal into death that was about to snatch his soul from his body. He fought against the contradictory forces but his strength was failing. He could see in that brief moment that the river calmed as it flowed away from the bend and then settled into deeper water. If he could reach it, then he might have a chance of survival. He filled his lungs with air, stretched every sinew and struck out for the middle. He cursed his waterlogged jupon that was as heavy as steel. There was no way to count the heartbeats that it took to reach the calm stretch but there was a sudden, soothing cradle that rocked and bore him along. His final effort had taken what little strength he had left. He raised his face to the sky and spread his arms. The evening mist rose, seeping through the trees: wisps of water spirits beckoning his soul. Robert Thurgood closed his eyes and surrendered to the river gods.

Killbere watched as the men settled around their fires. The captains went among them organizing the night watch. A man had died, but nothing changed in how seasoned fighters went about the ritual of creating warmth and food. Cooking pots nestled into embers and the smell of pottage steamed into the night. They had been lucky. The rain held off and only one man had drowned. It was a small price to pay. The fighting force that Blackstone led was still intact.

Killbere peeled off his mail and lifted his shirt. The wound was now only a blemish on his skin. The girl's skills had rid his body of poison, but he suspected she had infected the men with something more lethal. Fear.

'Your wound has opened again?' said Blackstone as he approached and settled his blanket next to the fire.

'No, it's like an infant's arse. Smooth and unblemished.'

'A pity she couldn't have treated your face then,' said Blackstone and accepted the dark piece of food offered by Killbere.

'Blood cake,' said Killbere. 'I kept some. It's good. I would not welcome a face without blemish. A man's face tells the world what he is about. Ask anyone who gazes on your features. The German knight did you a favour that day at Crécy. Had he not scored your face with his blade you would have grown into a pretty man. The women would have swooned and men would have spat at you in the street. There's nothing more troubling than seeing a man who looks like a woman.'

'You forget Guillaume,' said Blackstone, remembering his young squire who had died a vile death at the hands of the Savage Priest.

'You're right,' admitted Killbere. Guillaume Bourdin had often been teased for his boyish looks but his courage was without question. 'My God, that boy had a lion's heart,' he said and bit into the blood cake. 'We lose good men, Thomas. It's to be expected, but some of them deserved life into old age so they could tell the tales.'

'We leave that to the scribes and their exaggerations,' Blackstone said, falling into silence. Each of them gazed into the fire.

'And drunken old veterans who can lie better than most,' Killbere said after a few moments. 'Thomas.' He looked at his friend, knowing what had not been said needed to be spoken. 'She brings bad luck with her. She's cursed. Perhaps those people at Balon were right about her and her father. They scorched the evil from him but perhaps his malevolence passed to her.'

Blackstone raised the wineskin to his lips and then passed it to his friend. 'You've become as superstitious as an old crone, Gilbert. The man healed others, just as she healed you.'

'But I was lying between earth and heaven. I knew nothing of what she did to me. Magic is a powerful tool that conjures forces we cannot understand.'

'She healed you with herbs and potions. I stayed with you throughout and when I left the room another man took my place. She knew she could have died had she not saved you.'

'You know she has other powers though. You can see it. She draws men's desires to her like a beggar to a money-lender.'

'She stays under my protection, Gilbert. Thurgood died because he tried to save a woman from drowning, nothing more.'

Killbere shrugged. 'Perhaps. But she spins a web, Thomas. Who's to say she did not draw him to her? Eh? Witches do that, you know. When their own souls are being pulled from them they suck a man's spirit from him like a spider sucks an insect's juices.'

Blackstone stood and retrieved the wineskin. 'Do you feel less of a man since she healed you?'

'Me? No. Never better. All I'm saying is –'

'Listen to me,' Blackstone insisted. 'I watched her force the bile and poison from you. I saw what she did. If she was a sorceress she could have drawn the life force from you too, Gilbert. She touched your cock, not your soul.'

Killbere's jaw dropped, the food on his tongue falling to his chest.

'That's right, Gilbert. It was no dream of your nun. She straddled you that night.'

Blackstone strode away. No matter how much he wished otherwise he knew Killbere was right. Thurgood's death caused ill feeling towards Aelis. He needed to be rid of her.

The man-at-arms who guarded Aelis sat on a fallen tree a dozen paces behind where the girl's fire burned and the canvas shelter that had been put up for her. She sat wrapped in a cloak, knees drawn up, holding the warmth within the weave, the tin plate of food untouched at her side. The sentry got to his feet as soon as Blackstone approached.

'You've eaten, Collard?' he asked. He knew the name of every man who served him. Collard was under Meulon's command and had been with Blackstone since Italy. He was a veteran like every other who had sworn allegiance to the scarred knight. The man's pockmarked face with its uneven beard was as patchy as a moth-eaten cloth. The swordsman scowled.

'Later, my lord. There's time yet when my watch is over.'

'Very well,' said Blackstone. 'Has anyone approached?'

'None, lord. And they would not get past me if they did.'

'You fear her?' said Blackstone.

'I fear no one, Sir Thomas.' He grinned, exposing broken teeth through the patchwork. 'Except you, lord. You would loosen any man's bowels if you faced them with Wolf Sword in your grip.'

Blackstone spoke lightly. 'There are many who have tried to separate me from it and they showed no sign of fear. I ask you again, do you fear her?'

Blackstone's quiet insistence unsettled Collard. He nodded reluctantly. 'She says nothing to provoke a man to be fearful, but there's... something not right. I don't know what.'

'This woman has done nothing to harm any of us. If anything she is a force for good with her healing skills. She saved Sir Gilbert. Remember that,' Blackstone said, despite his own uncertainty.

He moved next to the fire. Aelis raised her eyes. Her toes peeked beneath the cloth that she had wrapped around her and he wondered whether she was naked beneath the cloak, but there was no sign of her clothing drying next to the fire.

'You are dry and warm?' Blackstone asked.

She nodded.

'You haven't eaten,' he said. 'The cold will bite and we all need food when we can get it.'

'I have no hunger,' she answered. 'Not after a man died trying to save me. What was his name?'

'Robert Thurgood. He was an archer. He was young and he was strong and one of the few men who could swim. It makes no sense to let his death starve you of good food. Eat.'

She shook her head and hugged her knees closer, her toes now covered. Blackstone picked up the plate. 'Collard, take this food for yourself.'

The man-at-arms strode forward and took the plate. 'Thank you, Sir Thomas.' He turned back to the fallen tree. He would eat, but keep watch on his sworn lord and his charge. If the woman was a sorceress she could strike Blackstone down with a spell. It was well known that a woman like her could do such a thing. If Blackstone fell he would slay her without another thought.

'The men fear me even more now,' she said. 'You have lost a good man. A valuable man.'

'Every man who serves me is valuable. We mourn every man we lose because part of us dies, because we share much together. We turn our backs on death until it has to be faced. It awaits us all. You bear no blame for what happened. The horses faltered. It was expected.'

'What of tomorrow? Do you search for his body?'

'No. He will have been swept downstream. I need to catch up with my King.'

The gloom had settled across the forests that stood behind and to the sides of the open land where they camped. The horizon was barely a smudge as the damp air settled. She shivered.

'Get under cover – the dew will be heavy tonight. There might be rain by daybreak.'

She turned her face to him. 'Robert Thurgood did not seem like a man who would die easily, Sir Thomas. When he was close to me in the water with his body pressed against mine and his breath was on my cheek I looked into his eyes through the fear in my own. We cleaved together like lovers caught in a maelstrom. There was a strength in him that would be hard to kill.'

'All my men are hard to kill. Don't dwell on him. Even you cannot resurrect the dead.'

CHAPTER TWENTY-FOUR

After two hours' slow travel the following day they were still uncertain of their location, dependent as they were on the dull glow of the rising sun behind the clouds to guide them westward. They skirted the vast swathes of forest that lay to their left and which curved a mile ahead, riding far enough from the treeline to avoid any ambush from routiers' archers, but close enough to escape into the trees should horsemen attack across the open plain. There had been no sign of the enemy or of marauding bands of brigands, but Blackstone knew that they roamed far and wide and he wished that he could find signs of the English army. There was no scent of man or horse on the breeze, and no smoke from any fires carried and lingered in the forest. They would soon lose the protection of the trees as they eased their horses across the open ground.

Killbere rode at his side with John Jacob and Henry following. Aelis rode alone with Meulon and Gaillard behind her. There was no idle talk among the captains but further back in the column archers and men-at-arms bantered as always. Banter that soon stopped.

Blackstone saw the figure far ahead. Eight hundred paces to his archer's eye. The man burst from the gloom of the trees and with a staggering gait ran hard towards them.

Blackstone halted.

'Perhaps it's a villager from somewhere around here,' said Killbere, peering across the dully lit landscape.

Blackstone kept his eyes on the man who stumbled and fell, then raised himself up and continued running. 'We've seen no village for days,' he said. 'That's no peasant,' he added. At six hundred paces the man took some form and at five Blackstone knew who it was. 'That's Robert.'

'A turd always floats!' shouted Killbere to the men. 'It's Thurgood!'

Men cheered and their horses jostled as they began to move forward to greet him.

'Hold fast!' shouted Meulon. 'You have had no command!'

'It's Robert!' Halfpenny said. 'He's exhausted. I'll take his horse for him.'

'No!' said Will Longdon. 'Stay here. Meulon's right. Why's he running? An exhausted man stays where he is and waits for rescue.'

At four hundred paces Thurgood fell and did not rise. Halfpenny yanked his horse out of the column but Gaillard reached out and snatched his rein. 'Jack! Listen to Will. Your friend runs from something.'

Halfpenny cursed but contained his impatience. The likely truth of what Gaillard said cut through the men's relief at seeing one of their own back from what had seemed certain death.

A slash of red like a bird taking flight fluttered through the distant treeline beyond the fallen archer.

'A pennon,' said Blackstone.

And then there was another as the dark treeline's shape shifted. A line of horsemen emerged. A rider came forward at the trot bearing a flag and then halted a hundred yards from his own men.

'I'll be damned,' said Killbere. 'Those are Lancaster's colours. It's Pegyn. He's been raiding and doesn't know it's us.'

Killbere raised himself in the saddle. 'You blind old bastard! It's me!' He turned to one of the men behind him. 'Raise our pennon. Let him see who we are.' He pointed to the lone horseman. 'Thomas, Pegyn is as wary as a fox. It will be good to have his men ride with us.'

Blackstone had not taken his eyes from the gathering horsemen. They waited on the edge of the forest. Why? They outnumbered Blackstone's men; that was plain to see. Pegyn's caution was understandable but why did he hold back once Blackstone's pennon was raised? And why was Robert Thurgood lying face down in the grass having run himself into exhaustion like a wounded deer from a ravening wolf?

'It's a trap, Gilbert. They're waiting for us to ride out further. It's not Pegyn. Get the men in the trees,' commanded Blackstone. 'Will! Wait until you're in cover and only then unsheathe your bows. Whoever they are they don't know there are archers among us.'

Killbere needed no further command. He wheeled his horse, as did those behind him. Blackstone spurred the bastard horse forward. 'Thomas!' Killbere shouted.

'They'll kill him!' said Blackstone. His shout made it clear he intended to rescue Thurgood.

John Jacob pointed at Henry. 'Go with the men!' He dug his heels into his horse's flanks and followed Blackstone's great war horse whose galloping hooves tore up clods of earth.

Thurgood lay face down. He felt the earth tremor and somewhere in the darkness of his wearied mind knew that it was not the roar of water that had swept him downstream until his body scraped against the shallow gravel bank that formed a small promontory jutting out from the shoreline. He had no sense of how long he had lain on that shore but as the first chill of dawn summoned the river's mist he had awoken. The gnarled and twisted tree roots that still clung to the muddy bank were rotten but afforded enough grip to pull himself up the bank. He had stumbled into the forest and felt despair defeat the joy of having cheated death in the water. It was dense, bramble-choked woodland with no sign of path or animal track. He had felt no pain or hunger and any thirst had long been satisfied by the copious amount of river water he had swallowed. It was the cold that would slow him down and although he had cursed the weight of his jupon in the water he now knew the padded jacket would keep him sufficiently warm. He stripped naked and wrung out his breeches, shirt and jupon with as much strength as he could muster; and then he put the wet clothing back on his shivering frame. There had to be a way through. The sun was still behind the clouds, and obscured further by the forest canopy, so he could not determine which direction he faced.

Gathering his thoughts he placed himself back at the crossing where he had plunged into the river. He remembered the dawn, pictured the bend in the river and then whatever images he could recall that gave him clues to the river's direction. He had to move west to try and find Blackstone and his companions. He forced his mind to ignore the uncertainty about where the river had taken him. There were ferns growing close to the water's edge; they were unfurling after retreating during winter. It was still early in the year so that meant it was likely that they had warmth early in the day. Morning sun. East. That way. Back across the river. Boyhood hunting lessons were never forgotten. The trees' branches soared upwards but others reached horizontally towards any warmth the sun might offer. He sought out trees with lichen growing on one side of their bark. It was not always the case that this meant they faced north. He had been fooled by nature's trick too many times as a boy when he poached the hunting grounds of his manorial lord along with Jack Halfpenny. Heading in the wrong direction then would have put him squarely into the arms of his lord's reeve and certain hanging. The skill he had been taught was to find where moss grew. Moss needed water to thrive. He forced himself through the undergrowth, following what few spears of light he could discern in the forest. Tumbled boulders rose above him, and good fortune proffered him the sheer face of rock he had hoped for. Pushing through the undergrowth, he ignored the brambles scratching at his legs. Edging around the rock's sheer surface he ran his hands across its flanks like a man assessing a horse. He found the covering of green that crept up one surface. This surface would never have the comfort of the sun's warmth: it was always in the shade. The sun spent most of its time in the southern sky. Therefore the rock's moss-covered surface faced north. The trees and moss had given him a bearing. He broke off a slender branch the right length for a staff. Now he had something to help push through the undergrowth and, he comforted himself, a means of defence against creatures that lurked there, and in his mind.

As he pushed through the bracken his eyes scanned the trees for any sign of movement. Because he was looking ahead not down, he caught his foot in a root and went tumbling headlong. He plunged into a ditch; black slime smothered him. He choked and cursed and spat the foul-smelling mud from his mouth, and with a desperate lunge clawed himself free from the boar wallow. Scraping the mud from his eyes he cursed his bad fortune. There was no point in stripping again. No stream offered itself, just the underground spring that had formed the perfect pit for wild boar to roll in. He blew what he could from his nostrils and pushed deeper into the forest.

He had no means of gauging how long it had taken him to penetrate the depths of the woodland. He found a path that cut through the thickets. The musky smell of deer and the animal's droppings told him the beasts had moved through hours before, probably going to ground just after first light, seeking shelter and safety from predators. And then another smell caught his nostrils. The woodland had thinned out and there was more light: his hunter's gaze flitted from one tree to the next until he found he could see more than a hundred yards ahead. There was movement in the half-light. And then the unmistakable sound of a sword being drawn from its scabbard. The distant movement slowed and became what looked like a single mass of men. The breeze barely penetrated the forest but the sickly smell of death needed no help to assail his senses. He had instinctively half crouched when he saw the men and in so doing his focus changed and fell on the disturbed ground to one side. He scurried quickly towards it and then stopped suddenly; unbalanced, he tumbled forward into the bracken. He was lying among dead men. A vast swathe of death where bodies had been piled up. The men bore no insignia to identify them. Heart thudding, he clambered over their bloodied corpses until one man's death stare halted him. His mind raced.

He had seen that face before. But where? The man's mottled beard exposed a rictus grin. It was Sir Walter Pegyn. He and his men had been slaughtered and stripped of their blazon.

The jangling of horse bridles and rustle of men preparing for battle startled him back to the immediate danger. Horses had been brought forward from further back in the forest. It was impossible to see how many men were readying themselves, but he knew that if they had slaughtered Sir Walter and his eighty men then they must number at least a hundred or more, and if they were scouring the countryside as a raiding party then they posed great danger to any smaller group. A half-dozen men eased their horses near the grave, their voices low, barely murmuring. They were almost on him. He lay without flinching. The horses were so close he could smell them. The men stopped, and through half-opened eyes he saw them staring down at him. He prayed his thumping heart would not give him away. The men said something to each other and then smiled as they gazed down on their victims. Thurgood realized that the dried mud obscured his jupon's blazon and disguised him. The men heeled their horses. He waited until the silence of the forest settled again.

He pushed through the undergrowth directly away from the gathering men. If Blackstone and the others had followed the line of the forest then they would ride into an ambush. He tripped and fell a dozen times, his face and hands were scratched, but he forged through the undergrowth towards the light that brightened the edge of the forest. He dared not go further. To try and escape into the open would invite death. A lone horseman could quickly ride him down or a crossbowman fell him.

His body trembled from exhaustion. Fear dried his mouth and throat. He waited ten feet from the forest's edge. The open ground beyond it showed no sign of movement. Crows cawed and bickered in the treetops. Nothing else stirred. The killers made no sound other than their movement: no voice was raised, no commands uttered and that told him that they were seasoned men who knew the value of silence. If the horsemen were readying themselves then it meant that they must have scouts beyond the forest who had warned them of others approaching.

His eyes blurred. He rubbed the tiredness from them and swept his gaze across the horizon. A smudge on the skyline became a knot of riders who were moving at walking pace. They had to be unaware of the men in the forest and if they stayed on course they would soon be too far in the open to escape back into the trees that lay on their flank for cover. He stared hard, using his archer's skill to focus on the approaching men. They were too distant for him to identify the blazon on their shields. Then the dark shape of the horse in front, its bulk and size and the misshapen head, told him who led the men. He cursed his exhaustion, knowing he did not have the strength to run all the way to warn Blackstone and the others. But there was no choice. He had to time his run carefully so that he could make enough ground before those who lay in ambush were forced to reveal themselves. Slowly but surely Blackstone's men approached and his mind's eye measured the distance. At what looked to be eight hundred paces he sucked air into his lungs and burst from the trees' protection.

Blackstone saw the shimmering treeline burst into life as the horsemen spurred their horses towards him. He had the advantage of being at full gallop, whereas they needed to gain momentum from a standing start. As he threw back his weight to pull the war horse to a halt John Jacob surged past him. Blackstone dismounted and went down on one knee to turn Thurgood's body face up. The leading horseman from the ambush had a fifty-yard advantage over his companions and he was the immediate threat. Blackstone gripped the front of the fallen man's jupon and shouted his name. The archer's eyes fluttered and Blackstone slapped him across the face. The shock made Thurgood half raise himself, a fist swinging unconsciously against his unknown assailant. And then realization dawned on him.

'On your feet!' Blackstone yelled, dragging the sturdy archer upright. He mounted and hauled Thurgood behind him, but not before the bastard horse had swung its head and tried to snap at the clambering man. As Blackstone turned away he saw John Jacob attack the fast-approaching horseman. The man barged his horse into Jacob's and swung a chained mace. Blackstone's squire took the blow on his raised shield and as his opponent regained his balance Jacob wheeled his horse tightly, yanking rein and kicking with his opposite leg into the horse's side. He had little time to kill the man-at-arms. More than a hundred riders had spurred their horses from the thickets. John Jacob came up slightly behind the man, denying him the chance to swing the mace again, but offering himself with a lowered shield to make him think he could swing the spiked ball behind him into Jacob's face. As he raised his arm to strike, John Jacob ducked and rammed his sword beneath the man's armpit.

As Blackstone urged his horse on he looked back and saw Jacob a hundred yards behind. The horde of men would catch him if they did not come within range of Will Longdon's archers soon. He could feel Thurgood's arms wrapped around him but knew the archer would not be able to hold on much longer, especially with the horse's awkward gait. As he came within 150 paces of the forest he felt Thurgood fall. He turned the horse. John Jacob was racing towards him. Blackstone felt a sudden rising fear. Had they chosen the wrong place? Where were Killbere and the other men-at-arms? There was no sign of them in the trees. And if Will Longdon did not have his archers on the edge of the forest where they could loose their arrows without the branches impeding them then he and John Jacob would have no chance against so many.

Blackstone halted the bastard horse in front of the fallen Thurgood and drew Wolf Sword. There was no time to fasten a blood knot to his wrist. He held up his shield and readied himself for the bone-crushing force of the charge that was now less than two hundred yards away. John Jacob swerved; sweat lathered his horse's neck and flanks. Its nostrils flared and for a moment it seemed he would not be able to control the stallion. Then Jacob turned the horse and, twenty paces to one side of Blackstone, prepared to meet the horsemen head on. The charging men seemed intent on galloping through him and Blackstone and then riding down the few men they thought to be retreating into the thickets behind.

Blackstone focused on the man he would kill first. The bastard horse strained, ever eager to attack, but as Blackstone was about to ease the reins and spur forward he saw a movement from the corner of his eye. The attacking horsemen suddenly leaned back in their saddles, hauling on their horses' reins, the shock of what they had seen causing instant panic. These men wore only jupon and mail and had no plate armour. The ranks of archers who strode ten paces from the forest on either flank of Blackstone and John Jacob were already drawing their war bows. Will Longdon had divided his archers ready to catch the horsemen in an enfilade. The bows creaked: yew staves bending under the enormous pressure from the archers' strength and skill born from years of training.

The ash-hewn arrows tore through the sky. The horsemen were already barging into each other as they tried to escape. No sooner had the archers loosed than their second arrows were flying and moments later a third. Three waves of yard-long, bodkin-tipped arrows fell into horse and man. It was carnage. Horses whinnied and screamed as the shafts pierced deep into muscles and flesh. They tumbled, legs breaking as they went down, eyes wide in terror and pain. Where moments before the horsemen had been sweeping down confidently on those weaker in number, they now were felled, cursing and shrieking in agony, some pierced by more than one arrow. Flailing hooves smashed bones and skulls. Men writhed; some tried to turn and run. Most could not.

Blackstone tasted the lust of killing on his tongue. As the fourth volley of arrows was let fly he felt the sinews in his back and arm relive the moment when he too had been a master archer. Before that German knight had sliced through his face and broken his bow arm at Crécy. But here and now, like that slaughter at Crécy fourteen years before, the chaos was almost complete. From certain victory to certain death in less than a minute.

Blackstone heeled the bastard horse and a heartbeat later John Jacob followed. Behind them Killbere and the mounted men-at-arms burst from the forest with blood-curdling yells. Within seconds Blackstone and John Jacob were among the foundering men; still dazed from the archers' unexpected assault they offered Blackstone's men little resistance. Killbere raised himself in the saddle, giving himself extra height to bring his sword down onto the collarbone of one of the horsemen. The man's mail did not save him. The blade angled and caught him beneath the ear. Half his jaw was sliced away and the edge of Killbere's blade almost severed his head. Blood gushed across Killbere's arm, but he was already spurring his horse forward. It needed little encouragement. The scent of blood was turning it wild. Like many war horses in battle it would run uncontrolled through the enemy lines, but once a blood-crazed horse did that the enemy could surround the isolated rider and bring him down with spear and axe.

Sir Gilbert wheeled and kicked the horse into submission and tried to reach Blackstone, who had already cut his way through the horsemen twenty yards ahead. Iron and steel wrought a deafening clatter but men's cries soared above the clamour.

'Thomas!' Killbere yelled. Blackstone had burst through the enemy lines and was pursuing three men who had broken free and were galloping across the open plain. He saw that John Jacob was fighting a determined opponent but would soon better him. Grinning, Killbere turned his horse to follow Blackstone, exulting once again in the joy of battle.

The pursued men looked back over their shoulders and saw only one man chasing them, with another rider two hundred yards or so behind. One shouted something to the others and they wheeled their horses to attack. Blackstone saw that they were riding too hard to make a neat turn, and as the men peeled away left and right they were too far apart to make their intended assault effective. The predator, Blackstone, locked his gaze onto his intended victim. The man in the middle had been obliged to slow his horse from a gallop to a canter. Under different circumstances that could have given him more control to fight. But with the weight of the bastard horse charging at him his own horse fought the bit, wrenching his head from side to side in a desperate attempt to escape. The horseman cursed and struck its flank with the edge of his sword blade and the pain made the horse whinny. It ducked its head unexpectedly and pulled the rider off balance.

Blackstone was on him. He parried a blow with his shield and as the man raised himself in the saddle to strike again Blackstone rammed Wolf Sword into the soft muscle of the man's buttocks. His scream was muted by the vomit that spilled from his mouth. His head dropped, body curled in pain, and Blackstone cleaved his shoulder from his body. Released from the tension of the reins the horse panicked and ran; the swaying man still saddled until moments later the corpse tumbled to the ground.

The two survivors drew closer together but now they had Killbere attacking from their left and Blackstone from their right. The sight of the raised shields bearing Blackstone's coat of arms caused them to hesitate. One of the men-at-arms was more courageous: he kissed the crossguard of his sword and urged his horse towards Killbere. The other panicked and tried to turn away but as his horse swerved he fell sideways out of the saddle. His foot caught in the stirrup for a few seconds but the horse's momentum soon released it. He clambered to his feet to find the charging war horse that was bearing down on him moments before now stood thirty paces away, flanks heaving, nostrils billowing cold air, the sheen of white sweat flecking the saddle and its rider, who stepped down, sword in hand.

The man fell to his knees, threw aside his sword and raised his eyes to the scarred face that now stood over him. 'Lord Blackstone, I crave mercy.'

'You know me,' said Blackstone.

'Your blazon,' the man answered as behind them the clash of steel told Blackstone that Killbere had engaged the second man. The fight soon ended and the kneeling man's reaction told Blackstone who had lived and who had died.

'You're routiers,' said Blackstone. 'You slaughter Englishmen and steal their colours. You lure others to their deaths under falsehood.'

The man shook his head. 'No, lord. We are French. We serve the King and his son the Dauphin. We fight as Frenchmen against you.'

Killbere's horse approached at a steady trot and stood off from Blackstone.

'No French knight would steal an enemy's colours and hide behind them. It goes against every code of chivalry. Even your Dauphin would not allow such dishonour.'

The man sighed. 'Sir Thomas, it was his command for us to ambush and kill them. Our captain was instructed by a man who counsels the Dauphin. His name is Simon Bucy, a man of great authority. Our captain died in the first assault. He was a squire, no more, but he led us well. We were to kill any English patrols and take their clothing. None among us took pleasure in such deception but we followed our orders.'

'Your name?'

'Paul de Venette.'

'You have a family?'

'In the suburbs of Paris, lord. Two sons and a daughter. And a good wife who fears the approach of the English King.'

Blackstone glared at the man, who had begun to shiver. 'Get to your feet,' he said.

The man attempted to stand but he trembled too much. 'I fear death,' he said. 'Here, like this, in an open field without a weapon in my hand. I do not wish to die like a butchered beast.'

'You will not die,' said Blackstone. 'At least not at my hand.'

The man tried to express his gratitude but Blackstone's sword point rested beneath his chin and raised his head. 'You will identify your captain among the fallen and you will take a message back to the man who ordered this deception. If you do not, I will hunt you down across the whole of France. I will find your family and I will slaughter your children in front of their mother and then I will give her to my men. Edward will soon be your King and so I will know if you break your pledge.'

'I swear I will do as you command. On my family's lives I swear it.' Still shaking, de Venette got to his feet.

'Walk to where we killed your captain,' said Blackstone.

Blackstone watched the man shambling back towards the killing ground. Blackstone tugged the bastard horse's reins and settled into the saddle.

Killbere spat. 'Slaughtering children and raping women now, are we?' He grinned.

'You know that I had to make sure he would do as I said,' Blackstone answered. 'Just because a snake hisses doesn't mean it's going to strike.'

CHAPTER TWENTY-FIVE

Meulon and Gaillard had pulled Aelis into the forest and told her to stay as far back in the trees as she could in case the attacking men penetrated the woodland. And then Killbere had shouted a command for Henry to stay with her as the two Normans joined the others readying themselves for the attack. The young page obeyed and remained mounted with sword drawn. He watched as Will Longdon quickly dispersed his men and Killbere gathered the horsemen ready to attack. His heart beat quicker and his palms sweated. Aelis looked at the boy who might soon be her only defence. He set his jaw firmly and concentrated on the men's rapid movement in front of them.

'Give me one of your knives,' she said.

Henry glanced quickly at her and shook his head. 'If they break through and kill me you have a better chance of staying alive if you don't try and fight them.'

'I'll die anyway,' she answered. 'Do you know what was done to me at Balon?'

Henry nodded.

'I will not endure that again,' she said.

The charging horses shook the ground and Henry looked through the trees to where his father protected the fallen archer. Nothing, it seemed, could halt such a charge. Even Will Longdon's archers, he thought, could not save his father or John Jacob out there in the open. Once again in his young life the boy thought he faced death. He tugged free the knife from his boot and handed it to her. She nodded her gratitude and together they waited for the assault.

What Henry Blackstone and the woman had never witnessed before was the efficient killing of man and horse by English and Welsh bowmen. Henry's shock at the terrifying slaughter was mixed with excitement. And when Sir Gilbert Killbere charged from the forest beneath the rainstorm of arrows the boy's stomach tightened and the gorge threatened to momentarily choke him. And then his father was lost from view as he plunged into the enemy ranks.

Once the French attack had failed, the men-at-arms dispatched the dying. He watched as his father followed a lone survivor towards the fallen. The man went among the dead and then pointed to someone lying half beneath his fallen horse. It was one of the men who had led the charge. His father quickly decapitated the corpse and beckoned one of the men to put the head in a sack, which was then given to the survivor. Henry could not hear what was being said, but the man grasped the bloodied hessian and then went on one knee before Henry's father. Blackstone took his knife and cut a blazon that was stitched to one of his dead men's jupons. He thrust it into the survivor's fist. Then a horse was brought forward and the man allowed to ride free.

'Your father sends a message to his enemy,' said Aelis, and without waiting for the boy's response went forward to help with the wounded.

'Four of ours dead,' Meulon reported to Blackstone. 'A small price, Sir Thomas. There must be a hundred or more of theirs. Our numbers become fewer in every fight,' he added. 'I hope we find a weaker enemy next time.'

Killbere was busy wiping the gore from his blade. 'It is not in Sir Thomas's nature to prey upon the weak,' he said and grinned at the big Norman warrior. 'You're injured,' he said quickly, noticing the blood that seeped beneath his coat of mail.

'A sword thrust. It's nothing.'

'Aye, and nothing becomes something. Get fires lit and water boiled. Clean and bind the wounded now, Meulon,' said Blackstone.

'Have the woman use her balm and dress it. We need to take a few hours and let Thurgood regain some strength. Move the men upwind from the stench of the dead. We camp until tomorrow.'

'And keep an eye on the girl,' said Killbere. 'She might do more than heal you.'

Meulon's bushy eyebrows creased in uncertainty.

'Never mind,' said Killbere and waved him away.

When Meulon was out of earshot Killbere said, 'Perhaps I was wrong about her. It might be that she brings us good fortune.' He looked across the killing field. What horses had escaped the carnage had run free but grazed contentedly within sight. 'Horses and supplies for plunder. Not much silver to be had other than Walter's belt, which I found on the man whose head you took. I'll keep the belt as a memento of our friendship.' He scrubbed a hand across his sweaty scalp. 'Until I need money for whores and drink,' he went on, grinning. 'I'll go down into the forest and see where he and his men lie. Perhaps there's more to be taken from them.'

'No, Gilbert. Whatever they had these men will have taken when they killed them. Leave them. We can't bury them. The creatures will feast on them soon enough. Same with these Frenchmen.' He spat the cloying taste of death from his throat. 'The French must be desperate if they're hiding behind English colours.'

The two men watched as Jack Halfpenny and Will Longdon helped an unsteady Thurgood to his feet and then sat him down at the edge of the forest. Halfpenny gave his friend a wineskin and Thurgood drank thirstily. Aelis walked towards the archers.

'You warm to her, then, Gilbert?' said Blackstone.

'I have a fevered memory of that night. That doesn't mean I intend to wed the girl.'

Blackstone gave him a warning look. 'Don't be like Will Longdon and let your cock rule your brains.'

Killbere sighed. 'Have no fear of that, Thomas. My cock is like a diviner's stick. It seeks out that which is hidden, not which is offered freely. A man needs a contest even with women.' He took the reins of his horse and walked to where the men had begun moving upwind of the dead.

Blackstone watched Aelis reach Thurgood and the archers. Her rescuer rose quickly to his feet and Blackstone saw her reach out and take his hand, then raise it to her lips. She was thanking him for saving her life. She then turned away and began helping one of the wounded. Blackstone saw the look of lust on Thurgood and Halfpenny's faces. Uncertainty lingered in his mind. The girl was among them like a fox in the hen house, and she already cast her influence – good or bad – over his men. Her spell would strengthen the longer she stayed. He regretted bringing her with them and the reason for doing so was beginning to seem less certain. He had wanted to save her life from the retribution that would surely have been inflicted on her once he and the men had left Balon.

More than that, he told himself. She had already started spinning her web. He promised himself that she would not entrap him.

They buried their four men-at-arms who had fallen in the attack. They were a Hainaulter and three Englishmen who had served in Blackstone's company for two years. Collard had been friendly with the Hainaulter but knew nothing of the man's family. These men lived and died anonymously, but Blackstone allowed their bodies to be buried and marked their graves by scratching a stone with each of their names. Before they had left Balon all his men had been shriven by the crow priest so their souls were ready to meet their maker in the hereafter. Only Blackstone had remained unshriven. He would not confess sins to a God who already knew them, and who had allowed his wife and child to be murdered. Defiance ran ever deeper within him. Arianrhod, the goddess of the silver wheel, hung at his neck next to the small crucifix Christiana had given him. Both symbols offered comfort in their own way. The pagan moon goddess was created by the Almighty as surely as any man, woman or beast. He felt her presence in every tree and river. But God hid in the shadows.

* * *

After two more days they had left what they believed to be Burgundy. It was soon apparent that they had left the land where the peace treaty had been signed with the Burgundian Queen. Devastation was widespread. They came across three burnt and plundered villages within the space of a day. The ashes were cold, the blackened timbers cool to the touch. Here and there bodies lay scattered across fields: victims of Edward's soldiers' raids who had tried to escape. If Blackstone and his men followed the trail of destruction they would soon find their way back to the King. Instinct and the occasional pall of smoke on the horizon led them towards the great army that by now must be ready to attack Paris.

'My lord?' Henry said late in the third day, as Blackstone was about to lay down his blankets by the fire. Killbere looked up from where he sampled pottage from the blackened pot.

'Henry, you've food enough?' he asked.

'Aye, Sir Gilbert, with John Jacob. I've skinned a coney that Will Longdon trapped. He caught a half-dozen and gave me one.'

'Then he favours you, damn him. He never gives us rabbit, does he, Thomas?'

'What is it, Henry?' Blackstone asked.

'May I speak with you?' his son said.

'All right.'

The boy looked uncomfortable in Killbere's presence and Blackstone caught the boy's look of anguish. 'Walk with me. I want to check the captains have placed the pickets.'

Killbere barely stopped his snort of derision. Blackstone trusted the captains with his life; there was never any need to check the sentries. He bit his tongue. It was obvious the boy needed to speak privately with his father.

Blackstone and Henry walked across the gently sloping ground. Rain had fallen the day before and the evening clouds threatened more to come in the following days. 'Rain will be on us again,

189

Father,' he said, allowing himself to address Blackstone as a parent rather than his sworn lord, now the two of them were alone.

'You didn't want to talk about the weather, I hope. My supper grows cold.'

The boy shook his head. 'No. More than that. I wondered why you have brought us to this place?'

'Here? We camp in safety. We are on high ground. There are no forests close enough to draw out night creatures. There's water in the stream and our backs are to the east wind.'

'Father, do you not recognize where we are?'

Blackstone gazed across the hillside. The copse of aspen in the valley at the stream's edge meant nothing; neither did the shadows cast from the weak sun. 'I do not,' he said.

'Then it is fate which brings us here,' said the boy in a defeated tone.

Blackstone felt a bristle of irritation. 'You've been listening to the ramblings of that woman?'

'Mistress Aelis? About what?'

'That my past lay somewhere in this land once we cross that river.'

'She said that?' Henry whispered, clearly shocked by Blackstone's answer.

'Henry, enough of this now. What is it you want?'

'When Mother and Agnes were killed at Meaux we travelled south.' He pointed to the opposite direction from where they stood. A slim scar of a track meandered past crippled trees, bent from age and wind. 'We came from the direction of those trees.' He pointed to their intended direction of travel the following day. 'If we travel across the crest of that hill we will be at the Abbaye de l'Evry.'

Blackstone felt a cold grip seize his heart.

Memories haunted him. Before the battle of Poitiers he had sent his wife and children to safety at Avignon under the Pope's protection. Christiana had been raped on their journey there. Henry Blackstone had been in his ninth year and had tried to save his mother from the attack but it had been John Jacob who had cut the rapist's throat and thrown his body overboard from the barge that carried them. After Poitiers Blackstone had been exiled for trying to kill the French King but when they were about to cross the Alps Christiana had told him she carried the rapist's child and that she would not abort it. It was not the unborn child's fault, she had declared. The rift tore them apart but eighteen months later, when Blackstone returned, days before her murder, they had reconciled. Days when they cleaved to each other like the long-lost lovers they were. And he had promised to claim the child as his own and to go to the convent where it had been placed for safety. After her death he kept his promise. The Abbaye de l'Evry was found, the child named and claimed as his own, but he paid for the nuns to raise him.

'Then... then we shall present ourselves tomorrow and see how... the child fares,' he said reluctantly. He was still bound by the promise to Christiana.

Now, he thought, the wound was reopened.

And not only his.

He saw the look of alarm flash across Henry's face. He had stabbed the boy's heart.

'Merciful God, Henry. You know, boy, don't you?' He realized that the lie he had told about the rapist's child being his own when they had previously visited the convent might have been believed then, but the boy had grown in knowledge.

Henry's face tightened as he held back the tears. 'I know whose child it is,' he said.

Father and son stood alone on the darkening hillside, the cold bite of wind ignored. It could cause no deeper chill than what they already felt.

'I promised your mother,' Blackstone said, his voice little more than a whisper. 'I honour her, still.'

Henry's chin sunk to his chest. Silent tears fell.

Blackstone took his son into his arms and they both wept for the woman they had loved.

CHAPTER TWENTY-SIX

The Abbaye de l'Evry rose sheer from the ground, windows set high in its walls. The abbey had been fortified a hundred years before and blessed with stipends from the nobility and knights who sent wayward daughters and unwanted offspring behind its walls to be forgotten. Their fate was left in the hands of the nuns who inhabited the sprawling convent.

The edifice stood rock-like in the barren landscape. What had been a village of a few hundred souls who had grown food and helped sustain the convent now lay in ruins. King Edward's orders that no church or convent be desecrated had been adhered to. The command had not included those who lived beneath its walls.

Killbere and John Jacob waited half a mile back from the convent gates as Blackstone and Henry were granted entry. Their weapons had been surrendered to Killbere who rubbed a thumb across the silver penny embedded in Wolf Sword's pommel. The sword carried Blackstone's history better than any scribe's manuscript.

'Just as well the King had no desire to scale these walls,' said Killbere. 'Not just for Thomas's sake but ours. It would take a siege engine to reach over them.'

'The men ask why we came here,' said John Jacob.

'There's no need for them to know, John,' said Killbere. Only he and John Jacob were aware of the reason.

'I've told them Sir Thomas owes a debt to these nuns. That they offered prayers for his wife.'

'A good enough explanation,' said Killbere. He spat and then blew snot from his nose. 'Were the bastard child mine I would leave it to its fate.'

'The boy is well?' asked Blackstone as he followed the abbess through the colonnade. 'There is nothing wrong with him?'

'We neither accept nor keep any child of deformity or idiocy. We allow only those whom we believe to have the potential to be a vassal of God,' she said as she briskly led Blackstone and his son along the stone-floored passageway of the open cloister. The convent was built so that the open ground faced south and gathered as much sun as possible and its walls ensured protection from the northerly and easterly winds. There were gardens and a well within the walls and nuns went about their duties hoeing and working in the potagers, but there were other women dressed in more fashionable clothing than a nun's habit who sat on benches enjoying shelter from chilling wind. They wore furs and fine cloaks and it was doubtful their hands had ever scrubbed a cooking pot.

'And women of entitlement bereft of their husbands,' said Blackstone, as one of the better-dressed women stared at him with open hostility.

'Widows and those who choose to live here in safety,' the abbess answered. And then without any sense of embarrassment: 'They pay well. They lie on feather mattresses and have clean white sheets. They have carpets on the floor and freshly cut rushes beneath them that are changed each season so that their dress hems do not trail in the dirt. Their food is as rich as they desire. Since I took the veil forty years ago I have seen many such women come and go. It is not for me to judge,' she said. 'Your King protects us behind these walls as much as our lamented King Jean, but your barbarian soldiers would be happy to storm the walls if they could and dishonour us all. It is well known to God and all his angels that our innocence is like that of the sacrificial lamb.'

How innocent? he wondered. Fornication with monks or priests was not uncommon and the abbess wore two or three jewelled rings on her fingers. Protection came from many places: a pious king who would see no harm come to nuns and an abbot who would ignore misdemeanours and irregular bookkeeping in return for sexual favours. It was not only money that rich women used to pay for indulgences.

'This is a religious house for women,' said the abbess. 'We are secluded from men other than the abbot and the priests of the Church. We do not usually permit men to enter into our sanctuary but we know your intentions are honourable.'

'The boy... my son... what of him?'

'When you were last here after your wife's death, may God rest her soul, we had a wet-nurse from the village attend him. Now we let him stay with the older children placed in our care so that he might learn from them. He is a willing child and even tries to copy them in their chores.' He was a pace behind her as she turned a corner. A door was slightly ajar and Blackstone saw it was the refectory. It was plain and unadorned, a place where food would be eaten in silence, perhaps with a reading being given. A far cry from the raucous scene when his own band of men ate. The abbess led him to where a narrow passage went past the chapter house. The slype led in turn to a heavy oak carved door where she stopped. 'Your wife wished us to keep him only until she was out of danger from the Jacquerie. That she died would have caused you pain and loss. She was a good Frenchwoman who saw fit to marry... you. But you paid us to keep the child and we have honoured the bargain. Please restrain yourself from calling out your son's name. He must not be upset by a wayward father's desire to know his offspring,' she said and pushed the door open.

The room was large and illuminated by cresset lamps which were barely sufficient to cast their light around the vastness of the space. The vaulted ceiling's beams flickered with shadows and added to the eerie silence surrounding what seemed at first glance to be twenty-odd children of different ages sitting on wooden benches at long tables where they stitched cloth. They worked in silence. Boys were dressed in loose-fitting shirts and girls in shifts; all wore a knitted woollen vest for warmth. The youngest seemed to be about three years old, the oldest eight or nine. The great slabs of cut stone on the floor had no covering of reeds for warmth underfoot.

'They sew clothes that we sell,' said the abbess. 'We teach practical skills as well as scripture.'

'It's cold in here,' said Henry. 'There's a brazier – could it not be lit?'

'We must all learn to endure,' she answered, giving Henry and his father a disapproving look.

The children had glanced up at their arrival in the hall but a nun quickly laid a strop onto the tabletop to bring back their attention. Henry flinched at the abbess's sharp retort. It was not difficult to imagine punishment being meted out for any slight infraction of good behaviour or convent rules. Henry knew the children's life within these walls would be strictly controlled. Which was the better existence? This life or the harshness that beckoned outside: sent into the fields by the age of three or apprenticed into a knight's care to be trained as a page? Harshness of one kind or another came as surely as night followed day. Every child endured whatever it must.

Like his father he searched out the child who might be his half-brother. 'I don't see him,' said Henry. 'Father?'

Blackstone shook his head and wished he had not honoured his wife's memory. It served no purpose to be in this place, looking to identify a bastard he could never love. But he knew why he had come. He desperately wanted to see Christiana's face in the child. That hope tempered the pain of going once again into the convent.

'There,' said the abbess, pointing to the middle of a bench and a dark-haired boy, his body hunched over the bench, his nimble fingers gathering pieces of cloth that he passed from one older child to another as if it were a game. His face was bright and round, cheeks flushed with the cold or good health – it was impossible for Blackstone to determine which. The boy was working quickly but then he raised his face to another child and his face broke into a grin. Dark eyes sparkled with mischief as he pricked the other boy quickly with his needle. The older child winced but did not cry out, and with a quick glance to see that the nun was not watching pricked him back. A child's spitefulness expressed as play. Nothing about the boy reflected Christiana's warmth. Her autumn-coloured hair and green eyes were absent.

Blackstone turned on his heel. 'I've seen enough,' he said.

The abbess escorted him to her office where a novice sat with quill and parchment. A leather-bound ledger, as tall as the table was deep, lay open. Blackstone instructed Henry to wait outside.

The abbess faced Blackstone as the door closed heavily behind him. 'Our King forces our people to burn their own villages. Those that do not are destroyed by your soldiers. I lose rents. It might soon be impossible to keep... all the children. Their care is expensive,' she said, trying to hide her slyness by glancing down at the neatly written columns in the ledger.

Blackstone spilled out a purse of gold *moutons*. A small fortune to the likes of the abbess. Enough money to cover ten years' rents.

'Betray me and the child and I will return and scale these walls that you think cannot be breached. And I will slaughter every living soul within them,' said Blackstone and watched the colour drain from the abbess's face.

She quickly regained her composure. 'There is no need to threaten us, Sir Thomas. The boy's welfare will be to the forefront of our minds and hearts.'

The novice counted the gold's value and was about to enter the amount in the ledger when the abbess fingered a dozen coins from the pile.

'The abbot would not look so kindly on such a generous donation, Sir Thomas. He would take more than usual for his priests'... wellbeing. We must have a contingency for unforeseen events. After all, there is a war being fought.' She tapped the table with her finger, instructing the novice to enter the amount that remained.

'How long will you keep him?' said Blackstone.

'Another five years – no longer; then he will be too old to live with women.'

'And then?' asked Blackstone.

'A monastery, I would think.'

That would shut away the child for ever. He would be lost to the world, no doubt to become a tonsured and pious begging wretch in rough-sewn habit. Blackstone felt torn. He was about to abandon the child. It would take nothing more than those few gold coins to ensure that he never heard of the bastard again.

'You would keep records of where he is sent?' Blackstone asked, glancing at the novice nun.

'Of course. We are held to account by the bishop.'

Let him go, the voice in his mind urged him. But Christiana refused to abandon her hold on him. He relented.

'I've decided that for the boy's own good he should not bear my name. I have too many enemies,' said Blackstone. 'He should be known by his mother's family name. De Sainteny. Let it be recorded that he is William de Sainteny. My wife had no other living relative. No claim will be made against him and he in turn will have no cause to seek out the family.'

Such a request was not unusual. Children were disinherited; shamed girls were abandoned and bastard children forgotten. The abbess glanced at Blackstone. The scarred face was stern. It told her that her suspicions had been right all along. When Christiana had brought the baby to the convent gates seeking protection she had suspected then that the child was illegitimate. The mother was no harlot; that had been obvious. So the child was either the result of rape or an illicit affair. It mattered not.

'It shall be as you wish,' the abbess answered. The Englishman had paid enough to have her forget original sin, let alone that of a dishonoured woman.

He watched as the novice erased his name from the ledger and replaced it with Christiana's family name.

The ink dried; the ledger thudded closed.

CHAPTER TWENTY-SEVEN

Blackstone made no mention of what had happened at the convent as he led the men towards Paris where he expected the King's army to be. The weather changed seemingly by the hour as the wind drove the rain into their faces and then veered so that the dry cold air chilled them further. Killbere and John Jacob kept their silence, but Killbere had Aelis on his mind. It would just take him some time to broach the subject of the woman with Blackstone.

'When the King is crowned and holds France, will you return to Normandy?'

'Why would I?' said Blackstone.

'It was your home with Christiana and the children.'

'It was my home when she was alive. No longer.'

'Where then?'

'If we survive the war... Tuscany, I suppose. I will have Father Torellini find a tutor for Henry in Florence. It will be a good time for him to return to his education. Another year of serving as my page at John Jacob's side will have toughened him and given him the skills he will need to become a squire one day.'

'You trust a Florentine priest in the pay of the bankers of Florence too much. One day his grace and favour towards you will run out and on that day he'll sell your soul to the highest bidder. Florence is a city-state that cares only about itself. Like any king or ruler. We count for nothing when deals are made, Thomas.'

'He has been a true and trusted friend. I'll count on that for as long as it lasts. Besides, Tuscany will suit us all. Elfred is still there with several hundred of my men. Our contract still holds with Florence.'

'If Elfred is still alive. He was old when we invaded in France in '46: Italian women and wine might well have planted him in the ground already.' Killbere grimaced. What lay ahead offered little compensation once Edward became King of France. 'Well, I suppose Tuscany is as good a place as any unless a crusade comes up, though I cannot bear the cries of the righteous when it comes to slaughtering heretics and non-believers. Best let a man face God on his own terms is what I say. Italy will at least be warmer, which is in its favour. And there'll still be some fighting to be had. Here, it will soon be over and if I'm to die in a good fight then I would rather choose the company I die in.'

'You complained when we were in Italy. You had had enough of the winters. They were colder than here.'

'I changed my mind.'

'Like an old woman.'

'When you were a boy and I took you to war I swore to Lord Marldon that I would offer you my protection. Now that I'm an "old woman" it will soon be time I am looked after. You owe me that.'

'I'll find you a fat peasant woman to feed you gruel and keep you warm in your bed.'

Killbere said nothing for a moment. It seemed unlikely a better time to discuss Aelis's fate would present itself. 'Talking of women, Thomas, we must discuss the witch girl, and what is to be done with her. Perhaps we should have committed her to the convent,' he said.

'She's no witch, Gilbert, nor was her father.'

'She predicted you would come here. She survived the water. If she's a witch she has the power to cheat death.'

'She did not name this place,' Blackstone answered.

'And yet we ended up here. Which is where your past lies.'

'A turn of phrase. She doesn't know anything about me. Every man's past lies down the road. It's where we meet our maker when we die. I thought you would be the one who would want to keep her. Are you not grateful to her for your life? And that she bedded you?'

'My life is in God's hands, not those of some herbalist who is banned from practising her skills and obliged to mix herbs and potions in a cellar out of sight of the King's officers. That she straddled me – if you are to be believed – I will consider to be moments of fevered pleasure. I did not know it was her. I will not allow myself to be beholden to a woman who finds me irresistible.'

'You have the good grace to smile. A ravening wolf might find you irresistible. I doubt many women would unless enough silver was pressed into their hand,' said Blackstone.

'All right, all right, I might jest but what do you intend with her? We ride into the King's camp with a woman who could snare an army with her bewitching eyes.'

'I don't know what to do with her, Gilbert. I'm at a loss. If I abandon her to her fate I sense I'll be cursed.'

'You fear her?' said Killbere.

'Not fear. A voice inside urges me to keep her with us. It tells me she is important to us, but I don't know why.'

'God's tears, Thomas. Has the visit to the convent and the boy addled your brain? Voices? I hear voices when I am lying drunk on rough wine and you have not been drunk since we dragged you from that piss-reeking room at the inn in London. The voices are your own. No pagan goddess, no angel on your shoulder – you!'

Blackstone tugged his cloak closer around him. It was already soaked, but it provided some warmth as he sat unmoving on horseback. 'She can treat our wounded. I'll keep her for a while longer.'

Killbere relented and fell silent. He turned in the saddle and looked back to where Aelis rode alone, boxed front and back by men-at-arms in the middle of the column. He shuddered. It was not from the cold rain that dribbled down his neck. Her eyes were on him and a smile played on her lips.

As if she knew he had been talking about her.

They were within a day's ride of the King on the outskirts of Paris. Their misery from the rain was compounded by the food running low. The forest's branches dripped incessantly and an acrid veil of smoke from the damp kindling stung eyes and caught men's throats. Blackstone rode the bastard horse at walking pace beyond the forest the length of the men's camp. The figures moving about looked like phantoms, ghost soldiers that hovered between two worlds. *We are already dead. This life is the journey towards death.* Strange words that came from somewhere in his thoughts. He could not remember anyone speaking them, or hearing them in any sermon spewed forth from a priest. A cloaked figure stepped out of the trees and stood waiting. Another followed her but stayed in the treeline.

'Aelis,' he said as he pulled up his horse.

She pulled the cloak's hood back from her head, ignoring the fine soaking drizzle. 'We're close to your army,' she said.

After they had crossed the river she had changed back into her skirt and bodice and once again the soft folds of her dress allowed men's eyes to settle on the fullness of her body.

'Tomorrow we will rejoin the Prince's division.'

'Am I a prisoner?' she asked. 'There is always a guard placed on me.'

Blackstone looked beyond her to where the shadowed figure stood. 'For your protection,' he told her.

'You cannot protect me all the time, Sir Thomas. I said that to you before at Balon.'

'But I did and I will. Men lust after you. Enough wine and my orders can be forgotten.'

'I am unafraid,' she told him. 'I would prefer to be left alone. I can defend myself should I have to.'

He remembered her desire to castrate the men who had raped her. There was little doubt she would not hesitate to use a knife if she had one. 'No,' he said and pressed his heels into the horse.

It took a few strides, but she stepped in its path. He pulled the horse up.

'Sir Thomas, I will be at greater risk once we reach the army. If you let me go my own way I will find refuge somewhere. What difference between now and then when you will be obliged to abandon me?'

'Now, I am here. Then, remains to be seen. I might place you with the barber surgeons.'

'Those butchers?'

'They help the wounded.'

'I would rather take to the road and become a wayfarer,' she said.

'Then accept my protection and stay with my men under guard,' he said.

'If I agree will you let me practise my skills? If I cannot save a wounded man I can ease him out of his pain and give him a clean death. I use the treasure given to me by my father and the blessing of a merciful God.'

Despite the darkness there was sufficient light for her to see his scarred face scowl with contempt. 'No one goes into the darkness silently. We die screaming in pain. We cry tears of agony from shattered bones. There's no final breath eased from our lungs – we gurgle and choke on our own blood. There is no merciful God, only a vengeful one.'

He eased the belligerent horse around her. He and his men were close to Paris and the French should by now be drawing up their army to protect that great city, the heart of their nation. The war banners would be unfurled and the last great battle would be fought. He would be glad to quit France and its misery.

Her voice carried behind him. 'Vengeful only for those who deserve it.'

He turned and faced her. 'My wife and child carried no sin,' he said, his voice cold, the words spoken deliberately. 'You think you are blessed with the power of healing and the sight to see the future? I am blessed with a greater vengefulness than even God.

Take some care what you ask of me. If I abandon you demons hidden in the hearts of men will hurtle from your merciful God's underworld. They will savage you.'

'I bear the scars already,' she said.

'You're alive,' he said. 'Scars and pain are proof of it. You will stay under guard until I decide what to do with you.'

He heeled the horse and sought the company of his men, silently cursing the memory of her nakedness and the desire it brought.

PART THREE

DEATH OF THE INNOCENTS

CHAPTER TWENTY-EIGHT

Failure bludgeoned the Dauphin Charles. The shock was as potent as if armed men had breached his chamber and attacked him. In reality only one man stood before him: Simon Bucy.

'The attack on England has ended in a rout,' said Bucy. 'And because of it our noble lord and King has been removed to another place of safety, far from the coast. The English will unleash their fury now.'

The Dauphin glared at his most senior aide, whose experience and presence he had inherited following his father's capture. In truth Bucy held more power than the Dauphin. It was Bucy who always searched for a way forward to secure a peace with the English. It was he who had liaised with the papal legates seeking an accommodation between the two warring kingdoms. And now the tone of the man's voice was accusatory.

The Dauphin sniffed. 'We cannot be held responsible for this failure,' he snapped. 'If thousands of men lacked sufficient courage to strike into England's heart then it cannot be laid at our door.'

Bucy was in no mood to coddle the boy. Decisions had been made against Bucy's advice. Hard-won years of experience serving the King of France and overseeing Parlement had been ignored. Whether it was the father or the son who went against his counsel their behaviour often stretched his lawyer's training and skills. And now the walled island that was Paris was soon to be completely surrounded and was being ruled by a boy who was at times as intemperate as his father. Well, if they were to have any chance at all of overcoming the great army that was trudging its way towards their beloved city then the Dauphin would have to be told the facts.

'The raid was bravely led, sire. They did not lack courage. But the English will come at us now and if their rage is greater than their caution they will lay their siege engines and towers against our walls and throw fire and missiles until we burn.'

'Let them come! Let them be provoked! The English army would never rise again: they would die in their thousands if they breached us.'

Bucy acknowledged to himself that the Dauphin, despite his immaturity, made a sensible point: his defensive position was strong. But... always a but, always a doubt... what if they were all wrong and the English threw caution to the wind?

The Dauphin paced nervously. Bucy remained unmoving. Best to let the boy spill out his thoughts and if pacing like a caged beast helped, then so be it. The Dauphin blew his nose and glared watery-eyed at Bucy. 'We are being assailed from within as well as from beyond these walls. Every day you bring me petitions from knights who wish to ride out and confront the English. How long before they raise their voices so loud that they cannot be ignored?'

'They're fighting men who do not wish to be held captive behind the walls, highness. Their honour demands confrontation.'

'We cannot afford to lose them but their ill will grows daily.'

'Then let them go out and fight. Let them issue a challenge – if that's what it takes to appease their blood-lust and misguided sense of honour.'

'Let our knights leave the city? Are you mad?'

'Highness, give them something... a gesture... succour for their wounded pride. A hundred knights can be spared.'

The Dauphin shook his head. 'We cannot afford to lose them,' he repeated.

'They might beat the English in a challenge. That would be good for morale in the city,' said Bucy.

'And if they do not?'

'Then it will convince the other knights to stay and ready our defences.'

The Dauphin could see that it made some kind of sense. The lawyer's mind had weighed the odds and offered a solution.

'Very well,' said the Dauphin, and Bucy could have sworn that the Regent had squared his shoulders as if pride had suddenly straightened his spine. 'They can issue the challenge but only when the time is right, when the English reach the walls. But not a hundred, that's too many. Fifty or sixty. No more.'

'A very wise decision, highness,' said Bucy with a nod of feigned respect. If the Dauphin now felt more confident it was a good time to deliver a more worrying message. 'There's more news, highness. Oil has been poured on the fire.'

An hour before, after he had read the document that related the disaster of the invasion of England, the royal captain of the guard had summoned Bucy to the courtyard. A dishevelled soldier stood clasping a sack darkened with dried blood. The man had refused to relinquish either the sack or the message he carried to anyone but the man who had given the orders to the raiding party in the Dauphin's name. Paul de Venette had travelled cautiously back to the city and had decided to delay his report and seek out his family in the Faubourg Saint-Jacques, one of the great suburbs that stretched from the countryside to the city walls. He had collected what possessions they could carry and brought his wife and children into the city where she would stay in the safety of her cousin's home as he did his duty and joined others on the walls to face the onslaught that would surely come.

Bucy had tugged the ermine collar of his cloak around his neck and shivered when he realized what was in the sack. Violence and the men who perpetrated it always stirred revulsion within him. He had commanded de Venette to relinquish the sack to a guard as he listened to the message from the man whose blazon he now clutched in his hand. The stitching on the badge showed the cruciform design of a sword and the words *Défiant à la mort*.

Bucy's stomach squirmed. He remembered a time past when he had commissioned the Savage Priest to slay Thomas Blackstone and his family, and now the Englishman's revenge reached again for those responsible

'I am to tell you, my lord,' said de Venette, 'that Sir Thomas Blackstone has slain our men and spared only me so that I may deliver his words exactly as they were spoken and which are meant for his highness, the Dauphin. I am to say this – and I recite it with disgust in my heart and the wish that I had not been so commanded. Forgive me, lord. These are his words: "There is no honour in the vile King's son, the Dauphin Charles of the house of Valois. He sends dishonourable men to do his bidding, who are prepared to slaughter in ambush disguised as their enemy; it is he who deserves to die after being dragged naked through the streets of Paris and then to face execution in the Place de Grève, and then for his severed head to be kicked into the Seine and his body cast before swine so they might feast on his foul flesh. I, Sir Thomas Blackstone, am the sworn enemy of the house of Valois. I am the sword of vengeance for all the wrongs done by that ignoble house. I come for you."'

Paul de Venette's head had remained bowed as he recited the message. He raised his face to that of the inscrutable Bucy. He could not know the fear that had gripped the older man's heart when he held the blazon and heard the words of the Englishman they had tried to kill.

'Forgive me, lord,' said de Venette.

Bucy looked at the forlorn man. 'You bring me the head of your captain and the words of the man who slew him. You say you regret being obliged to speak such foul words.'

'I do, my lord.'

'Then why was it not enough for you to bring your captain's head and remain silent?'

De Venette looked nonplussed for a moment. And then confessed: 'Lord, the Englishman's reputation is fearful. He swore that if I did not deliver the message he would hear of it and he would hunt me and my family down and slaughter us all.'

Bucy sneered at him. 'So you would malign your King and his

210

son at an Englishman's command in order to save your family? Traitors have no place within these walls.'

He nodded quickly to the captain of the guard and before de Venette could protest his innocence the captain's knife blade cut his throat.

'There is to be no mention of this man or the message he brought. Understand?' he said to the captain.

In the sumptuous king's chambers, warmed by braziers and carpets laid across the stone floor, a far cry from the dank and bloodied courtyard, the Dauphin waited for Bucy to relate the further bad news.

'Sire, the men you sent out to raid against the English and disguise themselves in Englishmen's colours: they have all been slaughtered.'

'How many?'

'One raiding party is all we know about, highness. They were formidable men anxious to execute your orders. They slew enough Englishmen to cover themselves in honour,' Bucy lied. Killing eighty Englishmen was hardly a major success but embellishment was always a good way to help smother bad news. 'They had the misfortune to come up against...' Was there any point, he wondered in his hesitation, in telling the Dauphin any more lies about the glorious dead who had died at the Dauphin's ill-conceived orders? Bucy handed the blazon to the Dauphin, who quickly cast it aside.

'He says he is coming for you,' said Bucy.

CHAPTER TWENTY-NINE

Simon Bucy clattered down the palace steps towards the royal captain, who waited with an escort of fifty men.

'Your name?' he demanded of the captain.

'De Chauliac, my lord.'

'You will escort me to the gates. To each gate and every defence. There is little time. Have some of your men ride ahead and clear the way.'

The royal captain turned on his heel and gave his men their orders. The closest city wall lay less than seven hundred yards from the palace to the west. The Faubourg Saint-Germain was already burning, but Bucy wanted to see for himself how close the English were behind the smoke and flames. Knights and their commanders were born liars. Soldiers never conceded that they could be beaten: there was no glory in that. They would insist they could hold the walls no matter what the English threw at them. Bucy had reports on his desk of the supplies held in the city grain stores. There was enough to sustain them; livestock could be slaughtered and the city's wells could not be poisoned by an enemy outside. If the English laid siege Paris would survive, but if they attacked then panic had to be avoided at all costs and the people's fear harnessed to fight their aggressor.

He made his way across the broad wooden bridge where silver- and goldsmiths and money changers plied their trade. The Grand-Pont spanned the River Seine from the Île de la Cité into the streets. It was unthinkable how much plunder the English would seize if they breached the walls. His beloved Paris was renowned throughout Europe for its luxury trades: her painters, jewellers, goldsmiths and furriers. There were Italian bankers on the right bank of the Seine, merchants' houses and churches stretched all the way north up the paved Grand'Rue. He could see the smoke and flames in his mind's eye, worse than any conflagration he would soon observe in the suburbs. The English King and his sons, banners unfurled, would ride down the city's great thoroughfare with renowned knights following. Merciful God, he thought, it would be the end of civilization if the English unleashed their war dogs into the streets.

The horses clattered onto the Grand'Rue, past the Châtelet and the church of Saint-Leuffroy. The butcher's foul-smelling quarter lay down the narrow alleyways to the right, where heavy-set men went about their bloody business. Crude, foul-mouthed men, members of the oldest of the city guilds. For once he was thankful for them. Knives and meat cleavers with belligerent hearts behind them would punish the English.

The captain wheeled the horses left towards Porte Saint-Honoré, the first great entrance into the city closest to the palace. As they approached a sergeant at the gates barked orders, an officer appeared and sentries poured out of their guardhouse. Bucy had no time for formalities: he raced up the steps to the ramparts behind the royal captain. No suburb touched the walls on the other side, it was still open countryside, but it gave an advancing army a clear line of attack. The gate was fortified and would hold, he told himself, and the English would be exposed. He looked over his left shoulder along the line of the city ramparts. A thousand yards distant, or more, the Faubourg Saint-Germain pressed itself against the south-east wall like a needy child against its mother's skirts. Refugees were still trying to gain sanctuary as they fled from the surrounding countryside beyond the city walls. Smoke billowed, buildings already falling to the Dauphin's command that nothing must be left to Edward and his marauding men. Bucy gripped the rough stone wall. He took a deep breath, thankful that he had decided to inspect the defences himself. His own eyes did not lie.

Two years before, the marshals of the army had ordered troops into the city to help protect the Dauphin against the usurper to the throne, Charles of Navarre, and the surge of the Jacquerie uprising. Now those troops would be needed should the English storm the city. It was unimaginable. But the royal captains had reported that King Edward was now closing in on all the suburbs that lay outside the walls. The huge city gates would soon be closed to any who sought refuge. Although, unlike smaller towns, Paris could not enhance its defence with ditches, this great city had its walls as well as its size and population to deter any attacker. But if Edward was so enraged by the failed assault on England then who could say what action he would take in revenge? One thing was certain, the villages and towns beyond the walls were already being burnt. If the English had brought sufficient supplies across la Manche then they could lay siege to Paris for years. But what King would want to exhaust his treasury thus? Everything favoured the city: no matter the size of the English army it was still not large enough to besiege Paris. However, every precaution had to be taken. Nothing could be left to chance. The city's commanders had already placed bowls of water on top of the towers to watch for vibrations on the surface in case the English tried mining beneath the walls. If they did mine a concerted assault was also likely. They would hurl themselves from the forests and burning suburbs and push hundreds of scaling ladders around the city walls and main gates. One huge attack all at once. But then if the pestilent English poured into the city it would take them weeks to fight through the streets and reach the Île de la Cité. The Dauphin would remain safe on the island and the English would still be denied the French crown. There was a permanent body of two hundred professional crossbowmen employed within these walls as well as full-time knights and sergeants. Each municipality had their own archers. Yet they were too few to man the walls so in the final fight for life it would come down to the citizens themselves to defend every alleyway and thoroughfare. Every adult male living within the walls and the suburbs was liable for military service.

Those with wealth would have armour and weaponry that suited their status; others would carry bucklers, padded jackets, sword and spear; any fighting weapon to hand would be raised against the English horde. Bucy momentarily relished the thought, seeing in his mind's eye the fifty-strong groups of men assigned to each of their city areas ready to ambush and cut down English soldiers in the narrow streets. The citizenry was charged with the defence of a particular sector of the walls. He regretted not being able to convince the Dauphin that each of the suburbs beyond the walls should stand firm and fight until the bitter end. Anything to slow the English advance would have been welcome.

The suburbs would be a great loss for it was where some of the richest sites awaited the English. Churches and abbeys of the Dominicans and Franciscans, forbidden by the Pope to establish themselves within the walls of the city, would lose their silver plate and religious relics. And what if by some great misfortune the English *did* breach the city walls? Damn them, they would perish in the streets, of that he was certain. But could enough of those barbarians reach into the very heart of power and cut it out? It occurred to Bucy that one of the safest places to be was the leper colony that lay beyond the north wall.

He turned to the captain. 'Now, the next gate, and the next. And then I report back to the Dauphin.' Let King Edward try to take my beloved city, he thought. His assault would be as worthless as the scarred-faced Englishman's threat. Blackstone would not enter the city sword in hand; he would come because Simon Bucy would entice him with an offer that could not be refused.

CHAPTER THIRTY

The cold wind banished the rolling clouds and the sun's warmth began to dry the men's sodden clothing. Knights' squires, mounted archers and hobelars eased the saddles from their horses' blistered backs and hoped the warmth would heal man and beast as the King prepared to descend on Paris. Blackstone's men were quartered within sight of the Prince's pavilions on the rising ground of the vine-clad hills above the left bank of the Seine. Will Longdon and his archers, stripped to the waist, dried their clothes over their fires. The archers had waxed their bow cords against the constant rain even though they had been kept dry beneath their caps, for the ongoing fighting caused wear and tear and a taut bow cord ensured their arrows flew the greatest distance. The English King was using ineffective bombards to try and break down town walls but it was his archers who still caused the most death and fear in their enemy. Jack Halfpenny and Robert Thurgood shared their cooking pot like the thousands of men encamped around them. The smoke from distant burning villages smeared the perfect blue sky.

'Salted fish. I'm sick of it,' said Thurgood. 'I've a mind to sneak into the Prince's food tent and see what's to be had.'

'Your balls on a plate is what'll be had,' said Halfpenny, his skin prickling from the cold air. 'Those shirts dry yet?'

Thurgood reached out and squeezed the cloth. He shook his head. 'At least we haven't had the shits,' he said, and then tasted the pottage. He grimaced and pulled something stringy out of his mouth. 'God's tears, this tastes like fletching glue,' he said. Goose-feather shafts were bound with adhesive that was water

216

soluble – boiled wild plant bulbs or fish glue – and whipped with silk or twine.

'It's what we have,' said Will Longdon. 'We'll get meat and bread, that's been promised by the King himself. The ships from England will soon be in Honfleur; then we'll have our bellies full and you'll spend half the day squatting in the bushes 'cause you've gorged. A man has to learn how to look after his guts.'

Jack Halfpenny sampled the pottage, letting his tongue roll around his mouth. 'Not enough wild garlic but it will bind your belly to your ribs. Besides, we'll soon be in Paris, I reckon.'

Thurgood swallowed the gruel-like pottage. 'I won't know what to go for first: the whores or the wine. And I'll wager they have cellars filled with smoked hams.' He sifted the food through his teeth and lowered his voice. 'The witch has tits that could make a man sell his soul and I'll wager her cunny is as slippery as eel skin.'

Halfpenny shared his friend's desire. 'And I would lie with her like a dog with a bitch.' He grinned eagerly. 'As if men like us had any chance. Besides... how do you know what her tits are like?'

'In the river I was pressed against her. Hard. Hard as a man could get against a woman. My arm gripped her, squeezed her tits; she made no objection.'

'She was drowning, you fool,' said Will Longdon.

'She pressed her face against mine is what she did. I swear I heard her moan.'

'Merciful Christ, spare this deluded fool.' Longdon sighed. 'Robert, the woman was near death and you weren't that far from it yourself. Best get any thoughts of her out of your head.'

Halfpenny grinned again. 'And cock.'

Thurgood looked stung. 'It's the truth!' he hissed. 'I swear it. And look what she did after I came through the forest. She took my hand and pressed it to her lips. You were there. You saw it. She desires me, I tell you.'

Halfpenny nearly choked. 'Robert, I fear your brain is still awash from all that water that ran through your ears.' He and Will Longdon were unable to withhold their friendly derision.

'She offered her thanks, you turd,' said Will Longdon.

'You saved her life and your courage was seen by us all,' said Halfpenny, 'but if you think she's taken a fancy to you then you're no better than a blind man in a brothel. Squeeze a tit here and there and you think you have found paradise.'

'I know what I know,' Thurgood complained, retreating from his friends' teasing.

Halfpenny and Longdon could barely keep a straight face.

'Aye, well, if you say so, Robert,' said Halfpenny. 'The truth is that you saved all our lives when you warned us about the attack. That's worth a drink when we breach the walls. And I'll wager every man will buy you one. I'll even pay for your whores myself.'

Will Longdon gazed across the vineyards. 'I wish to Christ they'd come out and fight, then we'd finish this war once and for all.'

'They won't,' said Blackstone, who had come up behind them carrying a sack. The men turned, clambering to their feet.

'Stay where you are.' Blackstone squatted with the men. 'The Dauphin knows he can't beat us. There's no glory in hiding behind his walls but he's doing it out of necessity. Unless he sends his army soon we'll have to starve and burn them out.' He dipped a spoon into the broth, tasted it and swallowed. 'Jack, it serves no purpose to wash your stinking shirt in the cooking pot. It will be a close-run thing as to who starves first. Them or us. It needs more garlic.'

'Aye, Sir Thomas, and a lump of meat,' said Halfpenny.

'There's no game for us to poach around here either,' said Will Longdon.

Blackstone pushed the sack forward. 'The bread's stale but will soak up the pottage and there's a smoked boar haunch. Cut the meat fine and share what you can. John Jacob and I went foraging. Each of the captains has a sack.'

Halfpenny and Thurgood tore into the sack and lifted out the contraband. 'Bless you, Sir Thomas,' said Thurgood.

'We owe you, Robert. Our lives were near enough forfeit,' said Blackstone.

'That's what we've been telling him,' said Halfpenny.

Blackstone got to his feet. Longdon grinned at him. 'I'll wager there's a knight's table less laden tonight, then.'

'More than one, Will. Better I run the risk of being caught than have any of you thieving bastards arrested. Eat and get ready. I'm summoned by the Prince and that means more fighting. Perhaps the French army has arrived.'

The captain of the guard escorted Blackstone into the Prince's pavilion. The stout canvas walls offered some protection from the cold as did three braziers burning charcoal. The air felt damp as the warmth penetrated the wet canvas. It was heavy with scent and the smell of cooked food. For once it seemed the King's son was not displeased with him. He waved the guard commander away and beckoned Blackstone forward and thrust a goblet of wine into his hand. 'Thomas, your men have fought harder than most. And we and our father are pleased with you.'

'Your grace, we do what you ask of us.'

'But you defied Chandos and killed the lord of the town,' said the Prince, though there seemed to be little chastisement in his voice.

'It was necessary to secure the town for the King,' said Blackstone.

'Chandos was aggrieved,' the Prince said. 'He felt you had defied us... yet again.'

'Sir John is a knight of the realm who holds you and the King close to his heart. He was aggrieved because he thought I had denied him a ransom. I secured the gold and the town, and then I went in search of help for my wounded friend, Sir Gilbert Killbere. And then I secured that town in the King's name also. It seemed a fair bargain to deny Sir John Chandos extra revenue from a ransom. Two towns, gold and a loyal knight in Sir Gilbert to continue fighting.'

'There's nothing to forgive, Thomas. You did more than was asked. We are grateful. So, too, is our Lord Lancaster. You revenged Sir Walter Pegyn's death. Lancaster himself will thank you personally in good time. Pegyn rode under his colours and was held in high regard. Rumour has it that the French were trying to infiltrate our lines. They would have killed more of us had you not stopped them.'

'I doubt any Frenchman has hidden beneath his enemy's colours before.'

'The French have become more sly by the day. The Dauphin is desperate; his father is furious that his son has rejected our father's treaty with him. But... they will give in.'

'Has the French army appeared?'

'No. And we cannot understand why it has not. The Dauphin needs to fight us to hold on to the crown. If he does not, he loses all honour.' He sipped the wine and said carefully, 'We understand you have returned with a woman.'

'She's a healer. She's the one who saved Sir Gilbert's life.'

'A woman shamed, from what we have been told,' said the Prince.

'Shamed by cruelty and men's lust. She was chained, beaten and raped. She is no lascivious woman, your grace. Her father was burnt at the stake. I avenged them both. I would ask a favour from you if you would permit it.'

The Prince nodded his assent.

'When we move against the French I would welcome a place of safety for her. She has skills an apothecary might use.'

'Very well, we will see that is done. And in return your King has more to ask of you.'

Blackstone's stomach tightened. The Prince had made the bargain knowing he would be giving Blackstone another mission that few would relish. The strategy of a war-loving King and his son could at times be badly executed, especially if those lords who advised them were ignored.

'The King will advance north on the Orléans road,' said Prince Edward. 'We will destroy everything that has not yet been destroyed by the French themselves up to the walls of Paris. The city will be encircled. You will lead the vanguard into the suburbs that lie outside the walls. Clear out any resistance. Burn everything. We kill whoever we find.'

'You will be with us?'

'We will strike on your flank. No one will escape the blade. Our father has ordered that terror is to be inflicted on man, woman and child.'

The Prince's enthusiasm was obvious but Blackstone sensed the danger at being hurled into enemy positions without further explanation. The suburban gardens were hedged and walled and made ideal ambush sites, and the streets were narrow. And he had heard worrying news of the King's activities. 'My lord, yesterday was Good Friday. Why did his grace the King strike when a treaty is being negotiated by the Pope's legates with our ambassadors at Longjumeau? The King is camped close to the delegates. It's barely a few miles away. Does his attack not signal a betrayal of his own goodwill?'

'The Pope's peacocks will have had their preened feathers ruffled. *Our* attack on the suburbs will sharpen their desire for peace on our terms.' His eyes studied Blackstone over the rim of the goblet. The defiant knight appeared uncertain, and he knew that Blackstone would have a valid reason if he raised any objection, even though it would irritate him like a scab being picked. Blackstone was a fighting man who used his intelligence. God forbid he, the Prince, should have to admit that the King had listened to Blackstone's opinion among others such as Lancaster, and realized that the siege of Rheims was unsustainable. 'Killbere's strength has not deserted him?' he asked, probing as to whether Blackstone's caution was simply that he did not have the men he needed at his side.

'No, sire. He's a bull-baiting dog on the end of a chain. But to attack these suburbs –'

'Thomas, do not question what we do,' interrupted the Prince, his tone of voice a check on Blackstone's impertinence.

Blackstone bowed his head and bit his tongue. There was going to be mass slaughter and he was being commanded to slay women and children. He resisted the urge to question the Prince for less than a couple of heartbeats.

'Killing women and children brings us no honour. No glory.'

'It inflicts terror and forges a path to peace.'

'It lets loose rape and murder. Acts I expressly forbid my men on pain of punishment,' said Blackstone, unable to keep the edge from his voice.

The Prince held himself in check, refusing to show Blackstone his sudden anger. 'You vex us, Thomas. You question us time and time again. You do not know the facts.'

'Even so, my Prince. What facts would allow us to slaughter townspeople who would run before our advance, who would flee inside the city walls and become a greater burden on the Dauphin who would have to feed and water them. Is it because of what happened to Sir Walter and his men?'

The Prince tapped a finger on the goblet's rim, and swallowed what was left of his wine. Blackstone had not yet raised his to his lips. 'We told you the French have become more devious in their desperation. Reports have reached us from England. Two thousand or more French troops launched a savage attack. They went ashore at Winchelsea. They desired to rescue their King. They failed. They wished to force us to withdraw to defend ourselves at home. They have failed. They wished to deny our father King John's ransom. They committed murder, rape and massacre of our people before they were thrown back into the sea. They are godless men who we are told ate meat during Lent. We will inflict our reprisals.'

The Prince placed the goblet down on the trestle table that bore the remains of his meal. Blackstone remained silent. 'I was told you had no mercy for those at Balon.'

'They deserved none. I only punished those who deserved it.'

The Prince sat down on his padded stool next to the brazier and pulled his cloak around him. 'And that is what we will do. The French must be punished.'

CHAPTER THIRTY-ONE

Killbere spat with disgust when Blackstone informed his captains of the King's intentions.

'I came here to seize the crown not slay babes. No man here relishes that. I'd rather feign illness and take myself off to a monastery and offer my arse to a monk.'

'We cannot defy our King's commands,' said Will Longdon. 'Our archers can kill from a distance, but I'm with Sir Gilbert. Killing crow priests or townsmen who stand against us is one thing but women and children can make a man's guts squirm. These people aren't Jacques like we had back at Meaux. They're not doing their own slaughter.'

Blackstone looked at the disgruntled faces around him. Meulon and Gaillard said nothing but they lowered their eyes when he sought their opinion. It was plain enough. 'I could not convince the Prince otherwise,' said Blackstone. 'The King wants revenge. There is a fortified priory at Arpajon, garrisoned by French troops, so I have told the Prince that we will take it and leave the rest to his men.'

The captains murmured their approval.

'It's a stronghold?' said Killbere.

'It's the suburbs' outer defences. Once we breach it the people are without protection.'

'Then their lives are already forfeit because we will kill the troops who hold it,' said Killbere. 'That is a fact, but I will lose no sleep over it.' He stood and looked at the gathered men. 'We serve as we must, but Sir Thomas is our sworn lord. We forge a legend of war with him and we die as men of honour at his side.

Kill the bastard French because they are unworthy of anything more. Leave the slaughter of innocents to others.'

Flames soared into the sky chased by billowing clouds of black smoke as the French burned houses and barns. Their granges had been emptied and the livestock that remained were herded through the narrow streets in an attempt to slow the attacking Englishmen. The suburbs of Faubourg Saint-Jacques and Faubourg Saint-Marcel burned with furious heat that delayed the English as they sought a way through the narrow streets and gardens. No French civilian remained to fight as the fires gave them the chance to escape into Paris, but those who were too slow or tried to salvage anything that might be used to barter for food were put to death. Beyond the suburbs the stronghold at Arpajon held out against the English assault. The Benedictine priory had been turned into a fortress garrisoned by French soldiers. Those townspeople and villagers who fled the suburbs and could not reach the city gates took sanctuary in its church, dragging what few possessions they could salvage. They were trapped. The English Prince stormed the surrounding villages and the King's bombards hurled their missiles without success against the walls. Blackstone and his men fought on foot, forcing back the defenders from their ditches and fences. The place of honour in the centre of the attack was given to the scar-face knight and his men. They fought across two ditches and then clambered forward towards the pikes bristling behind the burning defences, their spikes lowered ready to impale Englishmen.

Blackstone was three paces to Meulon's side as the Norman rammed his shield against the burning palisades. The flames scorched his beard. He cursed and brought his shield arm up to wipe his whiskers. A French pikeman loomed over the palisade to one side and rammed his halberd down towards Meulon's hunched shoulders. The fifteen-foot shaft – a lethal weapon in the open fields of battle – was too unwieldy to be effective at close quarters. The eighteen-inch blade scraped across Meulon's helm, but the spike's tip caught the mail coif that protected his neck, which gave Blackstone the chance to strike first the pole and then the man. As Wolf Sword severed the haft, Blackstone's shield smashed into the helpless pikeman, who fell forward. He floundered, trying to draw his sword, but Blackstone was already thrusting Wolf Sword's point into his chest. Blackstone stepped on the corpse and fought his way across the palisades into the troops who had hoped the pikemen would have bought them time and taken more English lives. Choking smoke caught men's throats and eyes but those that saw the surge of Blackstone's men turned and ran for the protection that the next ditch offered.

French crossbowmen brought down half a dozen men. One of the men-at-arms who had forced himself between Meulon and Blackstone went down with a crossbow bolt through his helm. It struck with a dull thud as it pierced steel and bone. At close range the crossbows were lethal whether a man wore armour or not. Blackstone felt a quarrel thump into his shield, its lethal tip protruding close to his arm. John Jacob was at his side, unscathed as he slashed away at the defenders. Though determined, they were no match in the open for Blackstone's men. The ditch held men in a tight slit of earth that hampered blows, so men had to grapple with bare fists. Kicking and screaming they wrestled each other. French and English curses were spat with blood. Helmets cleaved beneath axe and sword; legs fell severed, leaving ragged stumps and bewildered men in shock soon to yield to death from blood loss or an enemy's blade. Men's faces rose, gasping for breath, exposing parched throats; Englishmen with knives slit cartilage and bone and turned their own faces away from spurting blood.

The Prince of Wales had led his assault against the village three hundred yards to Blackstone's flank. Those who had left their retreat too late ran before his men's swords. The English hacked into anyone who was not fast enough to clear the narrow streets or who turned begging for mercy.

The smoke blew clear for a few seconds and Blackstone saw the defensive trenches ahead had been reinforced with fresh troops determined to stop the English advance before they reached the monastery. Blackstone knew he and the men would be hard pressed to clamber up and over more ditches without suffering greater losses than they had already endured.

'The flag!' Blackstone yelled. 'Now!'

The enemy crossbowmen were fifty yards away, their positions briefly exposed by the shifting smoke. Now that Blackstone could see them he ordered his bannermen to raise his pennons and mark their location.

'Thirty yards, Will,' he had instructed his centenar before the attack. 'When you see my flag you rain death down on these bastards thirty yards ahead of my flag. Anything less and you slaughter us. Mark the distance well. And if you see me bring two pennons to the centre then you will need to have your archers mark their flight only paces ahead. Our lives are in your hands, Will, should that happen.'

No sooner had the pennons been raised along the line of advancing men than a rustling quivered overhead like wind through leaves. The hail of arrows fell between Blackstone's men and the strongly defended trenches fifty yards ahead.

'Shit!' said Gaillard as they peered over the ditch. The harvest of arrows prickled the ground. 'Sir Thomas, he needs to shoot closer.'

'Aye,' said Meulon. 'Let's take him nearer.'

Blackstone nodded. 'Pennons! To me! Meulon, Gaillard, come on!'

The three men, bigger than any other among them, raised their shields and clambered up the face of the ditch. They ran shoulder to shoulder, their shields side by side, raised and extended to their front to protect against quarrels. One of the flag bearers ran with them but not close enough to the men in front. He fell, hit by three quarrels. John Jacob crawled across the top of the trench. He rolled and crawled five yards, and then stood and jigged left and right as he lofted the pennon and caught up with Blackstone and the other flag bearer.

'Raise both pennons!' Blackstone ordered.

'Merciful Christ, I hope Longdon has marked his distances well,' said Killbere as he caught up, and hunched down as John Jacob waved the pennon across his body, then followed Blackstone and the others' example as they crouched behind their shields. They were too close to the enemy lines. One quarrel punched through and struck Meulon on the shoulder, but his armour deflected its tip. The force of the strike twisted his body, creating a gap that exposed the three men who led the advance. They were barely twenty paces from the French lines and had seconds to live before the crossbowmen reloaded and shot again. They were saved by a swarm of arrow shafts that thudded down almost upon them. The closest fell a body length in front of their faces. The sudden shock of the bodkin-tipped shafts struck the dirt with such force the goose feathers quivered. Meulon cursed. That self-same arrow could have slammed between his own shoulder blades. He glanced at Blackstone, expecting a similar expletive to escape his lips, but instead Blackstone was smiling. He was enjoying the archers' skill, remembering when he too could place a yard-long shaft into such a small killing area. Such feelings never left a man weaned on an archer's war bow. Meulon began to rise but Blackstone snatched at his arm and held him back.

'One more, Meulon! Don't move!'

The ground to their front thudded again. The second volley loosed from near enough two hundred paces to their rear was the enemy's death knell. The French fell screaming, the last chance their crossbowmen had to stop the advance suddenly thwarted. No sooner had the lethal storm fallen than Blackstone and the two Normans got to their feet and ran into the stragglers. They jumped down into the ditch and began the killing. The men followed, bellowing to bolster their own courage and to put the fear of the Almighty into their enemy. The French braced themselves for the onslaught but were already dying underfoot as the two Norman captains struck down the smaller men. Blackstone had given chase to the retreating troops, forcing the French from their defensive positions around the front of the church, and those that retreated now made a final stand between church and town walls. That narrow gap would let them hold out longer. These French had reached the priory gates, which Blackstone knew would open long enough to let the soldiers in. John Jacob yelled for men to follow as he raced after Blackstone. The gates barely allowed fifty French troops in before being almost closed leaving thirty or more men abandoned. By the time John Jacob and the men caught up with Blackstone he had already barged into a half-dozen men with a fury that strangled the screams in their throats. Their bodies fell between gate and frame, stopping those inside from fully closing the portal. Those who were left outside, weary with fatigue and fear, could not muster the strength to fight on and their resistance quickly crumbled beneath Blackstone's men's assault.

A dozen men put their shoulders to the gate and Blackstone squeezed through the gap. He pulled back moments before two crossbowmen loosed their bolts, which slammed into the wood next to his chest. And then he was inside. It was very much like the convent he had visited. The French had no ramparts, so they had barricaded rooms with benches and stools and formed a shield wall, with spears poking through to keep swordsmen at bay. The two crossbowmen had run for the cover of the cloisters. More men pushed through the gates behind Blackstone, saw the shield wall and ran at it. They half jumped, half rammed it. Boots and shields hammered at it until it cracked like an egg on one side and Blackstone's men stormed through.

He stood to one side allowing their blood-lust to carry them onward without him.

As the close-quarter fighting continued against pockets of resistance he gazed across the courtyard gardens. The monks had planted a small orchard, not unlike the one he once had at home. There were no more than a dozen trees, perhaps to give them a few sweet apples in the spring. The blossoms had emerged, white against the grey sky and dark stone walls. Beneath the trees small thumb-sized flowers with colourful wax-like petals had forced themselves free of the earth, resurrected after winter.

As the clash of fighting and screams of dying men echoed down the colonnades Blackstone sat on a low stone wall and pulled free his helmet.

The orchard would soon be destroyed, the flowers trampled. He wanted the pleasure of it for a few moments longer.

CHAPTER THIRTY-TWO

The killing did not abate for hours as King Edward's troops scorched through village and town in a merciless rampage. Blackstone pulled back his men once the religious house used as a garrison had been secured. His men drank what wine they could and scavenged food not taken by the French from the priory's kitchens. Bloodied and exhausted they sat or lay at the priory walls sluicing sweat and blood from their faces and hands and aiding each other to dress their wounds. A few had died but the cost had been slight thanks to Will Longdon and his archers. Blackstone sent word for his archers to join them and to leave Henry with the other pages at the baggage train. He and his men-at-arms cleaned their weapons. They had done as expected and claimed the garrison; now it was up to the Prince and his men to sweep through his flank and push aside the few stubborn defenders at the suburb's walls.

Blackstone waited with his men at the gates as the English swarmed forward in another attack. Those villagers who had fled into the nearby church for protection no longer had the garrison troops to defend them, and although Frenchmen still held their ground around the church and suburban walls it was obvious the English would soon be among them. Cries of surrender from those in the church could be heard across the killing field. For a moment Blackstone thought the villagers had a chance. As the first few ventured out, stepping fearfully in front of the Prince of Wales's men, women and children shuffling behind their menfolk kept up a constant plea for mercy. The Prince's commanders halted their men a few hundred paces from the church.

The attack came from behind, from the very men who were supposed to protect the villagers. French troops, crying 'Traitors!' suddenly launched themselves at those surrendering. Stricken, the villagers panicked and ran back into the church. The English held back as the French did their work for them by setting fire to the sanctuary. Smoke suddenly appeared; it took only a short time for flames to take hold. The shrieks of the dying soared above the noise of fighting beyond the church. Blackstone and the men watched as villagers jumped from the windows, bones shattering when they hit the stony ground. Some lowered ropes and began climbing out. By the time the roof was ablaze Blackstone thought there were three hundred or more people below the walls, huddling uncertain which way to turn, although hundreds more must have still been trapped inside the burning building. Children cried for their mothers and women screamed for mercy. The men called out, arms raised; some fell to their knees in front of the English host before them as their countrymen, who had tried to kill them, retreated slowly back into the suburbs they were sworn to defend.

The English waited until those beneath the church walls began to shuffle away. And then they attacked and slaughtered them all.

Killbere eased his aching body up from where he sat in the dirt and gave a final wipe of his sword's bloodied blade before sliding it back into the scabbard.

'Come, Thomas. Let's be away from here. The Prince will want to celebrate his glorious victory. We'll all get pissed elsewhere. Let's find a tavern that has enough wine left to swill that shame from our throats.'

Blackstone and Killbere led the men into the burning suburbs. The walls of Paris were less than a mile ahead. Merchants' and peasants' houses alike were gutted and ransacked by those soldiers who had gone ahead of them but somewhere there would be an alehouse left standing. Which he and his men would not be by the time darkness fell.

The stench of burnt thatch and the dead wafted with the smoke from the burning suburbs. Bodies lay in the streets alongside slaughtered animals. The tavern Blackstone's men found had been a roadside inn before the killing started; now it was half destroyed, the doors ripped from their hinges and the windows smashed. The ceiling had been pulled down by soldiers most likely searching for hidden loot. Broken tables and benches lay strewn across the floor along with smashed glass, clay pots and empty half-barrels.

Meulon pulled aside the butchered bodies of the innkeeper and his wife who lay in front of the empty casks.

'Perhaps he served bad ale or gave short measures,' said Renfred.

Another woman lay spreadeagled in the corner, her clothing pulled above her bloodied waist, her head lying crooked to one side, her glassy eyes still open. She had been dead for hours.

'Most likely their daughter,' said Killbere, glancing back to the middle-aged innkeeper and his wife. Gaillard crossed himself and lowered the girl's dress and then carried her body outside where he laid her next to three slaughtered dogs and a horse. Nothing had been spared. There would be no burials that day, and by the time any survivors dared creep back there would be little left of her.

Will Longdon and Jack Halfpenny dragged aside a man's corpse and beneath it found the trapdoor to the cellar. Expecting people to be hiding there he went down into the darkness bearing a knife in one hand and a flickering candle in another. He emerged with Halfpenny and two wooden boxes of dark glass bottles swaddled in straw.

'Stupid bastards just killed the innkeeper and pissed away the wine in them barrels. This is where they should have looked.'

The bottles were shared among the men as Thurgood and a few others came back from foraging. Victoriously they carried a large round cheese and a smoked ham.

'All we need now are some women and we can celebrate,' said Thurgood.

'Aye. I'm not sure what, though,' said Killbere.

'Being alive is enough,' said Blackstone, and raised the bottle to his lips. The sharp brandy cut across his throat.

They stayed at the inn and spread out into the stables and barns. There was enough straw left to use for bedding and what remained of the roof gave some shelter from the drizzling rain. As the men ate and drank and then found a place to lie, a contingent of eighty or so English troops made their way towards them. Led by a banner knight, their clothing and faces were streaked with blood and smudged with soot. When the knight saw Blackstone's men he demanded: 'Get off your arses. There's more killing to be done.'

Will Longdon was sitting with his archers stuffing a piece of ham into his mouth. He raised his eyebrows at Halfpenny and washed down the meat with a slug from the brandy bottle. The knight scowled and looked about him, unused to being ignored. Meulon and Gaillard lay propped against a wall; the other men-at-arms sprawled here and there. Some raised their heads but then immediately went back to dozing.

'You men will come with me! On your feet!' demanded the knight.

'Fuck off!' a voice called from inside the inn.

The knight sidestepped his way past the indifferent men into the tavern. Blackstone and Killbere sat on a bench, helmets at their side, scraps of the cheese and ham on the rough-hewn table in front of them. They each nursed a bottle. In a corner John Jacob sat sharpening a knife blade. To the knight they looked no different than the men-at-arms who lounged outside. They wore no armour and were dressed piecemeal. Brigands perhaps, he thought, paid by the King.

'You scum will do as you're ordered,' he said. Half a dozen of his men had crowded behind him in support.

'And I said you can fuck off,' said Killbere. 'Now get back to your slaughter of the innocents before I ram my sword up your arse.'

Blackstone spat phlegm at the feet of the knight. 'My friend is more drunk than sober and that makes him doubly dangerous. I would obey him if I were you.'

The knight had not recognized Blackstone's smudged blazon and he took a step forward, grasping his sword hilt, half drawing the blade in threat. Killbere lunged, grabbing his helm from the bench at his side and smashing it into the man's face. He fell back into the men behind him, teeth shattered, jaw broken. The shocked men immediately drew their weapons but Blackstone already had Wolf Sword in his hand and John Jacob was at his side, knife at the ready.

'This could be your day of glory. Who among you would challenge Sir Gilbert Killbere?' said Blackstone.

Killbere had already flopped back onto the bench and raised the bottle again but the men's uncertainty was plain to see. Killbere's reputation in the army, especially among the veterans, might well have been chiselled in stone. The men pushed their blades back into their scabbards. One of them, older and more grizzled-looking than the others, gestured for those next to him to drag the unconscious knight away.

'My lord, I serve this knight, Sir Oswald de Chambres. We beg your forgiveness.'

Blackstone lowered his sword. The knight's name meant nothing to him and he had not recognized his colours. He was just one of hundreds of knights in the army. 'Take him and find a surgeon to bind his jaw.'

'Aye, and tell him to learn some goddamned manners,' Killbere added.

The grizzled man-at-arms bowed his head in acknowledgement. 'I would not dare, Sir Gilbert. My lord is a favourite of the Prince.'

'Well, he's no favourite of mine,' said Killbere and waved the men away. The sound of Blackstone's men jeering de Chambres's retreating soldiers reached into the inn.

Blackstone sighed. 'God's blood, Gilbert, did you have to go so hard at him?'

'He was an arrogant little shit. He needed to be taught a lesson. I swear, Thomas, some of the so-called knights that ride with the Prince must lick his arse every morning. Who wants men like that around them?' He tossed aside the bottle. 'Let's get back to the lines before more of his kind come looking to murder babes in arms. I pray this devastation spurs the Dauphin to let loose his army. Let's get at them. What kind of man is he to let his people die unprotected? A hundred troops or more in a garrison, a handful in the suburbs who turn on their own kind. The Holy Virgin's tears wouldn't be enough to wash away such a sin of neglect.' He stretched his aching body and steadied himself on the edge of the table. 'I'm pissed. Let's get back. This place reeks of shame from both sides of the damned walls.' Blackstone reached out to steady him but Killbere snatched his arm free. 'I stand on my own two feet, Thomas. For a while longer at least.'

They stepped outside. 'Come on, you idle bastards,' said Killbere. 'Sir Thomas and I will find you a battle to fight even if we have to start one ourselves.'

The men clambered to their feet.

Will Longdon and Jack Halfpenny hauled Thurgood upright. 'We could float Robert down a sewer and have him open the Paris gates; then we'd have a fight on our hands,' said Longdon.

Killbere took a few uneasy steps towards the archers and lifted Thurgood's face. His bleary eyes tried to focus.

'Aye, he floats like a turd right enough, but by God this lad saved our skins that day,' said Killbere, and gently slapped the semi-conscious archer's face. 'You find him a dry blanket for the night but don't put him too close to the fire. He's drunk enough to roll in it and with all the brandy in him he would light up the night.'

'He never could hold his drink, but he has a weakness for it,' said Halfpenny.

Killbere rubbed Thurgood's hair. 'Blessed are the weak for they shall inherit the wine barrel,' he said. The men laughed. The young archer raised his head.

'Weak I am, Sir Gilbert... but... what the river could not drown... the drink... will.' He grinned foolishly. 'But... you cannot... drown a man's love... not that... not ever.' His head flopped.

Killbere stepped back and scrubbed a hand across his face. 'When an archer starts talking of love then it must be for his horse, for who else would let him ride for free?'

The men-at-arms jeered and the archers laughed with them. The fight at the priory garrison had been hard won and those with sword in hand in the ditches had needed the bowmen at their backs. It was enough that both groups knew it. Blackstone and Killbere led them back to the lines. Behind them the killing would go on throughout the night, illuminated by the fires of the burning houses. The cries of the dying carried over the walls of Paris where the crown of France waited to be seized.

CHAPTER THIRTY-THREE

Robert Thurgood rolled out of his blanket and stared uncomprehendingly for a moment at his surroundings. The dull glow of fire embers was muted in the mist that had settled across the camp. Men lay snoring, tucked beneath their blankets. The rain had ceased some hours before, but the wet grass and the damp night air held the smell of the burnt-out suburbs of Paris. He shuddered and pulled his tongue, thick from the drink, from the roof of his mouth. He was not used to brandy and regretted not searching out wine when they reached the inn. The last thing he remembered was laughing with Jack Halfpenny as the archers teased the men-at-arms about how close their arrows had been to them when they assaulted the priory. It had been harmless banter and then he and Halfpenny had talked about the whores that would be waiting for them once they breached the city walls. Now he looked about him and realized his friends had carried him back to the lines and wrapped him in a blanket. His war bow had been put safely into its waxed linen bag and his sheaf of arrows tied neatly next to it. He needed to relieve himself. He clambered free from the blanket wrapped around his legs and staggered carefully between the sleeping men. He found a place in the trees and rested one hand against the tree trunk while fumbling at his clothing with the other. Thurgood felt the fuzziness ease from his head. He yawned and then did up his breeches. He turned back the way he had come and realized he did not know where his blanket and comrades lay among the many others. He stared, trying to peer through the mist, and felt the shiver of the night chill. He skirted sleeping bodies and began to curse silently as it dawned on him that he was unlikely to find his place until daylight.

As the faint breeze shifted the mist slowly here and there he saw the glow of a brighter fire than others and the figure of a man stooping to lay more wood onto the flames. It served as a beacon and he turned towards it, grateful he would not have to spend the rest of the night shivering in the dank forest. As he approached he realized it was the man-at-arms Collard who attended the fire. The knowledge stopped him in his tracks. Collard was part of the guard that stood over Aelis. Thurgood stood unmoving. His mind danced across a hundred thoughts in a few shallow breaths. He licked his lips and tasted the image that had presented itself in his mind's eye. It was not chance that brought him to Aelis's tent, but destiny. He would whisper his feelings for her and then caress her and she would cleave to him. He looked quickly around, fearing his thoughts might be heard by others, because such a clarion call could surely not be confined within his head alone. His heart thudded as he felt warmth flood into his groin. He would never have such an opportunity again, but Collard would stop him. As he thought the man's name Collard looked back and stared in his direction but Thurgood had quickly dropped to the ground the moment he sensed the man-at-arms begin to turn. He lay motionless as Collard pulled his cloak around him and went back to sit next to his fire.

Thurgood's mind played devil's advocate. Would Collard let him lie with the woman who had shown her gratitude for him saving her life, and her obvious affection? Could he be bought off? With what? The gold coin from Thurgood's share of the raids was still in his purse but Collard had also been given a cut. Besides, he reasoned, Collard would not risk disobeying Sir Thomas. Not him. No, the man-at-arms would stop him before he even reached for the woman's tent flap. Thurgood gnawed his knuckles because now the blood that pumped through his veins and warmed his body was prompted by a picture of himself lying on her with his face between her breasts. He yearned for them as an infant desires a mother's nipple. Saliva slaked the dryness in his mouth. The mist cloaked him. He was unseen and unknown to anyone. He was a ghost who could move undetected through the night. How to tell her, though, how his heart yearned for her? He had saved her and she had told him with her eyes that she was his. No words were needed. He rolled onto his back, his hand squeezing the erection that threatened to burst through his breeches. There was a clear sky above the mist. Here and there a star twinkled in the moist air and the moon's glow dressed the pale veil around him. There was risk; of course there was. But the regret that had assailed him when the river swept him away prodded him again. Life had not yielded enough pleasure. It had offered fear and death and good friendship with Jack Halfpenny. But now he had something more to hold close. As he turned over onto his stomach his arm pressed against a rock. He picked it up. It fitted neatly into his fist. Without further thought he silently got to his feet and strode through the mist towards the fire glow. The figure that sat hunched, head down, was breathing heavily. Collard was asleep. For a moment Thurgood hesitated. Could he lie with Aelis and not wake him? His fist answered the question before his mind did.

He stepped carefully across Collard's sprawled body and eased aside the tent flap. Enough light filtered through the canvas from the fire for him to see Aelis lying on her back with an arm thrown across her eyes. She slept in her chemise; the ties down the front were loose, exposing the cleft of her breasts. Thurgood knelt at her feet, uncertain how to wake her without her being alarmed. He wiped his palm across his mouth and eased himself gently forward. He smelt her musty fragrance and his heart thumped louder as he carefully leaned over her. Too loud, he thought. She'll hear it. Her breathing was deep and even and he suddenly felt confident. With a delicacy that belied his stubby fingers he lifted her chemise tenderly away from her breasts and gazed at her brown nipples. The linen had chafed them in the night and they stood proud of her flesh. Thurgood swallowed hard and lowered his face close to her cheek. He whispered her name. There was no response and he blinked in the shadows, not knowing what to do next as his erection pressed against her thigh. The touch of her warm body enticed him further. He lowered his lips to her cheek and kissed her. The weight of his chest against her breasts startled her awake. She gasped in fright, her body bucking against him. He saw the terror in her eyes as he smothered her face with his callused hand. She started to wriggle and he rolled further on top of her.

'Aelis, it's me, Robert. It's all right. Be quiet. It's me,' he whispered urgently.

She shook her head violently from side to side and now panic struck him. Why did she not recognize him? He had been so careful. Surely she knew he would cause her no harm? He tried to quieten her and pressed his body tighter against hers. His confusion increased with every movement of her thighs as she tried to kick him free. Her shift crept up her legs and then, without him realizing that he had pressed his free arm across her throat, she quietened, her struggles easing. Her eyes closed as if falling asleep.

'Aelis,' he whispered again. But she had gone limp beneath him. 'It's all right,' he repeated. But he knew it wasn't. His hand had gone from smothering her mouth to between her legs, and the urge to push himself into her became unbearable. He pressed his lips against her breasts and releasing his arm from her throat squeezed their fullness. It was too late to stop. His fingers desperately began to undo his breeches and as his body shifted from her she suddenly lurched, half rolling from under him, her outstretched hand plunging a small knife into the back of his shoulder. It pierced the thick archer's muscle and hit bone. Thurgood bellowed with the shock of the sudden and unexpected pain and rolled clear into the sides of the tent. She forced herself past him out of the tent as, dazed, he made a vain attempt to snatch at her. His fist caught the hem of her shift. It ripped but she was free of him. He stumbled into the night. It had gone wrong; nothing was as he had planned. He didn't understand anything except that he had to run.

She had stopped on the other side of the fire clutching her torn clothing as she looked down at Collard's sprawled body. The mist swirled and added to Thurgood's confusion. There was so much he wanted to say to her but the jumble of misplaced thoughts would not form into words. Voices were raised in the pale night as figures emerged, swords and knives in hand. Ignoring the pain in his shoulder he turned to run. The mist would be his friend. The night darkened as a large figure blocked his path. He looked up and then felt the added pain as Meulon's fist felled him.

Thurgood shivered. He opened his eyes and saw the blue sky above him. He was lying on the wet, dew-laden grass. The muscle in his back knotted where he had been stabbed. At first he couldn't remember why he was in such pain and then the shadows from the night before cleared from his mind. The daylight hurt his eyes. Someone kicked him in the ribs and he half raised himself and stared at the men who surrounded him. They were faces he had known for years but the scowls that greeted him caused him unbearable sadness. These were his friends.

'Get up,' said Jack Halfpenny.

Thurgood rolled onto his side, and then his knees as he stood unsteadily. His head pounded and he trembled in the cold. Someone had fashioned a bandage across his wounded shoulder.

'Christ, Jack, I'm sorry,' he said. 'I didn't mean no harm. You know that. Don't you?'

Halfpenny made no reply at first. He lowered his eyes and shook his head. 'Robert. You fool,' he said.

Will Longdon stood at Halfpenny's side. He strode forward, grabbing Thurgood by the collar and yanked him through the gathered men. Thurgood looked around him and saw where Blackstone's men had camped the previous night and felt a tinge of regret when he realized where his own bedroll had been. He wished he had never left it. Longdon shoved him forward to where Blackstone and Killbere stood flanked by John Jacob and the other captains. Merciful Christ, he thought as he remembered

241

the assault on the girl, at least he hadn't raped her. Blackstone would punish him for trying though; he knew that. There was no doubt he would be banished from serving with him. They might even take the gold coin from his purse as recompense for the girl. Thurgood went down on his knee in front of Blackstone.

'Sir Thomas, I beg forgiveness. My passion for the woman got the better of me. My heart was true in its feelings for her, but after the drink I lost my mind. I will make amends and also beg her forgiveness.'

Silence greeted his admission of guilt. He kept his head lowered a moment longer but when he heard the men's feet shuffle he raised his eyes. Blackstone and the others had stepped aside. Thurgood's stomach heaved. He brought a hand to his mouth. The acid from the spurt of vomit burned his throat. The shock of what he saw nearly felled him as had Meulon's fist hours earlier. Aelis's collapsed tent and the cold, blackened embers of the fire outside it were revealed. Lying next to the fire was Collard's sprawled body.

Thurgood's mouth opened and closed. His mind screamed denial.

'You killed a comrade-in-arms,' said Killbere, his voice subdued with tightly controlled anger.

Thurgood shook his head. He looked desperately from face to face staring down at him. 'No. I couldn't have. I swear it. I only hit him once. Only the once,' he implored.

'Stupid bastard. You don't know your own strength,' said Killbere.

Thurgood got to his feet, a hand outstretched towards Blackstone, begging. 'Sir Thomas... I would never... I could not...' he mumbled.

Blackstone remained silent, but Thurgood saw there was pain in his eyes.

'You were drunk, Robert, and your cock ruled your brain,' said Killbere.

Blackstone nodded to those behind Thurgood. Will Longdon and Halfpenny stepped forward and gripped his arms.

He was one of their archers and his fate was already sealed.

'I won't hang you,' said Blackstone. 'You have earned the right to be given a chance for what you did at the river.' He looked across the open meadow. It sloped gently away for a mile, the pockets of forests flanking its breadth of eight hundred paces. 'You forsake your war bow, food and water. You run hard and fast, Robert, and you might escape your centenar's arrow. A hundred and fifty paces is what I give you.'

Thurgood twisted and looked at Longdon. He never missed. Before he could say anything more he was pulled away from his sworn lord. He twisted his head back, eyes searching out Blackstone. 'Forgive me, lord. I don't beg for clemency but for your forgiveness. I served you loyally. I swear it.'

Blackstone's hardened gaze offered no compassion. Thurgood felt the loss as deeply as his regret for the night's events. He stumbled, grief almost claiming him.

'Keep your feet,' Will Longdon growled at him. Twenty paces away from the gathered men they stopped and turned him to face the long run that might offer a chance of life.

'Will, a moment with him,' said Halfpenny.

Longdon nodded. These two men were lifelong friends. He turned away and took up his bow and then searched out an arrow whose fletching satisfied his need for an accurate flight.

Halfpenny shoved a wineskin into his friend's hands. 'Drink,' he insisted. 'You'll need it.'

Thurgood nodded gratefully and drank thirstily until he had had his fill. When he had finished Halfpenny took his friend's face in his hands and pulled it close to his own. 'Robert, you stupid bastard, you have robbed us all of a good man.'

'I didn't mean to kill him, I swear.'

'No, not him. You. We have fought the battles over the years, my friend. We were a part of history. And now you must run for your life.'

Tears welled in Thurgood's eyes. 'Will Longdon never misses,' he whispered.

'Listen to me. You run straight for a hundred and thirty paces. You need to cover ground. Then go right for ten. Run straight and then left for another ten. Understand. Only go ten paces each side. Once you have got past a hundred and fifty you can make the trees. You understand?'

Thurgood was trembling and nodded vigorously. 'We'll get back home, Jack. You and me both. London. The Dog and Moon tavern. Like old days.'

'Like old days,' said Halfpenny and embraced him. He kissed his friend's cheek. And whispered: 'I won't let any man here harm you. I swear it.'

Thurgood pulled his face away, questioning what he had just heard. 'Jack, don't cause yourself trouble. I'll take my chances.'

Halfpenny nodded to reassure him. 'I swear it,' he repeated. 'Run hard, Robert. Think of home.'

Blackstone's voice carried across the gathered men. 'It's time.'

With a final glance and smile of regret, Thurgood stepped away from Halfpenny. He glanced at the men he had served alongside these past years. Different countries, different enemies, but always side by side. He wished he could find some words of farewell but could not. He focused on the long meadow. Will Longdon held his war bow, the arrow ready to be nocked.

Thurgood ran.

His eyes blurred in the cold morning air but the forest's sanctuary beckoned him. The torn muscles in his shoulder nagged but he used the pain to drive him on, relishing it, turning it to fuel his desperation. He did exactly what Halfpenny had told him. His head was clear enough now to think of survival. Straight, right, left... straight... arms pumping, sucking in great gulps of air. Pace by pace, yard by archer's yard. The arrow would come soon if his friend failed to stop it. He wouldn't hear it, he knew that. There might be the flutter of a bird's wing as the fletchings quivered through the air. He was strong. His legs carried him; the strength was there. The forest grew closer. He wished he could turn and wave because he knew he had won. Perhaps when he reached the trees he would look back and raise his uninjured arm in farewell. Elation soared through him.

Will Longdon watched Thurgood's run. His eyes followed every movement the man made. There were markers within that field. A rotten tree stump, a hump of ground, a patch of winter grass taller than the rest. Every one a measured distance to an archer's eye. Mind and hands knew instinctively where to aim. Legs braced, his back bent, the muscles and momentum of his body drawing back the arrow towards his cheek waiting to see which way the running man would turn next.

The sudden release of a bow cord a few paces behind him startled him into lowering his bow and like every man there he turned to see Jack Halfpenny watch the flight of the arrow he had loosed. Moments later it struck with deadly accuracy into Thurgood's back.

The young archer faced Will Longdon and Blackstone. 'I made my friend a promise,' he said quietly, and began the long walk to where Thurgood's body lay.

CHAPTER THIRTY-FOUR

They buried the young archer who had yet to see his twenty-first year next to the man he had killed. He and Collard were carried to the priory and monks were summoned and paid to bury the two men side by side and pray for their souls. Jack Halfpenny stayed a while longer than the archers who had knelt in prayer at Thurgood's grave and then turned his back on the chanting monks. Will Longdon gave no orders for Halfpenny and allowed his ventenar to attend his usual duties. The archers kept their distance as Halfpenny took an axe to Thurgood's war bow and burned the yew on his campfire. It was better that no other should feel its power.

Aelis de Travaux stood in the open clearing, her bedding rolled and tied, her cloak fastened around her against the cold north wind as Blackstone's men prepared to move with the Prince's division towards the walls of Paris. Edward's vast army was about to assault the city.

'Where did she get the knife?' Killbere asked the captains who gathered around Blackstone. The men looked blankly at him.

'Does it make any difference?' asked Blackstone.

'If Thurgood knew she wasn't willing to have his cock in her then he might have abandoned the attempt. It's only because she stabbed him that we discovered him. We'd still have a good man fighting for us.' Killbere spat. 'Get rid of her, Thomas. She's a curse.'

'And we would still have a murderer in our midst. Collard died under his hand.'

Before Killbere could answer Henry called out from where he stood with the horses. 'My lord. I gave the woman the knife.'

The group of men turned and stared at the boy. Henry stood unflinching.

'Why?' demanded Blackstone.

'You ordered me to stay with her when the attack came after we crossed the river. When Robert warned us. We thought the French would break through and she begged me not to let her face them undefended. She said she did not wish to endure the same fate as had happened to her at Balon. So I gave her my spare knife. The one from my boot. And then... then I forgot about it.'

Killbere turned his face away from the boy. 'You can't blame him for that, Thomas,' he said quietly.

Blackstone knew that Killbere was correct. 'Attend your duties,' he ordered his son. 'There's no guilt in what you did.'

'And the woman?' Killbere said.

'The Prince says he'll place her with the apothecaries. She's no longer my concern.'

Killbere pulled on his helm. 'I'll believe that when Edward's trumpets blow loud enough to bring down the walls of Paris.'

King Edward's progress up the Orléans road cut off the city from the south as his other commanders pressed their advance in the north until Paris was surrounded. The steady rhythm of the army's drums told the French that the English were coming. The pounding reverberated around the advancing men as the footsoldiers trudged behind the mounted archers and men-at-arms. Blackstone rode ahead of his men watching the bulk of the army move forward. The Prince of Wales rode leisurely forward too, surrounded by his knights and their retainers. Despite the cold and intermittent gusts of wind that swept rain across their lines, the great war banners of the English army unfurled in all their glory.

'If flags could win a war we would be masters of the world,' said Killbere. 'The damned French are nowhere in sight. It will be a sad day if they surrender and throw open their gates.'

'And you think they'll do that?' said Blackstone.

'It would save us having our shirttails lifted and being abused by the Pope's legates. I'll wager there's a deal being done. Have we had any orders? I don't see siege engines or scaling ladders.'

'They'll be brought up from the rear in good time if it comes to that,' said Blackstone. 'We're riding east. There's open ground between the walls and the Faubourg Saint-Marcel. If those suburbs are already destroyed the King'll make his assault against the southern gates first. Then we'll know what street fighting is about. This is a damned foolish plan, Gilbert. We'll lose thousands of men in those warrens.'

'Tell the King, Thomas. I'm certain he'll be pleased to hear your opinion,' said Killbere sarcastically.

They broke clear of the forests and saw the great walls loom up six hundred yards ahead. As the army advanced bugles and trumpets blared the English King's arrival. The rolling thunder of drumbeats thumped through the air and the splendour of banners and pennons of the English nobility paraded a history of conquest before the walls of Paris. The cacophony went on as heralds approached the great city's southern portal. Smoke from the burning suburbs still drifted on a veering breeze and Blackstone could only imagine the thoughts of those who gazed down from the city walls on the destruction around them and the host that lay ready to besiege them.

'You think they could be hiding ten thousand men or more in there ready to fight?' asked Killbere.

There had been a time when another great city had held such an army in its streets. Blackstone had been in Rouen more than a dozen years before and seen that the hundreds of streets could be crammed with an army waiting to go to war.

'They could be in there,' he said. 'And now would be the time for the French to show their hand and put their army into the field. And then this matter will be over.'

The stationary horses shifted their weight as they watched the challenge being delivered at the gate. Killbere grinned at Blackstone. 'Bastards might just do it. It would be like Crécy and

Poitiers all over again. Do you not relish the thought, Thomas? Face-to-face with them again? Eh? My God, let the trumpets blow. We'll cut them down as we did back then.' He sniffed and spat and chuckled to himself. 'I can feel it in my bowels, Thomas. What king's son would turn his back on honour and the chance of glory if he's to rule one day?'

Blackstone watched the heralds turn back from the gate and ride back to where the King's standard fluttered.

'This one,' he said. 'He's no backbone for a fight. And who can blame him? I've been in Paris, Gilbert: the city's too difficult to take so why should he risk a fight? Besides, he may not have an army camped in there.'

They watched as the heralds delivered the French response to the King. There appeared to be a ripple of excitement among the King's retinue. The Prince of Wales turned in the saddle and said something to his father.

'Y'see,' said Killbere. 'You were wrong. Look at the King, bless him, he'll have the Prince and us in the vanguard. That pledge you made to protect young Edward will have us in the thick of it. By God, Thomas, I believe we're about to confront the French.' He grinned. 'Perhaps I was wrong about the girl. Perhaps she brought us good fortune after all.'

Blackstone did not share Killbere's joy. The Prince had turned away from his father and pointed in Blackstone's direction. A herald spurred his horse towards them.

'The girl has nothing to do with it, Gilbert. It is what it is, and if that herald is coming for us then I doubt he's bearing glad tidings.'

Killbere turned his gaze to the fast-approaching rider. He grunted. 'You are a miserable wretch at times. Find joy in anticipation. I say my prayers as much as any other. I'm confessed, my clothes and saddle are dry now that the damned rain has stopped, and we stand before the walls of Paris waiting to fight. Cheer up.'

The herald reined in his mount. 'Sir Thomas, I am obliged to have you and Sir Gilbert accompany me to our lord, the King.'

Killbere looked with glee at Blackstone. 'Ha! We're at your command. Ride on!' The herald wheeled his horse and Killbere slapped Blackstone on the shoulder. 'We will write history again, Thomas, and your name will be writ large. I know that to be a fact because I will pay the scribes myself to make certain of it. You and me!'

By the time they reached the King's retinue, more knights had gathered in the background, brought forward on instruction of King Edward. They were mostly young, newly knighted men, and their eagerness to prove themselves was apparent.

The King had more than forty retainers behind him. The great knights were at his side. Cobham, Lancaster, Chandos: men of proven courage and intelligence in the field. Warwick, Stafford and the King's sons. The banners and pennons that fluttered in the ranks bore the blazons of every fighting knight known to Blackstone. Before this moment he and his men had seen only segments of the army, those close to the Prince as they shared the battlefield, but now the ten thousand stood on the open plain, their ranks curving away around the wall, encircling Paris.

'My lord,' said Blackstone, lowering his eyes respectfully as the King settled his gaze on him.

'Sir Thomas, we are told you have engaged with our enemy on numerous occasions and we are comforted by the sight of our trusted servant Sir Gilbert at your side.'

'Thank you, sire. We have been fortunate,' said Blackstone. He was wary of being in the royal company. Each time it had happened in the past he had been drawn too close to the heart of power.

'And God was with you,' said King Edward. He touched his neck and then indicated Blackstone. 'God and your pagan goddess. Many of our Welsh archers are comforted by her.' There was no hint of criticism in his remarks.

'She is a spirit of nature created by the Almighty, sire, and every fighting man who is prepared to die for you must take comfort wherever he finds it.'

'A good answer, Thomas,' said the Prince. 'My lord, our father, has a question for you.'

The breeze curled the royal banner. The dragon standard fluttered like a living beast moving through the air. It was a silent moment when the world held its breath. The flags were the only moving things. That and the snuffling horses chomping their bits, shaking their heads, shifting weight. Saddles creaked. The stillness, Blackstone realized, was anything but. His thoughts had been arrested for a few moments because when the Prince had spoken to him he had a look on his face that glowered a warning. He was expected to give the King the answer he wanted.

'You have been inside the city walls, Thomas. You know the streets and the danger that lurks within them,' said the King. 'If we assault how do we secure it?'

Blackstone hesitated. The army was drawn up. If the time had come then the attack had to be driven forward without delay.

'Sire, this weather will not hold. You can smell the change in the air. We'll be bogged down soon enough. We should strike now and make what gains we can because the next few days will have us back wheel-deep in mud.'

The King studied him a moment longer. 'Thomas, let us not consider when we attack, we wish to know what awaits us behind those walls.'

The memory of searching the streets of Paris when Christiana had been used as bait by the Savage Priest was as clear in his mind as the time he had rescued her and escaped through the warren of alleyways and across broad boulevards.

Blackstone surrendered to his own honesty, knowing full well it was not a truth the King wanted to hear. 'Sire, in truth I cannot imagine such an assault. To have thousands of men gathered in their mail and armour at the bottom of scaling ladders being punished with missiles and oil would slaughter far too many before you even breached the walls. If you succeeded and our men have had sufficient food and rest before such an undertaking, then they would have to survive savage resistance. Paris has sixteen quarters and each of those is divided into tithing groups. The city's militia are rotated every three weeks as night watch on the city walls, and they cannot shirk their duties because each militia is commanded by a royal captain and the guild contingents are supported by mounted troops. Every corner of every alleyway will be defended. It will be a charnel house for the army.'

Killbere failed to hide his look of despair as Blackstone delivered his verdict.

'But we would seize the damned place no matter the cost,' Killbere blurted.

King Edward's expression betrayed no sign of anger or disappointment at Blackstone's answer. He glanced kindly at Killbere. 'Sir Gilbert, we know we could cast you into hell itself and you would wrestle the devil and his imps into submission. Like you, those who fight under our command, with love and loyalty, are the finest England has ever witnessed. Their courage is never doubted.'

He turned his attention back to Blackstone. 'We are content with your answer, Thomas. Our dear friend and adviser Lancaster has already assured me of the bloodbath that awaits us should we scale those walls.'

'The Dauphin will not come out and fight, sire?' said Blackstone.

'He will not,' said the Prince.

'Then do we go in?' said Blackstone. Perhaps, he suddenly realized, it was his men's expertise at escalade that had prompted his summons. His heart squeezed tightly. To bring up tall ladders against those walls was, as he had just told the King, little more than a death sentence.

'We do not,' said King Edward. 'Not yet, at least. It is in our favour to find victory by another means. They must be taunted to come out and face us. The French have offered sixty knights to fight *à l'outrance*. They seek glory in a fight to the death. We will agree and have chosen young men newly honoured with knighthood to contest them. Their sixty against our thirty. That way when they are defeated they will know that every Englishman is worth two

252

Frenchmen. Then perhaps the Dauphin will be unable to resist bringing out his army to reclaim French honour. It is the least any king, or any king's son, would desire.'

'Sire!' Killbere begged. 'Young knights need a veteran to lead them in a contest to the death.'

King Edward put a finger to each nostril and blew snot free. 'Gilbert, how could we deny you the pleasure? Though it is unfair on the French. You and Thomas are each worth ten of them.'

CHAPTER THIRTY-FIVE

Simon Bucy stood with the Dauphin, who tugged his robes tighter around his neck against the chilled air.

'Sire, these men fight for the glory of France in your name. If you and members of the court were to accompany me to the walls they would be cheered by your presence. And it would be a grand gesture of defiance.'

The Dauphin shuddered. 'They fight for their own glory, Simon. We gave our permission; let that be enough. The people do not need to see us; they know we are here. If Paris falls we all fall. Let them take heart from the knights who ride out.'

Bucy knew it was hopeless trying to budge the Prince Regent from the comfort of the room that looked out beyond the Grand-Pont into the city. The coolness of the day and the clear sky would make the blazons and colours of those who fought beyond the walls more vivid. The pageantry would stir men's hearts, but the Dauphin's refusal was to be expected. The Pope's prelates were still trying to negotiate a peace settlement and if the city could hold out long enough then the English would be forced to make concessions and scale back their claim to vast territories. The Pope's prelates were scuttling back and forth between Paris and King Edward. France, the Dauphin knew, could not endure the great tribulation and poverty that would follow should Edward's demands be met. Clerks had committed his thoughts to parchment and sent them to the prelates. A final appeal for a treaty had been sent. It acknowledged the older treaty, made before Edward had increased his demands. The King of France, desperate to return from captivity, had signed France away, but his son had resisted. And the English army baying at the gates was the result.

'Then I shall bear witness to their bravery,' said Bucy.

The Dauphin was deep in thought, gazing across the city, and made no reply.

'Highness?' said Bucy. 'With your permission?'

'What? Yes. Yes, do as you please.'

Bucy bowed and left the chamber, walking quickly to where the captain of the guard, de Chauliac, and his escort waited. 'Where are they?' he demanded.

'The English have surrounded the city and have thirty knights waiting beyond the gates at Porte Saint-Victor,' said the captain.

A thousand yards from the palace, less in some places to the walls, where the English host were gathered. Bucy felt a tinge of anxiety mingled with anticipation. If the French knights did not succumb it would be a futile victory but might prove an important morale boost to the people of the city. Bucy and his escort's horses clattered across the Petit-Pont that connected the Île de la Cité with the south bank. By the time they dismounted and went up onto the walls the bugles and trumpets from the English were reverberating again. It was an act of intimidation. Bucy looked to where the French armoured knights waited impatiently behind the gates. Their visors were still raised, but their swords were held ready and shields tucked close. The war horses sensed their riders' anticipation and some of them jostled, cursed by the squires and stable-hands who kept a firm grip on their bridles. As soon as the gates were opened the horses would surge and it was likely that some of those doing their best to hold their masters' beasts in check would fall beneath their hooves. The horses were large and strong enough to knock aside the strongest of men, let alone these boys.

Bucy reached the top of the walls and gasped when he saw that the English army stood like another great encircling wall. In the near distance the renowned place of learning the Abbaye de Saint-Victor had remained undamaged. Its great library and scriptorium were still intact. Perhaps it had been spared because the English King's savagery had been sated by the slaughter in the suburbs. The noise and the spectacle caused Bucy's heart to tremor. He was aware of Edward and his standard in the distance but his eyes sought out the English knights who waited less than five hundred yards from the gates. They sat on their war horses in the shape of a broad arrowhead. The knight at the formation's tip waited with an open-faced helm gazing up at the walls. Bucy could not see his face, but he saw that this man and the knight a few paces behind on his left bore the same blazon on their shields. Bucy gripped the wall.

Thomas Blackstone.

'Open the gates!' a voice commanded.

'Let them come,' Killbere said, turning in his saddle to the eager young knights who waited behind him. 'Watch how they attack. They'll form up across us and then hope to ride into us and flank us. The French want personal glory. That splits them up.'

The nearest man was struggling to control his horse. Richard Baskerville was the son of one of the Prince's companions who had fought with him at Crécy and Poitiers. 'Hold him, boy,' said Killbere. 'When they charge, spur him on. Tight rein. Saw the bit. Otherwise his blood will be up and he'll run you into the damned walls.'

The young knight nodded nervously. Killbere pulled down his visor. Blackstone's horse raised its head, ears pricked forward. Its muscles quivered. Blackstone felt the tug on the reins. The horse was as keen as its master to strike the enemy, who now fanned out in extended line two hundred yards from the English.

Blackstone turned. 'Gilbert. Let's end this.'

Without waiting for an answer Blackstone spurred the bastard horse forward, its boiled leather breast armour creaking under the strain of its power. He heard Killbere curse at being caught off guard: he had been waiting for the French to get closer. Now Blackstone had gained forty or more strides on them all and would plunge into the fray unprotected.

* * *

The captain of the guard standing next to Bucy swore beneath his breath. 'Bastards are outnumbered,' he whispered to no one in particular. The French soldiers and militia manning this section of the wall cheered loudly. Bucy ignored the chilled air seeping beneath his cloak's collar and stared transfixed as the sixty French knights rode en masse towards the English. Two to one. They would inflict misery on them. He saw Blackstone spur his horse forward. Did the man have a death wish? He would be overwhelmed. Bucy's throat tightened in panic. He did not wish Blackstone to fall beneath French swords here, outside the city walls. Bucy had already planned a more fitting end for the scourge of the house of Valois.

The remaining English knights quickly put spurs to their horses. The trumpets and bugles suddenly fell silent. The deafening roar of the English army rose up. The horses thundered across the open plain, kicking up great clods of dirt. The French rode with swords at the high guard, ready to slash down, as did the English, who now urged their horses at the canter. Except for Blackstone. He rode as if out for a day's hawking. Bucy could not take his eyes from him. The unusual rhythm of Blackstone's horse rolled like a wallowing boat, but Blackstone was upright, sword arm low. What in God's name was he doing?

A handful of the French had forged ahead of the others and the attacking knights behind them became more scattered. They had lost their formation, whether deliberately or not Bucy couldn't tell. What held his gaze was the sight of the two knights who now vied to kill the scarred-face Blackstone. They had dug their heels into their horses' flanks and were now at full gallop but Blackstone's beast still lumbered at a canter. And then Bucy understood why. The slower-moving horse changed course. It angled away from the two knights bearing down on it, forcing the Frenchmen to jostle each other as they attempted to steer their horses at speed. The outer rider was being pushed by his companion by which time

Blackstone had crossed their line of travel and raised his sword arm. The Frenchman had no protection. His shield arm was on the opposite side, almost being barged by his companion. He kicked his horse to try and turn it but Blackstone was too fast: he had half twisted in the saddle, bringing a sweeping cut upwards. As the French knight slashed downward Blackstone's blade caught him beneath his raised arm, which suddenly flopped uncontrollably. Blood gushed from the near-severed arm and the knight tumbled from his saddle. By the time the dead man's horse had galloped past, the knight's companion had been forced to veer to one side and was suddenly under the swords of two Englishmen.

Bucy's mouth dried with the horror of the efficient killing. His stomach lurched but his grip on the rough stone wall kept him focused, now more against his will, but also with macabre fascination. Blackstone's horse barged a French knight. The man struck down repeatedly and Blackstone made little effort to halt the strikes: he simply parried with his shield, turning away the attacker's blade. It seemed impossible to Bucy's untrained eye that so many strikes could yield no result. Instead, as Blackstone's shield forced the knight to half raise himself in the saddle to deliver a killing blow, Blackstone leaned forward and thrust his blade into the man's exposed groin. His scream soared above the English cheers, and as he slumped, mortally wounded, Blackstone had already urged his horse into the other Frenchmen, leaving his victim to fall, head severed, beneath the blade of the knight who followed Blackstone.

Bucy nearly gagged. He clamped a hand against his mouth. His mind flashed with the imagined picture of the Savage Priest fighting Thomas Blackstone years before. He too had failed and his skeleton still hung as a warning to anyone who dared take up the challenge against the Englishman. And then a more sickening realization swept over him. If the English did breach the walls Blackstone would scorch the streets like uncontrolled fire. He would come for the Dauphin and, more importantly, for Bucy himself.

He abandoned his plan to lure Blackstone into Paris. Better to rid himself of the threat now.

'Kill him!' he heard a voice bellow. 'Kill him!' And felt no sense of shame as he realized the voice was his own.

Blackstone's attack had slowed his progress, allowing the other English knights to catch up with him. Two Frenchmen attacked Blackstone, kicking their horses into position left and right, shields raised, mace and sword hammering down on him. Blackstone wore light armour: shoulder and arm pieces and thigh guards. His open helm sat on a gorget to protect his throat and left exposed his face and eyes, which terrified the Frenchmen more than the violence that swept over them. Blackstone's gaze was unflinching. It was focused solely on killing.

Blackstone caught one strike on his crossguard and twisted the French blade away. The man's gauntlet could not hold the wrench against his wrist and unlike Blackstone he wore no blood knot tying the sword's grip to his wrist. The sword fell; his head half turned; Wolf Sword swept through the air with enough force for the hardened steel to cut into his helm and skull. The Frenchman reeled, his horse skewed away out of control as the blinded knight fought the pain and blood in his eyes and fell onto the swords of the Englishmen behind Blackstone, who now struck the French with concentrated violence.

No matter what the second French knight tried he could not deflect Blackstone's rapid blows. They came too quickly and there was a power behind them that tore at his back and shoulder muscles. The Frenchman was no stranger to trial by combat. He had fought valiantly at Poitiers and defended garrisons and towns for the French Crown against marauding routiers in the years since. But then one of Blackstone's blows forced aside his shield and the Englishman reached forward and backhanded his sword's pommel against the French knight's helm. The force made his head recoil and although he righted himself in the space of a heartbeat Wolf Sword's blade pierced his visor.

Bucy watched as the mêlée became a slaughter. Other than Blackstone the English seemed to fight in pairs, hemming in the French knights who fought alone, eager to claim personal glory. Even Bucy could see that. He cursed their arrogance. No wonder the English army was unstoppable – they were disciplined. If French courage had been matched with the same strategy they would have prevailed. Riderless horses galloped here and there across the plain. French colours lay bloodied in the dirt. Knights hacked to death lay like butchered beasts.

A French knight rammed his horse against Blackstone's. It made little impression. The bastard horse wheeled. Blackstone swore at the belligerent animal and gripped tightly as it bucked, its iron-shod hooves smashing into the other horse's legs. Blackstone heard the bones crack and the horse whinny. Its body folded; the French knight pitched forward, screaming curses at his mount. As he struggled to stay in the saddle Blackstone seemed to wait a few leisurely moments before plunging Wolf Sword's point into the gap in armour between chest and shoulder. The knight fell writhing but as he tumbled to the ground he bravely tried to regain his balance, staggering to his knees despite his pain. Blackstone halted the bastard horse and waited for the dying man as he pushed back his visor, gulping air. Blackstone saw that he was a young man, barely any whiskers on his face, perhaps newly knighted like the English squires who were slaying his comrades. The young knight grimaced. The agony was getting the better of him. He cried out, forcing his body to keep attacking. He was within half a dozen paces of the scar-faced Englishman who gazed down at him. He raised his sword but the effort defeated him. He fell to his knees and succumbed to death.

Killbere swung his mace, knocking a knight senseless despite the padding within his helm, and then struck again. The Frenchman's head whipped back and forth from the blows. His arms slackened as his head was pounded. His ears leaked blood and his brain, battered by the ferocious attack, plunged the man into darkness. He was as good as dead, and soon would be. He tumbled from the saddle and as Killbere wheeled his mount its hooves smashed into the man's back. Killbere saw the young English knight Baskerville lose control of his horse and fall. The last surviving French knight had gained the advantage and as he turned his mount, preparing to go in for the kill, Killbere kicked his horse forward between him and the fallen man. Another knight dismounted to help Baskerville onto his feet while the Frenchman faced Killbere, who blocked the first two blows against him and then swung his chained mace around the man's neck, hauling him from the saddle. Baskerville and his helper fell on him.

The killing ended.

Simon Bucy stood transfixed at the sight of the defeat. The cold blue sky highlighted the carnage. The blazons and surcoats were scattered like a trampled field of wildflowers. Blood seeped into the churned grass. English knights raised their visors and their sword arms, turning to the English host who roared in triumph.

All except one man.

Blackstone sat astride his war horse and faced the walls of Paris. He stared up at those who had witnessed the defeat. Bucy stepped back involuntarily. He knew it was an impossibility but it seemed as if Blackstone's eyes had sought him out. And marked him for death.

It would not be so, he assured himself, gathering his confidence as he made his way down the steps to the waiting escort. As pages and stable-hands ran out from the courtyard to retrieve the fallen knights and recover their horses, Bucy comforted himself with the knowledge that he had the information and the means to cast Thomas Blackstone into the arms of a monster in a place far from the French court where he could never again pose any threat. French swords had failed to slay Blackstone but he, Simon Bucy, would ensure the troublesome knight's death with the stroke of a pen.

CHAPTER THIRTY-SIX

Blackstone always rose before dawn even though after the previous day's contest against the French knights he and Killbere had roundly celebrated their victory. The Prince of Wales had sent barrels of wine for Blackstone and his men and he and Killbere had drunk them dry with their captains. It served to ease the regret of the killing of Robert Thurgood and Collard. Now, as he walked among his men who stirred from their blankets and poked kindling into their campfire embers, he believed that this would be the day when the King of England would assault the walls of Paris. Here and there men stretched out the stiffness from their bodies and went into the trees to relieve themselves before warming the cooking pots and supping what remained of their contents.

The sky was still clear but the cold air pressed a veil of snaking mist across the treetops. It would need the weak sun's warmth to lift it, but if it did not then it might help obscure their attack. It was madness, but they were all caught up in it and the future of England lay within such madness. They were all lunatics of war. He had wandered through his own men's encampment and now realized he had been drawn towards the rear where the wagons were stationed and the barber surgeons would ready themselves to receive the wounded once the battle began. The apothecaries were back here and so too, somewhere close by, was Aelis, now that she had the Prince's protection. He questioned why he had come this far with the unformed thought of seeing her again. Her image tugged at him, because he knew that if they got beyond the walls then the thousands who waited in the streets held the advantage no matter how strong the English. And death was more likely than not, even with the protection of Arianrhod. The silver goddess would ease his journey from this life into the next but before she did he wanted to see the witch-woman again. The previous night's drinking had brought him dreams that scattered to and fro, will-o'-the-wisps, taunting and defying him to hold on to the visions that hovered before him. He had seen Christiana again but she was beyond his reach, held by unseen hands. She had smiled and the joy from it had flooded him with warmth until she faded into an amber-leaf forest, the wood spirits drawing her away. And as the shadows took her a cold hand clutched his heart. Wind swept the leaves from the trees and another woman stepped out and stared at him. It was Aelis, standing in the half-light as if she had been responsible for drawing away Christiana, denying him his love. As the witch-woman's cloak fell open he saw that she was naked and the fullness of her breasts and the tilt of her chin challenged him. He had awoken in panic, the dream already escaping. The reality of where he was and the barren existence without Christiana was quickly brought home as he rolled free of the blanket, nearly kicking a snoring Killbere.

The wagons were gone. He stood for a moment searching the clearing for anything that might tell him why so many supply wagons had been moved during the night. The King, he reasoned, must be repositioning them in case of counter-attack.

Trumpets roused the men and by the time he had made his way back to his own lines priests were standing before men-at-arms and hobelars alike as they said mass. It was Sunday and if a man had to die perhaps it was better on the holiest day of the week. Killbere emerged from the trees tying the cord on the front of his breeches. 'I'll say this for the Prince, he has good wine. Not that gut-rotting stuff. Thought he might have sent some brandy though. Perhaps he has a celebration planned once we clamber over the walls.' He shook a couple of wineskins, found one that still held some wine and then drank thirstily.

'You suck like a cow at the teat,' said Blackstone, buckling on his sword.

'A man has little else to suck these days. I shall be glad to find a brothel before Edward's men flay the city. We must ask the Prince's indulgence and get ourselves in the vanguard. His blood will be up, you'll see.'

'You're anxious to have us killed. Your tongue wagged like a washerwoman's yesterday and had us in enough trouble. Learn to let the Fates decide.'

Killbere swilled his mouth and spat. 'Thomas, you and me, we should take what we can when we can because we're in need of some comfort in this damned campaign.' He tossed aside the empty wineskin. 'Are you going to mass?' he said, tugging on his jupon and shrugging off the chills. Blackstone made no answer as Killbere reached for his sword belt. 'No. I thought not. The devil will catch you unaware one day, Thomas. He'll snatch your soul when you least expect it and you won't be confessed. A man should not die unshriven.' He stamped his feet to get the circulation going.

Blackstone raised his face to the breeze. 'Wind's shifting. If he's going to attack we shouldn't wait. The good weather will be gone by tomorrow. Can't you taste it?'

'My mouth is like the floor of your horse's stall,' Killbere said.

Henry arrived with a leather pail of water. 'My lord, Sir Gilbert. I've brought water from the stream.'

'Ah, good lad,' said Killbere and cupped his hands into the cold water and splashed his face. He snorted and spat again. 'Now I can try and stay awake while the black-hooded crows mutter their incantations.' He strode away towards the gathering men and a priest who was already blessing them.

'You've eaten?' said Blackstone.

'Later, Father. John Jacob had me bring this water first.'

'All right. Be off with you. Eat when you can, boy, you don't know when the next mouthful is coming your way.'

'Yes, Father.' He left the bucket. 'Father, I watched you fight yesterday and... I was frightened.'

'We all know fear, son,' said Blackstone gently, 'some more

than others, but we hide it so that the man next to us does not get infected. Fear can destroy an army quicker than the plague.'

'I meant that I was frightened that you would be wounded or killed. I was fearful of that. I would not wish to be alone, Father.'

Blackstone studied his son. He showed no sign of trepidation; there were no tears in his eyes. 'Henry, I will always be with you, no matter what happens. Just as your good mother's love protects you.'

Henry nodded. And then he shrugged. 'It's not the same as having her here, though, is it?'

'No it's not. We find our courage in her memory though, don't you think?'

The boy nodded. 'She was brave. I will try and remember what you have said, when I'm afraid.'

Blackstone reached out and gripped his son's shoulder. 'Listen to me, Henry. I have seen you look death in the eye and I have been filled with pride at the way you faced it. Every man here who serves with me has seen it as well. These men are warriors who respect you. Carry that knowledge with humility and use it as your shield against fear when you must. This is the truth of it, and you would not be here with us if it were not.'

The boy looked uncertain for a moment. To hear such praise from his father and to be told that the hard-bitten men who served him regarded him with esteem was an honour he could not have imagined.

'I had better get back to my duties. But I still hope that you do not die.'

Blackstone gave him a reassuring smile. 'I'll do my best,' he said.

Within the hour trumpet calls and the shouts of the army commanders had men strike camp. All along the line banners were raised. The archers were placed ready to shower the walls with their lethal missiles. Blackstone's captains quickly had their men in position as Will Longdon ran with his archers and placed them in a sawtoothed formation between them. It was a tried and tested disposition that had defeated the French in two major battles.

'Why are we doing this?' said Killbere as he fussed at the strapping on his saddle. 'This is a defensive formation.'

Blackstone was already mounted. He looked down the line of the army's ranks. It swelled and shuffled as sergeants and captains barked their commands. Flags signalled the King's orders. The drums began a steady beat, building in volume until the ground began to tremble. Men would soon march across the open plain to their rhythm.

'I don't know,' said Blackstone. 'If the French are going to attack then we're in a good position, but if we're to make a run for those walls, then I'd rather be closer. And there's still no sign of scaling ladders.'

'Well, the whoresons are waiting for us,' said Killbere and pulled himself into the saddle.

The walls were thick with defenders.

Further down the line the Duke of Lancaster eased his horse forward, leading his men.

'Lancaster's taking the vanguard,' said Killbere. 'Merciful Christ, are we to sit on our arses and let the King's favourites have the glory?'

'Don't be so impatient to get us all killed. He's not attacking.'

They watched as Lancaster's division rode out into the open and then turned.

'Where do they think they are? It's like they're parading at a tournament,' said Killbere.

Trumpets and bugles blared, the cacophony rising up to those on the walls.

'It's a show of strength, Gilbert.'

'What?'

Blackstone gestured down the lines where ranks of soldiers had followed their commanders and began to troop across the open ground. 'Battalions are marching beneath the walls.'

Killbere looked perplexed. 'Showing our peacock feathers is one thing. Where will we strike?'

Blackstone eased back into the saddle and pulled off his gauntlets. The truth had slowly dawned on him. 'There'll be no attack. The supply wagons left in the night. The King is covering their withdrawal. This is all for show while they make some distance.'

'Bollocks,' said Killbere. 'He's here for the crown.'

'No, Gilbert, I'll wager we'll soon be following them. He needs more time to negotiate but he had to show his strength to help him get what he wants.'

Killbere scowled and watched the pageantry parade before him. 'This is your damned fault, Thomas. You told him it was impossible to fight through the city and he's listened to you. It's you who should bite your tongue.'

Blackstone slapped his friend on the shoulder. 'I can be blamed for many things, Gilbert, but stopping this attack cannot be laid at my door. The King knows when common sense prevails and when God is on his side.' He turned his face to the freshening north wind. 'The moment has gone, and so has this good weather.'

CHAPTER THIRTY-SEVEN

The vast column of men trudged and rode south-west across the vast plain on the Chartres road. By the following day they were within sight of the towers of Chartres cathedral. The army had made impressive time in covering the seventy miles to where the King would encamp and continue negotiations with the Pope's envoys. Blackstone and his men rode halfway back on the army's flank. For the first time he could see why the King might have decided not to assault Paris. Food had been in short supply and fodder was still desperately needed for the horses. As the army passed by him he realized Edward could not fight a major battle unless supply lines were established more effectively from England. Blackstone's instincts had proved correct: the weather had shifted and great rumbling thunderstorms pursued them. Had they launched an attack the army would soon have been brought to its knees when the threatening storm struck them.

Blackstone turned and looked at his men. They were spread out using the open ground to ease their horses' passage, not following in the churned ground of the mount in front of them. Veils of steam rose from the animals as they laboured through the heavy mud, turning the riders into ghosts. A small town lay a few miles to their right.

'John,' Blackstone called. 'How far to Chartres, do you think?'

John Jacob rode close by, Henry behind him. 'Twenty miles, perhaps a bit less?' Jacob answered.

'There'll be little for our comfort there,' Killbere complained, 'except more damned priests.'

Blackstone asked the same question of Will Longdon. 'A dozen miles,' the centenar answered once he had gazed at the distant towers.

'It's between the two,' said Blackstone, 'but it makes little difference. We'll not get there before this storm breaks.'

'It would be better if the French army had numbers twice those of us and were in pursuit rather than that storm chasing us across the sky,' said Perinne.

The heavens were now as black as death.

Blackstone turned away from the column. 'We need shelter,' he said, his breath already steaming against the sudden drop in temperature. Urging the bastard horse into a fast canter, his men wheeled and followed without question. Spikes of cold rain were already being hurled from the strengthening wind. As Blackstone raced for the shelter of the town the army trudged on, heads lowered, shoulders hunched against the impending storm. The vast plain offered no shelter but if the advance guard of the King and the Prince were already in Chartres then they were safe from the threat.

By the time Blackstone's men had reached the town the rain had turned to sleet that flayed their skin and obscured some of the buildings on the far side of the small town. Fearful faces appeared at doors and windows that were quickly slammed closed as the horses surged between the buildings. Blackstone rode straight for a large barn in the centre of the town and quickly dismounted. 'Find shelter for horse and man! Anyone resists, kill only in self-defence!' he commanded. Some of the men followed him while others led their horses into nearby cow byres and stables and whatever cover they could find as the wind whipped the smoke from roof vents. Men stayed with their horses trying to calm them as the thunder rolled and lightning cracked with terrifying force, tearing aside the black clouds. No one dared venture out as the sleet turned to salt-like hail that stung and blinded anyone caught outside and death-rattled against doors and stone walls.

Sixty-odd men had pressed their horses into the vast barn. Blackstone threw his cloak over his horse's head and every man did the same with jupons, blankets, anything that would help calm the frightened animals. The men muttered words of comfort to their mounts, their hands close to the beasts' soft muzzles so they might be calmed with a familiar smell. John Jacob pulled Henry to stand between him and Blackstone. The boy would be crushed if the horses panicked.

Steam rose from beast and rider as a cold surge of air swept over them. The temperature plunged and the hail became stones the size of a man's fist that punched through thatch and slate, thankfully slowing their impact before striking man and horse. The ice hammered louder than the rolling thunder, a drumbeat heralding heaven's destructive power. As it tore through the roofs some men were struck and went down beneath the impact. The violent wind tore the barn doors open. Half a dozen horses broke free and ran into the storm only to be felled by the icy missiles. Blackstone saw Meulon use his great strength to stop two horses bolting and Gaillard and Perinne laboured to pull the barn doors closed again.

Men crossed themselves and prayed while others cursed. The wind gusted, its eerie malevolent howl making the bravest men tremble as it tore away more of the damaged roof. Three women and two men ran desperately from their house only yards from the barn. Their abandoned children ran after them screaming for their parents. Hailstones had destroyed the family's roof but before they had taken a dozen strides towards shelter the hurtling ice felled them. Their skulls broke from blows heavier than a mace and their scalps were torn into a bloodied mess. One of the children, a small girl, stopped in her tracks at the horror of her parents being bludgeoned. She survived for a few moments longer; then the storm's dark angels, showing no mercy, battered her head and face into the ground.

The great storm took thirty long minutes to sweep across the plain. As the clouds and thunder eased the sound of dripping wet thatch and the gurgling of flooded streams through the town's streets enticed the men outside. The saturated bodies of the fallen family lay bedraggled on a bed of hailstones. One by one the men led their horses into the open and called out to those who had sought shelter in other buildings. Three of the men in Blackstone's barn had been knocked unconscious but they were alive, unlike four others who had been sheltering in a flimsy lean-to on one of the houses. Not one roof remained undamaged in the small town. Blackstone had his dead men tied across their horses and then led them away, ice crunching underfoot, to the edge of town. The gentle slope leading down to the English army's route glistened with packed hail and soon showed the devastation wrought by the freak storm. Some of the men in the column had dashed for shelter in nearby woods and had survived, while others lay scattered across the plain like fallen leaves. Wagons had sunk up to their axles in mud; mules lay dead in their traces. As far as the eye could see men lay slain; and horses: the mud on the great plain they crossed had sucked away the last breaths from their flaring nostrils. Survivors staggered from one body to the next, searching for anyone who might still be alive; it was obvious to Blackstone's eye that, amidst the vast army, some thousand men or more had perished. Perhaps as many horses, weak from lack of forage, had gone down beneath the heavens' onslaught. Soaking-wet survivors gathered their weapons but abandoned their plunder and supplies. Already weak before the storm, now the freezing air and battering had nearly brought Edward's great army to its knees. Leaving behind their dead comrades they made their way towards Chartres.

Blackstone followed the survivors as they poured into the city, his horse's hooves clattering onto the cobbled street, leaving the muddied dirt highway outside the gates. Men jostled through the arch of the Porte Guillaume, whose tollhouse leaned as if pushed by the wind. The whole world seemed askew after that storm. The army had divided and entered Chartres through each of the twelve gates around the city. Gabled houses leaned drunkenly over the river, the upper floors clear of those below. Women gaped as the battered soldiers shuffled their way into the city walls and then, after long moments of hostile stares, threw their slops into the river in a gesture that told the English what they thought of them. Windows slammed closed. Chartres would not be assaulted or burnt; its occupants were safe from violation. The ancient city of pilgrimage had been spared by the English King, but that did not lessen its citizens' hatred for the invaders.

As Blackstone rode beyond the gate into the city the outline of the ancient cathedral on the rising ground in the distance became clearer in the late afternoon light. The air sparkled after the storm and etched its towers on a tauntingly blue sky. The streets between the half-timbered houses were already overcrowded. Soldiers squatted and lay in doorways despite loud protests from French householders, but the exhausted Englishmen's crude responses and threatening tones quickly made those who hurled the insults slam closed their doors. Who among the citizens would risk aggravating such stinking, mud-stained men? Their fearful appearance would have the burghers on their knees praying even harder in the town's churches.

A sergeant-at-arms, bearing a blazon of three golden lions on a red background topped by a bar sporting the fleur-de-lys, clattered his horse over a small humpback bridge that spanned the narrow river. He drew up a dozen paces from Blackstone's advance and said, 'Sir Thomas. My Lord Lancaster's compliments. You and your men are to camp close to the Prince with the other lords.'

'The King and the Prince, they survived the storm unharmed?'

'By God's grace, yes,' said the sergeant. 'As did my Lord Lancaster, who has secured some of what little food there is for you and your men.'

'I have four dead of my own,' said Blackstone.

'Then they will be accorded the dignity of a burial. There are a number of churches here and priests who serve them.'

Blackstone and Killbere glanced at each other.

'Food? Is this favour for our work at Paris?' Killbere muttered with quiet disbelief, unheard by the waiting sergeant-at-arms.

'Lancaster's the King's right-hand man, but every time our arses are warmed by fires close to the Prince's pavilion we end up in a shit pit of trouble.'

'Gilbert, you're becoming an old crone,' sighed Blackstone with good humour. 'Unhappy if we are watered and fed and not fighting or miserable when we are tasked to do our King's bidding.'

'I'm suspicious of grace and favour is all I'm saying,' said Killbere. He faced the sergeant, who was waiting patiently. 'We thank the Duke of Lancaster for his generosity. We will follow your lead.'

Blackstone and Killbere urged their horses after the sergeant-at-arms as footsoldiers leaned precariously against the bridge's low parapet to avoid Blackstone's horsemen.

'You aren't that concerned about shit pits then?' said Blackstone.

'I'm thinking that if it's an act of gratitude there will be the best of wine and fine cuts of meat. Where my stomach leads, I follow.'

CHAPTER THIRTY-EIGHT

They followed the sergeant through the lower part of the town along the street named after the city tanners; then, skirting the river that ran between the narrow buildings, they edged their way through the areas where artisan guilds practised. The streets the horsemen rode along were named after the city's tradesmen, felt makers and cordwainers, which merged into narrow passageways where cobblers, saddlers and harness makers plied their skills; here the alleyways also bore the name of their trades. Then they left the artisan area behind and dismounted two streets from the great cathedral where the merchant classes and those who governed the town lived. The open ground around the cathedral was already a field of colour from knights and noblemen's blazons. The royal standard rose above them all from the King's pavilion.

Blackstone had not taken his eyes from the towers, each different in design, one slightly lower than the other in its reach for heaven. Gaillard and Meulon barked their orders as the horses were led away to be hobbled on a picket line.

'There's fodder for the horses?' said Blackstone to the sergeant.

'There's little to be had, Sir Thomas. The beasts suffer more than us. We at least have victuals here. I'll see to it that your men get supplies.'

'We carry enough to feed ourselves, sergeant,' said Blackstone, never wanting to depend on others.

'I carry out my orders as they are given,' he answered and with a nod of respect left the men to camp.

Killbere surveyed the area. 'It's good, Thomas. The buildings offer protection from the wind; the open ground allows pickets to stop anyone with a grudge from approaching. And' – he rubbed a hand across his itchy beard – 'where's there's royalty and nobility there's usually hot water. A decent soak to rid myself of crotch lice and whatever creatures nest in my beard would be welcome.'

'I'll ask the Prince if we can have his bathwater after he and his retinue have used it,' Blackstone said with a grin.

'I'll take the King's bathwater and be honoured even if his hunting dogs have been through it. A man feels better if he's scrubbed the dirt from his skin before battle.'

Blackstone pointed to a house that stood beyond the open ground. One side of its walled garden abutted a lane. 'We'll get ourselves and the horses in there,' he said and raised an arm to John Jacob, who in turn alerted the captains.

Killbere and Blackstone began to lead their horses away from the vast square that pressed against the front line of merchants' houses. There were already more than two hundred horses hobbled there; stable-hands and pages ran back and forth securing their masters' mounts. Some had feedbags; many did not.

'The stench of horse shit will soon bring delegates from the better-off citizens to the King's officers,' said Killbere.

'Much good it will do them,' said Blackstone, tugging at the bastard horse's leading rein. 'What battle are you planning to fight that you need to be scrubbed and dressed in clean braies and undershirt?'

'It's obvious why we've come south twenty-odd leagues. The King threw down the gauntlet at the walls of Paris and then made it look as though we were withdrawing. The French will think we are weakened. The Dauphin will give chase, especially after that damned murderous storm. He'll be dribbling spittle down his chin at the thought of butchering us. Now we're here we'll form up and meet them on that damned great plain we've trudged across. They'll come for us, you see if they don't. We can rest for a day or two, and then be ready for them. There's space to swing a sword out there.'

Blackstone put his shoulder against the garden wall's double gates and heaved them open. A chicken shed and an open barn stood at the end of the long garden. As they trampled the garden's potager a woman screamed at them from an upper window and a portly man suddenly appeared from the downstairs kitchen area. The irate Frenchman cursed the Englishmen, his face flushed, his fist wielding a carving knife. He did not stray beyond the threshold once Killbere turned his eyes on him. He faltered even more when he saw that another half-dozen vandals were also leading in their horses. His wife berated him but he threatened her with the knife, spluttering with anger, and she pulled her head back inside. With a final, useless curse, the householder slammed closed the door.

'John,' Blackstone called to John Jacob. 'Perinne and Halfpenny are to join the captains in here. This is where we'll camp. Henry, you help Will Longdon cook us a meal. Half a dozen of those chickens and some eggs will make a start.'

Blackstone led the bastard horse to a stall at the end of the barn and unsaddled it. The others knew to keep their distance.

'Lancaster will take this as an affront,' said Killbere.

'I'll take his gratitude and food, but we look after ourselves. You're right, being so close to nobility is never a good thing. Have the woman in the house boil water. I could do with a bath as well.'

'And me,' said Meulon.

'Aye, be good to scrape the last week's filth away,' said Gaillard.

Killbere glared. Sharing his King's dirty water would never have happened, but allowing the men he fought with to share his bath was another.

'You'll wait your damned turn,' he growled. 'I'll test the water first and then Sir Thomas can follow.'

'Be careful of the woman of the house, Sir Gilbert,' said Will Longdon as he dumped his blanket and saddle panniers. 'If she puts mustard seed in the water your cock will boil and your arse will squeal.'

'And if we used the bathwater as broth it would taste better than anything you're likely to sacrifice in the cooking pot,' said Killbere.

'Get about your damned business and wring some chicken necks and try not to think of your own puny cock when you're doing it.'

The men turned away, smiling; even Will Longdon knew there was no venom in the veteran knight's words.

'And you?' said Killbere to Blackstone.

'I'll go and check on the men outside,' he answered.

Killbere grunted. 'The men. Ah. If you lied as well as you fought we'd be better for it. The woman will be with the baggage train if she survived the storm, and I wouldn't be too sure she didn't cause it.'

Was it so obvious? thought Blackstone as he turned for the gate, feeling Killbere's stare boring into his back as sharp as a bodkin.

Blackstone picked his way through the tents and pavilions and the scurrying servants who ran back and forth to attend to their lords' requirements and comforts. The common soldiers and men-at-arms looked worn and exhausted. Many sported injuries from the storm but armour and mail was being cleaned, weapons sharpened and fires blazed with dry kindling that had probably been requisitioned from city merchants' houses. The smell of herbs wafted from the steam on cooking pots but it was poor fare. The kitchens had been destroyed in the onslaught of the storm, cooking utensils devoured by the mud; there was no tentage for the common soldier – along with saddles and arms they had also been lost. The men stank of rancid sweat. Unwashed clothing clung to bodies pockmarked with sores and chafed skin. Horses were lame, weak from lack of fodder, broken down from the weight of armoured men and their weapons. The army stank: it reeked of death and another stench that was more powerful than that of the latrine pits. Defeat.

Perhaps Killbere was right, Blackstone thought as he watched squires honing their knights' swords on grinding stones and blacksmiths who had already fired up the coals on the mobile forges that had survived the journey. The rhythmic beating of hammer against anvil meant that iron horseshoes were being replaced. It seemed to Blackstone's eye that despite the army being flayed by the storm that Edward was preparing for battle. One last time.

It took Blackstone fifteen minutes to find the baggage train and the pitifully few wagons that had got this far and which bore the barber surgeons and apothecaries. There were at least eighty wounded men, victims of the great storm, lying in rows on the ground ready to be treated by the surgeons. Blackstone noticed that most of them were archers who wore the green and white colours of Cheshire men. They had formed the main body in the centre of the column and had obviously been caught in the open without any chance of running for cover in the forests or clambering beneath the heavy timbers of the supply wagons as many others had done. They had broken arms and legs; bones protruded but the men's muted agony was testimony to their grim determination not to cry out. Many had suffered head wounds and were unconscious. If they survived the barber surgeons' treatment they would be counted as lucky, given the swathes of bodies that still lay out on the open plain. Unless the sergeants-at-arms could find churches and monasteries in the area and pay the priests and monks enough to cart away the bodies and bury them in their own churchyards, King Edward's men would be left to village dogs, crows and wolves. The horse carcasses would already be bloating and the stench would soon follow the King's retreat from Paris.

Blackstone walked along the rows of wagons searching for Aelis, and then quickly stopped when he saw her less than fifty paces away bending down to tend an injured man. Her cloak's hood was pulled back, revealing her dark hair, which had already grown to smooth the hacking it had suffered at Balon. Blackstone took a step backwards and used the tattered flap of one of the few pavilions to shield him as he saw her stand when beckoned by one of the surgeons. He stayed a while longer watching as she obeyed the surgeon's instructions. Her face glowed from the cold air and Blackstone could see that she was being put to good use despite the obvious lack of supplies. She seemed tireless, going from man to man helping wherever she could. After a few minutes she directed the servants to carry some of the injured closer to the blazing fires for warmth. Perhaps they were soon to die and she was offering them moments of comfort, Blackstone thought, or they were the ones who might have a chance of survival. Either way it was Aelis de Travaux who had issued the orders. Perhaps she had already proved her worth to the surgeons and apothecaries and they had begun to trust her judgement.

Blackstone felt a sense of satisfaction that he had spared the woman's life. She had already repaid the gift by saving Killbere and now she was giving relief to men-at-arms and archers who otherwise would have received nothing more than rough-and-ready treatment from the surgeons. He also felt, he acknowledged to himself, a sense of relief that she had survived the storm, though he did not know why that mattered to him as much as it did. He suddenly felt conspicuous standing among the pavilions; those going about their business had already given him the occasional questioning glance. It was time to leave. He hesitated a moment longer and observed as she ducked into a tent and then emerged a moment later without her cloak but wearing a jerkin that gave her more freedom of movement. So that was where she slept, he noted, and for a brief moment thought of Robert Thurgood making his way through the night to try and lie with her. A young archer not understanding his own heart or the strength in his arm when he struck Collard. The warning was plain. The woman could entice a man by her presence alone.

Blackstone meandered back through the encampment, moving closer to the great flying buttresses on the side walls of the cathedral that sheltered sentries patrolling their stations. Blackstone skirted the soldiers and reached the cathedral's front doors. An escort waited in the broad open square in front of the sacred building: squires held a half-dozen saddled horses, draped in trappings and obviously meant for men of rank and importance. Something was happening inside. He gazed up at the great rose window in wonderment, awed by the skill of those masons centuries before who had created such a magnificent tribute to God. Below the carved lintels three portals remained closed; of these three heavy wooden doors it was the larger centre one that began to creak open. Men stood up to get a better view from where they tended their fires; knights of the King's retinue stepped out of their pavilions to see who would leave the church. A procession of heralds and squires led out three papal legates; they were accompanied by the Prince of Wales and the Duke of Lancaster, who escorted them towards the waiting horses. The first of the Pope's envoys wore a black cloak over his white habit. He was gaunt-looking; his demeanour befitted the Dominicans' reputation. One of the men next to Blackstone spat in disgust.

'Black Friar. One of the Hounds of God, Sir Thomas,' he said quietly. The Dominicans insisted the sobriquet denoted their obedient service to the faith, yet it suited, too, their dedication to the pursuit of heresy. It meant the same thing to common men.

'Aye, and they'll sniff out sinners like us,' said Blackstone to reassure those around him that he was no different than them. 'Who else is here, do we know?' he asked as the two other envoys stepped towards the horses.

'No idea,' said one of the men. 'But they're dressed fit to be kings. Sumptuary laws don't mean much to these holy men. Reckon they're from Avignon and the Pope is trying to convince our good King to stop killing the French.'

'Well, he would, wouldn't he?' said his companion, and turned to Blackstone. 'Don't you reckon, Sir Thomas? A French Pope will side with those who bred him.'

'A whelp knows its bitch,' said another.

Blackstone moved away as the Prince and Lancaster bade farewell to the envoys. The great doors closed with an echoing thud. A treaty was still being discussed although the last time the envoys met, the English took up the sword to convince the Pope's legates and the Dauphin that Edward would settle for nothing less than the treaty that had already been settled and had since been reneged on.

If the look on the delegates' faces was anything to go by, Blackstone thought as he skirted the cathedral walls, Edward would need to loose his men on every town between here and Paris and scorch his royal seal on French souls.

As Blackstone strode on a sentry turned to relieve himself in the corner of a buttress and Blackstone saw that another twenty paces beyond him a small side door was left unguarded. Drawn to see for himself the glory that had been hewn by stonemasons, and with a quick glance to make certain he was not observed, Blackstone reached the door and tested the heavy iron latch. It turned. Stepping into the near darkness of a small entranceway he quietly closed the oak door behind him.

It smelt like a crypt. The dank, heavy air clung like a damp shirt but within two strides he was free of the entrance porch and thoughts of the dead lying beneath his feet were forgotten. He stared up at the vibrant colours of the immense stained-glass windows. Like a child at a country fairground mesmerized by an unfamiliar spectacle he walked into the vastness of the interior. There was a blue within the glass that made these gifts to God unlike anything he had ever seen before. They pulsed with light and for a moment he stood beneath their glow as if being caressed by an unnatural power.

Vast circular pillars soared a hundred and more feet into the curved ceiling; coloured light flooded the transept and the choir. Wings fluttered somewhere high up: a bird trapped in this sacred place. Silence bore heavily down on him as he stepped through the shadows, but somewhere ahead he heard a softly muffled rustling that sounded like cloth against stone. A murmur hung in the air, barely a whisper, softer than the darkness beyond the broad pillars that guarded the expanse of the nave. Blackstone stepped around one of the pillars and saw a man dressed only in shirt and breeches, barefoot, arms outstretched, lying prostrate on the cold stone floor. Blackstone blinked. The figure of a humble monk stood half-in half-out of the shadows cast by the pillars. His hands were clasped in prayer, his head bowed, what light there was barely illuminating his tonsure.

The prone man on the ground was still sixty-odd paces from where Blackstone stood transfixed. Suddenly the figure rose to his knees and began to shuffle in a circular direction. It made no sense for a few moments until Blackstone realized that there were markings on the floor. He looked hard, blinking in the poor light. It was a great circular labyrinth laid into the stone that covered the floor of the nave and the shuffling man appeared to be doing penance.

Blackstone was drawn to the shuffling figure whose soft murmurings resolved into the familiar sound of prayer. It was Latin and though Blackstone did not understand the words the man's humility and devotion were obvious. And then, once he was within twenty paces, the man turned within the labyrinth's curve. Blackstone saw the weather-beaten features draped with long fair hair and beard and realized with a cold stab of fear why sentries had been posted around the cathedral to stop any intruders. They had not only been for the meeting that had taken place.

The man on his knees who now stared at Blackstone was the King of England.

CHAPTER THIRTY-NINE

Blackstone dropped to his knee and kept his head bowed, silently cursing himself for encroaching where he was clearly not meant to be. He heard the sound of the King getting to his feet and a moment later his unmistakable voice.

'On your feet, Thomas,' he commanded, his words unhurried and without rancour. His voice was gentle, perhaps because he had spent time in prayer.

Blackstone obeyed. A hand clapped in the shadows, resulting in a scuffle of feet. Blackstone's hand was on Wolf Sword. He relaxed his guard when three of the King's servants arrived bearing his clothes. With practised ease the men quickly dressed their master, buttoning his embroidered jerkin and fastening a silver-buckled belt around it. A dagger's handle was visible from its black leather sheath.

'Sire, I apologize. I meant no disrespect or intrusion.'

The King's servants finished their duties, finally reaching for his cloak, which lay across a bench, and securing the gold clasp that held the ermine-collared garment. Edward raised a hand and the servants melted away. He signalled the monk to leave also. As Blackstone watched the monk disappear from view, his shuffling footsteps fading into the darkness, he thought he could see another figure in the deep shadows, but the light played tricks and made him uncertain.

'You always appear where least expected, Thomas,' said the King. 'Even here in this venerated church of pilgrimage.'

'I was drawn to this place, highness. I have never seen anything like it.'

The King adjusted the clasp on his cloak. 'Built to the glory of God. A reflection of God's creation. Do you know your scripture, Thomas?'

'A little, sire.'

'I doubt there's great need for such studies when you fight as well as you do,' said Edward. 'But a king is divine and must be versed in all that is holy, even though we defer to Mother Church and God himself for guidance. Did you know that God is considered a geometer and that creation is a mathematical act?'

'No, my lord. My master mason was learned enough in Latin but it was practical geometry that guided us in our skills.'

'Then, as a stonemason, you would have seen plans drawn and buildings raised so you will understand the words of St Augustine when he wrote: "Thou hast made all things in measure, number and weight."'

'The creation is beyond my understanding, sire. I live day to day as best I can in service to you and the Prince.'

'And we are glad of it. But all are joined to the Almighty, Thomas, even you with your pagan goddess at your throat whose outstretched arms within her silver wheel embrace the small crucifix that you also wear. You confound us as well as God,' said the King, stepping towards one of the vast pillars. 'Masons and builders who labour over a place such as this to mirror God's mathematical creation of the universe are co-creators with Him. Sacred geometry was understood by the Greeks and God is worshipped through man's labours.' The King smiled. 'Thomas, every time you chiselled a block of stone for chapel or church you were honouring Our Lord.'

Blackstone bit his tongue. Every time he had chiselled stone as a young man it had been to earn a few pennies to keep starvation from the door and the master mason's switch off his back.

The King gazed up at the stained-glass windows and pointed them out to Blackstone. 'They dispel the myth that we are victim to the wheel of fortune. Every window shows us the glory of the creation and the story of Christianity. No words are needed: these windows are for the common man to understand. Pilgrims come here to sleep beneath their glow. It is said they heal a man whether he is sick in body or spirit.'

Edward studied Blackstone for a moment, then appeared to think of something and gestured him to come closer. He laid a palm against the hewn stone. 'Feel that,' he said.

Blackstone let his palm slide across the surface. He felt something etched under his fingertips.

'Look closely,' said the King, 'and you will see a stonemason's mark. Every man who followed those before him left his mark. This place took centuries to build. First it was a druid place of worship, and then Roman and then Christian. It is a kingdom built upon a thousand years of faith.'

Blackstone had little idea why the King was sharing this knowledge, but he had not been scolded for his intrusion and the King seemed calm and his mood indulgent.

Edward stared across the voluminous cathedral's nave. The labyrinth on the floor encircled them like an arena. 'We built a kingdom, Thomas. England. It was laid over the foundations of our father and his father before him and they in turn imposed the power of their rule over those who had gone before them. We abase ourselves before God and we pray that when we fight it is a just war. Our bishops and archbishops declared this war to be just. That we had God's blessing to bring our army here and to take what was rightfully ours.'

'And you will succeed, sire.'

The King sighed. 'Those envoys who were here were from the Pope. One of them was the Abbot of Cluny. He uses many fancy words but he is unworldly and lacks negotiating skills. The other two men, did you see them?'

'I did, sire,' said Blackstone. 'They looked to be venerable men. One was aged – was he not full of wisdom?'

'Yes. And they propose peace. The Dominican was Simon of Langres, a Frenchman favoured by the Pope. He is harsh in his demands but we will not yield to him. He's too blunt and has not the finesse needed to bring a king to the negotiating table. The old man was Hugh of Geneva; he has spent more than sixty years talking to kings and listening to God. He fought at my side back in '39 in the Low Countries. I made him our Lieutenant in Gascony. He is forthright and honest in his opinions. Like you. You told our son that we should abandon Rheims and that Paris could not be taken.'

'It was an impertinence, my lord.'

'No, it was practical advice echoed by Lancaster. Plain talk and understanding cut through the shroud of doubt. You were right to say it. And Lancaster and Hugh have both advised that we now throw ourself into peace as we did into war. It is our final chance to agree a treaty. The storm was a sign of the Almighty's displeasure. More than a thousand dead men; three, four times as many horses. We take heed of God's voice. He punished our pride and the slaughter of the innocents. We acknowledge divine providence.'

'Then... then we will no longer fight?' said Blackstone.

The King looked benignly at his troublesome but favoured knight. 'No longer. The reality does not suit us, Thomas. We do not govern for our own selfish needs: we do so for the people. Our belligerence demands we continue to inflict violence on those who oppose us, but we are father to our people and must now bring stability and prosperity to our nation. We crave the cessation of a war that began more than twenty years ago.'

Blackstone felt the weight of the cathedral's arched ceiling fall on him. He had known nothing but war since a boy, had been baptized at its high altar. In that moment it seemed little consolation that there would always be a place for him to fight – Florence still held his contract to defend it against its enemies. But the great battles were over.

The hand of God had done what no French army could have achieved – it had swept aside the pious King's ambitions.

Silence laid itself over both men until the King spoke gently. 'Thomas, you saved our son's life at Crécy and that makes you dear to us. Our mother entrusted the Prince's safety to you before she died. You are held in great esteem but this peace comes at a price to us both.'

'How so, my lord?'

'There was another priest who journeyed with the Pope's envoys.' He turned and raised a hand.

Blackstone's instincts had not failed him. There had been another man in the gloom. As the figure emerged from beneath one of the great windows, sunlight speckled its colours across the floor and the older man who trod across it.

'Father Torellini,' Blackstone whispered disbelievingly as the Florentine priest emerged from the sparkling light. The man who had cradled his savaged body at Crécy and since shadowed his life embraced him.

'Thomas, my heart glows at seeing you again.'

Blackstone almost laughed aloud. It was a joy to meet his friend again. The last time he had seen the trusted priest had been in Italy when he'd brought news that had taken Blackstone back to England.

'Thomas,' said Torellini, his hands still gripping the knight's arms, his eyes intent upon impressing the importance of his words on Blackstone. 'Once again you are in danger.'

Blackstone grinned. 'Father, I'm always in danger.'

Torellini looked to King Edward, who nodded his assent.

'You are about to be delivered to your enemy,' said Torellini.

'How so?' said Blackstone, looking at the stern faces of the two men.

'As part of the peace negotiations the Dauphin demands that you are delivered to him in Paris,' said the King. 'You and your son.'

CHAPTER FORTY

'He throws you to the dogs!' hissed Killbere. 'You can see what this is, Thomas. In God's name, tell me you can see it? The French will kill you and Henry and make sure the Blackstone name dies with you.'

The two men squatted in the shelter of the barn; the fire's smoke smudged the air. Killbere pushed aside the chicken that Will Longdon had cooked when Blackstone had returned from the cathedral.

'Perhaps not,' said Blackstone, taking a mouthful of the chicken leg. 'The King said he would insist on my safety.'

Killbere growled in disbelief, keeping his voice low because Blackstone had not yet told his men what had happened. 'And the bastard Dauphin agreed of course. He'll not let a soldier kill you – it will be an assassin in the crowd. A crossbow bolt in the back. A dozen butchers rushing you with meat cleavers.'

'I don't think he would risk the peace negotiations by killing us. Not yet at least.'

'Not yet at least,' Killbere repeated. 'Do you think it makes a difference as to *when* he kills you? You ride into Paris, he creates a situation, you lose your temper. The next thing you know you're at the Place de Grève with your head on the block because it will be made to look as if you've brought about your own downfall. It won't be worth a nun's tits to the peace negotiations. You are not that important.'

Blackstone sat quietly chewing the chicken, gazing across the garden to where Henry sat and ate with John Jacob. 'They wouldn't kill Henry,' he said after some thought. 'That would be a step too far.'

Killbere scrubbed a hand across his beard and slapped the dirt. 'You are blind, Thomas Blackstone. I did not give you my protection all those years ago for you to turn out to be a king's fool. They could behead you and then poison him, or make his death appear to be an accident. You swore to kill the King of France and threatened his son. The Dauphin's balls will be tighter than horse chestnuts at the thought of luring you into Paris.'

Blackstone smiled. 'Perhaps I'll get the chance to kill him first.' The look of despair on Killbere's face made him relent. 'Gilbert, I won't even try. Not when Henry is with me. Father Torellini –'

'The Italian priest always brings trouble to your door,' Killbere interrupted.

'He's the King's confidant and my friend.'

'I'm your friend, Thomas, but I don't send you into the jaws of hell.'

'You're right, I usually follow you there.'

Killbere shrugged. 'I like to fight the French and if I get ahead of you in the battle I apologize.' He made a final solemn plea. 'Thomas, say no. If you go in there alone with the boy we can't help you.'

'The King desires peace, Gilbert. I'll play my part.' He reached for Killbere's half-eaten food. 'Do you want this?'

'My appetite has deserted me. Take it.' Killbere sucked on a piece of chicken bone. 'Peace is no good to the likes of us, Thomas. If they let you live what then?'

'We still have our men outside Florence. We can go back there.'

'The winters are cold. We could go to the King of Naples – I hear the weather is better down there.'

Blackstone tossed what was left of the chicken leg to an emaciated cur that had been lying hopefully a dozen paces away. It snatched the offering and scurried away. 'We take what scraps are offered, Gilbert. Florence still holds our contract. After that... we'll see.'

'I should ride with you into Paris. Me and John Jacob. Squire and companion knight,' Killbere said hopefully.

'The way you antagonize the French?'

'I will stay silent,' he said, raising a hand in oath.

'You would test God's patience once too often,' said Blackstone. 'If I end up with my head on the block it will be because of what I do, not you. Once we reach Paris you stay outside with the men. They need you, as they always have. You taught me that our word was our honour, Gilbert. And I swore to protect the Prince and serve the King. I have no choice in doing as he asks. You know that.'

Killbere nodded reluctantly. 'I taught you well. I pray I don't live to regret it.' He gathered straw under his blanket and reached for a leather flask of wine. 'God's tears, Thomas, no more war. I think I'll drown my misery.'

Blackstone said nothing to Henry; it would serve no purpose. Let the boy get a night's sleep and then next morning he would ride back to Paris and they would enter the city together. The King and Torellini would begin negotiations with the French ambassadors and Pope's envoys. It would be heralded with all the pomp that the English could muster, with renowned noblemen in attendance. The Duke of Lancaster would be at one of the King's shoulders, the Prince at the other. It would be a show of force and pageantry. Hundreds of servants and bodyguards would be present, flags and pennons would be raised and the royal standard unfurled. The English might agree to the peace treaty but they would let it be known that they were the overwhelming force and that they could still wage war. The great English King would bring the long-running war to a close and return home in triumph, but would secure the right to inflict his wrath on the French should they dare renege again. Edward would renounce his claim to the French crown and the vast territories that he had demanded previously but he would hold Aquitaine as a sovereign independent state. History, Blackstone realized, was being made and he still had a part to play.

By the time all these thoughts had passed through his mind he had reached the barber surgeons' wagons. There was no sign of

Aelis. The night's chill would soon be upon the wounded; the clear sky already held the promise of a bright moon and crystal-clear stars. Everyone relished the dry cold; anything was better than the saturating rain which they knew would soon return.

A surgeon told him that the wounded had been taken inside the cathedral on the King's orders. Aelis was with them, administering her potions and balm. Blackstone made his way to the great door on the west portal and eased through its half-open gap. The chill still seeped from the stone floor but he could make out the injured men lying on blankets with coverings over them beneath one of the rose windows. For a moment he was once again held by the rich hues despite the failing light outside. Candles had been lit and their warmth softened the depth of the church's shadows.

Aelis had her back to him, grinding something in a pestle and mortar. Her hand stopped; her head raised, sensing a presence. She turned. He was barely a dozen paces behind her.

'I have been waiting for you,' she said.

Blackstone went to her. 'I had no reason to come here,' he lied, knowing full well the attraction she held for him.

She showed no regret, and she spoke matter-of-factly. 'Then why are you here now?'

Blackstone couldn't find a satisfactory answer: he would not openly admit his desire for her.

'It is because I called to you,' she said. 'I could not leave my place here and find you, so I put you in my thoughts and beckoned you to me.'

'I came here of my own accord,' he insisted. 'I do not hear your voice in my head; I do not see images of you in the shadows luring me like a siren. I came to see that you were not being mistreated. Nothing more.' Another lie, yet close enough to the truth to satisfy his own uncertainty. He realized he was standing too close to her. Her back was pressed against one of the pillars. He felt foolish and half turned, determined not to give in to whatever pull she exerted on him. 'But I see you don't need my concern.'

She quickly reached out and gripped his arm and this time her voice was urgent, barely above a whisper. 'You must take me with you.'

It took him by surprise but she did not let go of him. 'Am I going somewhere?' he said.

'Yes. Across the mountains.'

Blackstone knew she could not have spoken to Killbere, and none of his men would have gossiped about the future, idly wondering what was to become of them after the war which had to end sooner or later.

'Who told you this?' he said.

She shook her head. 'It comes to me. These feelings. They are not conjured with magic. They are given to me. And all I know is that I must come with you. You... and the boy,' she said finally as if surprised to realize the full extent of what lay ahead. Her hand dropped from his arm and she touched his face. Fear made him step back. A witch's touch could poison a man's heart and seize his soul. He brushed her hand aside.

'Leave me be,' he said.

'I cannot,' she answered. 'You saved my life and I am indebted to you. We are bound together until that debt is repaid. I do not ask for what I am given or what must be done.'

He glanced away. Darkness had settled. The night had drawn in quicker than he had realized – unless, he reasoned, she had held him in a spell and the night's mantle that now cloaked the church's chambers was part of it. Neither spoke but he still could not step away from her.

'There is no debt between us. You saved Sir Gilbert; that was enough. Who has told you about Paris?' he finally said.

'Paris? No one. There are no mountains to cross going back there.'

He could not shake the uncertainty from him. Finally, reason returned. 'You hear gossip and rumour around the camp. You imagine mountains where there are none. I am going to Paris with my son and after that I do not know where.'

292

She accepted his rejection without apparent rancour and turned back to her pestle and mortar. 'After that you will face betrayal and death.' She gave a backward glance: there was pity in her face. But he was already making his way through the moonlit veil of colour shimmering from the north rose window that glorified the Virgin Mary with the child Jesus on her knee. Perhaps, Aelis thought, the surrounding pear-shaped droplets of multi-coloured glass represented the twelve apostles? Their glow might protect Blackstone, but she felt certain that the dove of peace that appeared to flutter within the glass would never bless the Englishman.

CHAPTER FORTY-ONE

The rolling clouds felt as though they touched the top of the city's walls. Men swore the darkness they brought was a portent of ill tidings and when they smothered Notre-Dame some said that God had abandoned them. The English horde had melted away days before but they lurked somewhere like the plague. Now a handful of Englishmen, no more than a hundred, waited beyond the north gate and at their head was the man who had sworn to slay their king. Rumour spread that he was there to challenge the Dauphin to mortal combat and it was only when town criers had gone from square to square declaring a truce had been agreed with the English King that the mood of despair changed to one of hope and joy. No longer would the city dwellers have to eke out their food; no longer would wine be so expensive that a man could not share it with a friend. Fear had held them in its grip for too long despite their certainty that they would resist – and prevail – if the English stormed the city. The scar-faced Englishman who waited at the Porte Saint-Denis for escort through the city was an envoy of the English King. He had been summoned by the Dauphin. And the Dauphin had been obeyed. Power was back in the hands of the French. Or so they were told.

Blackstone and his men had travelled back across the plain still scattered with the dead. The fallen men's clothing had been stripped by scavenging villagers and their flesh by crows and beasts. The charnel house was no different from any battlefield except this time the violence had been inflicted by the Almighty.

'The King has sent us into the heart of our enemy,' Blackstone had told Henry. 'We do not know why. Perhaps it is to inflict humiliation onto us.'

'Or kill us,' said Henry.

'Have you been speaking to Sir Gilbert?'

'No, Father. But they are your sworn enemy and you theirs. It would make sense for them to claim you as a prize of war. But I know you will not let that happen.'

Blackstone didn't know whether to be impressed by the boy's logic or fearful that he did not comprehend how dangerous it would be inside the city walls.

'Mother told me how you once rescued her in Paris, and that you fooled the sentries at the gates by telling them that you were a mason working on the walls,' said Henry.

'That's right. We were running for our lives.'

'She said that you cut your initials into one of the blocks that went into the new ramparts they were building.'

'I did.'

'Do you think we will be able to see it?' said Henry, his air of excitement plain to see.

'Son, I will be happy if we ride in and out of Paris without catching a chill in our bones let alone an arrow in our backs. Stay alert at all times. Our lives may depend on it.'

They waited in front of the great gates. Somewhere beyond the walls they heard the sound of clattering horse hooves.

'You think they'll attack us?' said John Jacob. 'If them gates open and French men-at-arms come at us we don't have much defence out here.' He turned in the saddle to look back to where Will Longdon and Jack Halfpenny stood with their archers a hundred paces to the rear. 'Even with Jack and Will at the ready.'

'There'll be no killing today, John. This is the King's business we're on.' Blackstone smiled. 'Still, no harm in having archers at the ready. Just in case.'

The gates opened and the royal captain of the guard, de Chauliac, rode out ahead of his men. Forty of them flanked the

Grand'Rue behind him that reached down through the throat of Paris.

'Sir Thomas Blackstone?' said the captain.

Killbere muttered his remarks aside. 'Well, they look very pretty, Thomas. I'll wager the only conflict those clean surcoats have seen is at the hands of a laundrywoman.'

Blackstone's men had ridden hard through the muddy fields the past three days and their splattered horses and clothing made them resemble vagabond brigands. Unshaven and dirty, hair matted with sweat, mail coifs pulled back from bare heads, they looked like the bunch of fearsome men they were. Which was what Blackstone had intended.

'I am,' Blackstone answered the captain.

De Chauliac's eyes gleamed for a moment. He had witnessed the fight against the sixty French knights from the walls. He'd felt a sense of relief he had not been chosen to go out against this murderous-looking knight. Respect, though, was due.

'Sir Thomas, I am Bernard de Chauliac, captain of the royal guard.' He bowed his head. 'We are sent to escort you and your son.' He hesitated and glanced at Killbere and John Jacob and the two huge bearded men who loomed behind them on horseback. 'You and the boy alone. As agreed.'

Blackstone nodded at the captain and spoke quietly to Killbere. 'Camp well away from these gates. Find a place in the forest so you can watch the road. There's a leper colony behind us. Choose your ground well in case the Dauphin betrays us and sends men for you. They won't venture into the place of lepers so you can trap them on the road.'

'If they cross us, Thomas, we will wage war on them with or without our King. I hope that pagan goddess of yours is wide awake.'

Blackstone eased the bastard horse forward with Henry a couple of strides behind so that the belligerent beast would not turn its head and snap at the lesser horse next to it. Bareheaded, Blackstone entered the city and saw the gathered crowds who thronged the great boulevard. For once he was glad of having French troops near to him, for without the royal guard he and Henry would have been torn from the saddle and beaten to death. As it was the crowd vented their hatred for him by yelling abuse and shaking fists. None dared hurl missiles or weapons when the guard rode escort but it was plain to see that the Dauphin had ordered them to ride along the length of the Grand'Rue, through the heart of Paris, so that Blackstone would have to endure the population's abuse.

'Do not meet their eyes, Henry,' said Blackstone. A mob could form quickly and if anyone did not fear the royal captain's sword then there was always the chance of the Dauphin's command of safe passage being ignored. Blackstone kept his own eyes straight ahead. A sudden surge would swamp them but the swaying crowds did not encroach onto the wide boulevard. What was it that held them back, other than the passing escorts? He turned and looked at the faces nearest him. Eyes flared back, mouths baring blackened teeth as they shouted. And then he saw the reason why. As his gaze fell on them their courage failed. Their eyes lowered. Fear of Blackstone controlled the mob.

'There,' said Blackstone. 'That's Les Halles. It's the city graveyard. I found your mother there when we were being hunted. After I chiselled my initials in their new wall we escaped past soldiers through a breach.' He glanced at the boy who kept his back straight and shoulders square. 'This place must hold no fear for you, Henry. Your mother ran at my side. She was a woman of great courage.'

Henry Blackstone glanced at his father. The baying crowd frightened him, but he nodded.

'Let them howl,' said Blackstone. 'They cannot harm us. They have every right to hate me. I killed many of their countrymen.'

Simon Bucy stood with the Dauphin watching from one of the high windows that showed the Grand'Rue's straight line from the palace's bridge across the river to the north wall. It was thronged with bystanders whose roar could be heard even from that distance. Bucy's mouth salivated. The Englishman was getting closer. Part of Bucy wished the crowd would disobey and tear him apart but his cold-hearted and rational side relished the fact that it was he who would soon send Blackstone to certain death. He felt aggrieved that he could not decide which option was the most satisfying. He closed his eyes. The Dauphin's ceaseless pacing had begun to wear on his nerves. If Bucy felt conflicted about Blackstone's fate then the Dauphin was positively racked with nerves at the prospect of meeting Blackstone face-to-face. Peace was at hand but that did not mean that retribution could not be meted out to a blood enemy.

'Sire,' said Bucy. 'Would you prefer that I deal with this matter alone?' He spoke with considered calmness, although he did not relish facing the Englishman either. Did Blackstone know that it was he who had unleashed the Savage Priest on him and his family years before? He must know. He must, he told himself.

The Dauphin stopped and thought about the offer and then shook his head. He had to face Blackstone. It was a matter of honour – before he sent the Englishman to his death.

'We are not afraid of one man, no matter how violent his anger towards us and our father. And Edward has our word that he will not be harmed.' He paused. 'Here, that is. We must extend sanctuary to him and then we can use his violence to our benefit. It is you who have planned his death, Simon. We have agreed to arrange the means of it, so as to leave ourself as the innocent party. Let him come.'

Bucy kept his eyes on the approaching escort. They clattered across the bridge and between the guards flanking the palace entrance. Blackstone dismounted and a stable-hand from the royal stables ran forward to take his horse's rein but the mottled beast yanked back and kicked out. Two of the escort's horses reared in defence. The stable-hand fell, but Blackstone quickly brought the horse under control and then helped the stunned boy to his feet. Bucy saw the Englishman tip a coin from his purse and hand it to the shaken lad. The captain of the guard said something and pointed towards the royal stables and Blackstone led the big horse forward followed by a boy of about eleven or twelve years of age.

Every step closer dried the spittle in Bucy's mouth.

'He's here,' he told the Dauphin.

There were only about two hundred officials serving the royal household, a corps of royal administrators often there through marriage or patronage, men who could be trusted and controlled. All strove constantly for higher office but the hierarchy in which they served meant that they were dependent on each other for their success. And that gave Bucy almost complete authority over them. He had the ear of the King and, being the dominant member of the Prince Regent's council, influence over the Dauphin. The one thing Bucy was certain of was that there would be no dissent from those officials when he brought their King's enemy into the beating heart of France. A heart that now pounded with anticipation. Simon Bucy had made his plans, but still he felt the fear of impending violence.

He had been raised in lowly circumstances, so far removed from the wealth and influence he now held that it was almost impossible to recall his family's penury. His father had been a humble legal clerk, obliged to work by the half-light of a candle, his eyesight fading, his body hunched in an unheated, windowless room. One day a rat had found its way under the floorboards and its scurrying became so intrusive that Bucy's father laid a trail of breadcrumbs into a box whose lid was propped with a stick. He held his young son behind his desk and, with a finger to his lips, pointed. The rat took the bait and the trap was sprung. Bucy's father leapt forward in victory and battered the helpless rodent to death with a brass candlestick. Bucy remembered that moment only too well. He had vomited from the sight of it and his distaste for physical violence had never left him. The vision of his mild-mannered father relishing the kill reminded him of his own loss of control on the city walls when he saw Blackstone fight. Now he had carefully laid an enticing trap of his own for the Englishman and he prayed his own intemperate desire to see the man dead did not betray him.

The Dauphin sat and waited, his embroidered silk-cushioned chair raised on a dais. Beyond the chamber's ornately carved oak doors lay a long passage of pillared arches, an entrance grand enough to subdue any man's hubris. Footsteps echoed closer and then halted. Bucy glanced back at the Dauphin. He seemed unconcerned about who was about to step into the room. A sword's pommel was struck against the wood. Bucy stood between the Dauphin and the doors as they swung open. The royal captain of the guard and his men flanked a man who stood head and shoulders above them and who stared at Bucy, and then at the Dauphin. The Englishman's presence seemed to fill the room. And what was it in Blackstone's gaze, Bucy tried to determine in those seconds, that created such a tremor of fear in him?

The captain of the guard requested Blackstone relinquish his weapons and the Englishman unbuckled his belt and wrapped it around Wolf Sword's scabbard, which he then handed to the captain. The boy at Blackstone's side followed the knight's example and handed his belt and sword to one of the guards.

Bucy squared his shoulders and set his face. An air of authority was essential. He dragged his eyes away from the hulking, weather-beaten Blackstone and spoke to the captain of the guard. 'The boy stays outside for now. He will be summoned in due course. See that he is seated by a fire for warmth and given whatever food and drink he desires,' he said and, with a glance at Blackstone, added, 'Father and son are our gracious Dauphin's guests.'

Blackstone did not look at Henry and neither did the boy seek any assurance from his father. Blackstone stepped into the chamber accompanied by the captain and half a dozen of his men, who flanked the walls, far enough away not to impinge on the Dauphin's presence but near enough to rush Blackstone if he made any attack against him. The doors closed heavily behind them. Bucy moved to one side, which suggested to Blackstone that he was required to move further towards the Dauphin Charles. He stopped twelve paces from the raised dais. The French Prince and the English knight stared at each other for a moment and then Blackstone dipped his head. Bucy noticed the Dauphin's eyebrows rise. Surprise that Blackstone had not knelt before him or, Bucy wondered, because the Englishman had at least dipped his head in respect? After a few moments during which the Dauphin and Blackstone studied each other, Blackstone broke the silence and the protocol of waiting for the royal prince to speak first.

'You have changed, my lord, since I last saw you at Rouen. Then you were a boy.'

The Dauphin's mouth opened and closed with uncertainty, a frown furrowing his brow. 'Rouen?'

'Back in '56. You sat with Jean de Harcourt and the Norman lords before your father burst into the room and accused de Harcourt, my sworn and loyal friend, of treason and then had him butchered.'

The memory of the event caused the Dauphin to lurch in his seat. His body bent forward, arm outstretched. 'You were there?'

'In the gallery. I had gone to try and warn him, but a traitor got there before me and betrayed them all. I heard you, my lord, plead with your father not to harm your guests.'

'And when de Harcourt was beheaded –'

'Butchered,' Blackstone repeated.

The Dauphin allowed the impertinence. '– that was when you swore vengeance and tried to kill our father at Poitiers.'

'I was within five strides and a sword stroke.'

These recollections of the past upset the Dauphin. He stood but kept distance between himself and Blackstone. 'And I was in the wave that attacked you before I was withdrawn from the field. We saw you defending that gap in the hedgerow. That was a day that changed our world.'

'And mine,' Blackstone acknowledged.

The Dauphin returned to his chair. 'There will always be bad blood between us, Sir Thomas.'

Blackstone glanced at Bucy, who held his robes close to his chest, gripping the material for comfort. An obvious sign of anxiety and most probably guilt. 'Especially because your father set the Savage Priest on me and my family,' he replied.

The Dauphin nodded. 'He was a vile creature who was at my shoulder at Poitiers, charged with protecting me... and killing you.'

Blackstone smiled. 'His remains hang in a mountain pass. And the corpses of those sent recently to kill my Prince disguised as Englishmen lie in an open field as carrion. Another vile act of dishonour.'

The Dauphin lowered his head. Blackstone's taunt had struck home.

'Why am I here?' Blackstone demanded.

Simon Bucy took an involuntary step forward to chastise Blackstone. 'You will be told in good time,' he said.

'Who are you?' said Blackstone, setting Bucy back on his heels. 'Was it you who advised your King to set the Savage Priest on me? And you who advised your Prince to send men dressed as Englishmen into our ranks?'

Bucy's face drained of colour, but he kept his air of authority intact. 'I am your enemy as you are an enemy to France. I would do anything to protect my King, my Prince and my country.'

'And your fine clothes and status, I'll wager,' said Blackstone.

'Enough,' said the Dauphin. 'It was never our intention to cause your Prince harm by sending those men.' He glanced at Bucy. 'No matter how ill advised the act might have been.'

'My lord,' said Blackstone. 'You have me and my son at your mercy just as my King has the crown of France at his.'

'We are not defeated,' snapped the Dauphin. 'It is your King who has agreed to the truce and a treaty.'

'He could still destroy Paris and take what he wants,' Blackstone said, knowing this action would never be taken, but happy to antagonize French royalty and pride. 'He is a great and pious king, my lord, but if you harm my son, no matter what happens to me, he will bring his wrath down upon you.'

The Dauphin blew his nose and dabbed his eyes. Was it from anger or the chill that crept up from the Seine? Blackstone wondered.

'We have brought you here...' The Dauphin's voice trailed away, and it was only after he glanced at Bucy that he managed to finish the sentence. '... to thank you.'

It was Blackstone's turn to feel the blow of incomprehension. And the Dauphin saw it.

'Yes, your enemy thanks you. When France endured the Jacquerie uprising you fought to save the women and children at Meaux. Our father's family and our own wife and infant were there and your actions saved them. You have our thanks.'

Blackstone sensed the Dauphin's gratitude was genuine. 'My lord, it was not only my actions.'

'We know,' said the Dauphin, 'but there is more than our gratitude that needs to be offered.' The Dauphin nodded at Bucy, who in turn gestured to a servant who stood next to a side door of the chamber. The servant opened it and another entered carrying a small ornate cushioned chair. He placed it close to the Dauphin and then went out of the same door. No sooner had he left the chamber than a girl that Blackstone took to be about ten or eleven years old came in, followed by two ladies-in-waiting. The quality of her clothing and the fact that she sat on the chair provided meant she was of the royal household.

'Our sister, Princess Isabelle. You escorted her to safety from Meaux after the fighting.'

'I did,' said Blackstone, remembering the brief glimpse he had had of her after the siege, the memory also serving to remind him of the circumstances of his wife and daughter's death. The child stared at him without any sign of fear and then turned to the Dauphin. Her voice was gentle and barely raised above a whisper, so Blackstone could not hear what she said. The Dauphin smiled and nodded and addressed Blackstone.

'She asks where her *petit chevalier* is.' Without waiting for Blackstone to comprehend the Dauphin raised a hand and the chamber's doors opened again. After a moment Henry Blackstone was brought into their presence. Blackstone caught his son's glance as he quickly bowed before the Dauphin and then, deliberately, to the Princess, who smiled in recognition.

'My little knight,' she said.

'Highness,' said Henry. 'I am pleased to see that you look well.'

Blackstone struggled to keep the look of a fool from his face.

'And I have not forgotten your kindness,' said the Princess. 'You served me well.'

The Dauphin raised a finger to his lips to silence her. His kindly smile soothed the girl's urge to say more.

'Boy,' said the Dauphin and gestured Henry to him. He stepped forward as the Dauphin raised a hand to a servant who stood against the wall. 'Our sister tells me that when you were at Meaux you expressed a love of reading.'

'Yes, sire,' said Henry.

'Good. To read creates a greater understanding of the world. I have a library containing many books and manuscripts here.'

The servant approached carrying something wrapped in a purple velvet cloth. He unwrapped a book which he presented to Henry.

'It is a book of chivalry,' said the Dauphin with a glance across to Blackstone. 'And honour.'

'Thank you, highness,' said Henry and stepped back to stand at his father's side.

'Sir Thomas, you serve your King loyally,' said the Dauphin.

'My sword is his,' said Blackstone.

'Then now is the time for you... and your sword... to serve him still. Your King continues to demand a great deal from us to release our father from captivity in England. We are soon to sign a treaty but the amount required is... exorbitant. To secure the three million gold écus for his release a marriage has been arranged between Isabelle and the Visconti of Milan's son, Gian Galeazzo. This marriage confers great prestige on the Visconti and serves to secure the payment for your King.'

'I don't see how this involves me, or my son,' said Blackstone.

'It is our wish that you and your men escort our beloved sister to Milan.'

'Milan?' Blackstone said. 'My enemy? I defended Florence against them. I have killed their captains. They would like nothing better than to have me fall into their hands.' He looked at Bucy, who remained inscrutable. 'A plan to rid yourself of your sworn enemy without dirtying your hands and keeping the peace treaty intact with my King.'

Bucy stepped closer. 'Sir Thomas, the Prince Regent's gratitude to you is an honest expression made in good faith. His sister, when she was told of the arranged marriage, asked if her *petit chevalier* might accompany her. It seems that your son served her well at Meaux.'

'I will not take either of us into that vipers' nest,' said Blackstone.

Bucy played his part well. He glanced with regret at the Dauphin, who nodded his understanding. Would the nose-dripping youth play his role with equal skill? he wondered. The Dauphin raised a hand, as if to stop Bucy from saying anything further.

'We understand, Sir Thomas. But your reputation is such that if you agreed we feel that our sister's safety would be guaranteed. And that in turn would secure your King's ransom.' He dabbed his nose with the lace handkerchief, then chose his words carefully. This, Bucy knew, was the bait that had to be dangled perfectly.

'We are aware,' said the Dauphin with what seemed to be genuine regret, 'that when you escorted our sister into safekeeping from Meaux your absence was used by an assassin to murder your wife and child.'

No matter how often Blackstone had tried to banish the image of his butchered daughter and wife, it lurked in his tortured memory. Any word spoken of Christiana and Agnes scraped the wound like a blunt knife blade and made the picture rear again like a harpy.

'And I put an arrow through him, and our horses trampled him into the dirt. He screamed as every bone broke,' said Blackstone.

The Dauphin nodded. 'We understand such grief and desire for vengeance. And in gratitude for your service to our family and your saving the life of this child, and many others, we wish you to have the information that has come into our possession. Those who sent the assassin are in the court of the Visconti.'

Bucy was barely able to suppress a smile of success.

The rat trap was sprung.

PART FOUR

THE SCENT OF BLOOD

CHAPTER FORTY-TWO

Blackstone told Killbere and the others little of the mission he had been charged with – to Killbere's frustration – so the journey back to Chartres was full of speculation and anticipation among the men. Blackstone's own thoughts had grappled with everything the Dauphin and Bucy had told him. The insistence that he take Henry to Milan to accompany the Princess flagged up a warning. They could both be killed once they were in the grip of the Visconti. To slay the father and not the son would risk leaving a desire for revenge when Henry became old enough to inflict it. Blackstone had Henry brought forward to the front of the column as they neared the English camp.

'When we were at Meaux you told me that you had nothing to do with the royal family and now, years later, you and the Princess are friends and you're her *petit chevalier*. How much time *did* you spend with her?'

'I worked with the other pages and took water to the women and children but one day I was sent to the royal chambers and she spoke to me.'

'Why? You were little more than a servant to her.'

'You suspect something, Father?'

'I suspect everything that the French do and say. They lay a trap for us, boy. I need to see why they are using you as part of it.'

Henry shook his head. 'I don't know. She spent a lot of time on her own and one day she asked me if I could speak and read Latin because she was at her studies and I helped her.'

'Then why didn't you tell me that?'

'It was only on two occasions that she asked me. Maybe three. I think.'

'You think?'

'I don't remember, Father.'

'Then why does she call you her little knight?'

'She was frightened, and one day when I took the water to their rooms I could see she had been crying because she was so scared of the Jacques. I told her that I wouldn't let anything happen to her.'

'And you didn't think this was important enough to tell me when I asked you at the time?'

'No, Father.'

Blackstone thought on it for a while. The reason behind the French demand that Henry go with them was probably that innocent and nothing more should be read into it. Perhaps a young princess simply needed reassurance. However, it did land them both in the Visconti's grasp. 'All right, go back to John Jacob.'

'Is it true that the Visconti sent the killer?' said Henry.

'I don't know. But we will find out,' Blackstone told him, his tone gentle, because the boy had shown no sign of anger at the thought of those responsible for murdering his mother and sister. 'We'll find out,' he said again by way of reassurance.

The mud slurped beneath Blackstone's boots as he made his way through the camp towards the cathedral at Chartres. When he had returned from Paris he had reported to the King and the Prince of Wales what was expected of him and why he had been summoned by the Dauphin. King Edward had said little and asked that he meet with Father Torellini the next morning. But first he sought out Aelis.

She was putting the small glass bottles into her satchel and as she raised one to eye level to check the contents she saw Blackstone approaching.

'Sir Thomas, you have returned safely, I see,' she said.

'As you knew I would,' he answered.

'Nothing is certain,' said Aelis. She settled the bottles carefully and then fastened the satchel's straps.

'Magic potions?' said Blackstone. 'More alchemy to distort a man's mind?'

'Think of it what you will. Some of them ease pain, others heal and still others help a man slip away into the darkness when the angels abandon him.'

'Are you abandoned?' he said. 'You have the sight and I wonder if it's a curse? Perhaps from the dark angels.'

'Or a blessing from God,' she said calmly.

'How did you know? About Henry and me?'

'It is not something I understand. It is given to me.'

'Do you see anything else? Now? The future? What will happen to you?'

'I am in the Prince's hands now. His protection will end when the treaty is signed. He will go back to England and I will go from town to town and offer my skills to those who want them.'

'Or get burned as a witch,' he said.

'That's not how I will die,' she answered, and the way she said it made Blackstone sense she knew the truth of how her own life would end.

'Then you are abandoned,' he said.

'I am.'

'And I see the future more clearly than you,' said Blackstone. 'You were right: there are mountains to be crossed and danger to be faced. You are going to come with me.'

She slung the heavy satchel over her shoulder and smiled at him. 'I know,' she said.

Her words lingered in his mind as he stepped into the cathedral. The rainbow light streamed from the windows and he saw stretcher-bearers carry the wounded to lie in their glow. Speckled colours flickered across the men as a dozen monks went among them and ensured each man was made comfortable. Father Torellini stood to one side observing the monks' activity. He saw Blackstone emerge from the shadowed pillars across the nave.

'Thomas, walk with me. We have much to discuss,' said the Italian priest when Blackstone reached him.

'What's this?' Blackstone asked, looking at the wounded men.

'Healing light,' said Torellini. 'This is a sacred place of pilgrimage and it is believed that the light from the stained glass holds magical properties. The blue glass is rare, Thomas, it is the Lord's colour. Artisans grind lapis lazuli, which only comes from Afghanistan, and use it in the glass. It is more valuable than gold.' He glanced up at Blackstone. 'Perhaps you should bathe in the light and let it heal the pain that you carry in your heart.'

'We all bear scars, Father. Mine are no deeper than those of other men.'

Torellini smiled and shrugged. 'So you say. I think not. I wonder why we have been brought to this place, and why the King was led here. Look at the colours that decorate these walls. These pigments are there for a reason; those who built this place were trying to bring a vision of heaven to this squalid world. The windows unfold stories for the illiterate so that they understand more of the richness of the angels and Our Lord.'

'I didn't come here for a lesson in architecture or the working of the scriptures,' said Blackstone, barely able to keep the irritation from his voice.

'You would deny even the beauty of God's comfort to those desperate for it?'

'A stonemason's chisel and men's sweat built this place. Nothing more. There's no religious magic to be had from men's backbreaking labour. How am I to get to the Visconti and do what I must?'

'Which of the Visconti will you kill?' Torellini answered. 'Galeazzo or Bernabò? They are the Lords of Milan. Which of them sent the assassin to inflict the horror on you? There is no knowing.'

'I will kill both of them if I have to.'

'And die trying.'

'The French have given me the information about them so they may rid themselves of me. Do you expect me not to go?'

312

'It is a condition of the peace talks. The King knows what's being asked of you.'

'Then is it true? Did the Visconti send the assassin?'

They reached a side chapel and Torellini sat on a bench gazing at the gold cross on the altar before them.

'It is so rumoured,' he admitted, persuaded by the holy icon to admit what he knew.

'Father, I'm about to take my men into the den of the beast. Rumour?'

'Listen to me, Thomas. I have spies and informants in the court at Milan. It is hearsay, no more than that. Yes, the order came from Milan, but from whom we cannot say. You were an enemy and you were brought down, which is exactly what they wanted. They killed Christiana and Agnes and you were cast into the pit of drunkenness and despair.'

'But I am back.'

Torellini nodded. 'And they know it. So what do we make of it all?'

'I don't know. That's why I need you to tell me, and if you can't then I need you to find out.'

The Italian priest opened the palms of his hands in a gesture of acceptance. 'And so we must discover the truth. The English King desires peace and a ransom. The first cannot be achieved without the second. Galeazzo, the Lord of Milan, pays the ransom and buys the Princess to marry his son. The Visconti gain immediate prestige and an alignment with France that will protect disputed territories. And a bonus. The opportunity to have the man who killed their assassin in their hands. Moreover, now the treaty with France is to be signed, you are still a danger. You still hold a contract with Florence against them. Another reason for them to try to kill you. But who? Galeazzo or his brother Bernabò? Both? Or someone who serves them? Someone who was rewarded by them for sending a killer after you who murdered your family? Whom did he serve, this man who controlled the assassin? The clever Visconti or the mad one?'

Blackstone looked away. The puzzle could not be answered. After a few moments he turned to the older man who had shadowed his life since the day he lay a whisper away from death at Crécy. 'By the time I get to Milan, I have to know who it was, Father.'

Torellini sighed and his chin settled on his chest for a moment. 'Both brothers are formidable. They are men of strong passions and violent character. Galeazzo is the greater statesman. He extends his power and influence by negotiation and diplomacy, although you should have no doubt of his ability to inflict violence; however, he favours the English. One day he will reach out to our own King for alliances. Bernabò is less predictable. He is physically strong, as tall and broad as you. He leads his men in battle. He's fearful of neither man nor God. He rejects the Pope where his brother courts him. You can see how, between them, they rule. Bernabò's ruthlessness is feared but respected. He is not simply a violent thug, Thomas. He is educated and that, combined with ruthlessness and a volatile temper, makes him the more dangerous. His punishments are savage, but the citizens of Milan are grateful. Their streets are free from crime; officials do not take bribes. You will find no one there who would cross the Visconti to offer you refuge or help should the need arise. As to who paid the killer of your wife and daughter: I will send word to those who spy for me in Milan to find the answer, but if I cannot discover it in time then it is more than likely that you and your son will die there.'

'No, I won't take Henry into Milan. Once we have escorted the Princess across the Alps I will send him to Florence and place him in your care. I killed the assassin who murdered Christiana and Agnes, and now I will kill the one who sent him.'

'If he can be found, Thomas,' said the priest. 'And if he is found then you must declare vendetta. It might give you a chance. No city-state in Italy will deny the legitimacy of it: their law recognizes and sanctions private justice.'

'I'll burn Milan to the ground if I have to. Not even God will save the man I aim to kill,' said Blackstone.

He took his leave of the priest and walked through the cathedral, stepping across the glittering veil of light cast down from one of the windows. He stood for a moment and raised his face to the healing beams, letting himself bathe in the brightness. Nothing happened. The pain he bore would be eased only by vengeance.

CHAPTER FORTY-THREE

Simon Bucy gathered the ermine-collared cloak around his neck. Blackstone had agreed to go to Milan and the Visconti were not even aware of the prize being laid at their city gates. He and the Dauphin had not dared to let the information reach the Visconti: to have told them could have jeopardized Isabelle's safe arrival. What if the mad bastard Bernabò threw caution to the wind and ambushed the Princess's retinue in order to kill Blackstone? What chance then of the French King returning home? No, better to deny themselves the satisfaction of telling the Lords of Milan in order to secure the child's safe passage and the ransom. He allowed himself a moment of self-congratulation. In no small way, he believed, he had been the saviour of France. Within days the arrangements for the signing of the treaty had been decided and he was to attend as representative of the Dauphin and Jean le Bon, King of France. It was momentous. Of course there were others who would preen themselves in the same mirror of success: the Count of Tancarville had been released as a hostage from England and he would think himself more important because he was a soldier who had accompanied the King into imprisonment. But he could be managed with judicious flattery. The irritating and at times insufferable French Chancellor, Jean de Dormans, would no doubt soon whisper in Bucy's ear that it was he who had finally secured the terms of agreement. Bucy mentally chastised himself for the foul language that crept from his thoughts onto his tongue. When the King came home he would know whom to reward. Bucy had held the Dauphin in check, had arranged the meeting between the Prince Regent and his blood enemy; had prepared him, tutoring him how to behave and respond when facing the scar-faced Englishman. And he had banished Blackstone from the kingdom by throwing him poisoned bait. Sending him right into the jaws of that madman Bernabò Visconti.

'My lord?' said a servant as Bucy cast a final eye over his attire and adjusted his mink hat. 'It is time.'

Bucy nodded and waved the servant away. He had eaten a good breakfast, his clothing was appropriate for the occasion and his mood could not be better. The great noblemen and knights who were close to the King of England would represent the English monarch: the Duke of Lancaster; the Earls of Northampton, Warwick and Suffolk; Cobham, Burghesh, Walter Mauny. Legends on the field of battle. They would see themselves as the victors. Let them delude themselves. The ransom would soon be paid and France would have her King returned. And Blackstone would soon be dead.

It was, at last, a day to bask in the warmth of his triumph.

The preparations for the royal journey south took many weeks, a period that gave Blackstone and his men time to rest and recruit. King Edward had given him and his captains the pick of men to replace those who had died on the campaign. It had been a hard-fought selection for those who desired to ride with him. Hard fought because he and his captains had made them face each other in hand-to-hand contest and chose only those who withstood the ordeal, but now Blackstone had a hundred men at his back.

The royal litter swayed gently between the two big pack horses, chosen for their strength and endurance. At least, Blackstone thought, the litter was not as cumbersome or as slow as a carriage. The Princess's servants rode behind the litter, ready to administer to the child's needs. The disparity between them was an act of God. When Henry was her age he had been fighting for his life at his mother's side. And yet there the boy was, at the Princess's request, riding alongside the litter. If a King and his offspring were divine, chosen by the will of God, then what use did God have for the rest of them? To serve, was the answer his thoughts gave him. To serve and die if necessary. They had a hundred leagues to travel and every step along the way could pose danger, Torellini had warned him. But from whom? The Visconti wanted the child-bride; the routiers who roamed the hills would not dare snatch the King of France's daughter. It made no sense to Blackstone. The Visconti wanted their revenge on him for killing their assassin as much as he did on them for sending the killer.

'What?' said Killbere at his side.

Blackstone looked quizzically at him.

'You were muttering and sighing like a drunkard,' said Killbere. 'Is the boredom driving you to holding private conversations with yourself? Merciful God, this is a journey we should have refused. We've been riding for ten days. Damned near three hundred miles of arse-aching monotony. We should have taken ourselves off on a crusade or gone back to Florence to fight the Visconti. They won't be going anywhere. Why do we wet-nurse this child?'

'It gets us into Milan under Edward and John's protection.'

'Aye, and much good that will do us,' answered Killbere. 'If your Italian priest doesn't get the information to us in time we will be drawn and quartered and parts of us seeing Milan the other bits won't.'

Blackstone grinned. 'They would need more than hardened steel to separate your stubborn head from your body.'

'Thomas, don't jest with me. I'm serious. We have no say in any of this. The route is not ours. We play into others' hands. They can do with us what they will. This handful of French troops who ride with us wouldn't put fear into a gang of street urchins. And Amadeus? Merciful Mother of God, he's no friend of yours. He's got noblemen with knights and men-at-arms at his beck and call. Who's to say he won't surround us once we get down to Chambéry? He's the Visconti's brother-in-law by marriage,' said Killbere, pointing towards the litter, 'and uncle to the Visconti's brat that she's going to marry. He's got hundreds of cavalry under his command and do you see one of them here? No. Not one. It's a pig's arse, Thomas. And it smells like one.'

Blackstone knew that Killbere had every right to be wary. Amadeus, the Count of Savoy, was one of the transalpine princes. The twenty-six-year-old was the sworn enemy of the Marquis de Montferrat whose territory lay across the Alps and who was allied to Florence; and Montferrat and Florence were bitter enemies of the Visconti of Milan. Montferrat was also Blackstone's ally and held the mountain pass where Blackstone had slain the Savage Priest years before. But the route through the mountains that Blackstone and his men knew well and which took them into the safety of Montferrat's territory was denied them. Instead the Princess and her escort of French troops and Blackstone's men would travel south to the city of Chambéry, held by Amadeus, and then through the pass at Mont Cenis before the winter snows.

'He formed an alliance with the Visconti,' said Blackstone. 'The Pope wanted him to side with him. But the treaty between the Lords of Milan and the Count strengthens the territories they each hold. And it keeps Montferrat in check.'

'And leaves us sticking out like a whore's nipple on a winter's day,' said Killbere. 'Vengeance is one thing, Thomas, but suicide is another. These men follow you in good faith and affection. You're their sworn lord. They won't desert you because you've a mind to inflict misery and death on those who sent an assassin to tear your heart apart.' Killbere drew breath and spat. 'They'll die for you. But it needs to be a fight worth fighting. That's all I'm saying.'

'Much more and we'll have you giving morning prayers. You've become a preacher in your old age, Gilbert.'

'Dammit, Thomas. I'll not be mocked. When men die their blood is on your hands.'

Blackstone knew Killbere was right and he decided that when the time came he would give all his men the option of going into Milan or staying outside the walls. Before he could answer Killbere a shout went up.

'Riders!' yelled a voice from the front. Blackstone drew the column to a halt and watched as a troop of horsemen, a hundred or more, pennons fluttering, emerged from the forests that smothered the rolling foothills in the near distance. Killbere signalled Perinne and the outriders to rejoin Blackstone. By the time they had reached Blackstone the approaching knights and men-at-arms had divided and formed two columns. The knight who led them wore a green silk tabard over his breastplate and two ostrich feathers dyed the same colour were attached to his helm. His horse's caparison was embroidered with green patterns.

'They flank us, Sir Thomas,' said John Jacob. 'Though the way they're dressed they look as though they're going to a tournament.'

Will Longdon had already ordered the archers into extended line and Gaillard and Meulon had gone left and right with their men behind Blackstone. What had appeared to be a lethargic moving column only minutes before was now a spearhead of fighting men. Only the French troops remained static and readied themselves for a charge. No wonder they kept losing battles, Blackstone thought fleetingly.

'Come on, John, let's see what this popinjay wants,' said Blackstone and spurred the bastard horse forward.

Killbere stayed at the head of Blackstone's men, sword drawn and ready.

Blackstone reined in a dozen paces from the extravagantly dressed knight. His visor was open and Blackstone saw that the man was somewhere in his twenties.

'You are Sir Thomas Blackstone,' said the knight cheerfully. 'Wonderful! I am honoured to meet you. I recognize your coat of arms and its challenge: *Défiant à la mort*. And from what I have heard you have defied death on many occasions.'

Blackstone remained stony silent, giving the ebullient man no cause to think him friendly or agreeable. Then: 'You have a hundred men at your back. If you've a mind to fight my archers will have you dead where you stand and my men-at-arms will finish the job. You're blocking the road.'

Blackstone's curt response punctured the flamboyant knight's enthusiasm and his demeanour became more solemn.

'Ah, yes, I can see how so many heavily armed men would cause you to be wary, especially with such a precious cargo,' he said.

'Your time runs short,' said Blackstone. 'My archers use me as their mark and you and your men as targets. State your intent.'

'Everything I have heard about you is true. You are rude, ill mannered and spoiling for a fight.' He laughed. 'All the qualities one needs to escort my sister-in-law. I am Count Amadeus of Savoy and I thought the child should be greeted with the honour she deserved.'

Blackstone thought he heard John Jacob curse under his breath at their bad luck – they had threatened a nobleman – but he chose to ignore it. 'My lord,' said Blackstone and bowed his head. 'You'll forgive my ignorance and ill manners but I am sworn to protect Princess Isabelle and anyone who approaches poses a threat.'

'And it would be a foolish man who sought to cause her harm while she is under your protection. I am here to personally escort you into Chambéry where you are to be made welcome and to dine at my table and share with me stories of your exploits. I am keen to be entertained, Sir Thomas.'

'I would be honoured, my lord,' said Blackstone with as much enthusiasm as he could muster, hoping that his despair at the thought of being in the Count's company would not be noticed. He turned his horse. He winced when he caught John Jacob's gaze. Insulting and challenging a transalpine prince was a poor start.

321

CHAPTER FORTY-FOUR

They were within half a day's ride of Chambéry when they saw black smoke mushrooming in the distance.

'Is there fighting here?' said Blackstone.

The plumed Count shook his head sombrely. 'No, Sir Thomas, we have had an outbreak of the pestilence. It is another reason why I chose to ride out and meet you: to ensure you did not stumble into the diseased villages. The plague is one enemy that could strike you silently. We burn every place that has been stricken.'

Thought of the death sweeping through the countryside made Blackstone fearful. 'And in the city?'

'So far it has not reached us. And I have banned from entering anyone who shows signs of fever. The sentries at the city gates check everyone. The markets are closed until the pestilence moves on.' He glanced at Blackstone. 'The danger will not end here, Sir Thomas. It is across the Alps in Lombardy as well. We will offer our prayers for you and the Princess.'

Bad enough, Blackstone thought, that there were those who wished to see him butchered, now the great pestilence had cast its barbed net across the land waiting to snare unsuspecting travellers. No matter how forewarned they were, even a chance encounter with anyone infected would inflict an excruciating death. He instinctively turned in the saddle and looked back to where Aelis rode with the captains. She returned his gaze without expression. Just how much did she see of the future? he wondered.

He watched the smoke struggling to rise in the cold mountain air and sensed the stench of burning flesh it would carry. He pressed Arianrhod to his lips and, as the silver goddess caught the light, he saw Count Amadeus glance his way.

'Perhaps, Sir Thomas, you will need more prayers than most.'

The pale stone castle loomed over the roofs of the town that spread out from beneath its walls. Killbere pushed open the shuttered window and looked down the sheer walls of cut stone. There were no places for a grappling iron to find purchase and no hand- or foothold. He had a sheet wrapped around him that absorbed the water from his body. A brazier burned in one corner adding its heat to the room, already heavy with steam from the two large wooden bathtubs.

'This place is impossible to escape from, Thomas. Look how high we are. Almost as high as the damned mountains.'

Blackstone luxuriated in the hot water. Count Amadeus had been extravagant in his hospitality. And that raised immediate suspicion. 'He won't cause us harm but his welcome is more generous than expected. He wants something, but I don't know what.'

'Listen, he's a strange one, and riding around like a parrot on a horse, all feathered and draped in silk over armour. Makes me think he's a bit touched.'

'He told me it's what he wears for tournaments and he wanted to greet the Princess in all his finery.'

Killbere unwrapped the sheet and stood naked in front of the brazier. His body was as scarred as Blackstone's; some of the wounds were deep and the skin puckered. He scratched his balls as he warmed them. 'One thing it tells us is that a man who dresses like that is a good enough fighter to put an end to anyone who mocks him for it. We must be careful when we go to this dinner tonight. It isolates us. I wish we could have stayed with the men.'

Blackstone's captains and John Jacob had been billeted next to the stables, the French troops separated from them by inner curtain walls, effectively reducing his fighting force. Meulon and Gaillard would have already seen where they could make a stand if cornered by a duplicitous Amadeus, and Will Longdon and Jack Halfpenny would, by now, have decided how best to defend the men-at-arms if an assault came. Fighting at Blackstone's side over the years gave every man the knowledge and instinct to survive. They would be ready.

'He's aligned with the Visconti: he won't deny them the pleasure of having me in their clutches. We're safe enough. For now.'

Killbere grunted. His nose wrinkled; he raised an armpit and sniffed. 'There's perfume in the water, Thomas. I swear we have fallen into the hands of a brothel keeper.'

The great hall was decorated with colour-washed walls and tapestries; the fireplace had bundles of stacked kindling the size of a man's body on one side and wood on the other that would be laid across the iron grate. Oil lamps and candles threw their warmth and light into the room as big as any Blackstone remembered from the time he lived at Jean de Harcourt's Norman castle, except this nobleman had richness and comfort rather than unyielding austerity surrounding him. The Count approached them from the far side of the table, which was adorned with silver plate overburdened with meat, bread and fruit tantalizingly within reach of the hungry men.

'No sign of dried fish, thank God,' whispered Killbere.

'Your stomach growls. We are at a nobleman's table,' Blackstone said quietly in admonishment.

'I greet you with an unreserved welcome, my honoured guests. Sit, here and here. Close to me so we may speak without raising our voices across the length of the table,' said Amadeus effusively.

Blackstone and Killbere sat either side of the Count. Servants poured wine and then discreetly stepped away.

'I am in a joyous mood. Not only do I play a part in bringing the Princess into a marriage with the Visconti, an act that has far-reaching consequences for all concerned – a cessation of war, a ransom paid and an alliance between the Lords of Milan and the French – but our beloved lady wife gave birth a few months ago to a son. Our first. After five years of waiting the good Lord finally blessed us.'

'Sir Gilbert and I offer our congratulations, my lord.'

Killbere nodded in agreement.

'My thanks. Now, your men are quartered under cover because even at this time of the year our summer can carry a chill wind from the Alps, and they and your horses are fed. Your son and squire are quartered above the stables with my master of horse, and your woman has been sent to your quarters and bathed with one of my wife's ladies-in-waiting in attendance.'

Blackstone was about to protest that Aelis was not his companion, but the look Killbere shot across the table quietened him. It served no purpose to offer lengthy explanations. The Count raised a hand and the servants stepped forward and laid meat and bread on each of the men's plates. Blackstone remained silent, agreeing that the Count's presumption was best left uncontested. At least he knew where she was and that she had been kept away from the French troops. It took little imagination to see how an incident could escalate. Perhaps this resplendent Lord of Savoy should be credited with anticipating trouble before it began.

'All of which we are grateful for, my lord. We are undeserving of such hospitality.'

The younger man pulled his fingers back through his hair, and as if his hand had swiped away his pleasant expression he suddenly became sombre.

'I have the blood enemy of the French royal house at my table, a man who tried to kill their King. You have been helped in the past by my own enemy the Marquis of Montferrat who controls the pass you used when you fought your way in and out of Italy. I should find it repugnant but we are all cursed at some stage of our lives with an overwhelming desire for justice. I know your story, Sir Thomas. I know what you were and what you have become through your own honour. Alliances are made and lost. Times change. Enemies become friends and brothers become enemies.' He smiled and shrugged as he brought the silver wine goblet to his lips. 'It is what our good Lord determines. Now, enough of my pretence of knowing how God's world works. Let us eat and talk about the great battles seen across this ravaged land.'

For the next few hours they ate and drank but it was Killbere who spoke about how they fought at Crécy and Poitiers with exaggerated gestures that became more animated as more wine was consumed. The young Count was a receptive audience and laughed with gusto as Killbere used the room as his stage. The veteran knight finally finished his performance to applause from Amadeus. Blackstone had made little mention of the times he had faced danger alone, and as the storytelling faded to a satisfied ending it was obvious to him that the Count had not drunk as much as it appeared. Killbere's head settled on his chest as he gave in to fatigue from the day's travel and excess of wine. There was no shame in it and Blackstone reached across and eased the goblet from his hand and then placed his arms on the table and his head to rest on them.

'I have never heard him talk as much,' he said kindly. 'He's a fighting man, my lord, and one of the best I have ever seen. No one I know has as much courage. He has been guardian and friend since I was a boy.'

'Then you are more fortunate than most,' the Count said.

'I am, lord. I have the best men at my back. I could wish for nothing more. Loyalty is everything.'

A servant quickly charged their goblets and was then dismissed from the room. The Count and Blackstone were alone, and Killbere slept. The Count eased his drink aside and leaned forward to Blackstone. 'You and your men are riding to certain death in Milan. And I...' He hesitated. '... do not wish to see it.'

'We fight on opposing sides, my lord,' said Blackstone. 'If I die then it would spare us having to face each other across a muddy field one day. And that is something I would not wish. You've been a gracious host to a common man.'

'I have my own selfish motives. You serve Florence and they fight for the Pope. The Visconti are of the anti-papal league. Two years ago the Pope asked me to align myself with him. I did not. It did not suit me at the time. There are matters of self-interest and territories to be secured and of course I have family connections with the Visconti. It's politics. Agreements that can undermine a man's true self. One day, in a few years, when I have what I want from these alliances, I will take the cross and serve the Pope on a crusade against the Turks and Saracens. That is a worthwhile fight. And if you live then perhaps you and your men might join me.'

'Perhaps, my lord.'

'Very well. This is what I know. Routiers pour down the Rhône valley. Their strength is increased by men released from the English army now that a treaty is signed. There is a possibility they may descend on the Pope at Avignon. I do not send troops to accompany you into Lombardy for good reason. Firstly, the Pope may call for the lords of the region to help him against these mercenaries, and secondly if the Visconti know you are accompanying the Princess then perhaps they will use mercenaries to attack and kill you and I cannot have my men slain trying to protect you.'

'That's if the Visconti know I am part of the escort. The Dauphin gave me information so that I might strike at those who caused my family harm. I seek revenge.'

'Then does it not follow that the Visconti know of it and would wish to strike before you reach Milan?'

'I don't know, lord. It's possible. But they would not risk causing harm to the Princess just to get to me.'

'Let us suppose they lie in wait: I suspect they would use routiers to attack you. No blame can then be laid at the Visconti's door. Your men and some of the royal escort would be killed, the routiers would make a pretence of ransoming the Princess and you would be delivered with your son to the Lords of Milan. Helpless, without any of your men at your back. And as much as I warm to your company, Sir Thomas, I would be unable to help you.' The young Count smiled without malice.

'Where would they attack if such a plan existed?' asked Blackstone.

'They could not do it on the pass, and they would not risk doing it on the other side and have Montferrat come to your aid. So it will be this side of the mountains. I will find out what I can.' He smiled. 'And if either of the Visconti brothers are responsible for your family's deaths and you kill him, then so be it.' He raised the drink to his lips. 'Who knows, it might even be beneficial to my own future.'

The carefree attitude had been brushed aside and a calculating provincial lord exposed. It made no difference to Blackstone. Whatever help he could get to reach the Vipers of Milan he would welcome it.

Amadeus pushed back his chair. 'It will take a few days but I will do what I can to find out more. Until then you stay as my guest. Goodnight, Sir Thomas.'

'Goodnight, my lord.' Blackstone watched the Count of Savoy leave the room; then he reached forward and plucked at the cluster of grapes. He sucked their sweetness to ease the sour taste of the wine left on his tongue. Or was it, he thought, to ease his distaste for the connivance of noblemen?

Killbere lifted his head. 'I thought he'd never leave,' he said, none the worse for the drink. 'I suspected he might blab about something of use to us and would only want you to hear it. Now we know. He's as big a bastard as the next lord only he enjoys himself and laughs a lot more.' He reached for the green glass wine decanter, half covered in leather embossed with the Count's blazon. 'And he is no beggar when it comes to his wine. It's from the best grape.' He grinned at Blackstone. 'I heard what you said about me, Thomas. My heart was warmed by your generous words.'

Blackstone turned for the door. 'If I'd thought you were really asleep I'd have told him the truth,' he lied.

CHAPTER FORTY-FIVE

Blackstone's quarters were welcoming and warm, a far cry from muddy fields and a wet blanket for cover. It could make a man soft having this much comfort, he thought, a faint memory stirring of a home he had once had and the way his wife had been careful to cosset her family. Candlelight flickered and the embers from the fireplace cast their crimson glow. Sheepskins were laid across freshly cut rushes and he could smell their sweetness. He glanced to where Aelis lay asleep on the feather mattress. He had rested on it when the servants had first taken him to the room and decided it was too soft for him and that he would sleep on the floor with his cloak over him and his back to the fire's warmth. Her head rested to one side on the bolster and the bed covering lay across her just above her breasts. The linen sheet crumpled against the rise and fall of her breathing. She obviously slept naked and the image in his mind of her body below the covering stirred desire in him again.

It would serve no purpose to bind himself to the woman; it might make him care for her and feel the need to protect her more than he was already doing. By holding a mirror to his life and seeing a truth he could not explain she had already enticed him closer. A voice inside him warned against staying in the same room. When darkness came witches turned to shadows and slipped into men's souls. He lit another candle, tall enough to last through the night. Witch or seer, healer or poisoner, was there any difference? he asked himself. He stripped off his clothing and placed firewood into the embers. They smouldered and flamed and he settled himself onto the sheepskin rug, the soft wool itching at first against his skin. The wine and a sense of safety lulled him into idle thought. The comfort of the wool made him think of the simplicity of being a shepherd. No battles to be fought other than those against wolves and bear. A hut and dogs for company and once in a while payment to a whore. And when a shepherd died a clutch of sheep's wool was put into his palm so that when he reached heaven the angels would know he was a good and simple man who tended his flock and that was why he could not attend church on a Sunday.

Blackstone let the image fade. What of when he died? Would Wolf Sword be in his palm still held by its blood knot on his wrist so the angels would know the kind of man he was? What excuse would he offer for not attending mass? Would he proffer the memory of childhood and the village priest's switch across his back? Or his father's skill in teaching him how every leaf took life from its tree and each animal they hunted was a gift from nature? Earth and sky, wind and rain. The silver goddess nestled at his throat. He raised her to his lips. She would take him across the dark abyss as surely as she had eased the soul of the dying Welsh archer who had pressed her into his hand all those years ago.

As his eyes closed he heard a soft rustle of the floor reeds, swift and almost silent; then the figure was suddenly upon him. In that instant he reined in his instinct to roll clear and reach for his archer's knife, for he wanted her. She slid next to him and he felt her arm around him and her needle-sharp fingernails on his chest muscles as the fullness of her breasts pressed into him. He turned and pulled her into the crook of his arm and let his free hand explore her. She urged him on as her hands sought him out and then tried to turn him away so she could straddle him. She bit his lips and clawed his skin but he easily overwhelmed her as she bucked beneath him. And as he pushed into her it felt as though his mind was held as it had been when he saw her with Killbere at Balon. Nothing was clear, the sensations overwhelmed him, and for a moment he thought he had been drugged again.

As he hungrily pressed his mouth against her raised nipples the spell was broken. She pulled his face to hers. She whispered something that he could not hear; her breathing was laboured, and sweat glided between their bodies. He took hold of her arms and the candlelight shimmered across her as he raised himself to gaze down on her. The burn marks on her breasts and belly from her torture had faded. Her eyes widened like a trapped beast, crimson from the fire glow, showing him the witch in her. He didn't care. If she was the devil's servant he would subdue her. She embraced him with her legs and pulled him deeper into her. And then once the fury eased and her body arched they settled into a slow rhythmic embrace. There was no telling how long the night lasted. The last thing he remembered was rolling off her as the candle flame flickered and died. Aelis lay in the crook of his arm, her breathing slow, her breasts soft against his chest. He breathed the fragrance of their sex and its potion eased him into sleep.

She was gone when he awoke. For a few moments he wondered whether the night with Aelis had been a drunken dream, but he knew it was not. He could smell her fragrance on him. He went down to the courtyard where his men were billeted and sluiced his body with the cold water from the well. Some of the men smiled knowingly.

'Sleep well, Thomas?' said Will Longdon as he cranked the well handle and poured water for his cooking pot.

'Well enough,' said Blackstone, wary of the archer's grin.

'Aye. I see you've been off in the Count's orchard early this morning. Have to be careful of those peach trees when you reach up: they snare a man's skin.' He gestured over his shoulder. 'Scratch your back and neck. Best to wear a shirt when you're foraging.' He turned away, carrying the pail towards the men who were tending their cooking fires.

'I could save you the long horse ride to Milan by kicking your arse over those mountains,' called Blackstone.

The men jeered as Will Longdon played the fool and hurried his pace.

'Thomas!' Killbere called from one of the palace doors and beckoned him.

Pulling on his shirt and jupon Blackstone strode across the yard. Killbere led the way inside. 'The Count's chamberlain sent me to find you. There's a problem. The child is sick.'

'The Princess?'

Killbere nodded. They climbed the stairs within the turret until they reached a broad landing. The Princess's companion ladies waited outside one of the doors. Their fearful looks said more than words. Pestilence.

'She has the fever?' said Blackstone.

Killbere nodded. 'In the night, or early this morning. The town's physician has not yet arrived.'

'He's been sent for though?' said Blackstone, keeping back from the door like Killbere. The very thought of the plague being in the room was enough to make fighting men fearful.

'He serves those who cannot pay in the town. It's his contract with the city council and the Count. The noblemen pay for their treatment and he tends the poor.'

'Has it struck the town yet?'

'Who knows?' said Killbere.

Blackstone gripped Killbere's arm and lowered his voice so the Princess's ladies could not hear. 'Gilbert, this child means nothing to me, but if she dies I can't seek my revenge. I cannot get into Milan. Find the damned doctor.'

Killbere turned his back on the women, who were now looking towards the two Englishmen. 'Thomas, if that child dies we all may die. Who knows how long she has borne the pestilence? They say it strikes quickly but who knows? She was coughing on the journey here and Henry said she has been shivering these past two days.'

Blackstone knew the situation could worsen. 'Henry was close to her. We need that doctor. Where's the Count?'

'With his family. They're staying in their private quarters until the physician examines her and the priest attends her.'

'Then why has he sent for me?' said Blackstone.

'Because Aelis is in there and he is fearful of what she might do. He wants you to get her out.'

CHAPTER FORTY-SIX

Entering the room felt more dangerous than defying night creatures in a forest. He eased open the door and saw Aelis bending over the Princess. The room was warm from the fire burning in the grate but the canopy that hung across the bed moved gently from the breeze that came through the open window. The child was either asleep or close to death, he decided as he heard the soft rasping of her breath.

'Don't be afraid,' said Aelis as she looked at him.

'If it's the pestilence I'll seal you in this room with her,' he said dispassionately.

She smiled. 'You're cold-hearted, Thomas. After last night I wouldn't have thought that of you.'

'Don't confuse lust with anything other than what it is. I've seen the plague before and I'll not expose myself or my men to it. Why did you come in here?'

'I heard the child's cries.'

'You should have waited for the physician.'

'I didn't know how ill she was. There are times you have to step into danger. Haven't you ever done that?' she said with a hint of teasing in her voice.

Why was she being so unconcerned? he asked himself. If she had the powers of a witch, did that protect her from the pestilence?

Aelis rinsed out a cloth and placed it on the Princess's forehead. 'Thomas, it's not the plague. The child has a fever. That's all.'

'You can't be sure of that,' he said. 'Look at those red blotches on her arms. I've seen the pestilence before.'

She sat on the edge of the bed and held the child's hand. 'Don't bring the physician here. Tell the Count she will recover.'

He had closed the door behind him but stepped no further into the room. 'If she dies because of what you have done to her I won't be able to save you.'

'Think clearly about this. I give her herbs to reduce the fever and I will feed her broth when she is able. The physician would bleed her and that will weaken her further. If the pestilence has reached the town then the last person you want in here is the man who has been treating those who have it. Her skin is blemished by the fever; that's all it is.'

There was a tap on the door. Blackstone opened it. Killbere stood close to the opening; behind him in the background, hovering with an impatient and worried look, stood the Count's chamberlain, and with him a valet, the Princess's chambermaids and ladies-in-waiting. A crowd of those who attended the royal child was gathering.

'They're talking about sending in some of the Count's men. She's a princess, for God's sake. They can't have a... a...' He looked at Blackstone, trying to find a description of the woman that would not cause offence to his friend. 'You know what I mean,' he said.

Blackstone glanced at the chamberlain, whose face clouded with concern. 'Tell them... tell them that the Princess was tired from the journey, that she has only a chill, not the pestilence, that she is recovering and that she has asked to be left in peace for a few hours more before her ladies attend her. She is content with the administrations of the... er...' Blackstone faltered.

'Apothecary?' Killbere suggested.

'Apothecary,' he agreed. 'And that if the pestilence is in the city then the physician should stay away. For everyone's sake.'

Killbere sighed. 'I'll stand at the door until you get her out. And that will give me enough time to pray that your lying tongue does not send us all to the devil's graveyard. If the child has it, Thomas, then you might as well stay in there with her.' He pulled closed the door.

Aelis looked at him. 'Not so afraid, then? Or cold-hearted.'

'I need that child alive. She serves a purpose.'

'Like me?'

He ignored her. She had predicted this journey. Whatever advantage he could gain from her would help him reach those who had sent the assassin that murdered his wife and child. 'Do not let her die,' was all he said. Because of their passion the previous night he knew he had been drawn closer to her than he had wished. Part of him felt guilty for having succumbed to his desire for her, haunted as he was by his dead wife's memory. Whatever magic Aelis had cast he had been willing.

'Help me,' said Aelis as she eased back the Princess's bed coverings.

He stepped around a chair and bench towards the bolstered bed. Isabelle lay unmoving and for a moment he thought again that her flushed face and hands were the warning signs of the plague.

'Lift her,' said Aelis.

He hesitated.

'She needs dry bedding and a fresh nightdress.'

'I'm not undressing a girl child,' said Blackstone.

'No one is asking you to. Lift her.'

He did as she instructed. The eleven-year-old girl was as light as a feather but her clothing was soaked with sweat. As he lifted her free of the bed Aelis stripped back the linen undersheet from the padded cover that lay on the feather mattress. Blackstone looked down at the helpless girl. Agnes, his own daughter, would have been her age had she lived. For a moment the unconscious girl in his arms was more than a means to an end and the tenderness he suddenly felt towards her caught him by surprise. Aelis quickly remade the bed and then eased aside the green coverlet stitched on one side with sable. 'Put her down,' she said.

Blackstone bent forward and placed her gently onto the mattress. His face hovered close to hers and he resisted the urge to kiss her forehead. His calloused hand eased away a lock of hair that had escaped from below her nightcap. Aelis nodded him away as she began to lift the child's nightdress.

'Close the window,' she said. 'There's been enough air to ease away the stale smells.'

He did as he was told and as he pulled the latch closed he saw the Count's captain of the guard talking to a horseman who had obviously been let through the palace gates. Will Longdon and the archers had gathered to one side and Meulon and Gaillard watched with the men-at-arms. The captain of the guard ushered the horseman across the courtyard towards one of the palace doors.

'All right,' said Aelis, making him turn his attention back to her. Isabelle had been changed into a fresh nightdress.

'What now?'

'We wait.'

'What for?'

Aelis's resigned smile triggered an alarm in him. 'To see whether she has the pestilence or not.'

By the time the palace chapel's bells rang for vespers, Isabelle's fever had subsided enough for her to sip water, and as the candles burned lower and the cresset lamps were lit she took a little broth. Blackstone fed the fire small pieces of wood so no great heat would build in the room; it was enough that any evening chill was kept at bay. The chamberlain had been told how Aelis had saved Killbere's life and of the child's progress. The Count sanctioned Aelis and Blackstone to stay with their charge until morning. Blackstone slept fitfully on the narrow bench, his back against the wall; he awoke when the chapel bell rang for the night's vigil prayers and he saw that Aelis had stayed awake at the child's side. She sat, head unbowed, her back straight, eyes slightly open, staring into the flickering shadows as if she was watching something unfold ahead of her. The muted sound of prayers whispered across the palace's walls, but Aelis made no sign of hearing them. Isabelle slept soundly. Settled on the child's chest was the crystal rock he had seen when she had healed Killbere. It had some significance but as it roused only mild curiosity in him rather than posing any threat, he let it be. When the dawn's rose light eased across the snow-capped mountains Aelis pressed her hand against the child's heart and lowered her ear to the sleeping Princess's lips.

'She's weak from the journey and the fever but if they let her rest she will recover,' she told Blackstone, who had slept a couple of hours since vigils and, as he had always done, awoken before the dawn.

'The Count will be grateful,' said Blackstone.

'I doubt it. I am already condemned as a roadside herbalist, banned by royal decree. I'll have my hand out for payment – that'll make sure I am appreciated. If you're not paid the service rendered is thought worthless, by the rich at least. They only permitted me to attend her because they were afraid it was the pestilence. It was your presence and your lies that kept me here to see it through. Now, she can sleep and I'm hungry.'

They had not eaten since breakfast the day before because Aelis had forbidden any food to be brought into the room except the broth she had ordered for Isabelle. Her fast had something to do with her powers of healing and Blackstone had borne the hunger well but now his stomach growled. When they opened the door a dozing Killbere fell off the stool that he had propped against it. The ladies-in-waiting, the valet and chambermaid slept on the stairs and in doorways. Startled, they quickly got to their feet as Aelis went ahead of Blackstone, her satchel of medicines on her shoulder, walking nose in the air as if she were royalty.

She addressed the gathered servants. 'These are my orders. See they are carried out or Count Amadeus will hear of your neglect. Broth only for the Princess when she asks for it. She must be allowed fresh air for one hour, the room must be kept warm – warm, not hot – and she must be given the liquid I have prepared in the carafe on the table in the room. I will visit her highness later to see that she is kept quiet. No chatter. No fuss. Understood?'

The cowed servants kept their heads bowed and quickly stepped aside as Aelis strode down the stairs without a backward glance.

Killbere rubbed a hand across his short hair. 'Witches can do that, you know,' he said.

'Heal the sick?' said Blackstone.

'Scare people shitless,' he answered and led the way from the chamber's door.

CHAPTER FORTY-SEVEN

Amadeus, the sixth Count of Savoy, was grateful that ten years earlier his sister, Bianca, had married Galeazzo II Visconti, Lord of Milan. Peace with Milan was secured and the marriage helped him protect his southern borders across the Alps in Piedmont. Good fortune had blessed her when she gave birth to Gian Galeazzo, now almost nine years old, who would marry the French Princess who lay prostrate in her bedchamber. This marriage between the house of Valois and the Visconti was too important to be lost. But something was wrong. That the girl had fallen sick had caused him enormous concern. Not only could she have died under his roof, thus jeopardizing his alliance with the Visconti, but if she had had the pestilence it might have spread and he could have lost the beloved infant son he and his wife had awaited for so long. And now trouble was lurking in the foothills of the mountains, but he could make no sense of it. Who would benefit from ambushing the royal Princess? His thoughts danced back and forth as Blackstone and Killbere stood before him. It had been only minutes since they had responded to his summons.

'How long before she can travel?' he asked.

'I don't know, my lord. The woman, I mean the apothecary, says she must remain undisturbed and cared for a while yet,' said Blackstone.

Amadeus pulled a hand through his generous mop of hair and looked out of the window towards the mountain peaks. 'You must get across the pass before the September snow falls. It can be early some years but you must be gone within ten days at the latest. And we are in danger of an early winter. It's in the air, Sir

Thomas. You can smell snow before it falls and those of us who live in the shadow of the mountains know the signs. Even the wild rabbits' coats have started to turn from brown to white. We all ready ourselves. The child must recover and it must be soon. The ceremony is planned for October. There is much to be done. This marriage is a momentous occasion.'

'We can only travel when her highness is well enough,' said Killbere.

'Of course, of course, there is no question of doing otherwise.' Amadeus hesitated. Was now the time to try and uncover who wanted to harm the girl? 'I have had men scouring the countryside to see that the route we planned for her is safe. They are thorough, and they have the ear of my subjects. But there is one I value more than most. He was a feral child I came across in the forest years ago – the circumstances are unimportant – but he has the sense of an animal and he knows these forests as well as any hunting creature. He has seen hundreds of men lying in wait – two hundred, possibly more – in a forest close to the road you will take. They are routiers who obviously mean to cause harm, yet they have made no attack on any traveller so far, although there are merchants who travel that route from Milan to Lyon and then north to Paris. They have not been assaulted.'

'But you control the pass,' said Killbere.

'I have sufficient men to protect my territory but they are scattered and, as I told you, I hold them in reserve to respond to a call for help from the Pope. And here I have only enough men to defend the palace. By the time I send orders to gather my vassals these routiers may have gone elsewhere. Why are these men there, I ask myself, and if it is not to seize you then the only answer I can find is the Princess.'

'To ransom her,' suggested Killbere.

'But how would common brigands know of her journey? Was it common knowledge among the English? Are these men released from service after the treaty who wish to seize wealth by taking the child?' said Amadeus.

'There is no knowing, my lord,' said Blackstone. 'Skinners will take their chances to seize a great prize and if your man saw two hundred then there will be more he did not see.' Blackstone couldn't discount the fact that these men might be waiting to ambush him. He had made enough enemies over the years: it might not be the Visconti's mercenaries who were waiting. 'Who would benefit from the Princess's death?'

The Count recoiled at the thought of someone wishing to kill the child.

Blackstone pressed his question. 'If the Princess dies. Who would benefit?'

'No one. Surely,' Amadeus said uncertainly, for a part of him knew that Thomas Blackstone might suggest the name of the one man who *would* gain from the death of the Princess. Galeazzo Visconti was politically astute and the marriage of his son into the house of Valois would give him the support of the French and the blessing of the Pope. There was only one man who would one day lose power because of the arranged marriage: Galeazzo's brother, the second Lord of Milan, Bernabò Visconti. The crazed, lustful one who relished torture.

Blackstone held the Count's gaze. Had they both thought the same name? 'Bernabò Visconti's future would remain secure if the girl dies,' said Blackstone, and saw that he and the Count had indeed reached the same conclusion.

'Christ,' said Killbere. 'He would murder a child to stop his own brother becoming more powerful?'

'Both have murdered members of their family in the past to increase their power. One pays the King's ransom for the privilege; the other will kill for it.' Blackstone looked back at the Count. 'We should find out whatever we can before we take her across into Italy and determine whether this fever was brought on by poison,' he said. 'I suggest you keep your quarantine in force. The gates should stay closed and no one be allowed to leave the palace until this matter is settled. If she is the victim of a poisoner then those outside may be waiting for news of her death. Will you give me the time and authority to investigate?'

'You have it, Sir Thomas,' said Amadeus, but the look of concern still wrinkled his young face.

Killbere kept pace with Blackstone as he strode from the Count's quarters.

'We have a hundred Frenchmen with us. It might not be enough if there are more of those whoresons in hiding,' said Killbere. 'Who knows how accurate the Count's reports are?'

'Have the men ready. If we go outside these walls we'll do it without the French escort,' Blackstone told him.

Killbere spat. 'Send the French. Rather them die than us.'

Blackstone grinned. 'But we kill better than them.'

Aelis was asleep, exhausted after the long vigil with the stricken child. Her arm was thrown across the side of her face. Blackstone gave her nakedness barely a thought. He shook her awake. She started but then calmed. He told her of his doubts about the child's fever.

'It could be poison,' she admitted as she dressed quickly. 'She vomited when I first went to her. If you are fearful then I must go back and stay with her. Keep everyone else away from her until she recovers.' She had made no sign or gesture of affection towards him, but he followed her to the Princess's chamber where the servants were waiting for Isabelle to regain consciousness. They looked alarmed as Blackstone and Aelis came into the room. Aelis went straight to the child, felt her heart and pressed a hand against her skin.

'Did you do as I instructed?' she asked the servants.

One took a step forward, an older woman who served with the ladies-in-waiting. 'She awoke for a few moments and I gave her the juice you left,' she said, pointing to the carafe. 'Then she slept again.'

Aelis looked at Blackstone. 'She sweats again and her breathing is shallow.' She faced the women, some of whom cowed before her. 'When I left her the Princess slept soundly. I had reduced the fever. What else has gone on here?' Her voice was laden with threat and the younger women shuffled back against the wall. 'Who prepared her food?' she demanded.

The older woman beckoned another of the women who were waiting obediently. 'This one, Angeline.'

Aelis made no move towards the girl. 'Come here,' she said.

Blackstone watched the other women. They shot glances at each other; their hands twisted anxiously. They were all frightened.

Aelis continued: 'Did you prepare any food different than usual?'

The girl shook her head, her expression anxious.

'No spices in her food?'

Again the girl's head went from side to side.

'She speaks the truth,' said the older woman. 'We have attended her highness for two years. We all know what she likes. She would not eat such food.' And then she understood what the suspicion might be. 'You think the child poisoned?'

The women gasped at the prospect. One, a middle-aged matron, crossed herself and kissed the crucifix at her neck.

'Spicy food would disguise the bitter taste of any poison. Of course,' the older woman said. 'But it is not possible. No one here, not one of us would cause harm to the child.' She looked at the chambermaid, who was little older than the Princess. 'And she has only been in attendance when her duties required her to be here. She is one of the Count's servants. Look at her. She has neither the wit nor the brain to even know about poison.'

'Then why is the Princess worse than when I left her?' said Aelis.

'She sickens, is all,' the woman answered.

'You,' said Blackstone to the lady-in-waiting who had kissed her crucifix. The other women looked alarmed as they stared at her. Why was she being singled out?

'My lord?' she said.

He beckoned her forward. The others stepped aside as she nervously approached Blackstone, her head craned upwards to meet his eyes.

'When you raised the cross to your lips the back of your hand came free from your sleeve. It's covered with red blemishes.'

Before the startled woman could answer, he heard Aelis speak. 'Wolfsbane. You've got it on your hands.'

The woman quickly stepped back, terror-stricken, but Blackstone grabbed her and Aelis pulled back the woman's sleeve. All saw the red blotches inflaming her skin.

'Clarimonde! You did this? To our child? To this innocent?' the older woman cried. 'Did you put it in the wine? Bitch! You always serve her the wine!'

The culprit snatched free her arm, but Aelis took everyone by surprise and slapped her hard. She sprawled. The sudden violence shocked the ladies-in-waiting into silence. Clarimonde looked at the stunned companions she had lived and served with over the years; then she scuttled backwards, snarling her own venom at them all.

'I owe the child nothing. When the Dauphin ran back to Paris after Poitiers he had my son executed. He accused my son of cowardice on the battlefield.' She spat at them, no longer a sedate matron but a vengeful creature who had harboured the venom of hatred within her every day since they had hanged her son. 'All these years I have waited to inflict pain. Four long years!'

Aelis turned on the other women. 'Find mulberry leaves, boil them in vinegar. Be quick.'

The women almost ran from the room. Blackstone looked at Aelis.

'It will help to stop the poison. I have my own potions but I need to slow the wolfsbane's effect first.'

Blackstone reached down and hauled the squirming poisoner to her feet. Her lip was already cut. 'You did this on your own?'

She twisted her head away, refusing to look at Blackstone. He grabbed her face and forced her to confront him. 'Why wait until now? You've served the child for years – why now?' He loosened his grip so that she could answer him. There was fear in her face now, and uncertainty, and he could see that she would not answer.

345

'Were you paid? Were promises made if you killed the Princess?'

The fight and bitterness deserted her. Tears welled in her eyes. 'He said I should wait... that I must hide my desire for revenge because it could be better served when the time was right. And then... when the child was betrothed... then he sent me word... Before we crossed the mountains, that is when I should make her ill so that she died.'

'Who?' Blackstone demanded. 'Is it the Visconti who sent you?'

She shook her head. 'He does not bear that name. Cataline, my daughter, serves in his house... that is how he used me, used my desire for revenge. She will die if the Princess survives and reaches Milan.' She slumped, as if her tortured soul was ready to flee from her, and wailed, 'I have no other child!'

Blackstone slapped her, forcing her back to reality. 'Who?' he demanded.

But the fear of losing her child kept her silent.

Blackstone eased her to the far side of the room. The cool air from the window seemed to revive her for a moment and as she glanced at Aelis tending the Princess the years of hatred and anger surged up once more; she found enough strength to spit on the floor at her feet. Blackstone pushed her down onto the bench.

'What do you know of others who wish to harm the girl? Are there men waiting before we cross the mountains?'

The look of puzzlement on Clarimonde's face told Blackstone she knew nothing of the routiers in the forest. She shook her head. Blackstone lowered his voice. 'You will be sent back to Paris and the Dauphin. There you'll be taken through the streets to the Place de Grève for public execution. You know they won't just hang or behead you. You'll die a thousand deaths first. They will rip the flesh from your breasts, arms and thighs with red-hot pincers, and the hand that fed the Princess poison will be burnt with sulphur. And where they have flayed your body they will scald the raw flesh with hot irons to sear the wounds, and then they will tie you to horses and have your limbs wrenched from your torso, and what is left of your body will be thrown into a fire and your ashes scattered.'

His quiet words held the woman as if in a trance. Her face was wet with silent tears.

'I can help you,' he said gently. 'I'll find your daughter and I will try to save her. What is the name of this man who used your hatred for his own purpose?'

The palm of her hand wiped away tears and snot. 'Antonio Lorenz,' she said quietly. 'He is one of the bastard sons of Lord Visconti.'

'Which lord? Galeazzo or Bernabò?' said Blackstone.

'Bernabò,' she said. She raised her head. 'How can you help me?'

Blackstone stepped back a couple of paces and looked at the open window.

It only took a moment for her to realize what he offered.

'Bless you, Sir Thomas,' she said and, clambering quickly onto the bench, pitched herself through the open space onto the courtyard far below.

CHAPTER FORTY-EIGHT

When Blackstone and Killbere sought permission to speak to Amadeus the Count's chamberlain demanded to know on what grounds they wanted an audience, insisting that anything that could be said to the Count should be relayed first to him. Blackstone extended a restraining arm to stop Killbere grabbing the old man's beard and tugging him to his knees.

'When Sir Thomas Blackstone requests an audience he does so with information fit only for your master's ears, you decrepit beggar.'

The insult made matters worse and the chamberlain turned his back until Blackstone threatened that unless the old man did as they asked the French royal Princess might not survive the day. The blustering fool ran as quickly as his spindly legs could carry him into the great hall where Count Amadeus berated him for standing between the child's bodyguard and his lord under whose roof she sheltered. Bowing with abject apology the chamberlain ushered Blackstone and Killbere into the Count's presence. Blackstone recounted the dead woman's attempt on the Princess's life.

'Did you throw her from the window?' asked the Count.

'I gave her the choice of that or the Dauphin's punishment.'

'She made the right decision.'

The young Count sank into silence. The complexity of the situation did not escape him. The child was in his care until she passed across the Alps.

'Do you know of Antonio Lorenz?' said Blackstone.

'One of Bernabò's bastards,' the Count replied.

'He is the one responsible,' said Killbere.

Amadeus gazed at the burning logs in the grate. His alliances could just as easily go up in smoke. After a few moments he became aware of Blackstone and Killbere staring at him. Each had moved slightly, as if ready to block any attempt he might have made to escape. It dawned on him that they might think him complicit. The realization spawned other fears. Blackstone and the French escort numbered nigh on two hundred men inside his walls. His own men were too few to ride out against a determined enemy but strong enough to hold out against an assault. But not from within. Not from men such as Blackstone led. They could kill him and seize the palace. Perhaps Blackstone had already alerted his men.

'You consider me a part of this?' said the Count.

'Your sister is married to Bernabò's brother. We reach your palace and an attempt is made to kill the child.'

'You dare to accuse me?' Amadeus said sharply.

His indignation had no effect on either of the men before him. The danger these men presented was immediate and he knew no matter how strongly he might protest their suspicions had to be allayed.

'Very well, I understand. But we spoke earlier of who would benefit from the child's death. We have no evidence to link Bernabò Visconti to this assassination attempt. And it was I who warned you about the men waiting on your route. I gain nothing from this,' he insisted. 'If anything I lose greatly. Think on it, Sir Thomas. My sister Bianca married to Galeazzo; their son betrothed to Isabelle. An alliance that strengthens my hand against those who try and attack my borders. My territory straddles the Alps. I need alliances but Bernabò Visconti is a man berserk with lust and an unquenchable desire for power. He cannot offer me anything except loss of influence and disgrace brought down on my name. If he is involved through his bastard son then he is our common enemy.'

His explanation was convincing enough to make sense to the two armed men.

Blackstone's hand eased away from Wolf Sword's grip, a move noticed by the young Count. Perhaps he had been closer to death than he had realized.

'It's obvious that if this woman failed to kill Isabelle then the men waiting are there to see it done,' said Blackstone. 'I cannot risk her again, so I ask you to allow us to travel south to the pass I have used before to cross the mountains.'

'Through the Gate of the Dead?' Amadeus said. 'Into Montferrat territory? No. Sir Thomas, he may be your friend but he is my enemy, and if he had the chance to seize the girl and hold her to ransom he would, and then whatever friendship there is between you could soon disappear.' Count Amadeus had regained his composure. 'No, I will help you snare these routiers. You must travel the way we have determined.' He walked to the far side of the room where a long table held writing materials, books and rolled parchments which he fingered until he found the one he wanted.

'Come here,' he said, unrolling the parchment. It was a crudely drawn map but easy enough to understand. 'I have been told there are already early falls of snow. It will soon become difficult for the child to travel if we wait too long. These men are here,' he said, pointing to a place on the map that showed forests and foothills. 'When you leave this is the route you will take. The valley of Maurienne turns sharply south at Saint-Pierre d'Albigny; you then follow the arc eastwards to the pass at Mont Cenis; once in the pass you will have left any chance of attack from routiers far behind. They will not venture further than the mountains to pursue you. On the other side you will be in the Val di Susa and soon after you will reach Ivrea. I have mountain guides waiting at the pass who are my vassals and in my debt. And I will send messengers to my sister so that she can tell Galeazzo of your departure from here. Once he sends his men out to escort you from Milan, Bernabò, if it is indeed he who wishes to harm the Princess, will not be able to reach her.'

Blackstone and Killbere left the grand hall and made their way to where Gaillard and Meulon had gathered the men.

'A galloping bull's bollocks would be less noticeable than us riding at a snail's pace,' said Killbere. 'We have to hit these skinners hard and fast before we take up the journey again. Several days to the pass and then if we're lucky another ten over the top until we reach Milan.'

'If we're lucky,' agreed Blackstone, 'and for once I'd be happy to see Visconti troops riding out to escort us.'

As they walked across the yard de Chauliac, the French captain of the Princess's guard, and two of his sergeants cut across their path.

'Sir Thomas, one of the ladies-in-waiting fell from the window. Is the Princess all right?'

'She's recovering from a fever. She's doing well.'

'This woman who fell: she had served her highness. Such an accident will be upsetting for her, but Count Amadeus has his men posted and I cannot even approach the room.'

'Those who nurse her haven't told her about the accident. The child needs rest. She's in good hands and she will soon be well enough to travel. You have your orders from the Dauphin, captain. You will follow them.'

'Of course, but when do we leave?'

'Soon, but you will escort her without me and my men until you reach the pass.'

The soldier reacted with despair. 'I have a hundred men and she has twenty servants with her who slow us more than a baggage train. If there is trouble I doubt I can protect her without your men, Sir Thomas.'

Blackstone eased the man aside from his sergeants. 'Captain, your discretion is important if we are to safeguard the Princess.'

'I understand,' de Chauliac said.

'There are men waiting in ambush. We cannot delay our journey much longer and the Count has barely sufficient men to protect the palace so he can offer no further help.'

'Better we ride together, then,' said the captain.

'No, better that you stay back and we will root them out and kill them. You are needed here for the Princess, that's what you are charged with,' said Killbere, barely concealing his obvious disdain for the French.

'Sir Gilbert, I have fought the English on the field of battle and served my King on crusade. We know how to fight,' said the man, insulted. 'We were defeated but we fought hard.'

The last thing Blackstone needed was dissent among the men who rode to protect Princess Isabelle. 'All right, de Chauliac, you shall help us. Keep half your men here and the rest of your men will ride out bearing the Princess's litter, and I and my men will snap shut the trap.'

The man looked confused. 'Use the Princess as bait? I cannot.'

Killbere sighed. 'Holy Mother of God you dimwitted oaf, not the Princess, just the damned litter! Can't you grasp even the simplest deception?'

Abashed, the captain bore the slur and bowed his head to Blackstone. 'I await your orders, Sir Thomas.'

'Stay silent on this matter, captain. Say nothing to your men or anyone else. Not yet. Understand?' said Blackstone.

'Even I am not that stupid,' he said with an ill-concealed venomous look at the veteran knight.

'I wouldn't wager on that,' said Killbere as they watched him stride back across the courtyard to where the French troops were quartered. 'Thomas, these men's thinking is more rigid than the planks on my bed. They'll cause us trouble in the fight.'

'No, they'll serve a purpose, Gilbert: they'll take the skinners' eyes off us. I should have thought of it before.'

'Then you're becoming as dull-witted as the French. I despair for you. No wonder you've needed me at your side all these years. This whoreson Bernabò and his bastard might not be able to harm the Princess once we kill these skinners,' said Killbere, 'but after you're inside the walls of Milan you're at the mercy of a man who would strip the skin from your bones before he kills you.'

'Then I'd better find him before he finds me,' said Blackstone. 'Now, let's think on how we kill the routiers. They aren't blind or stupid; they'll see how horses walk carrying an empty litter. She has to be in it and they need to see her before they attack. Let's get the bait dressed.'

CHAPTER FORTY-NINE

Two days later Meulon and Gaillard led thirty of Blackstone's men-at-arms along the route towards the mountains. They were five hours ahead of the royal escort, but a full day behind Blackstone, Killbere and Will Longdon's archers. They too had been split into two groups, with a rearguard held by Jack Halfpenny and his twenty bowmen, but there was no sign of Blackstone on the road. Meulon and Gaillard's men had taken unmarked shields from the Count's armoury and their rough, makeshift clothing made them appear just like any other band of roving brigands seeking opportunity now that the war was over. They rode under a clear blue sky, the chill wind from the snow-capped mountains funnelling down into the foothills. They travelled at a steady, unhurried pace across the valley that bellied out from the forests before the road narrowed a mile further on into a highway wide enough for a wagon and two outriders on each side. Halfway across the valley was a small stone-built shrine, big enough for one person to kneel before the makeshift altar and the modest crucifix fashioned from wood. It guaranteed the icon's safety from theft. Were it made of silver or gold it would have been stolen by heretic mercenaries. The faded fresco painted into the plaster inside was of the Madonna and Child and might have been there a hundred years.

'It would be here,' said Gaillard as they moved across the open meadow. 'This makes a good killing ground. They'd attack from over there.'

Meulon studied the ground. The forest, 350 paces to the left, was the obvious choice for anyone lying in ambush. To their right, the rising ground was embedded with boulders and twisted tree roots clinging to the uneven terrain. There could be no retreat up there.

'Ahead,' said Gaillard as he saw horsemen filter out from the treeline half a mile in front of them. A group of riders sixty or more strong eased their mounts across the narrowing meadow to block their way.

Meulon turned to the men riding behind him. 'Be ready, but remember what Sir Thomas told us. We're not looking for a fight.' He turned to Gaillard. 'Let us hope that if there are Englishmen among them they don't recognize any of us.'

They slowed their horses as they approached the waiting men who, like themselves, wore a mixture of armour and mail and whose shields, slung on their saddles, displayed the scarred blazons of various French and German lords. These were fighting men who had abandoned those who had once rallied them to war. Those blocking Meulon and Gaillard's route posed an initial threat that Meulon and Gaillard could deal with despite being outnumbered two to one. The greater threat lay with the rest of the brigand's force hidden in the forest. The leader of the men who blocked their route raised a hand to stop Blackstone's men.

Meulon and Gaillard waited as the mercenaries eased their horses forward. 'This road is guarded,' said their leader.

'It's a road into Lombardy. We don't pay tolls; if we were prepared to do that we would go south into Montferrat territory. We need to pass,' said Meulon.

'In good time,' said the mercenary. 'We need to know your business.'

'It's ours to know,' answered Gaillard. 'If it's trouble you want, we'll oblige.'

'Steady, stranger. We make no threats. Tell us who you are and where you're going and there'll be no trouble.' He had eased his horse closer to observe the men and cast an eye on the shields slung on their saddles. 'You wear no blazon. You serve a lord?

Amadeus, perhaps?' The man eased his horse around them. 'No blazon, no lord. Are you routiers? You've booty perhaps?'

'We serve no one except ourselves, and if you don't clear the road we'll shed blood and be gone before the men you've got hiding in that forest can put their arses into their saddles. Then you'll see who has the right of way,' Meulon growled at him. He studied the man's pockmarked, broken face: bones badly set from past fights. The hands holding the reins were similarly scarred. He would be unafraid of grappling and fighting a man close in, Meulon thought as the routier's eyes glared at him.

'You think we've men in the forest?' said the mercenary.

'You'd be a damned fool to ride out to challenge us if you didn't,' said Gaillard.

The man grunted. The men he faced were obviously experienced fighters.

'We're skinners,' said Meulon, 'and if we've taken from the lord you serve then bad luck to him. Whatever we took we've spent in taverns and whorehouses and now there's nothing left in this godforsaken country so we're riding to the Visconti. They need fighting men and they pay well.'

The man grinned. 'Brother, we ride the same road. I am Grimo. You have heard of me? Grimo the Breton.'

Meulon looked at Gaillard. 'Have you heard of a foul-breathed shortarse who goes by the name of Grimo?'

The mercenary scowled as Gaillard shook his head. 'I heard of a butcher's dog called Grimo when we rode with the Savage Priest years ago.'

'Hey, that's me! The butcher. You rode with de Marcy? Merciful God.' The mercenary leader crossed himself. 'That priest could put the fear of Christ into the devil himself.'

'The Savage Priest *was* the devil.' Meulon grinned, drawing the man in, gaining his confidence, having insulted him as any routier with self-respect would have done, damning the consequences.

'Butcher's dog, eh? Well, maybe he honoured me,' said Grimo. 'I had a reputation back then for fighting like a bear-pit dog.'

'And what's your reputation now? A toll collector?' said Meulon.

Grimo laughed. 'Yes! Why not? I serve Visconti. I collect heads as a toll for the Viper.'

The man's bragging confirmed what Blackstone had told his men about Visconti's plans to lay an ambush for the Princess.

Grimo considered the two men. He too was playing the game that dangerous men played. 'Are you all Frenchmen?'

'No, there are English and Germans among us.'

The mercenary turned and called to one of his men who then came forward.

'Bring one of your Germans up,' said Grimo.

Meulon called to the men behind him. 'Renfred! Come here!'

The man-at-arms spurred his horse forward to where Grimo waited with his chosen man. Grimo hid his face with the back of his hand and whispered something. The routier nodded and called out in German to Renfred. Neither Meulon or Gaillard understood what was said.

Renfred glanced at Meulon and Gaillard, and then nodded, and answered back.

Grimo's man seemed satisfied. 'He says these two are men who should not be challenged. They are killers. They rode with the Savage Priest right enough and they fight for whoever pays the most. Now they ride to Milan to offer their services to the Visconti. One is known as the throat-cutter and has a bounty on him.'

Grimo was satisfied. Men at the back of the column that faced him would not have heard him questioning their leaders at the front. The men's story needed to reflect each other's.

'You could do worse than stay here, with us,' said Grimo to the two big men.

'We don't know you,' said Gaillard. 'What can you offer us that the Visconti cannot?'

'We're waiting for a prize to come our way. She will be under escort. I'm going to take her head and when I drop it at the feet of the man who's paying we'll have enough gold florins to keep us through the winter and beyond.'

'She's special, this woman?'

'No woman, a girl. She's royal blood.'

'Then she'll have an escort,' said Gaillard. 'You'll need more than the men you've got here. And I don't like being on the losing side. I've had enough of that thanks to the whoreson English.'

'Every sword helps,' said the mercenary, 'but I've got damned near three hundred men back there in the forest. And every traveller who makes their way across the mountains stops and prays at the shrine. It will be an easy kill. Stay. We'll ride on to Milan together when it's done.'

Meulon made as if to consider it, and then shook his head. 'Count Amadeus already has men looking for us. He has a treaty with King John and the Dauphin. We're safer in Milan. Perhaps we'll see you there.'

'As you wish. We'll be the ones camped outside the walls with all the whores and with food and wine in our belly,' he said. 'Mention my name to the Visconti. He'll welcome you.'

'Which one? There are two of them. We know neither Lord of Milan,' said Meulon.

Grimo's lips parted like a wolf already tasting its prey. 'Tread carefully and show respect otherwise he'll break you on the wheel or throw you to his hunting dogs. You seek out the one known as Bernabò; he's possessed, but he has power and gold and he will kill for pleasure.'

'Then we are right to enter Milan without you because if you don't kill this girl we could all be thrown into the pit. Good luck to you,' said Meulon and edged his horse forward.

Grimo pulled back his horse and his men parted allowing free passage for Blackstone's men. 'Which one of you is known as the throat-cutter?'

'There's only one way to find out,' said Gaillard.

Grimo chuckled. 'Good answer, my friend. Who's to say I would not have turned him in for the bounty?'

As Meulon's horse eased past he looked into the man's broken face. Blackstone had briefed the men well: the lies told had carried them through the routiers' ranks. When the time came he would seek out Grimo the butcher and acquaint him with his knife blade.

CHAPTER FIFTY

Girard Goncenin could neither read nor write. From the moment he could walk his life had been spent in the forest, scavenging for plants and snaring rabbits to help feed the family. When he was six his father, a belligerent drunk who had been mutilated for poaching on Count Amadeus's father's domain, almost killed him. Later, when his mother and father died of pestilence, he ran away from home, preferring to let his two sisters and younger brother fend for themselves and to die if they could not. Over the years villagers told the story of a wolf boy, who ran with the pack and brought down deer, who snarled when cornered and lived as a beast. None of it was true. Girard could smell a wolf from half a mile away, that was the truth, and he could trap any living thing. But like the mountain bears that came down into the forests when the snow smothered their food, he favoured wild mushrooms and berries. He no longer spoke, and had almost forgotten how, but his mind recorded every leaf on every tree and he knew where the creatures of the forest lived. His small cave was set deep into a hillside and he had known nothing but self-reliance until he was caught by the Count's men.

It had been his own fault. The Count, who had by now inherited his father's title and lands, had been hunting and foolishly rode ahead of his party in pursuit of a wounded deer. The animal had collapsed deep in the forest, its last heartbeats pumping blood from the arrow wound, blood whose scent was easily caught on the air by not only Girard, but also by a hungry brown bear. The Count's horse had reared and thrown him and Girard, who had been keeping well away from the boisterous hunting party, saw the massive bear rise up to its full height, its muzzle already bloodied from the dead deer, and turn angrily on the human intruder who threatened its spoil.

The bear charged at the young Count, throwing down his mount, its great claws disembowelling the horse. The Count was momentarily helpless but Girard sprang forward and struck the eight-foot-tall beast with a fallen sapling, stinging its snout, forcing it to turn on him. But then his foot became entwined in the undergrowth and he fell, trapped, as the enraged bear came down on all fours and charged. Girard closed his eyes and pictured his cave and the safety and warmth it offered. He could not imagine death: he had not been told of salvation or damnation by any priest, he just knew that when animals died their eyes closed and their hearts stopped beating. And he would be no different. It was the way of the forest. Girard heard the bear bellow in pain and opened his eyes to see the young Count on his feet thrusting his spear into the animal. He jabbed and jabbed again, and then others were there cornering the bear that had only wanted to escape hunger and was now being stabbed by a dozen men. Girard's eyes filled with tears and he wept for the great beast's death.

Saving the Count's life changed Girard's. He was taken in, cleaned and fed, clothed and given a bed by the master of horse. He was visited daily by the Count, who spoke kindly to the boy, and after several weeks Girard began to talk again, but only to the man who had saved him. His room in the stable was little different from his cave and many a day he could not be found. He came and went, returning whenever he wished to the forest, but when the Count hunted, the boy, as if by some animal sense, was always ready to lead him to wolf lair and boar bramble.

And now he led another hunt, charged by the Count to take the tall, scar-faced Englishman and his men through the deep forest on foot so that those who waited to kill could, in turn, be slain. Since dawn Blackstone and fifty of his men had followed Girard through what seemed to be an impenetrable forest as he led them this way and that along animal tracks, across deep

361

streams and up boulder-strewn embankments. The men were scratched and bruised from their efforts as Girard weaved left and right, and on more than one occasion went down on one knee and signalled the men to follow his example. Like the boy, Blackstone was at ease in the dense woodland, but even he could not see what the boy saw, and only on one occasion did he catch a fleeting glimpse of shadows moving and his instincts told him that they were wolves seeking out prey. As they made their way patiently through the trees Blackstone was reminded how Robert Thurgood must have struggled alone through the forest before he warned them of the impending attack. He felt as though the dead archer's ghost were flitting between the saplings and great trees, a haunting reminder of the lad's courage, of his death, taunting Blackstone. He pushed Thurgood's image from his thoughts and concentrated on following Girard, who at every twist and turn kept those who followed him downwind. If the breeze shifted, so did his route; there was to be no risk of the horses waiting in the distant treeline catching their scent. It was several hours before Blackstone caught the unmistakable smell of men who had spent days in the forest. Their latrine pits stank and the stale odour of sweat and food clung to the foliage. Blackstone and his men were two hundred paces from the blurred figures who milled at the fringe of the trees. Blackstone moved his eye from tree to tree until he focused clearly on the men who were preparing their horses; some of the mercenaries were already in the saddle. Girard had brought them through the forest in good time. He glanced at the boy who crouched, shivering. Perhaps, Blackstone thought, he was as feral as the Count had described. His quivering body was like a beast's, sensing danger. He reached out and laid a hand on Girard's shoulder. The boy flinched and then, with a glance at the fifty men who crouched, weapons in hand, eyes fixed ahead on the shimmering treeline, he turned and moved silently back into the forest. Within moments he was gone from sight.

Blackstone crept forward.

De Chauliac led the Princess's escort into the valley's broad expanse. His back muscles ached from the tension of the expected attack. His men were the best the Dauphin's royal guard could offer and none were strangers to battle. What he feared was the Englishman's tactics. If Sir Thomas Blackstone was making his way through the forest in the hope of reaching the expected ambush site by the time he and the slow-moving litter got there, it wouldn't take much of a delay to find de Chauliac and his fifty men dead on the valley floor. If Count Amadeus's man had reported the numbers of the routiers accurately then they were outnumbered at least five to one. Perhaps more. Even if Blackstone did hack his way through that forest, they were still going to face greater odds than de Chauliac wished. When Blackstone had briefed his captains on what was expected and de Chauliac had raised the matter, the Englishman and his captains had laughed. He had been insulted. They seemed to have no care for their own lives and being outnumbered evoked no fear in them. It had required Blackstone himself to soothe his hurt pride, pointing out that de Chauliac had been granted the honour of drawing the first blood. Very well, he had decided, no matter what happened he and his men would acquit themselves with courage and...

The sight of the shrine interrupted his thoughts. The sons of iniquity would attack here when they stopped, and he had to pretend that it was not expected. He could not form up his men in battle order to meet any charge against them; they had to wait, as if unsuspecting. He raised a hand and brought the column to a halt. The litter stopped in front of the shrine and, as Blackstone had instructed, the Princess climbed down to pray, aided by her two ladies-in-waiting. De Chauliac licked his dry lips and kept his eyes on the forest. There was movement in the shadows, he was certain of it.

No sooner did the Princess alight and kneel in prayer at the shrine than the treeline shuddered as an extended line of horsemen surged forward.

'Make ready!' de Chauliac called as his escort turned to face the attack. He hoped the mercenaries did not have good enough eyesight from that distance to see the men's boots beneath the ladies-in-waiting's robes. Their wimples covered the men's beards and the litter concealed their weapons.

Henry Blackstone had laughed along with the others when Blackstone presented John Jacob and Perinne with the women's clothing.

'Sir Thomas,' Perinne pleaded. 'I have fought with you since you were a boy and we built that wall together at Chaulion to fend off the bastard killer Saquet. If I am to die at the hands of routiers I beg you not to let it be dressed as a woman.'

'Get the clothes on, Perinne, no one's asking you to become a whore and sell your arse to monks,' said Killbere. Perinne's face fell and the shame of it nearly defeated the fighting man.

'Sir Thomas?' he pleaded again.

'Perinne, I ask this of you so that you and John Jacob can protect the Princess. She must be seen by the skinners.'

'The French would be better suited to this task,' said John Jacob in almost a whisper. 'I have heard stories from Paris about brothels that keep boys dressed as women.'

'Idle gossip,' answered Blackstone. 'And can you imagine the insult rendered to the French if I asked de Chauliac to dress his royal escort in women's clothing?'

'They could charge more than you, John,' said Meulon and laughed along with the others.

'Aye, but if Perinne shaved that boar's stubble from his chin I could get him married off to a tavern owner,' said Will Longdon. 'And then everyone would be happy.'

'You'll have a yard-long arrow shaft up your arse before this day is out, Will Longdon,' snarled Perinne.

'Which is less painful than what you'll be getting!' he answered.

The men's laughter echoed around the courtyard.

'Enough of this,' said Blackstone. 'I can't afford to insult the French. Get the clothes on so we can all admire you.'

'And a cap and veil will be enough to hide a face even a wild pig would spurn,' said Killbere.

'I hope you pray for forgiveness, Sir Thomas,' said John Jacob as he was helped into the flowing clothes by Henry Blackstone.

'Master Jacob, I think you serve my lord well, though I would suggest a tightening of the belt to lessen the girth,' said Henry, smiling, 'lest anyone think you are bearing a child.' Which earned more laughter as well as a cuff around the head from John Jacob.

'A page would do well to remember respect for the squire he serves. There are a hundred creaking saddles that can be oiled,' he retorted, but with good humour.

'And Henry, this is for you,' said Blackstone as he tossed him a dress. 'You are to be our Princess.'

The earth rumbled from the attacking horseman.

'Not yet, not yet,' Perinne said from beneath the face veil. 'Let the bastards think they have us.'

'Stay behind us, Henry,' said John Jacob. 'We take horse and man. Be ready to finish the beasts before they kick us to death when they're down.'

Grimo the butcher and his attacking routiers spurred their horses on. The French and the women who served the Princess seemed rooted to the spot with fear as he sprang his ambush. It would be an easy kill. They were 130 long paces from the line of French cavalry when the first shadows fell from the sky. Horses whinnied and veered as arrows struck, throwing their riders; men gaped wide-eyed as the sudden shock of bodkin-tipped arrow shafts pierced neck and back. Screams and shouts of panic rose up from the valley and funnelled into the mountainsides, startling rooks and crows from the trees. Those same birds would soon be pecking the eyes and flesh of his fallen men. Grimo turned in the saddle and saw a line of men at the trees behind them half bent into their war bows as others raced towards them on foot with swords and shields raised. His ambush had turned on him like a wounded wolf. The sky darkened again and his eyes lied – the

Princess pulled free her veil and dress and grabbed a sword from the litter, as did her ladies-in-waiting, women transformed into fighting men like a magician's demons. Demons who now ran at him only to be overtaken by the charging French escort.

'Away!' Grimo screamed, waving his sword, ordering his men to split and run. Those that could peeled away from the French assault, but most were caught between the men attacking from the rear and the horsemen to their front. His horse barged another; he swung widely, skill and desperation forged into a bid for survival. The Frenchman went down. Those men who had worn dresses ripped them free and were fighting together, spear and sword, shield and mace, as they thrust into a horse's chest and then hacked the rider to death. Two men and a boy. Efficient and deadly, they stood their ground, chose their victim and attacked again. He had seen fighting like this before on the field at Poitiers and knew without doubt that they were Englishmen. The mêlée engulfed them all. The royal guard tore into his men but were initially outnumbered as his routiers divided their ranks, forcing them to fight in twos and threes. But that momentum was soon lost as more of his men fell writhing on the ground pierced with arrow shafts.

'Break left and right!' he screamed. If they made good their escape these attackers would be forced to separate and he and his men would have the chance to ride to safety. The silence of the men attacking on foot with their bared teeth and snarling faces was more frightening than if a banshee had howled its spectral scream and descended on them. Those who had swarmed from the forest behind them started to kill with practised efficiency. The big man leading the attack raised his shield to ward off a blow from one of Grimo's men on the ground. There were too many unseated horsemen, he realized as the attacker's shield smashed into the man, followed by a swift strike that cleaved the man from shoulder to chest.

Iron-shod hooves churned mud. Henry jumped lithely aside and killed a flailing horse as Perinne and John Jacob ran forward to pull a routier down from his saddle. And then Henry was separated as horses milled between them. A rider leaned down and swung a spiked mace at him; he ducked but slipped in the mud. The horseman quickly heeled his horse around in an attempt to trample him. The man bent low in the saddle, his arm brought back in a high, sweeping curve that would deliver a crushing blow. Henry's fear and desperation gave him strength. He lunged, forcing his sword point into the man's exposed thigh. The snarling face bellowed, spraying spittle. Wide-eyed with pain he swept the mace down. Henry felt the air whisper past his ear. Pain cut through his metal skullcap. He could smell the horse's sweat and saw the beast's terrified eyes rolling back at him as its shoulder struck him. Hooves clawed the dirt next to his face. As he rolled clear he saw the distant snow-capped mountains tinged with the sun's blood hue beneath the horse's belly. It was a glimpse of God's beauty and a moment's foolishness that took his eye from his attacker. Helplessly he tried to scramble clear, but the wounded man – who in his fury had dismounted, abandoning the advantage of his horse – rammed his boot heel into Henry's chest, pinning him down. Then he swung the spiked club towards the boy's face.

In an instant the man was pulled backwards by a blood-streaked Perinne and as the routier lost balance John Jacob fell on him, hacking him to death.

'On your feet, boy!' Perinne shouted.

Stunned and winded, Henry clambered to his feet. The screaming cacophony swirling around him made him dizzy. Colours blurred. John Jacob grabbed him by his jupon and was yelling at him. But he couldn't hear. And then as blood ran across his eyes his legs gave way and he slipped into blessed silence.

Blackstone ran twenty paces behind the arrow strikes. They ceased to fall the moment he reached the rear ranks of the horsemen. The heaving mass of riders barged and struck at each other. The French fought well, although Blackstone and de Chauliac were outnumbered. Blackstone realized there must have been three hundred routiers who had attacked, but the English archers had claimed a third of these and fear of the archers' skill caused panic among the rest. No sooner had Will Longdon's archers stopped shooting than they abandoned their war bows and, with buckler, knife and sword, ran to support Blackstone's men-at-arms.

Blackstone cursed as a rider heeled his mount around against him, wishing he was on his bastard horse, wanting its strength and belligerence. Killbere swept his blade across the mercenary's horse's leg, severing it completely. It screamed and went down, body rolling in agony, throwing the routier. Blackstone jumped clear of the thrashing hooves and Killbere plunged his sword into the man's neck as Blackstone put the fallen beast out of its agony. Blackstone's men swarmed past, shields high, ramming them against riders' legs, working in pairs; cutting and slashing the routiers down onto the ground where they attempted to defend themselves – without success. Blackstone had been right. His men knew how to kill better than most. The mêlée was bedlam. Madness gripped the fighting men as those who grappled on the ground beat each other with fists and rocks. In the eye of the fighting storm a dozen of the royal guard encircled some routiers, hacking them down. Two of the brigands half wheeled their horses and boxed in de Chauliac. He was at their mercy, unable to counter their wild blows. He took a strike on his sword arm; his mail stopped the sword point from cutting into bone but the blow was powerful enough to spill blood. His arm went limp and he was unable to parry the next blow. Blackstone had seen the attack, wove between horses and yanked the routier's reins, pulling him from the saddle. The man rolled clear, but Blackstone was on him and threw his weight onto Wolf Sword's crossguard; the blade pierced the man's throat.

De Chauliac's strength returned. He feinted and then plunged his sword point beneath the man's raised arm. He kicked the horse around and saw Blackstone was already attempting to outflank survivors who were desperately attempting to break free. Fallen bodies and thrashing horses slowed his pace and at least twenty men escaped. Others fled in the opposite direction. Suddenly the fight's energy waned and some of the routiers tried to surrender – without success.

Blackstone saw de Chauliac urge his men to pursue the escaping mercenaries.

'Captain! No! Let them go! Leave them!' he yelled, running to the horseman and snatching at his bridle. The Frenchman's blood was up and he tried to yank free but Blackstone held firm. 'My men will deal with them. You give chase, you might die with those bastards!' For a moment it seemed de Chauliac would wrench his horse free but the lust to kill calmed and he nodded.

'I owe you, Sir Thomas. It will not be forgotten.'

Blackstone barely acknowledged the Frenchman's thanks and rejoined his men.

The fight in the valley was over. Blackstone's men were already stripping the bodies of whatever plunder they could find. The dead routiers had gold and silver in their purses and some wore silver belts with expensive knives and swords, plunder taken from their victims. Blackstone saw the look of disgust cross de Chauliac's face.

'You and your men fight like demons, Sir Thomas, and I more than any other am glad of it, but it's common men who scavenge from the dead.'

'It's their reward, de Chauliac. Unlike you, they're not in the service of any nobleman or king. They must take their profit where they find it. See to your wounded.'

The Frenchman had watched Blackstone carve his way through the mercenary ranks, and the force of his attack had stunned the enemy. He and the veteran knight Killbere were formidable and de Chauliac knew that had they met face-to-face on the battlefield he would have been the one to die. He had no sense of false pride when witnessing the prowess of such fighting men.

'See to your own men, Sir Thomas. And your boy. I saw him fall.'

He steered his horse away as Blackstone's eyes scoured the killing field. He saw John Jacob and Perinne next to the small shrine of the Holy Mother. At their feet lay his son.

CHAPTER FIFTY-ONE

Grimo the butcher spurred his horse away from the killing. Twenty men had turned with him and a similar number had escaped on the road back towards Chambéry. The attack from the forest had taken him utterly by surprise. English whoreson archers. They had slain his men with a terrifying ease and then the swordsmen had swept into them with a fury that staggered even his men, every one of whom had fought in the great battles. How many men lay back there in the valley? More than two hundred was certain. He would have to build his force again. How had they known, those English? His paymaster didn't know where the attack was to take place; there could have been no idle gossip, no words loosened by drink. How had they known?

It made no difference now. He and a handful of his men had survived but there would be no payment from Milan and, worse, he would not be able to return in failure. Not to the monster who would tear the flesh from his bones with his bare teeth. He looked back. No pursuit. The road ahead narrowed and beyond its bend he knew there was a crossroads. He would decide where to go when he got there. He slowed their retreat and cantered down the curved track, but then quickly reined in.

'Sweet Jesus,' said the man at his side. 'It's a trap.'

Two huge men straddled the road with their men. The same damned men he had let through before. Men he could have slaughtered back then but who would now inflict losses on him. Desperation clawed at Grimo and his routiers. They couldn't go back: certain death lay there; they had to throw themselves forward and seize the road. Horses jostled. The odds were about equal. The butcher bellowed defiance, kicked his horse forward and brought up his shield, his raised sword ready to strike.

The road served Meulon and Gaillard better than it did those who attacked. Blackstone's men bestrode the broadest part of the track where the road bellied out, which gave them the opportunity to strike Grimo's men from the sides as they were forced to ride into the fray barely three abreast along the narrow road. Horses and shields clashed but the routiers had no power to drive through. Riders from the edge of the broad part of the road curled in on them in death's embrace.

Meulon parried Grimo's strike with his shield, waiting for the desperate man attacking him to deliver the blow that would expose an unguarded part of his body. Gaillard had already driven forward into the mêlée. Grimo's men were jammed together, yanking their terror-stricken horses' reins this way and that and spurring the beasts' flanks, cursing as their lumbering mounts could do nothing more than heave and push against the ones next to them, desperately fighting their riders. Snared like fish in a net, Grimo's men fell beneath a savage onslaught. Horses trampled those who went under their hooves and then broke free, tearing open the cluster of routiers, giving Blackstone's men the advantage as they forced their mounts into the gaps left by the panicked beasts.

Grimo grunted with effort, yet could make no impression against Meulon. He tried desperately to force his way past the big man, to where freedom lay, down the road towards the mountains. Sweat stung his eyes. He swung his sword wide with as much force as he could, but the shock of the strike against Meulon's blade shuddered up his arm. And then the big man moved so quickly Grimo failed to raise his guard in time and the massive blow from Meulon's shield knocked him backwards in the saddle. His feet slipped from the stirrups and his balance was gone. He tumbled to the ground. Avoiding flailing hooves he saw that there were fewer than half a dozen of his men still alive and they were being hacked to the ground. He staggered to his feet again, knowing there might be a chance to escape if he could run free into the forest where horses were unlikely to follow.

He shouldered past a riderless horse and for a moment thought fate had favoured him. And then a dismounted Meulon stood in his way. Grimo lunged; Meulon easily sidestepped. He swept his knife beneath Grimo's raised face. The pain came a breath later. A gurgling, choking, desperate inhalation of blood into his lungs. He fell to his knees, hands to his severed throat, eyes locked on the big bearded man who gazed down at him, bloodied knife in hand.

'Now you know,' said Meulon.

Henry Blackstone had not regained consciousness and the blood-soaked bandage, torn from the dress he had been obliged to wear before the fight, bore witness to his wound. Blackstone and the men gathered around the fallen boy. John Jacob held Henry's shoulders in his lap as Will Longdon unwrapped the cloth and inspected the wound.

'It's a gash is all,' he said, puckering the split scalp with his bloody fingers. 'Perinne, spill some wine on it.'

'Vinegar's better,' said one of the archers who had crowded around to see how badly hurt the boy was.

Killbere kicked him. 'This wine's vinegar at the best of times. Get yourself back with the others. You keep an eye out in case there's any more of those skinners lurking.'

The man scurried away as Will Longdon poked a finger in the wound. 'Can't see bone, and can't feel nothin'. No bits of cracked skull sticking out. Ah, the lad'll be fine. Here, pour it here,' he instructed Perinne, who poured red wine over the wound. 'Who's got the needle and thread?' One of the archers leaned into the throng of men proffering a curved needle like a fisherman's awl, its eye threaded with silk. Longdon took it and studied the length of silk whipping unwound from an arrow shaft. 'Perinne,' he said, holding out the thread. Perinne duly dribbled wine over it. 'Right, now let's give the lad a decent scar,' said Longdon, holding the flaps of scalp ready for the needle. When the stitching was done and the boy's face bathed clean of blood another bandage was tied round. The men had bickered among themselves whether the slash should be packed with manure as were most battlefield wounds, but Blackstone remembered how he had been cared for by the royal physician when critically wounded as a boy after Crécy, and of how Aelis had cleaned and treated Killbere's wound. His decision to leave the wound dressed only with the torn cloth had been grudgingly obeyed. Blackstone watched as the unconscious boy was eased onto the litter. A stab of fear and guilt made him place a hand on Henry's chest. The slow but steady beat of his son's heart assured him that the lad's courage lay deep within him despite his youth.

Some of de Chauliac's men had succumbed to their wounds and his losses now totalled eleven men. A small price, given they had been so outnumbered. Blackstone had lost four men and two others would not reach Chambéry alive. The dead would be buried by the Count's priest in the city's churchyard. Blackstone and the men rode back towards Chambéry, past the dead routiers brought down by Jack Halfpenny and his twenty archers who had waited to cut off any escaping survivors. They recovered what arrows they could from the scattered bodies and dragged the corpses to one side of the road; then they did as Blackstone had done at the ambush site and strung up the bodies from trees along the road. Eighteen bodies swung in the breeze, as did another thirty by way of example along the valley fringe. Meulon had rammed Grimo's severed head on a shaft and left it at the bend of the road along with his mercenaries' corpses strung from the trees. De Chauliac had protested. Merchants would travel this route between Lombardy and Paris and such barbaric gestures of victory would simply tell them they were entering a lawless land.

'Not so,' Blackstone insisted as he watched the last of Halfpenny's kills being hoisted. 'They show the merchants they are safe. At least when my men are around. Any routier will think again before he lies in wait on Count Amadeus's territory.' He studied de Chauliac for a moment. He and his men had accounted themselves well. They were a long way from the comfort and privilege of the royal palace. 'I send a message the only way I know how to these killers. You forget, de Chauliac, they came here to murder the Dauphin's sister, your King's daughter. We should have kept the wounded alive and had them drawn and quartered, but time is not on our side. Besides, by the time you return home from Milan this encounter will be known at court and your part in it declared a victory for the Dauphin. They'll honour you. Might even give you a reward. And you can tell them that you and your men did most of the fighting. I don't care.'

De Chauliac bristled. 'I would claim nothing that was not true.'

'Aye, I didn't think you would. You're a loyal and honourable man,' said Blackstone. He turned his horse for Chambéry and the hope that the Princess had not died of the poison that had been administered. Otherwise his men would have died for nothing.

'The boy was at our side, Sir Thomas,' said John Jacob. 'It's my fault he was injured. I should have kept him out of it.'

Perinne shook his head. 'John's right about the lad's courage, but he wasn't to blame. We were both fighting when it happened. Young Henry ducked and weaved after stabbing the bastard and the skinner was determined to have him.'

Blackstone turned to the two men who had fought alongside him over so many years. 'I hold no one responsible. You both know how a man needs luck to get through a fight. He's been blooded before; he's no stranger to the killing. You've both held my life and his in your hands before now. If you had not been there in good time he would have died. I owe you thanks. There's nothing more to be said on the matter.'

The men nodded and fell back to ride with the litter.

'If the lad's as thick-skulled as his father he'll be all right,' said Killbere. 'I've seen you take bareheaded blows that would kill men wearing iron helms. Though I suspect so many lumps might explain why you're such a mad bastard in a fight.'

'Only in a fight?' said Blackstone.

'I was being generous,' answered Killbere, and then drank thirstily from his wineskin.

CHAPTER FIFTY-TWO

By the time Blackstone and his men were within a day's ride of Chambéry, Henry Blackstone was awake and complaining bitterly to John Jacob.

'He says he won't ride in the litter like a girl. A knight doesn't ride in a wagon or on a mare, he tells me,' said Jacob, reporting to Blackstone.

Blackstone smiled. The lessons from the boy's childhood had stayed with him. 'Get him a horse, John. Tell him if he falls off because of his wound we leave him behind.'

'The lad will tie himself to the reins,' said Will Longdon. 'But I'm ready to surrender my aching arse to a hot bath and a serving girl to wash my back and vitals.'

Killbere squirmed in the saddle to look back at the grinning archer. 'Your damned vitals are barely enough to serve as bait for a river eel, let alone a serving girl.'

Longdon grinned. 'No serving girl will want to let my river eel slip from her grasp when it squirms, Sir Gilbert.'

'Archers,' said Killbere, and then spat. 'They think they're God's gift to kings and whores.'

'That's because we are,' said Blackstone, siding with his bowmen.

'Here's my arrow shaft!' called Jack Halfpenny. 'Stand ready, girls!'

'Nock, mark and loose!' Will Longdon and others chimed in, bursting into laughter.

Killbere glanced at Blackstone riding at his side. 'And you grinning like a priest in a brothel only encourages these cocksure peasants,' he said.

'And I know you would have it no other way,' said Blackstone. Killbere shrugged. 'As long as I get to the serving girl first.'

News of the killing had already reached Count Amadeus by the time Blackstone and de Chauliac led their men through the city gates. The wild boy Girard had witnessed everything and ran tirelessly back to his master like the half-creature he was. After the Count had questioned Blackstone he acknowledged that everything pointed to Bernabò Visconti being behind the attack but, he argued, there was no proof. The Vipers of Milan writhed with deceit and intrigue and using a man's name to blacken his reputation was common currency. The child Princess must be delivered to them and now that one attack had failed it was unlikely whoever was behind the assault would risk another, especially after the royal party crossed the mountains and entered Visconti territory. Blackstone and de Chauliac would ride into Milan but they would be shadowed every step of the way by the bridegroom's father's troops.

Back in the yard Blackstone sluiced water across his torso, scrubbing the blood from his stubbled face.

'Will he now give us men to strengthen our escort?' said Killbere.

'No. He's not even convinced it was Galeazzo's brother who arranged the ambush.'

'Damned idiot. Meulon had it straight from the horse's mouth. That skinner whoreson told him to serve Bernabò Visconti.'

'And that might have been a name to hide behind.' He tipped the bucket of cold water away and rubbed himself down.

'You'll not wait for the water to be heated?' said Killbere as Blackstone dressed.

'I don't want to see the Princess with blood on me.'

Killbere's eyebrows rose. 'The Princess,' he said flatly. 'Uh-huh. You stink of sweat no matter how hard you scrub with cold water and soap. Now, a hot bath, a fresh shirt and a comb through that rat's nest of hair, that would be fitting for a princess. But' – he grinned – 'the woman Aelis, she will no doubt embrace your stink.'

* * *

Blackstone climbed the stairs past Amadeus's guards to the Princess's chamber. There were voices inside. He stepped in and saw Henry on the stool at the child's bedside while Aelis stood watching. The Princess was propped up on pillows and seemed none the worse for the poisoning. The ladies-in-waiting stood diligently in the background.

He glanced from his son to Aelis. She smiled.

'Your grace,' Blackstone said, bowing his head to the child Princess. 'I see you are recovered.'

'I am, Sir Thomas. And it is thanks to your lady here. And *mon petit chevalier* has been telling me of a great fight. Have you seen his wound? It is terrible.'

'It is nothing, highness,' said Henry with a guilty glance towards his father.

'Nonsense,' said the Princess. 'I would have felt a great responsibility had you been mortally injured. And my good lady Aelis has examined the wound and tells me it was stitched by a good hand.'

'Did my son explain why we fought?'

'To ensure our path across the mountains was clear,' said the girl.

Blackstone breathed a sigh of relief. It would have served no purpose had Henry blabbed about any suspected attack commissioned by one of the Visconti. But the boy had kept his mouth shut and the information to himself.

'Exactly right,' said Blackstone. 'Henry, time to leave the Princess to rest now. No more stories of violence to disturb her sleep.'

'No, no. I asked for him to be here,' said Isabelle. 'He will tell me about the battle and how you killed your enemies and then he will read to me.' She laid a hand on Henry's shoulder. 'I am grateful for such courage.' She glanced at Aelis, the ladies-in-waiting and Blackstone. 'Leave us.'

* * *

'For once a royal command served me well,' said Blackstone as he and Aelis lay entwined in the sweat-creased linen sheets. They had returned to his quarters and no sooner had the door closed behind them than Blackstone pulled her to him, his hand cupping her breast, his mouth smothering hers. The aftermath of the fight still seared his blood, and tenderness was abandoned as she met his demands with equal desire. By the time darkness fell their passion had finally been quenched. He no longer felt any sense of betrayal or guilt as his wife's ghost passed through the shadows of his mind. Sinking into the deep river of darkness that drowned a man in passion, he almost called Christiana's name, but another face emerged, that of the woman who had bewitched him. He had dragged himself back from those depths and shaken himself loose from the abandonment of his climax. She felt it immediately but said nothing. Aelis's body was scarred from the torture she had endured, as was his from battle. Each had touched and kissed the other's wounds, but when she caressed his face and the scar that was now little more than a thin line her heart caught a beat. She closed her eyes for a moment and then looked at him.

'That is where your life started,' she whispered. 'The life you live now. I can feel the terror of that moment. So many of those you knew died that day but there was one who was special. Someone you guarded. Someone of your own blood.'

The image of his brother being slaughtered at Crécy formed in his mind's eye. He shuddered, not only from the memory but also from the unease that squirmed within him. Superstition was a constant companion for any man who faced the ebb and flow of battle. Wariness about luck and the fates that determined it crept inside every fighter's heart. A prayer, a false promise to the Almighty, or a blatant disregard for danger was every man's shield. Blackstone saw nothing but his enemy in front of him when he fought. His animal-like instinct and the Celtic goddess at his neck were what kept him alive. She could nudge a man this way or that, place him where an arrow fell or a blade sneaked under his guard. It was fate when she decided the time for him to fall; until then she protected him. But those like Aelis who professed to see behind the veil of a man's life – they could frighten the bravest of men and he was no exception. Did she talk to the dead or did God in heaven whisper in her ear?

She saw the shadow of doubt pass across his eyes. 'Do not fear me, Thomas.'

'Why shouldn't I? You recount my past as if it were written by a scribe on parchment. You speak as if you were at my shoulder over the years. No wonder they wanted to burn you.'

'There are no words I can ever say to convince men that I would not do them harm. I am no witch.'

'You put the fear of Christ into men because you can poison as well as heal and you were prepared to castrate those who violated you. You are capable of causing harm, Aelis. You look beyond the grave to see the ghosts of men who are not yet dead and predict what you see.'

'There are times I am taken by surprise, especially when my heart is touched. Perhaps that's what brings on the second sight,' she said as he gathered his clothes. 'You're leaving me? Because of what I said?'

He quickly dressed. 'I heard a rider in the courtyard. I should see if there's more news of our journey.'

She extended her arm to him, beckoning him back. 'You have captains to do that.'

He hesitated. 'You're beginning to know too much about me, Aelis. You could use it against me.'

She was shocked at the accusation and threw aside the sheet, kneeling forward so that her breasts swayed. Her nipples hardened in the cold air. His eyes fell on them and he tasted the spittle of desire again, despite her making no effort to seduce him. Not that much effort was needed.

'I am drawn to you, Thomas Blackstone. I cannot say why. You saved me and for that I am grateful, but I do not share a bed with you out of gratitude. If I see that you suffer or know that you are facing a danger that you are unaware of I cannot stop myself from sharing what I see.'

He had taken a step back into the shadow that lay on the edge of the candlelight. The further away from the tantalizing sight of her nakedness the better. There was another temptation that beckoned him now. Milan and the Visconti tyrants.

'You once said I would be betrayed. How do I know it won't be you?'

Despite the soft light he saw her expression change. She dropped her head. He felt the shock. She knew! In a couple of strides he was in front of her and tugged her short hair, raising her face to the light. A single tear from each eye trickled down her cheeks. 'Who?' he asked again, his voice barely a whisper.

'Someone who is at your shoulder,' she said quietly. 'Someone who owes you his life.'

He waited. The look of regret on her face spurred panic inside him. He and his men had fought shoulder to shoulder over the years. Could she mean one of them? Killbere? Meulon? Gaillard? Will Longdon? All of whom were like the brother he had lost at Crécy. All of whom had shed their blood for him.

'Who?' he asked. The need to know was painful.

Through her sadness a rueful smile creased her tears. 'The hand of friendship betrays you. I cannot see him, Thomas. I cannot save you. All I see is your blood.'

PART FIVE

THE DEVIL'S SON

CHAPTER FIFTY-THREE

Five houndsmen each held a half-dozen mastiffs on long leashes, the muscled dogs pulling them along Via Manzoni; each man needed all his strength to keep them under control. The dogs' powerful gait meant their handlers were obliged to run in order to keep up with their pace. A houndsman's life was short if unforeseen injuries befell any of his charges due to neglect or an accident that could have been averted. And now it was becoming more difficult to restrain the slavering beasts. Bernabò Visconti had more than five thousand such dogs billeted in the city. Hunting was one of his greatest passions and it was said his love for his hounds surpassed even his love for his wife, Regina. Bernabò's life was one of orgy and self-indulgence; his many mistresses and numerous bastard children were spread across the territory he had taken by force. Yet his beloved wife was his lodestone and she could restrain his wild fits of temper and rage; and despite his cruelty, murder and avarice being known far and wide, so too was his diplomacy with foreign rulers. Everything this contradictory man did was aimed at one day achieving complete power. Milan was mostly left for him to govern while his brother, Galeazzo II, spent more time in his *castello* in Pavia to the south of the city where he indulged himself planning great places of learning and building a bridge across the Ticino. It was a good arrangement. The brothers tolerated each other but Galeazzo found living in the same city as Bernabò exasperating. So while they shared control of Milan, it was Bernabò who saw himself as its true lord. He and Galeazzo had agreed long ago who would control which parts of the city. The city was divided. Of the eight gates into Milan Galeazzo held the western portion: Comasina,

Vercellina, Giovia and Ticinese. Bernabò held the eastern side of the city-state and the Porte Nuova, Romana, Tosa and Orientale, all of which gave him access to the eastern territories and their cities he had conquered. But no matter which gate Bernabò chose to use when hunting, when the baying hounds ran through the streets Milan's inhabitants pressed back to give them right of way. And when their self-declared God on earth, Pope and Emperor rode through the streets everyone was obliged to bend the knee.

With so many of Bernabò's hounds to house some of Milan's citizens were given one or two of his dogs to care for and feed, and the strict enforcement concerning the animals' welfare applied as much to the householder as to the houndsmen. Sometimes the dogs were taken to the hunt in cages that held twenty at a time, but today they were running ahead of their master, whose horse cantered behind the baying packs as they caught the scent of the countryside beyond the city walls where they would soon be unleashed to drag down deer or boar, whichever creature the beaters flushed out first.

A handcart lurched out of a side alley. The iron-rimmed wheels could cause injury to even the strongest of hounds. Citizens scattered from the paved streets as one of the houndsmen bellowed a warning. The cart was quickly turned and the dogs ran past without harm. The Lord of Milan reined in his horse. Those who pushed the cart knelt. Bernabò was a striking figure: his height and strength were impressive, even when he wasn't on horseback – enough to make any man cower, even if he had not been their ruler. Behind him ran a retinue of courtiers and footsoldiers and now they too stopped, lungs heaving as their lord gazed down at the handcart and the dead man it bore.

'What killed this man?' Bernabò demanded when he saw the broken body. His rule of fear meant that Milan was probably the safest of cities. No thief or murderer would risk the terrifying punishment Bernabò would inflict on any convicted criminal yet the man's bloodied corpse looked as though he might have been the victim of an assault.

'He fell from a scaffold, my lord,' said one of the men without raising his eyes.

'Then where are you taking him? He's beyond help from any physician. Why isn't he buried?'

'My lord, we were going to dump him in the river. His family do not have enough money so our priest refuses to bury him.'

Bernabò inclined his head to one of the courtiers who waited behind his horse. It was sufficient as a gesture to have one of them step to his side. 'Give this man coin for the burial,' he said, and then to the cart handler, 'Look up, man. Who is your priest?'

'Father Stefano,' said the man.

'Fetch him and have him wait here,' he commanded. 'I will see this man buried before nightfall.' He spurred the horse forward. His hounds were already baying in the distance for their quarry. Bernabò grunted with anticipation. The day was set to be one of gratuitous pleasure. There would be blood on the ground soon enough, and it would not be long before news reached his brother that the French Princess had died on her journey from Paris. Poison or waylaid by brigands? he wondered. Which had snatched her away from the promise of marriage and a French alliance with Milan? Which of the two plans had been successful? Nothing had been left to chance. Soon he would feign regret at the child's death while concealing his satisfaction that the arrangement to share the rule of Milan with his brother would remain intact a while longer. He acknowledged the satisfaction he felt at his own cunning in stifling any future power and influence the proposed marriage between his nephew and the French King's daughter would have brought. Thinking ahead to the day when he held absolute power meant long-term planning.

Sparks flew from his horse's iron-shod hooves as he drove the beast towards the Porta Nuova and the hunting forests beyond. Impatience was his greatest enemy. News of the child's death should have reached him by now. Urging his horse into a gallop he saw his mastiffs loosed. The quarry's scent was in the air and the half-starved dogs wanted the taste of flesh and blood. And

Bernabò was no different. Why hadn't he heard? Why? What could have gone wrong? His blood was up and he wanted to feed his passion for the hunt. And more than anything he wanted to be victorious.

Count Amadeus had sent his wedding gifts of silver plate and armour to add to the burden of Isabelle's slow-moving column. The first early snows had fallen on Mont Cenis's high pass but the Savoyard mountain villagers, exempted from paying taxes for their service, had been waiting to guide the party across the Alps. They were dressed in woollen caps and mittens and wore spiked boots to give them purchase as they pushed and hauled the Princess and her ladies-in-waiting safely along the slippery route on *ramasses*, large wicker sledges. Their passengers were covered for warmth with animal furs and the French commander and a half-dozen of his men gripped the side of each sled and did their best to keep up, much to the amusement of the Princess, who found the sight of her escort slithering at her side a distraction from the great height. Blackstone had let de Chauliac have the honour. If the damn sledge went over the edge taking him and his royal cargo with it, then no blame would fall on Blackstone or his men. As they approached the highest point the going became ever more uncertain and he instructed the French to do as his own men had done and bind their horses' hooves with sackcloth for grip and pull hoods over the animals' heads to stop any panic as they edged along the precipices. It was a blessing they had not been obliged to pass in winter. A year before northern Italy had been smothered in deep snowfalls. Further east, Bologna had been covered in thirty feet of snow, and although these trade routes across the Alps were kept open by villagers and monks, merchants and soldiers who travelled between France and Italy had suffered more fatalities than usual and the frozen bodies of those who died were often only recovered in the thaw.

Henry Blackstone gaped in amazement at the majestic scenery. Where the child Princess giggled with excitement and joy, Blackstone's son felt the power of the place awe him into silence. Great waterfalls plummeted thousands of feet down through pine-clad mountainsides. Rocks, hewn as if by a giant stonemason, were etched against the blue sky. And when the wind gathered and swirled, dust clouds of snow from the mountaintops danced through the air stinging their faces. Nothing could be more beautiful or humbling than these mountains, he determined.

'Close your mouth, Henry, or you'll have icicles hanging from your teeth,' said Will Longdon as he guided his hooded horse in line with the others. They were all walking by their mounts, no one daring to risk a horse losing its footing and plunging to the valley below.

'I didn't know it could be so beautiful,' said Henry.

'Aye, well, you watch where you're going. If the man in front stops your head'll be up his horse's arse, and then you'll see how beautiful it looks when you go over the edge,' said John Jacob.

'Tell him about when we came over last time. Merciful God, Henry, Sir Thomas brought us across a pass ten times worse than this,' called Perinne from two horses to the rear. 'Blizzards, ice, couldn't see a hand in front of your face, which was just as well being as high as we were.'

'And we didn't have no sledge to ride on. Look at them things. Bigger than a lord's bed,' said Will Longdon. He hawked and spat from the exertion of keeping a tight rein while powering himself up the incline. 'Worse going down. Hit ice beneath the snow and you'll go arse over tit and be the first at the bottom.'

Those who could hear the banter added their voices. Renfred, the German man-at-arms, called out, 'Notice how much space we give Sir Thomas and that beast of his? It loses its head and we could all go over the edge.'

'And if the damn thing farts we'd have an avalanche,' added Gaillard, half turning to look back at them from where he led Will Longdon's group.

'As long as you don't break wind,' said Longdon. 'I've heard they have earthquakes in these mountains.'

The men's chatter went on a while longer, but Henry closed out their crude jesting and let his eyes drink in the sights that rose around him. Books he had read told him that armies had crossed these mountains; the great Carthaginian general Hannibal had taken elephants over these passes. He looked beyond the horses' rumps in front of him and saw his father leading the men. His height and breadth set him apart from the French escort, and for a moment the boy felt a renewed admiration. Perhaps, he reasoned, his father could also be a great general one day, given an army by the English King and told to go out and conquer lands, to make England an even greater nation than it was already. And then, as a brusque wind swept up the path and found its way through his clothing, he shivered. Ever since he was a child his father had taught him to ignore the privations of the weather but this chill was different. It was fear. His father's shield, like his men's, was tied across his back so that no breeze could lift it from its usual place strapped to the saddle. The defiant blazon heralded his father's intention never to yield and now they were travelling into the Visconti stronghold, to the men whom his father believed had sent the assassin who had slain his mother and sister. How could his father avenge them? The men who rode at his back were too few to assault the great city-state of Milan. He felt panic rise in his gorge. His father was sending him to Florence when they reached the great plains of Lombardy. Sending him away so that the Visconti could not use his presence at his father's side against him. He would sit in a classroom while his father and his men fought what might be their last battle. A fight they could not win despite their defiance. In that moment Henry Blackstone vowed that he would give his escort to Florence the slip and find a way into Milan.

CHAPTER FIFTY-FOUR

Men cried out in fear and warning as the hulking beast of a boar ran directly at its tormentors. It stood as high as a man's chest and weighed as much as a small horse. Four of Bernabò's beloved dogs lay eviscerated on the forest floor along with two of his beaters. One of the dog handlers bravely tried to spear the beast in an effort to save his dogs. The boar turned surprisingly quickly. Its tusks caught the handler inside his thigh and tore upwards, ripping the man's taut stomach muscles and spilling his innards to mingle with the gore from his dogs. His scream was brief and death took him quickly and then the charging boar scattered the hunters. Those on foot plunged into thick brambles while others tried to scramble up trees. Half a dozen horsemen shared the hunt with Bernabò: three of their mounts reared and plunged out of control with their riders clinging desperately as they bolted through the forest. Two of Bernabò's crossbowmen shot the boar. It barely registered the impact of the steel-tipped bolts.

One of the remaining hunters launched his spear into the charging animal, which brought it down onto its snout, its razor tusks tearing into the dirt. But such was its power and perhaps its hatred for man and dog who had invaded its domain that it quickly found its footing and ran forward again, but its strength had been diminished. Another half-dozen dogs leapt at its throat and hocks. Their teeth clamped into sinew and artery; the boar's blood spilled over its flanks and the dogs who hung from it. The great beast swung its head and dislodged one dog, trampling it beneath its cloven hoof, but the hounds had done their job and slowed it so that another two men could leap forward and plunge their spears into its flanks, narrowly missing the blood-crazed hounds.

Bernabò heeled his horse clear of the carnage and tightened the reins in his left hand with such force that his horse's head was pulled up high, eyes rolling in terror as the boar swept past it. Bernabò stood in the stirrups and with all his strength plunged his spear beneath the boar's shoulder. It was a fatal blow and the crippled animal staggered to a halt. Two huntsmen dared to run forward and plunge their knives into the beast's spine, and then it went down. Houndsmen whipped the frenzied dogs away from the kill and secured them onto their leashes. The blood spoor through the forest told the story of the long chase. Bernabò bellowed out a roar of satisfaction at the kill. Men and dogs had hunted bravely and they would be rewarded: the men with good food and extra wine and the dogs with a haunch of the dead animal. Once the head had been taken as a trophy the boar would be spit-roasted.

Sweat stung Bernabò's eyes and he drank thirstily from a wineskin as the yelping dogs, denied their victim, lunged on their leashes, held tight by exhausted handlers. Those of the retinue who had scurried away returned, scratched and bruised from their desperate efforts to avoid the enraged boar. Bernabò dismounted – his reins were quickly taken by a servant – and stepped towards the dying animal. As he ran a hand over the prickly head its eyes rolled and it tried to slash sideways, but its energy was gone and its life was slipping away. The last thing the lord of the forest beasts saw was the Lord of Milan sliding his knife across its throat.

The hunting party journeyed back, blood-streaked and weary, through the north gate, but the city's lord showed no sign of fatigue. He sat upright in the saddle, smiling at those citizens who stepped aside and cheered his name. Not even seeing how the city was being inundated with Galeazzo's guests for the wedding dented his good humour.

A thousand or more thronged the city, renting houses, filling inns and taverns and keeping the brothels busy day and night.

Three days of festivities to celebrate the marriage had been planned, great pavilions had been set up outside the walls, food and drink on a huge scale had been arranged and tournaments would be held to entertain the guests. It was to be an ostentatious display, a vibrant tableau to show every noble house just how wealthy the Visconti were. Jewels, silk and the most expensive raiments had been sent from throughout Italy. They had bought a French princess: a humiliation for France, a victory for Milan. But when the Princess failed to arrive because of her untimely death the celebrations would turn into a great mourning. Galeazzo would be reduced in his ambitions and then only his brat of a son would stand between Bernabò and his gaining full control of the city-state and the income it generated.

By the time he was halfway down Via Manzoni he saw the figures of the men with the handcart, and now there was a priest standing with them. The joy of the hunt had caused him to forget his earlier command that they await his return.

'Success, my lord?' asked one of the men gathered around the handcart as Bernabò reined in his horse.

'Yes, he gave a good account of himself,' said Bernabò as the boar was carried past and he waved the courtiers to continue on to his palace. 'You're Father Stefano?' he asked as the priest bowed his head.

'I am, my lord,' he answered.

'Uh-huh,' grunted Bernabò. 'And the grave is now dug?'

'It is,' said the priest.

'Then I will accompany you and these good citizens and see that all is as it should be.' He gestured for the men to turn the cart and the priest led the way down the cobbled street. The slow jolting twitched the dead man's body in a final jig before the confines of the earth embraced him.

Less than three hundred yards down the narrow street the cortège turned into the suburban graveyard where the men lifted the corpse from the back of the cart and carried it towards the freshly dug grave. Bernabò stayed mounted and watched the proceedings. Finally, when the benediction had been muttered, he addressed the priest.

'Who was it that built this church?' he said.

'It was your grandfather's father, my lord,' the priest answered.

'And who furnished it with gold crucifix and silk altar dressing?' said Bernabò.

'You did, my lord. And your brother Lord Galeazzo furnished the new bell for the belfry.'

'Are we not generous to you?'

'More than generous, my lord,' said the priest.

'And yet the Pope calls me Son of Belial. If I am the devil's son then why am I so generous?'

'I cannot answer, my lord.'

'Is it because I fought his troops and won? Is it because I do not bow my knee as my brother does?'

'Again, my Lord Bernabò, it is not for me to speak for the Pope. But your generosity cannot be denied.'

'And yet you refuse to bury one of my subjects?' Bernabò asked, and for the first time the hint of approaching danger in his voice made the priest falter.

'I had other duties, my lord. I was obliged to attend those who needed my ministrations,' the priest answered.

'Not the whorehouse on Via San Damiano?'

The man's jaw gaped and it took a few seconds before he could find an answer. 'I do not attend such places, my lord.'

'You should. I recommend it.' He grinned but the priest remained solemn. 'Ah, but I'll wager you have obliged some of the nuns at Santa Maria d'Aurona convent to spread their legs. They've a reputation, those nuns. No, Father Stefano, you had no other urgent business. You denied a working man a Christian burial. These people are mine to protect and yours to pray over and to help pass into the next world. Their poverty should not deny them your blessing. You must embrace the common man,' said Bernabò and turned to his escort of footsoldiers. 'Help Father Stefano achieve more humility.'

Soldiers quickly stepped forward. They grabbed the frightened priest and threw him into the grave. His body slammed into the corpse and he cried out in fear and disgust, trying to get to his feet. His habit entangled him but then, using the walls of the grave, he found his footing. He gazed up at the men as Bernabò gestured to his soldiers.

'Bury him.'

'No, lord, no! I beg you!' Father Stefano cried, but the soldiers were already shovelling the loose dirt into the pit. Soil clogged the priest's eyes and mouth. He spat and floundered and raised a hand to try and protect his face from the dirt that poured down on him. He choked, fell to his knees, clambered back to his feet, but soon he was waist-deep in dirt. His spluttering cries for mercy faded.

Bernabò Visconti watched dispassionately as the man's face finally disappeared; an outstretched disembodied hand clawed at the air, but then that too vanished beneath the mound. Bernabò eased the horse aside. 'Make a marker,' he told the cowed men. 'Name the man who died and say that he lies embraced by a man of God.'

Bernabò heeled his horse away. No one would dare try and rescue the priest by digging him out. The Lord of Milan had delivered justice.

CHAPTER FIFTY-FIVE

The nearer Princess Isabella's retinue got to Milan the more the numbers of the escort swelled as they were joined by the local lords who were tasked to accompany her in a manner fit for a king's daughter. Every nobleman bore his banners and pennons proclaiming his status, not only to impress the French Princess but also to show Galeazzo Visconti that they had obeyed his command. Outriders from the city had been sent to report on the bride-to-be's progress and the day before the entourage rode triumphantly into the city Thomas Blackstone and his men had fallen to the rear of the column. The Italian noblemen would form the escort ahead of de Chauliac and his royal guard.

One of Galeazzo Visconti's heralds sent from the city held back as he watched the slow-moving procession make its way across the flat landscape. He made note of the Dauphin's royal guard, but it was the men who followed that held his interest. In previous years Visconti troops had been outfought and killed by English *condottieri* and now, as the light faded on the day before the convoy entered the city, the herald realized who it was that would soon ride into his master's domain. He turned his horse and spurred it for home.

The night's crisp, cold air settled on the encampment. Sparks from the fires flew upwards, quickly extinguishing themselves in the night chill. Blackstone's men had camped a quarter of a mile beyond the pavilions and tents erected by the Italian noblemen. De Chauliac was still close escort to the Princess and shielded the child from the constant flow of regional lords who wished to impress on her their joy at her marriage. Court jesters tied on a rope, Killbere had said when he saw the puffed-up, brightly dressed aristocrats standing impatiently in line during the preceding days, each vassal keen to ensure his name would be remembered and perhaps, if the Princess were generous enough, to mention their good wishes to the Lord of Milan. Blackstone's men had eaten and then set about sharpening their weapons. Blackstone huddled with his captains around the fire. Perinne pushed wood into the flames and its shadows caught the men's gaunt features. Like many times before when going into battle they each pondered what might befall them. But now no great conflict awaited: any fighting to be done would be at close quarters as in all likelihood they would be forced to fight their way through narrow streets, a battlefield that had them at a disadvantage. An unknown city favoured their enemy.

'We enter the city tomorrow. We are protected by the Prince of Wales's command and his flag but once we are behind the walls his letter of safe passage may be worthless,' said Blackstone. He turned to his centenar, Will Longdon. 'You'll keep the archers on the road to Florence; only the captains and a dozen men-at-arms will enter the city with me. The smaller the force inside the walls the quicker we can move.'

'Thomas, you ride into a vipers' nest. They can strike you at any time. The more of us the better your chances,' said the veteran archer.

'Your bows are of little use in the city streets,' said Killbere. 'Thomas is right. He needs you outside because if we have to escape we will be pursued and you and Halfpenny will need your hands off your cocks and your wits about you to cover us.'

Will Longdon looked at the other captains. The English bowman was always treasured by the fighting men. There was no point arguing. 'We'll be ready, Thomas, you can count on us.'

'Stay alert, Will. The Visconti would like nothing better than to kill English archers. The men-at-arms who remain with you will serve to cover your flanks should any attack be made against you,' said Blackstone. 'If the Visconti strike at us before we find the man we seek, they will come for you soon after.'

'At least there'll be no threat for the three days of celebrations,' said Gaillard.

'You're wrong, my friend,' said Meulon. 'If I wanted to kill my enemy what better time than when others are distracted? Am I right, Sir Thomas?'

'Yes,' said Blackstone. 'Whatever happens it will be in the next few days.'

'And we don't start any trouble,' added Killbere. 'No whores, no fighting in taverns, no matter if we are provoked. They will look for any excuse to imprison us and rid themselves of the protection we have from our Prince.'

Blackstone gave a final glance at the men around him. Who among these friends would survive the next few days? All of them were prepared to follow him without question even though the desire to avenge the death of his wife and child was his alone. Fourteen years of comradeship had brought them to this place together. He prayed he could get them out of the city alive.

Perinne rubbed a hand across his close-cropped head. The crow's-feet scars on his scalp were white against his weather-beaten skin. 'I say we get as drunk as monks when this is over,' he said.

The men murmured their agreement.

'Aye, but only if Sir Gilbert pays for it,' said Will Longdon.

The archer waited for the usual rebuff from the man he had known even longer than Thomas Blackstone. But none came.

'If any of us get out of this alive I'll buy the drink and the whores but I suspect I'll need few coins in my purse,' said a pessimistic Killbere.

Blackstone walked back to his tent. A few hundred yards away a glittering swarm of fireflies twinkled in the darkness. These were no night insects, but the torchlight from the Princess's encampment. His own camp's burning torches afforded enough light for his men to find their beds and stand their sentry duties. Being within a day's ride of Milan put Blackstone on guard in case of a surprise attack. Cooking fires flickered here and there as braziers gave warmth to small groups of men. As he made his way through the encampment conversations paused for the men to acknowledge their sworn lord. In the distance he saw Aelis open the flap of his tent and pull it closed behind her. Since they had left Chambéry their lovemaking had been no less passionate, but had been restrained because of the closeness of the men around them. Such constraint had made it more intense. Aelis had made no further mention of what might lie ahead but he sensed a slow withdrawal of her feelings for him. As though she was already preparing to mourn his death.

Two shadows emerged from between the tents; Henry led a man towards him. 'My lord,' said Henry, 'this man has been sent by Father Torellini.' The boy's anguish was plain to see even in the half-light. Father and son would soon be parted. And Blackstone had not yet embraced the boy or explained in more detail his wishes should he not return from his vendetta.

The man was dressed in a cloak that Blackstone recognized. He knew that if the man turned his back there would be a symbol that looked like an axe but in reality was the sign of the Tau. The man who stood before him bowed his head. 'Sir Thomas, I am Pietro Foresti. I have information for you.'

Blackstone placed a hand on his son's shoulder. 'Henry, attend to your duties with John Jacob. My jupon and shield need to be cleaned. See to it.'

'Yes, my lord,' said the boy, obeying without question. He would plead to stay with his father after his intended escort to Florence had delivered Father Torellini's message.

Blackstone guided the Tau knight to the edge of the camp. The man's clothing was mud-splattered and his hair was matted from dry sweat. He had obviously been riding long and hard to reach him.

'What news do you have for me from Father Torellini?'

'Sir Thomas, there have been whispers within Bernabò Visconti's court that he knew of a plan to harm the Princess Isabelle.'

'Your news comes too late. We already discovered such a plan when we were at Chambéry. They tried to poison her but they had also set an ambush. Both attempts failed, as you can see. Is there proof that Lord Bernabò ordered her death?'

The man shook his head. 'No, only that he knew of it. Lord Galeazzo would have had no role to play. But in the matter of the death of your wife and child Father Torellini believes that it could have been either of the brothers who sent the assassin. Perhaps both were in agreement to try and kill you. But there is a third man involved. It is thought the Visconti shield themselves behind him. It is one of their household or family. Nothing is certain.'

'No name given to you?' said Blackstone.

'A name, Sir Thomas, but no evidence of his guilt. He is a man who stands back in the shadows and does the Visconti's bidding.'

'Is it Bernabò's bastard son, Antonio Lorenz?' said Blackstone, hoping that the man who had planned the Princess's death might be one and the same as he who had sent the assassin.

He saw Foresti's look of surprise. Blackstone smiled. 'He commissions assassins on behalf of the Visconti but this time he is involved in trying to kill King John's daughter. That knowledge is valuable.'

'Father Torellini instructs me to tell you that if you get close to Lord Bernabò there is a servant who spies for Florence and who will know your name and will do what he can to help you. His risk is great because should he be discovered a terrifying death awaits him, so he will be cautious in his approach.'

'What's his name?'

'Only Father Torellini has that knowledge.'

'Then whom do I trust?'

'No one. If he has information or wishes to identify himself he will approach you and use these words: *Worldly fame is nothing but a breath of wind which blows now from one side and now from another, and changes its name because it changes direction...*'

'That's all?'

'It's from a poem, Sir Thomas, but they are words that can be spoken in conversation without suspicion when the time presents itself.'

'Very well. I know nothing of poetry but if that is how I recognize him, then so be it. Now, you must rest and I'll arrange food for you, and then we can discuss you taking my son to Florence.'

'I have already been instructed by Father Torellini in that duty. Sir Thomas, we have met briefly once before. You would not remember but two years ago in Lucca when we took the English messenger's body from the merchant's house, I was one of those who carried him. I served Fra Stefano Caprini then. He accompanied you when you returned to England.'

Blackstone remembered the night when the English courier had brought the command for him to return and serve the Crown. But he had no recollection of the man's face. 'Fra Caprini gave his life trying to save my family, but he was killed by the same assassin who was sent by the Visconti. I will avenge my family and your master.'

Blackstone held close the feeling of anticipation. The Visconti were his enemy and he sensed their nearness. They were protected by walls, moats and canals, and Milan's labyrinthine streets twisted and turned like the snakes' nest the city was, but the urge to finally kill the man responsible for his family's death surged through him. It would take more than desire, though; he would need clear thinking and luck. He raised the crucifix that nestled next to Arianrhod. The small gold cross had once sat in that small dip at the base of his wife's throat. He kissed the slender symbol, and then did the same with the silver wheel of the Celtic goddess. Thoughts of how to kill and escape with his life, and the lives of the men who would accompany him, refused to leave him. It served no purpose to die in Milan. His son needed him and there was still his pledge to protect the King of England's son, even though the Prince of

Wales rebelled at the duty inherited by Blackstone. But for now all pledges made would stand behind this one act of vengeance. Like a wolf relentlessly chasing down its prey, he had finally caught the scent and his senses were alert and his blood was up.

The moment Blackstone stepped inside the tent he smelled the musky odour of the woman who was unlacing her dress. She turned to face him as she held the loose garment at her shoulder. A candle burned, its warm glow making her all the more enticing. He glanced down at a silk dress and chemise that had been laid neatly across a small chest. A cloak with a fur-trimmed hood hung from a corner of the tent pole and shoes, fit for a lady, were tucked neatly below.

'It looks as though you've been courted by one of the Italian noblemen,' said Blackstone, his throat already thick with desire for her. He loosened his belt and dropped his jerkin onto the floor.

'Are you concerned?'

He feigned indifference. 'It's your life, Aelis.'

'No, Thomas, it's yours. The life you saved is yours to own.'

He stripped free of his shirt. The cool, bracing air added to his desire to feel her warm flesh against his. He pulled off his breeches and tossed aside his braies. 'I told you, I don't own you. You do what you wish.' He waited for her to drop her dress but she kept herself covered.

'Aelis, it's cold. I shrink by the minute.'

She glanced down at his manhood. 'So you do. Soon there will be nothing left of any use.'

He took a step towards her, eager to release her dress. She stepped back and gave him a warning look. 'No, my lord, I am not yours for the taking. Or so you have just said.'

Exasperated and impatient, he cursed. 'Christ's blood on the cross, Aelis, do you want me or not? I've a fight on my hands tomorrow. I don't have all night.'

'Sleep then. You'll need your rest.'

'Should I go out and sleep on the ground with my men?'

'If they can offer you the same comfort as I can.'

He grinned. 'All right. You win. I'll be patient.' He settled down onto the blankets and pulled the fur covering across him. 'But not for long.' She turned her back on him and dropped the dress, which settled in a pool around her ankles. A shadow drew a curve from the fullness of her buttocks that swept down to her thighs. Most of the scars and blemishes from her mistreatment at the hands of the witch hunters had faded, but some still showed the puckered welts. 'The clothes?' he said, watching as she stepped free of the fallen material, each movement gently shifting her contours.

Picking up the silk dress she turned, holding it to her, ignoring the chemise. 'They are a gift from the Princess for my service. Her ladies-in-waiting were made to show me their best wardrobe and I was given freedom to choose.' She bent forward to step into the dress. Her eyes staying on him. Her breasts falling forward. Blackstone was held. She pulled up the dress, which settled below her breasts, its low cut almost forcing them free of the fabric. It was a tightly fitted gown with a low waist and a wide, scooped neckline. 'It is silk woven on the finest loom,' she said and sat down with her back to him, exposing her shoulder. 'And silk, Thomas,' she said, turning to face him as he pressed his lips against the warm fragrance of her skin, 'could arouse a monk sitting in prayer on a cold mountain pass.'

She eased back into his embrace and kissed him; then she pushed him back onto the blankets and pulled back the fur covering.

'I'm no monk,' said Blackstone.

'And I see you are no longer cold,' she answered, straddling him.

CHAPTER FIFTY-SIX

The most powerful city in northern Italy had dominated Lombardy for a thousand years. It boasted paved streets and more fountains than the renowned city of Paris – six thousand of them supplied drinking water for more than a hundred thousand citizens. The population had long spilled over Milan's ancient Roman limits and the outer walls, built centuries before to defend against invaders, cocooned suburbs and their churches and hospitals. Ten thousand monks from all denominations offered religious comfort while fifteen hundred lawyers applied the rule of law. Workshops housed artisans who helped create the city's great wealth. A hundred armourers manufactured the legendary Milanese armour: swords, helmets and mail for knights of Italy, Provence, Germany and more distant lands. The Milanese mint struck over twenty thousand silver pennies a year. More than three hundred public ovens gave each district fresh bread daily, milled from wheat grown on the vast plains around the city irrigated by numerous rivers and canals.

All the city-state's wealth and the surrounding towns and cities were controlled by two brothers. And now Galeazzo, the older of the two, sensing not only the danger that was about to befall the intended marriage but also the future of treaties with the English, rode urgently with his escort through the streets, which were almost unnaturally quiet. No man dared stagger from a tavern for fear of being maimed by the night watch, who enforced the strict rules of the city ordinance. To stumble drunk and beg for wine or money to procure it was to risk being arrested and then enduring the punishment of having a foot hacked off. Under the clear sky the walls of Milan looked as though they shuddered from the shadows cast by the hundreds of burning torches and braziers that illuminated the great city as Galeazzo and his men urged their horses to his brother's palace nestled beside his palatine Church of San Giovanni in Conca. The irony of the debauchery in Bernabò's palace almost touching the walls of the ancient place of worship was not lost on him.

Neither brother would dare enter the other's palace with armed guards for fear of being misconstrued, so once his presence had been announced by Bernabò's chamberlain Galeazzo ordered his men to wait outside. Despite his gout Galeazzo was spry enough to push past the old retainer. Bernabò, dishevelled and wearing a long nightshirt, nursed a gold goblet of wine as he leaned over the balustrade from the palace's upper chambers.

'You'd wake the dead!' he called down, his voice booming across the marble floors.

Galeazzo reached him, grimacing from pain, then grabbed his brother's arm.

'My lord?' the chamberlain called up the stairs.

'Go back to bed,' Bernabò told him, and then muttered to his brother. 'I should rid myself of the old fart but I raped his daughter a few years ago. I felt I owed him. What do you want at this time of the night?'

'Inside,' said Galeazzo.

'No, not there,' said Bernabò, turning his brother away from one of the tall carved doors. His wolf grin told Galeazzo all he needed to know. There would be the remnants of an orgy in the room. He could smell the sickly smell of sweat, wine and sex. How Bernabò's wife tolerated his behaviour he never understood. Regina was a chaste and faithful woman who bore Bernabò child after child. Perhaps it was only bearable because she lived in her own palace at Porta Romana.

Galeazzo was ushered into another ornate room that offered a terrace overlooking the city. On a clear day the Alps were visible and had the dawn suddenly risen Galeazzo knew they would probably see the retinue of lords and soldiers accompanying the

French Princess. He didn't need to see them; he could picture them in his mind's eye. He accepted a goblet of wine. Bernabò stood at the open door of the terrace, impervious to the cold. He lifted his nightgown and let the air reach his private parts. Galeazzo, long used to his brashness, ignored him. 'Isabelle is close.'

'I'm happy for you,' said Bernabò, his sarcasm hiding his sudden shock at learning she was still alive. When Galeazzo's horses had clattered into the courtyard he had felt certain his brother was coming to tell him that the child had died on the journey. As he had anticipated. Now the terrace and the distant flickering of torches and braziers shielded his face. He drank and then turned to face Galeazzo.

'Then what's so damned urgent?' he said, unable to keep the annoyance of his disappointment from his voice.

'Not only does she have the Dauphin's royal guard accompanying her, but there are a hundred men riding under Thomas Blackstone's banner.'

Even Bernabò's demeanour could not disguise his surprise. 'Impossible,' he said, quickly gathering his thoughts. 'The Dauphin would have warned us. God's tears, it makes no sense. Blackstone is their bitter enemy as well as ours.'

'That may be, but he is hours away.'

Bernabò's agitation stopped him thinking clearly. 'Blackstone would not ride into our territory. He knows we would kill him.'

It was Galeazzo who applied reason. 'The French are not stupid. They have contrived this and they could not warn us because they knew that we might strike at him on the journey here. And that would have endangered Isabelle.'

Bernabò glanced quickly at his brother. Had he known of the attack in Savoy? No. He could not. The last they had heard was that she had left Amadeus's care, which was when the ambush had been planned. Beyond that, nothing. No word had reached Milan, either of the attack's success or failure. It was obvious to Bernabò now why the attempt had failed. Blackstone had defeated the routiers.

'So what? We kill him anyway.'

'It cannot be that simple,' said Galeazzo. 'There's another reason behind it all.'

'Then you figure it out. You're the clever one. I'll have his heart roasting on a grill and his head on a pole.'

Galeazzo shook his head. 'Why would he offer himself to us? Why was he escort to the Princess?'

Bernabò remained silent. He knew his intemperate manner might inadvertently trip him up. His brother would be sharp enough to seize on anything untoward he might say. Better to wait until the wine wore off and the cold light of day helped him decide what to do.

'The Dauphin offered him something that he could not refuse,' said Galeazzo, still thinking through the mystery of Blackstone's impending presence in Milan.

'Perhaps he thought he could ride back to Florence and rejoin his men. There are still several hundred of them down there guarding the roads.'

Galeazzo suddenly felt alarmed. 'Could they be moving north to attack us? For all we know Blackstone has sent word to Montferrat and the Pope. What better time to attack us than when our guard is down amidst the wedding celebrations?'

Bernabò hawked and spat onto the terrace. 'There's nothing. We would have heard. Montferrat is your enemy; the Pope is mine. I'm a boil on the Pope's arse and if he was going to try and lance it I would know. Blackstone is not gathering a force against us.'

Galeazzo calmed. 'Yes, you're right, we would have heard,' he said. He paused, letting his thoughts travel to the French court. Realization dawned. 'He saved the French King's family at Meaux,' he said simply. 'The Dauphin has told him we sent the assassin. It can be nothing else. The Dauphin repays a debt and Blackstone has the best reason there is to risk everything.'

Bernabò grunted. That made sense. Nothing but revenge would drive a man into the arms of his enemy. 'Neither the Dauphin nor he can know who sent our killer. We are in the shadows. Besides' – he grinned – 'he was *my* assassin.'

'They know!' Galeazzo insisted. 'Even if we did not pay him, we arranged it. Where is Antonio?'

Bernabò feigned ignorance but the sudden glance towards the orgy room betrayed him.

'Here?' whispered Galeazzo. 'You invite your son to your orgies?'

Bernabò tossed the goblet aside. His irritation had got the better of him. 'Attend to your wedding. I'll deal with Blackstone.'

'No!' Galeazzo got to his feet, ignoring the pain from his swollen foot. 'We cannot kill him. You fool, he's bound to have Edward's promise of safe conduct. He would not allow Blackstone to come here if he did not. I cannot risk upsetting the English King by killing him.'

Bernabò made his conquests through brute force and threat, but Galeazzo spent years forming alliances and agreeing treaties. The English court was no enemy of the Visconti. They traded with Milan; they sent ambassadors. Galeazzo was more wary in his dealings with the Pope, because the pontiff was French: he and the English Crown shared a mutual sense of distrust of the Holy See at Avignon. One day Galeazzo would propose even closer links with King Edward. He had secured one King's daughter – why not a son from Edward to marry into his family?

Bernabò was aware of his brother's ambitions. 'I'm not kissing any king's arse. Whether Blackstone comes into the city or not I'll kill him.' He knew there was no choice because if Blackstone reached Antonio and forced a confession even more truths might be exposed and his involvement in the attempt on the Princess's life would be hard to disprove. He stalked out of the room, leaving his brother standing alone in the chill night air.

Galeazzo watch the light flicker as his thoughts settled. The gold-encrusted statues, fine silks and frescoes that adorned the walls might be ostentatious but they trumpeted the Visconti's wealth. And the greater the wealth the more power could be bought. There was no doubt that Blackstone had King Edward's favour and Galeazzo was suddenly torn between wanting to protect the Englishman and seizing the moment with his brother to kill the knight whose men still stood between the Visconti family and Florence. Which temptation would he yield to? Reason once again came to his rescue. Neither he nor Galeazzo would raise a hand against Blackstone. Bernabò's bastard son had paid the assassin who murdered Blackstone's wife and child. The Vipers of Milan were complicit in their deaths and a snake can strike more than once. The Visconti serpent had many heads. Antonio Lorenz was more than capable of killing Thomas Blackstone – but would Bernabò allow his son to challenge the Englishman? Whether he would or not they had only days to kill Thomas Blackstone and the Lords of Milan must not be seen to wield the knife.

Bernabò slammed closed the heavy ornate door into the orgy chamber. The light cast by the dying candles and oil lamps was so dim that the figures who sprawled in varying degrees of undress seemed entwined in death rather than drunkenness. Figures loomed large and wide-eyed from the painted frescoes on the walls, glaring down on distorted shapes that writhed and grunted in the shadows, contorted creatures undulating in passion, copulating with heaving effort. The stench of sweat mingled with perfume and wine in a pungency nausea-inducing to anyone sober – a problem not experienced by those whose bodies littered the chamber. Bernabò kicked away two women who blocked his way, their sweaty embrace broken by his hard curse and the hurt he inflicted. The room's miasma clouded his vision.

'Antonio!' he bellowed, his voice startling the aftermath of the orgy into a degree of wakefulness. A naked man quickly pushed away the two women who squirmed over him.

'Lord, he's in the next chamber,' he said, pointing across the room to another set of doors.

Bernabò strode across the chamber and pushed open the doors. In each corner of the room a candelabrum illuminated more clearly the effects of the night's bacchanalia. Bodies sprawled in drunken stupor on the ornate marble floor, red wine spilled around them. The silk curtains around the great four-poster bed were open, exposing the entwined limbs of men and women. A young woman's body was tied to one of the bedposts; it sagged, held only by cords around her wrists. Blood from her torn flesh streaked her back, trickling down her legs to mingle with the spilled wine. A young man in his early twenties leaned back against a gold-encrusted cabinet. He was lathered in sweat with blood flecks across his face, chest and arms. In one hand he held a near-empty bottle of wine, in the other a short metal-tipped riding whip that he had clearly used on the woman's back. His glazed eyes turned away from the woman and settled on his father, who stood looking from him to the woman.

'Father,' said Antonio Lorenz.

Bernabò gazed around the room. 'Get them out,' he snarled.

For a moment it seemed Antonio would protest, but no one dared argue with the Lord of Milan. He nodded obediently and was still sober enough to walk among those on the bed and sprawled drunk on the floor, raising and lowering his whip against their flesh.

'Get out! Get out!' he bellowed, throwing the bottle at one woman. He snatched at another's hair, hauled her from the bed and then kicked her across the room. 'Leave! Now!'

The sudden violence galvanized the revellers: they ran for the door, tripping and falling, shoving each other aside to avoid falling victim to the blows. Finally when the room was clear Antonio slammed shut the door.

Bernabò had settled onto a silk-cushioned chair and watched as his bastard son lashed those privileged to partake in one of Bernabò Visconti's orgies – all members of the nobility. Antonio grinned and tossed aside the whip. He was lean and muscled, and his love of hunting and skill as a swordsman were well known. A cruel man, he had never shown pity towards any living creature. He nurtured violence and employed silent killers known only to him. He was, Bernabò knew, utterly malevolent. And he loved him for it.

Antonio found another bottle, tipped wine into a gold goblet and handed it to his father. Then he swigged from the neck of the bottle and sighed. 'Father, it has been a long night but I had arranged to bring more women as you requested.'

'Send them away when they get here,' Bernabò said. He gestured towards the girl tied to the bed. 'She's dead. Make sure you get rid of her before daylight.'

'I will,' Antonio answered. The death of a common serving woman carried no penalty. If she had family they would be paid and their lives would see some benefit from her death. 'What is it?' he asked, seeing the look of concern on his father's face.

'Princess Isabelle lives,' he said.

Antonio faltered as the bottle almost reached his lips. 'How can that be? We arranged poison and brigands.'

'You paid the woman to poison her; I arranged the routiers. Both attempts have failed.'

'God's blood! How hard can it be to kill an eleven-year-old child?' Antonio said disbelievingly.

Bernabò tugged his fingers through his beard. His brother's words still unsettled him. 'Galeazzo was here. And he brought more news. Thomas Blackstone rides with the Princess. The Dauphin sent him to us as a gift. Drove him like a beast from the forest onto hunters' spears and arrows.'

Antonio's face grimaced as if the wine had soured. 'He comes to kill me.'

'No, he has no knowledge of you or the part you played in trying to kill Isabelle. He comes for Galeazzo and me. The French have told him where the assassin came from who killed his wife and child. He comes for us,' he repeated.

'I can kill him,' said Antonio.

Bernabò nodded. Perhaps he could. No one had yet bettered Antonio at sword fighting, not even his own swordmaster, and he had gained a fearsome reputation in the lists. It would be a spectacle worthy of a king's ransom.

'Even at the wedding celebrations,' said Antonio enthusiastically. 'Imagine Blackstone being humiliated and slain in front of the thousands who have flocked here for the wedding.'

Bernabò moved to his son and placed a hand on his face. 'No. He knows nothing of you and it must remain that way. You are too valuable to me. You have an assassin's skill of staying in the shadows. That is your world and I will not...' He hesitated and patted the man's face before turning away. '... lose another son to Thomas Blackstone.'

Antonio bridled; his body stiffened. 'Father,' he said, 'I know my enemy.'

Bernabò poured a drink. There was no doubting Antonio's ability but the risk was too great. Two years before, when they had sent the assassin who went by the name of Bertrand to kill Blackstone and his family, the lithe young killer had been like a ghost. No one was better placed to kill Blackstone. Had he not been abandoned by the English that day when he had claimed sanctuary of the Church he would have returned and been useful again. The murder of Blackstone and his family had been carefully planned but had been only partially successful. That the assassin had been another of Bernabò's bastard sons was known only to the Visconti brothers and Antonio who controlled him. Bertrand had been a strange boy who could hide behind the mask of different characters. He had been so different from them all: a man who neither drank nor whored but studied the art of killing as a priest studied scripture. Bernabò shrugged at the memory. The rage and grief he'd experienced at his son's death had been short-lived. The love he felt for his illegitimate children almost matched the emotions he felt for his hunting dogs. Almost. And Bertrand had failed to assassinate Blackstone.

Bernabò looked at his son. 'Antonio, you will stay well away from Blackstone. He does not know you exist. I will deal with this. What's important is that Galeazzo must never know of what we planned. Understood?'

Bernabò stared into his son's eyes. There could be no misunderstanding. If Antonio's tongue was ever loosened by an excess of wine or any suspicion ever fell on him for his role in the attempt on the Princess's life, then his body would be found floating in the river with his throat cut – his murder most likely committed by his own father. No one was allowed to stand between Bernabò Visconti and his desire for greater power.

'I understand,' said Antonio.

'Good. Now dump that girl's body and pay her family well.'

CHAPTER FIFTY-SEVEN

They had had an early start. Mist rising from the far-reaching plains clung stubbornly to the forest treetops. Men hunched in the chill as they relieved themselves, small whispers of steam flagging their efforts. Soldiers crawled out of their blankets, coughed and spat, and rubbed cold hands over stubbled faces. Blackstone's men were already awake and ready. It was the French and Italian escorts who were stumbling around the camp.

'Small thanks that our enemies didn't strike while we have that lot for company,' said Killbere.

'We're safe enough now the sun's up,' said Blackstone. 'But I saw no sense in offering the Visconti an easy target. We're in spitting distance of them and the Princess has enough troops around her for protection.' He glanced behind him at his captains and the men they commanded. They waited patiently, letting the morning unfold. 'They know we're coming and I thought they might have struck at first light.'

'Seems they'd rather stay in their warm beds and give us enough rope to hang ourselves,' said Killbere. 'What about your woman?' he said, nodding towards Aelis, who stood in the distance tying her medicine satchel onto her horse.

Blackstone watched her. He had eased from her embrace before dawn to be with his men. He had felt her stir and then as he dressed saw a movement in the darkness as she sat up. 'So soon?' she had said.

'My men must be ready,' he had answered. 'Once we get to Milan you'll stay with Will Longdon and the archers. It's the safest place.'

She had remained silent for a moment and then whispered, 'I won't be staying, Thomas. I'm riding with the Princess.'

He tugged on his jupon, her sudden proclamation catching him unawares. He had assumed she would be staying with him. Hadn't she told him how she was attracted to him? At times he had used harsh words towards her and the memory of them suddenly taunted him. He didn't love her. She did not hold his heart as had Christiana. So why did he feel the tinge of regret?

'As you wish,' he said, refusing to tell her that he would prefer her to stay under his protection. And, he admitted, close to him.

The darkness hid their feelings.

'Remember when we spoke at Chartres? In the cathedral? You thought me to be abandoned,' she said.

'I have not abandoned you,' he answered into the gloom.

'I told you we would travel across the mountains and that I saw the future more clearly than you.'

'Then you've decided?'

'It is decided for me,' she said.

He noticed the catch in her throat. 'It is as it is then,' he said, and stepped out into the early dawn.

Blackstone tugged the bastard horse's reins. 'She goes her own way,' he said to Killbere.

'Not before time. We lost a good man because of her, and I'm thankful we didn't lose another,' said the veteran knight with a knowing look at Blackstone, his meaning clear.

'Ready the men, Gilbert. We'll ride on the flank and see what the Visconti have in store for us.'

Killbere watched as Blackstone turned his horse away from Aelis in the distance. She turned her face towards them. But Blackstone did not look back.

For over a hundred years there had been a hundred towers in Milan. There were more now – should a man take the time to set his back against a tree and begin counting when the sun rose he would barely be finished by the time it set – symbols of power thrust towards the sky. The city's encircling walls behind rivers and canals made it unlikely an enemy would attempt to lay siege. The great banners fluttered in the day's breeze, the languid caress creating the illusion of a living serpent on the blazon swallowing the child. The Milanese were soft in their comfort, their fighting done by paid troops: German and Hungarian, English and French; all had fought for the great city-state and over the years Thomas Blackstone had faced them and killed them. The scourge of Milan led his men aside as the royal column was brought to a halt by the Italian noblemen. Musicians dressed in colourful clothing oozed from a city gate like a shuffling caterpillar, the soaring cacophony of their trumpets and drums shattering the day's stillness and drowning out birdsong.

'Noisy bastards,' said John Jacob as he and the others sat waiting. The half-day's ride from the previous night's camp had been without incident but the men's growing sense of anticipation kept their senses and their eyes sharp. Despite the expanse of the flat plain ambush was not out of the question, even at this late stage of the journey. They watched as Visconti heralds rode out of the city gates escorting someone who looked to be important.

'Perhaps he's the head tavern keeper,' called Will Longdon from behind Blackstone and his squire. 'Probably about to offer the Princess a barrel of wine as a wedding gift. John, ride over and tell him she's too young, but we can oblige.'

Killbere looked behind him at the column of men. Blackstone had ordered that his pennons and banner be shown and that their shields be on their arms. The important-looking messenger had approached the Princess and then de Chauliac. After a brief conversation the Frenchman turned his horse and spurred it towards Blackstone. The music still bellowed across the plain.

'They play much louder and they'll bring down the walls for us,' said Gaillard.

'Let's see what de Chauliac has to say,' said Blackstone as the royal captain approached. He reined in his horse.

414

'Sir Thomas. We are to ride to the southern gate. The Porta Ticinese is the Lord Galeazzo's entrance into the city; you are to ride under escort to the Lord Bernabò's entrance, Porta Tosa.'

'What escort, captain?'

'I am relieved of my attendant duties when we reach the Porta Ticinese, and then it is I who will escort you.' The Frenchman paused. 'Is it meant as an insult, Sir Thomas?'

Blackstone shook his head. 'They mean to give me a sense of security. They will raise no hand against us while a royal guard is with us.'

De Chauliac looked at Blackstone and his men. With their shields raised they were not preparing for an attack at this late stage of the journey, they were proclaiming themselves to the Visconti. Look who comes into your city, they were saying. Feast your eyes on the men who have bested your troops. Gaze upon your enemy. Be fearful.

'You taunt the Visconti, Sir Thomas,' said de Chauliac. He couldn't help the grin that creased his face. He had learnt to respect the Englishman's courage. 'You defy them.'

'You don't tread lightly into a nest of vipers, you carry a big stick. Scare them away before they can sink their fangs into you,' said Blackstone.

Killbere spat. 'Except these serpents squirm from every shadow and alleyway so we might not see them coming. We're just letting them know we're ready for them.'

De Chauliac looked back to where the Princess's retinue had begun moving towards the city gate. 'Sir Thomas, I'm under the Dauphin's command. I am only relieved of my duties once the marriage ceremony is over. That's three days away. You saved her life and I will do what I can to serve you should you think you and your men are in danger.'

'I'm grateful, but this isn't your fight. However, you can hold this for me,' said Blackstone, reaching forward with a folded document. De Chauliac looked at the sweat-grimed parchment. 'You recognize the seal?'

The Frenchman nodded. 'Yes. The Prince of Wales.'

'Our safe conduct. If anything should befall us they would seize that and deny its existence and then we are abandoned. When the time comes I would ask you to relinquish it only to Lord Galeazzo. He's my enemy as much as his brother but with you as witness he might see the value in honouring the English Crown's demand for our safe passage.'

De Chauliac tucked the document into his glove. 'Very well, Sir Thomas. Let us hope that moment does not arrive and we can all return safely to our families.' The Frenchman must have realized that his words had a hollow ring to them for Blackstone. The scar-faced knight showed no sign of displeasure or regret. The royal captain searched for more appropriate words but few came. 'Back to our... duties,' he said falteringly. He dipped his head in salute and turned his horse.

'You put our safety into the hands of a man who, when his horse kicks him in the head, will realize that the Dauphin would reward him handsomely for *not* doing as you ask,' Killbere said.

'It's worth the gamble, Gilbert. Who knows, we might have French swords to help protect us when the time comes.'

Killbere snorted. John Jacob, Meulon and Gaillard couldn't keep from smiling. Blackstone grinned. 'God moves in strange ways. Will Longdon might even snap his bow and become a monk.'

They laughed.

'I'm doing what?' said Will Longdon from behind.

'Sir Thomas thinks there's a chance that one day you'll become a monk!' Gaillard shouted.

'Aye, well, unless these Italian women spread their legs I might as well,' Longdon grumbled.

'At least you'd be pleasured by the other monks,' Gaillard taunted.

'At least I'd have the pleasure of gelding you first,' Longdon answered.

Blackstone's raised hand halted their banter. The column was passing a hundred yards in front of them, the musicians leading the way, the Princess's litter swaying gently. Her hand appeared, lifting the gossamer screen covering, and then the girl's face, her gaze directed towards Blackstone. The child bride smiled and for a moment Blackstone thought it was meant for him, but as he lowered his head in acknowledgement he realized the gesture was directed towards the boy who rode beside John Jacob. Henry's face beamed with pleasure at being honoured.

'Dip your head, son,' Blackstone commanded. 'Only village idiots grin like that.'

As Henry obeyed the veil lowered and the procession continued towards the southern gate.

'At least we've bought ourselves good favour with one of the brothers,' said Killbere. 'Galeazzo should be rewarding us with some of his gold and silver for saving his son's bride.'

'He won't even hear of it,' said Blackstone, turning his horse to lead the column of men behind the entourage. 'All he might be told is that some routiers were stopped from stealing from merchants. The Princess knows nothing of the truth and de Chauliac won't even be questioned. He'll be billeted like us. No one will get close to the Visconti to say anything.'

'Then how do we get to the bastard we're looking for?' said Killbere.

'They'll come for us,' Blackstone answered.

CHAPTER FIFTY-EIGHT

Henry Blackstone sat astride his horse with the Tau knight Foresti at his side. They watched as Henry's father led his men around the southern walls of Milan. The exuberant colours of the musicians was surpassed by the clothing worn by the Italian noblemen and he knew it was unlikely that he would ever see such a spectacle again. And he realized that in a small way he had been a part of it. A princess of France was going to be married to a lord of Milan's son, and that was history.

When he had parted from the column those men who knew him, the men close to his father, had embraced him and wished him well. He had smelled the pungent sweat on Will Longdon's greasy leather jerkin when the archer had put his strong arms around him and told him slyly to watch out for the beautiful daughters of Florence. He had been nearly smothered by the two bears, Gaillard and Meulon, their garlic breath wafting over his face as they kissed each cheek. Perinne had simply grasped his arm, unconsciously almost crushing the bones. The fighting man seemed as strong as his stonemason father. John Jacob had quietly lectured him on his behaviour. Their long-standing bond stretched back years to when the tough Englishman had taken the boy into his care and protection after the night Henry's mother had been raped. John Jacob had cut the man's throat and Henry had helped tip his body into the river. John Jacob cleared his throat, his eyes welled with tears and he had quickly turned away. It was obvious to Henry that these men were saying their farewells in case they did not return from what might be their last fight at his father's side.

When the men's embraces were done Blackstone drew his son aside. He resisted the impulse to bend down on one knee so that he might embrace his son as if he were a child. The truth was Henry was growing quicker than he had realized and had he knelt the boy would have been taller than him.

'Henry, you know I am going into Milan to avenge your mother and sister.'

'Yes, Father. To kill the man who sent the assassin.'

'Your mother's strength was forged from love and I would not wish your inheritance to be anything less. Vengeance is not hatred; it is honouring that love. If I don't return you will complete your studies in Florence. Father Torellini will protect you but the day will come when you must honour your mother and sister.'

'And you, Father.'

'Yes, if that's what needs to be done, me as well. Bear your name with honour and pride, Henry, and remember that injuries to one member of a family are considered injuries to all. It is written in law that the family should take up weapons because vendetta is an obligation on kinsmen. It doesn't die with those who have been killed.'

He handed Henry a folded piece of parchment. It bore a blood-red seal.

'You carry this with you. That is the King's personal seal and it guarantees our safety. When the King knew what we were to undertake he gave us his safe conduct. As did the Prince. If one safe conduct was lost or destroyed the other would serve in its place. We live in treacherous times and we must think ahead for what might befall us. Fra Foresti will guide you to Florence but if anyone challenges you that safe conduct will save your life or ensure they know you are important enough to be ransomed. Guard it well and show it to no one unless you have no choice. Understood?'

'Yes, Father.'

'Good. Now let us embrace and go our separate ways. You carry my strength with you and the shield of your mother's love.'

'It is fifty leagues to Florence,' said Foresti. 'We will not punish the horses but I expect you to ride at least five or six leagues a day.'

'I understand,' said Henry. 'You don't have to worry about me. I have ridden at my father's side across France and I have a good horse.' He looked at the column of men who snaked their way past the Princess's entourage. His father, along with the French escort, would enter the city by another route, and the trouble was Henry had no idea how he could follow once he escaped the man tasked to lead him to the city of learning and art that was Florence.

Fra Foresti nudged his horse away from the city walls. Henry turned with him, gauging the man. He was much younger than the Tau knight who had once served Henry's father. Henry knew that like his predecessor this man would be an expert swordsman who would lay down his life for the boy at his side. 'Do you know the route well, Fra Foresti?'

'Of course. We are hospitallers who guide pilgrims on the Via Francigena. It is what our order does.'

Henry knew this, but wanted to engage the Tau knight in genial conversation so that he might gain his trust. If he could weaken the man's resolve and diligence by appearing to be less knowledgeable than he was, then the older man might lower his guard and not sense any threat of escape. 'So, do you prefer to be in the countryside or in the city?'

'Both,' Foresti answered. 'Each has its qualities.'

'But you prefer Florence to Milan?'

'Florence, yes. It is a great city and the Tuscan language is one that is more pleasurable to the ear.'

'So does Milan have more gates into the city than Florence has?' Henry asked, searching for the answers he needed.

'There are sixteen gates into Florence and each is opened at dawn and closed at sunset. Milan has six or seven gates but it also has other posterns so that local people can come and go more easily. Milan has more towers. They denote its power but Florence is the more beautiful. Towers are ugly.'

It seemed an impossible task to discover a route into the city that he might use. Henry could not think of a way to get the information he needed from his guardian without raising suspicion. He lapsed into silence. And then Foresti, keen to impress his young charge, began to talk.

'I spent some years studying in Milan before I took my vows with the Knights of Altopascio. Students can get into a lot of trouble so we always had to find a way into the city after being outside the walls in the village taverns. It is forbidden for a man to be caught on the streets leaving a tavern after dark and in those days we spent a lot of time in taverns, I can tell you.' He grinned and shook his head. 'I should be ashamed, but when you are so young... well... your time will come and you will understand. I remember there was a postern, Pusterla di Sant'Ambrogio, that we used all the time. We had to lie to the sentry – God forgive me but I did; we used to swear we were on a pilgrimage of confession to the basilica to pray for forgiveness. No one can deny entry to a pilgrim. We were so young, barely a few years older than you, but that's what we did. And then, well, then I did pray in the basilica and the saint spoke to me and I gave up my sinful ways. And, as you can see, my honour has been restored and I serve God and man.'

'Is that where my father will enter the city?' Henry asked, suppressing his relief at finding a way into the city.

'No, no. Porta Tosa is round to the east, Sant'Ambrogio is to the west. Different parts of the city.'

Henry looked over his shoulder. The sun would go down across the plain, somewhere beyond a small village church tower that he could see in the distance. If he used that as a landmark he would make good his escape but it would be made more difficult by Fra Foresti wishing to make good progress.

'Could we wait a while? I would like to watch the last of my father's men make their way beyond the walls.'

The music from the procession was fading but Blackstone's men could still be seen in the far distance. Foresti glanced at the boy. It was possible the lad would never see his father again. He looked around him and saw that a few miles ahead smoke curled from village fires. They could camp there for the first night, he decided, and make up lost time the following day.

'All right, Master Henry. We will watch until they disappear from view. And we shall pray for them. Would you like that?'

'Very much,' said Henry, already hoping his father, as well as God, would forgive his sly and wilful disobedience.

De Chauliac's royal escort rode into Milan beneath the Porta Tosa archway into the eastern side of the city. The horse's iron-shod hooves clattered on the paved street, their echoes drowning out some of the men's ribald cries and laughter. Blackstone and his twelve men-at-arms followed.

'What are they shouting?' Killbere asked.

'I can't hear,' said Blackstone.

'If they're laughing at us because we bring up the rear I'll kick de Chauliac's arse in front of his men.'

As Blackstone entered the archway he pointed and laughed. 'No need, Gilbert.'

Embedded in the gate's walls was a statue of a woman raising her skirts and exposing herself, a pair of shears in one hand as if about to cut her pubic hair.

'Clean whores!' shouted Killbere.

'Milan welcomes us with shaven cunnies!' cried Perinne.

The men laughed as had the French.

'It's meant as an insult,' called Renfred the German man-at-arms, who was riding behind Gaillard and Meulon. 'I've heard of it. Something to do with a war long ago. They call this the "door of the shaving lady". They say she exposed herself on the city walls when they were under siege.'

'Let's hope there are others who feel like insulting foreigners,' Meulon said.

The men's laughter reverberated along the curved walls and then died away as they entered the city. Faces peered from upstairs windows; the broad street ahead coiled like a sleeping serpent. Colourful signboards hung over shops identifying the wares they sold; shopkeepers stepped back into their doorways, some crossing themselves when they saw the scar-faced Englishman. They might not have known who he was, but he and the fighting men he led looked formidable and frightening. Shields on their arms, these unsmiling men gazed down on them from their large horses, forcing those less brave citizens to avert their faces. Blackstone's stonemason's eye swept across the tall buildings, their rich hue warm from the sun's rays. Master builders had built a fine city, declaring its wealth as brazenly and gloriously as a silk-threaded banner. Doves fluttered high across the walls. There were no swallow-tailed crenellations here like the battlements in Florence or Verona; Milan's history had dictated square, no-nonsense merlons. It was a formidable city and Blackstone knew that to escape from it when the killing was done might be an ambition too far.

Alleyways and side streets snaked away from the main street. Sulphur fumes from blacksmiths working at their forges hovered, trapped in the narrow passageways. De Chauliac had been met by the city watch commander and led off down one of the lanes. Blackstone followed until streets later they came to an enclosed cobbled yard. It was broad enough to accommodate three times the number of his horsemen, who now came to a halt. To one side were stables built into the walls and it was obvious from the cart laden with straw and hay there would be no problem feeding and bedding down the men-at-arms' horses. Stable-boys ran out, fifty or more of them ready to aid the riders. The stabling and the ostlers alone were enough to express a show of wealth. Curtain walls blocked any view beyond the courtyard, but beyond them Blackstone and the men could hear the baying of hunting hounds. He realized they must be on the lower fringes of one of the palaces. Tiered terraces rose up on the opposite side from the stabling and trees and bushes were visible in roof gardens. Several levels up faces peered down at them and he guessed they were members of the nobility because the speckled colours of their clothing denoted wealth. Blackstone eased the bastard horse around and saw that it would take very little to entrap them in the arena that this courtyard seemed to be. He assumed that beyond the curtain walls where he could hear the dogs barking there would be similar courtyards with kennels and exercise yards.

'Walls are low enough to breach, Sir Thomas,' said John Jacob, gesturing towards the curtain walls, and then, glancing up at the terraces, 'but we'd have eyes on us if it came to that.'

While the French had dismounted and handed their reins to the stable-hands, Blackstone's men had done as he had done and looked around them. They were few and they had all fought in city streets before now. They spoke quietly among themselves. A doorway here, an alley there. Low walls and doors that could be kicked down. They would need a way out when the time came.

'Sir Thomas,' de Chauliac called as he approached. 'We are to be billeted down there at the far side of the square. There is food and drink waiting for us. Give your horses over to the ostlers.' He pointed to a half-dozen Visconti footsoldiers and their commander, who waited to escort them. 'The city watch have handed us over to them.'

'Are there others?' asked Blackstone. 'Hidden perhaps in any of these yards or alleys?'

'I doubt it.' De Chauliac smiled. 'Don't look so worried, Sir Thomas, the Visconti will not harm us – at least not when we are together. They would not dare risk causing harm to the Dauphin's guard.'

The bastard horse snatched its head, trying to bite the Frenchman, who stood too close. De Chauliac stepped back quickly even though Blackstone held a tight rein.

'It's nothing personal,' said Blackstone. 'Where's the Princess and all those peacock noblemen?'

De Chauliac sighed. 'I don't know. Over there somewhere,' he said, looking beyond the rooftops. 'I will be summoned later so that she can instruct me on what to tell the Dauphin.'

Blackstone dismounted. 'Wait for us. We stable our own horses and then we'll join you.'

The royal captain turned back to his waiting troops.

Blackstone's men had followed his example and led their horses towards the stables. Killbere eased alongside. 'I smell dog shit from the kennels but there's bread and meat in the air as well.'

'Aye, we'll be fed and no doubt given dry straw for a bed under a roof. They'll suckle us like babes in arms and hope to lower our guard.'

'I wouldn't mind a bit of suckling myself,' said Killbere as they took the horses into the gloomy half-light of the stalls. 'Food and wine will do for now but a fat kitchen girl to serve it would at least give a man pleasure.' He glanced at Blackstone. 'Missing the witch?'

'She's no witch and you know it.'

'All women cast their spells,' Killbere said. 'Though I thought she might have lingered a while longer at your side. Women never know when they're lucky enough to have the favour of a good man.'

'She owed me nothing,' said Blackstone.

'Well, you could have passed her along, Thomas. I would have liked to see if the reality matched the dream when I thought I was humping my nun.'

'Gilbert, it's possible neither of us will ever lie with a woman again.'

'Aye, you're right. But she was good, was she?'

'Keep your memory,' Blackstone said and tugged the bastard horse into a stall.

The inner stables ran the full length of the courtyard. Every stall was boxed with chestnut planks, gated and secured. Deep straw covered the floor and troughs of water were placed every twenty paces so that the stable-hands had an easily available supply of water for their mounts. Sacks of oats sat off the ground on sturdy shelving, free from mould and rat infestation. Killbere had shouldered his mount into the neighbouring stall and tied off its trailing rein.

'I doubt even our King has such grand stabling,' he said, allowing a stable-lad to enter and begin unsaddling his horse.

Another boy, younger than Henry, waited as Blackstone lifted free his own saddle.

'It is my duty to care for your horse, my lord,' the boy said.

'Not this one,' said Blackstone. 'You keep the halter on him and the rein secure. He'll bite off your hand if you don't. Be wary of him: he'll try and kick you through the wall. Understand?'

The boy's eyes widened but he nodded and, grabbing a feed bag, bravely entered the stall.

Up and down the stable's aisle the men closed the gates on their horses.

'All right,' said Blackstone, 'let's share a table with the French and watch our backs with the Italians.'

CHAPTER FIFTY-NINE

Bernabò Visconti stood alongside his brother gazing down on the courtyard. The Princess had been received by the city fathers and Galeazzo's chancellor had shown her to her quarters. It was inappropriate to meet a royal princess the moment she had entered the city and so soon after such an arduous journey. By now she would have been fêted by noblemen and ambassadors and would have been dressed by her ladies. She would expect her future father-in-law to welcome her to his palace, which was why Galeazzo was dressed in his finery. A pearl- and jewel-encrusted tunic and an ermine-lined cloak, dyed in the richest blue, set off his features, more refined than those of the man next to him. Galeazzo usually wore his red-gold hair long in braids but today it rested on his shoulders in a silken net.

'It's time we left to greet Isabelle,' said Galeazzo.

'Not yet. I want to see the Englishman,' Bernabò answered, watching the group of men far below being led through lanes that meandered through the courtyards.

'Have you thought of what to do?' said Galeazzo.

'I told you before: I'm going to kill him. I haven't decided how yet. Perhaps I'll put him in an iron cage and roast him alive.'

It was no idle threat. Bernabò had inflicted such torture on the Pope's delegates in the past. The stench of roasting flesh and the sizzle of the victims' fat dripping into the flames had left a stench that lasted for a week.

'And what of Antonio?' said Galeazzo.

'No. He stays out of it.'

'You should use him.'

Bernabò shook his head, keeping his eyes on the men far below as they were taken through another alley towards their quarters.

'Don't do anything without discussing it with me first, Bernabò.'

'I don't need your permission, brother. I rule half this city.'

Galeazzo exercised patience. A misunderstood word could send Bernabò off into a rage whose consequences could prove disastrous. 'Of course you do not need my permission. But we rule together for the benefit of our name. There's much at stake. The French King holds out his palm for us to fill with gold. He's ours but we cannot risk harming either his men or antagonizing Edward by cutting down Blackstone in the street. Lure him into a false sense of security.'

'Hot food and a warm bed won't do that. He's a fighter.'

'Think, Bernabò. Let the desire for his death within you quieten. Lure him is what I said. Offer him bait. Bring him into the palace.'

'What?'

'Bring him to court.'

'A *condottiere* like him? In our court?'

'Your court, brother. I have a royal princess to entertain.'

'Why would I bring him inside my walls?'

'Because then you get the measure of the man and you offer him the chance to serve us. To command an army.'

'He would never accept – don't be stupid.'

'And if his anger is as volatile as his passion for revenge then he will try and strike. And then you can kill him in good conscience.' He readied to leave. 'In the right place at the right time with justification.' He eased a fallen hair from his cloak. 'Think, Bernabò. Use your brain instead of your balls.'

Bernabò grabbed his brother's arm as he turned away. Galeazzo knew immediately that he had provoked him.

'Curse you,' said Bernabò between gritted teeth. 'You bought yourself a virgin princess for your boy so go and welcome her. I have my own welcome for Blackstone down there.'

Galeazzo snatched free his arm. He did not fear his brother. Both could inflict violence without a second thought but it was he, Galeazzo, who stopped to think things through. He placated his brother. 'All right. Let's not argue. It's an historic day for our family and we are expected at my palace.'

'Wait,' insisted Bernabò and gestured to the yards below. A man had been dragged out of a building by guards. His voice was raised begging for mercy. He was less than twenty paces from the French and English men-at-arms who were being escorted to their quarters past the pens for the hunting dogs. Each of the yards held thirty to fifty animals, lean, sturdy, muscled mastiffs with crushing jaws that could bring down a boar and teeth that could tear into its hide. The dogs were fed sparingly; carcasses of freshly killed deer were usually tossed into their yard every few days. The dogs' taut skin bore witness to their hunger and their slavering jaws left little doubt as to the hounds' power. There was no need for Galeazzo to make any enquiry as to the man's crime or punishment. The first question would not have mattered; the answer to the second obvious.

Blackstone and de Chauliac were halted by their escort as they reached the struggling man. The half-walled dog pen was topped with iron railings, high enough to stop the dogs from jumping over but low enough for them to be seen and fed. As the guards had approached the latched cage door the dogs had erupted into a snarling pack. Two of the condemned man's guards lowered their pikes to stop Blackstone and Killbere from moving forward.

'Mother of Christ,' said Killbere. 'They mean to feed him to the dogs.'

He took a half-step forward, hand on his sword hilt, but Blackstone's arm stopped him. 'Wait. They mean to provoke us. It's for our benefit. He's condemned whatever we do.'

As he spoke his warning one of the dog handlers appeared on the far side of the pen to draw the dogs away from the gate and allow the guards to throw the man inside. As the handler whistled the confused dogs turned and in that moment one of the guards opened the iron gate. The man fought without success, his screams rising above the dogs' baying. In that instant of struggle and watching for the precise moment to fling the man inside, the guards' attention was distracted. Blackstone sidestepped one of the lowered pikes as Killbere grabbed the other, forcing its blade down. In a couple of strides Blackstone was an arm's length from the desperate man. A sudden gush of blood splattered the guards as his archer's knife slashed the man's throat. Blackstone quickly stepped back so the guards understood he was not attacking them. The dead man slumped, shuddering in his death throes. The Visconti men cursed and threatened to advance on Blackstone but their commander shouted an order and they slung the body into the pen. The dogs turned from their handler's distraction and fell on the corpse. For a moment there was a stand-off between Blackstone and Killbere and the disconcerted guards who thrust their spiked shafts towards them. Their commander demanded his men raise their weapons and they backed off. As they retreated he glanced over his shoulder towards the high terraces. Blackstone followed his gaze and saw two indistinct figures step out of sight as the dogs' noses buried themselves into the torn carcass, their macabre snuffling savagery holding everyone's attention – except Blackstone's. That fleeting glance was enough to tell him that he had finally laid eyes on his enemy.

A thousand candles, each the thickness of a man's arm, burned brightly from a hundred gold candlesticks and chandeliers that lit the great hall as Princess Isabelle de Valois was escorted by her ladies-in-waiting towards the raised dais where Galeazzo and his wife Bianca stood with their young son waiting to greet the royal bride-to-be. Bernabò, already bored with the fanfares and baubles, stood to one side with his wife and a chosen few of the many children he had sired. Antonio Lorenz was not on the dais but stood behind his father against a wall. As he looked out at the gathered nobility he realized that when Thomas Blackstone had cut the condemned man's throat before he was thrown to the dogs the Englishman had betrayed his own weakness. He would not allow a man to suffer unnecessarily. Such compassion could be exploited. He stifled a yawn as the trumpets heralded Isabelle's advance towards the dais. On both sides of the aisle diplomats and ambassadors, noblemen and rich merchants jostled shoulder to shoulder to catch a glimpse of the child-bride. The hall's blue and gold ceiling had been painted by Giotto, one of the greatest Italian artists, and the pictures on the walls represented a mixed collection of historical and mythical heroes. Over the years the Visconti had employed many accomplished artisans and renowned sculptors and created vast gardens with fishponds and fountains of animal heads gushing water. Surrounding the palace were courtyards of menageries full of animals foreign to Italy that included lions and monkeys and a vast aviary filled with chattering songbirds. The extravagance reflected the grandeur of the Lords of Milan.

The Archbishop's mitre bobbed as he chanted a prayer, and all present lowered their heads, except Bernabò. And the woman who stood behind the ladies-in-waiting, their features pinched in earnest worship. Of all the hundreds in the hall only she and the Lord of Milan had their faces raised. He gazed down at her and she stared back defiantly. He was suddenly pleased that he had been obliged to attend the ceremony. The woman's black hair peaked below her headdress and the tightly clinging dress pushed up her breasts. The moment passed when the woman averted her eyes and looked straight ahead towards Galeazzo and his family, who made the sign of the cross as the Archbishop ended the prayer. Bernabò convinced himself that he saw a smile tweak the corners of the woman's lips. As the droning voice of Galeazzo's chancellor delivered the formal welcoming speech he willed the woman to look his way again. But she did not. Bernabò's wife, Regina, heavily pregnant with their seventh child, glanced up at him, aware that he was studying the young woman in the Princess's entourage. No words were needed between man and wife; she knew that by that night the woman would be in his bed, willingly or not.

CHAPTER SIXTY

Despite being in the warmth and safety of the stables, Blackstone had ordered his men to stand watch. The nearby kennels had quietened as night had fallen and although the hunting dogs would have picked up movement and warned the sleeping men of approaching soldiers he relied on his own men to ensure their own safety. Other than the usual sounds of the city at night and the screeching of a catfight in an alley the hours of darkness passed without incident.

It was pre-dawn when Blackstone stood alone in the courtyard. His men were not yet free of their blankets but he saw that the sentries he had posted at the far corners of the yard were awake and alert. As he walked along the length of the men's quarters an iron-studded door in the wall he had thought to be bolted creaked slowly open. Thoughts of an attack raced through his mind and his hand reached for Wolf Sword but the figure revealed in the near-darkness of the tunnel made a small gesture at him to remain calm and then brought a finger to his lips. It was an old man with a white beard, dressed in a quality cloak, who beckoned him. Blackstone glanced at his distant sentries: they had not seen or heard the intruder. He stepped closer and the man took a pace backwards to accommodate his presence in the tunnel. Wary that this might be a ploy to entrap him Blackstone palmed his archer's knife. There would be no space within the narrow confines of the tunnel to wield a sword but the knife would give him a chance in a close-quarter fight.

The tunnel's fetid air washed over him as the man smiled in friendly invitation beneath the cloak's hood; but his expression became a grimace as Blackstone held the blade beneath his throat.

'Sir Thomas, your legend precedes you and yet... *Worldly fame is nothing but a breath of wind which blows now from one side and now from another, and changes its name because it changes direction...*' He waited a moment for his words to convince Blackstone that he neither offered nor brought any threat. 'I am not here to cause you harm.'

'You're Father Torellini's informant,' said Blackstone, easing the blade away.

The old man nodded. 'Indeed my tired old eyes are those of Father Torellini in this city.'

'Who are you?'

'I am Bernabò Visconti's chamberlain. That knowledge places my life in your hands.'

'It will never be revealed,' said Blackstone.

The old spy sighed. 'Let us hope not, but under torture... well, we must offer prayers that such a day never comes. My time is short: my lord's household is not yet awake, and I fear this may be the only opportunity we have to speak. How may I help you?'

'Father Torellini said he would try and find out who controlled the assassin who slew my wife and child.'

The man's face wrinkled. 'Impossible to know. This family's power is smothered in secrecy.'

'I believe it to be Antonio Lorenz.'

The old chamberlain's eyebrows furrowed. 'Why so?'

'A woman poisoner gave me his name in exchange for my promise to rescue her daughter from his household.'

'Her name?'

'Cataline.'

'Ah.' The chamberlain sighed, his head bowed. After a moment he whispered: 'She is dead, Sir Thomas. She was a victim in one of my lord's orgies. Indeed it was Antonio Lorenz who killed her for his sexual gratification.'

'Then I am even more convinced that he is the man I seek.'

'Yes. More than likely. Lorenz slips between the shadows.'

'Where do I find him?'

The old man shook his head. 'Impossible to say. One of several houses, rooms within palaces – he never stays long in one place. No one can be sure, not even his father – you know that he is Lord Bernabò's illegitimate son?'

'Yes. I must find where he is and then kill him.'

'Be warned if you do find him that he is a renowned swordsman. He will not be an easy man to overcome.'

'I'll find a way,' said Blackstone.

The old man ruminated a moment longer. 'I will try to throw light on this shadow for you but... in a city such as this... I don't know. He was at my lord's palace but now... Sir Thomas, I will do what I can but until such time as I have any information you are on your own and if we are unfortunate enough to meet under more... difficult circumstances I implore you not to show me any recognition.'

'You have my word.'

'Then God be with you. Now, go back to your men.'

Blackstone stepped back into the brightening dawn and the door closed behind him.

The first of the three days' festivities had already started as Blackstone ate with his men in the courtyard. In the west of the city trumpets and drums heralded the tournament where the Milanese would be treated to jousting, horse races and a fair with jugglers, acrobats, musicians and bear baiting.

'I would welcome some entertainment,' said Killbere as he cut a slice from the round of hard cheese onto a piece of bread. He filled his cheeks, the bread's burnt underside crumbling onto his beard as he spoke. 'Some bear baiting and dog fights enliven a man's day. We have already sat around here too long.'

Blackstone related what had happened earlier but made no mention of the informant's status within the Visconti palace.

'Then we are none the wiser as to which hole this rat crawls into.' Killbere glanced across the yard. 'Let's hope these two have some news.' Blackstone had sent half his men out onto the streets to gauge the layout of the city and to try and find where Antonio Lorenz lived.

Blackstone spooned pottage as John Jacob and Perinne joined him and Killbere. 'Anything?' he asked.

'There are two passageways that lead to the palace's lower entrances. They're guarded but there are other houses for members of the family. We won't get into the palace. But there's no word that he's even in there.' Perinne accepted the plate of food offered by Killbere and took a mouthful. 'I spoke to a saddler. Lord Bernabò has few court officers, unlike his brother, so he attends to the administration of his part of Milan with only a handful of courtiers. If we could find where Lorenz is he might be vulnerable enough for us to reach him but John's right about trying to get into the palace: we'd never make it. But Lord Bernabò rides out and hunts most days.'

Blackstone glanced at Killbere, who shrugged.

'We'll not stand a chance accosting him in the streets, Thomas.'

Blackstone wiped a sleeve across his mouth. The yard and outside kitchen did not demand the etiquette of a dining hall. 'It might be our only opportunity. John, did you find out where Antonio Lorenz lives?'

'Perhaps a grand house somewhere near the palace but no one seems to know which one or when he is there. He's going to be difficult to find.'

'The saddler was making a silver bridle for him in his workshop,' said Perinne, 'but Lorenz never comes down into the streets. I spoke to half a dozen people in a tavern and they couldn't even describe him. He's a shadow.'

'Then we keep looking until we find where he steps into the light,' said Blackstone.

One by one the men drifted back from the streets to share what they had learnt, each describing the layout of the area of the city they had reconnoitred. Postern gates might be used for escape, but the broad streets that led to the main gates carried a lot of day-to-day traffic. Whether they attempted to evade capture using side streets or main thoroughfares the city's vibrant commerce would slow them and militia could halt their progress long enough for Visconti troops to attack.

'Sir Thomas,' said Gaillard, tearing a chunk of bread and dipping it into the pottage. 'To get away from this place we would need a hostage. Someone important enough to stop them attacking us.'

There was a murmur of agreement among the men.

'There's no one important enough to stop the Visconti from killing us all, including any hostage,' said Blackstone. 'If we are to get out alive then we must do it by stealth. Let us all think on it because time is against us. Be alert because it's my belief they will strike at us soon. From what I have heard Bernabò Visconti is an impatient man.'

Killbere looked across to the far side of the courtyard where de Chauliac and his sergeants were striding towards them.

'There's my food spoiled,' said Killbere. 'Today might have been bearable without having them scurrying around like damned alley rats.'

De Chauliac bowed his head in greeting. 'Sir Thomas, I was summoned by the Princess so that I might give her report to the Dauphin when I return to Paris, but I have information which might be of value to you.'

Blackstone and the men stared and waited. If the captain of the royal guard expected any gesture of enthusiasm from the hardened fighters he was disappointed. Blackstone's men were thankful that the French had fought well in the valley and aware that if the Visconti thought them to be allies then the Dauphin's men aided their safety – at least until they left the city to ride back to Paris. It was then that the Visconti might make their move, once there was no chance of the Frenchmen being caught up in the killing.

'Well done, captain,' said Blackstone. 'I'm grateful. Tell us.'

De Chauliac allowed himself a brief smile of success. 'I discovered where Antonio Lorenz lives and how to get inside his house.'

He was gratified to see that this information caused some interest among the gathered men.

'How?' asked Killbere.

'A narrow set of steps between buildings. They lead to a walled garden and from there the house can be entered.'

'Guards?' said John Jacob.

'I am uncertain but from what I have been told there are very few men at the house. A handful patrol in the grounds but he does not feel under threat; he's just another of Bernabò's bastards. He has no official rank or status within the family.'

Killbere picked the food from his teeth and studied the captain. 'And how did a captain of the royal guard in an unfamiliar city come by this information?' he said.

'I gave my word that I would not divulge the man's name but he is a Frenchman who serves in the palace.'

'And what have you promised him in return for this information?' Blackstone asked.

'To take him back to Paris.'

Killbere leaned into Blackstone's shoulder. 'A good story, Thomas. But that is all it might be,' he whispered.

Both men remained expressionless.

'When are you leaving Milan?' asked Blackstone.

'In a few hours,' de Chauliac answered. 'I am preparing my men now. But I will lead you to the steps and have twenty men cover your back.'

'Why would you do that?' asked Killbere.

'Because I owe Sir Thomas my life,' said de Chauliac.

'Wait for us while I discuss this with my men,' Blackstone told him.

De Chauliac and his sergeants stepped away. Blackstone waited until the Frenchmen were far enough away across the yard.

'Sir Thomas,' said Meulon, 'he stinks of lies, this Frenchman. He serves the Dauphin. Let us not trust him.'

'That was never my intention, Meulon.' He looked to each man. 'If he's lying we will soon know. If it's a trap then we expect it. But if he is speaking the truth then it might be the chance we need to strike quickly. This is my vendetta, not yours. No man need follow me, you know that.'

Perinne threw the contents of his bowl into the gutter. 'Sir Thomas, we have followed you since you were a boy. If we turn our backs now we would be men without cause or honour. Let us kill these bastards who inflicted pain on you and young Henry.'

'Aye,' said John Jacob. 'Take their heads and toss them to those hounds.'

The men grinned in anticipation and picked up their weapons, tucking mace and fighting axe into their belts. With sword in hand they would be as well armed as they could be.

'All right,' said Blackstone, looking from man to man. 'We'll follow them. Sir Gilbert and I lead, then Perinne, John, Renfred, you and the others at our back, Meulon and Gaillard protect our rear.'

The men stood readying themselves. Meulon and Gaillard hefted their pikes. The ten-foot-long shafts would be too unwieldy to use in the narrow streets but would be effective enough as a rearguard weapon to hold an enemy at bay for a time.

Killbere raised a hand. 'If it goes badly we fight and hold the ground and let Thomas find his way to the murdering scum.'

There was a murmur of agreement, and then they were ready. Blackstone lifted his shield onto his arm and strode across the yard to where de Chauliac and his guard waited.

The royal captain led the way through the narrow passageways running alongside the caged courtyards that held the hunting dogs. As the men moved slowly in the narrow confines, barely wide enough for three men abreast, slavering dogs howled and snarled and leapt against the cage's bars. Blackstone saw that a hundred paces ahead the narrow alleyway widened into a passage. From where they stood terraces loomed out from the upper storeys of the building where he had seen the two men gazing down, suggesting that if Antonio Lorenz lived in one of the grand houses nearby then the steps that led up to the house might be close. As they passed the gate where Blackstone had cut the man's throat de Chauliac halted and turned to face Blackstone.

'A few minutes ahead are the steps that lead up to the gardens. There are narrow streets that intersect and once we are there I will keep my men at the crossroads until you have taken your men up.'

Blackstone looked ahead and saw that there was an increase in pedestrian traffic with handcarts being hauled along and shopfronts being set out to display their wares. The marriage celebrations were going on outside the walls but this vast city still throbbed with the noise of those going about their business. People would choke those narrow streets and if the city watch or the Visconti guards confronted Blackstone's men then the congestion might work in their favour. Or, he realized, stifle any attempt to move back the way they had come.

Blackstone looked back. His men were bunched but alert and ten paces behind followed twenty of the French guard. Blackstone's men bore their shields but their swords were still in their scabbards, which, Blackstone hoped, would avoid creating alarm among those on the streets when he and his men passed through them. If they held weapons that would have caused panic and brought Visconti guards down on them. Why then were the French armed? Were they nervous?

De Chauliac extended his hand to Blackstone. Both men clasped the other's. 'Sir Thomas, I offer my hand in gratitude and friendship and wish you success.'

In that instant Aelis's words struck him. A life owed. The hand of friendship ready to betray him. And in that same moment de Chauliac realized that the Englishman saw the betrayal. He tried to yank free but Blackstone's grip tightened.

De Chauliac cried out: 'Now!'

Blackstone rammed his shoulder into the captain's face and he fell, mouth bloodied, as behind them the French guard attacked. Meulon and Gaillard locked shields and thrust their pikes forward. Perinne and Renfred turned to lend their weight to the two big Normans. Dogs howled and barked. The first of the advancing guard went down, spear points in their throats. The odour of blood sent the hounds into even greater frenzy. Perinne and Renfred protected the spearmen as French attackers tripped and stumbled over the bodies. The two men-at-arms slashed and stabbed as Meulon and Gaillard thrust their pikes into the attackers again.

Blackstone stepped forward as de Chauliac writhed on the ground, eyes wide with fear, spitting blood and teeth. Blackstone pushed Wolf Sword into his chest. De Chauliac bucked, his hands grasping the hardened steel. Agony from the embedded blade. Blood. *The life you saved is yours to own*, Aelis's voice whispered as Blackstone pushed his boot into the man's neck to thwart de Chauliac's last desperate attempt to rise. He was already dead by the time Blackstone withdrew the blade.

The weight of the attacking Frenchmen began to bear down on Blackstone's men.

'Go on,' shouted Killbere. 'We'll hold them.'

Before Blackstone could answer or take another stride the ambush tightened. Thirty men bearing the Visconti blazon spilled from the narrow alleys. They had sprung their trap at exactly the right place. De Chauliac's betrayal had halted Blackstone's advance and given Visconti's men the chance to cut off any escape.

'Hold!' Blackstone yelled.

Twelve against fifty. Assaulted from both sides. Killbere and Blackstone took the Visconti attack head on. John Jacob was a pace behind and with him the others. Meulon, Gaillard, Renfred and Perinne battled the French guard. Blackstone's men were boxed in. They had no choice but to fight their way clear.

Meulon turned and saw the ambush close in on them. He desperately sought a way to fight back the way they had come but the French were scrambling over their dead and would soon overwhelm them.

'The gate!' Gaillard yelled over the shouts of men and howling dogs. 'The gate!'

Meulon looked over his shield rim. Help was at hand if they could reach the gate in the dog cage.

'Push them back!' Meulon shouted. 'Five paces! Five paces! Back to the gate!'

He and Gaillard leaned into their shields as Perinne and Renfred heaved their body weight into the big men's backs. Sheer brute force, stabbing spears and slashing blades bought the five long strides Gaillard needed. As they reached the iron gate into the dog pen he held the weight of the French attackers with his shield and slammed at the locked bolt with his mace. It snapped free. Yanking the iron bars he pulled the gate's hinges open towards him. It blocked the Frenchmen's attack in the narrow passageway as the dogs were set loose.

The French faltered as the savage beasts leapt at them. They slashed at the animals, severing limbs as the dogs snarled and bit. Blood from man and dog sluiced the path, making it difficult for the French to hold their ground. They slithered in gore and fell, and the half-starved hunting dogs tore into them. Jaws ripped flesh and muscle, crunching limbs.

'I'll hold the gate,' Renfred shouted. 'Help Sir Thomas!'

The German's strength held the iron gate fast, safe from the snapping jaws on the other side as the French retreated behind it from the dogs' attack. Meulon, Gaillard and Perinne turned and brought their weight to bear behind their comrades. Blackstone had brought down the first four Visconti men and Killbere another two. John Jacob hacked his way forward at their side. They fought in a seemingly unhurried manner. Brace, turn, stride forward. Strike, parry, thrust and kill. It was a deadly momentum of slaughter. Sweat stung their eyes, but now, with Perinne and the two big Normans, they formed a fighting wedge and slowly but surely pushed back the attacking Milanese. Howls from the rear told them that men were still dying viciously under the weight of the pack of dogs.

'The street and then left!' Blackstone called. If they could reach the crossroads they might have a chance to sweep in a great circle back to the stables and try to escape. Vengeance would wait another day.

They had carved their way through the Visconti men with such ferocity that Blackstone's men were less than fifty paces from where the streets met. Then thirty paces. And then the crossroads became a death trap. More Visconti men came from left and right. Like a sudden, gasping breath for life the fighting stopped. The surviving Visconti fell back to join the fresh troops. Blackstone and the others stood their ground, sucking air into their lungs, wiping sweat from their eyes. The groups faced each other, neither moving.

'Let them come to us,' said Killbere. 'I'm too old to attack them.'

Blackstone glanced at the blood-splattered veteran. 'You could always stay here.'

'You taunt a man to his own death, Thomas. Damn you,' he said.

'Stay or not, they'll kill us,' said Blackstone. 'This day had to come.'

He turned and looked at his men, who glared past him at their enemy.

'Better to die on our own terms. Better to let them remember it,' said John Jacob.

'It is what it is,' said Blackstone and smiled at his friends.

Killbere hefted his shield closer to his body and fell in step, and then, like the others, broke into a run as Thomas Blackstone roared in defiance and threw himself into the enemy ranks.

CHAPTER SIXTY-ONE

Henry Blackstone had slipped away from Fra Foresti in the night. It had been easier than he had imagined to enter through the western gate into the city. He had stabled his horse outside the walls along with many others belonging to those who had come for the wedding celebrations and joined the local traffic travelling in and out of the city through the postern gate. No one paid any attention to a boy carrying a bedroll across his back. His cloak concealed his sword and the hood his face.

He was jostled as he made his way through the busy streets. His stomach growled with hunger but he ignored the food sellers and bakers who touted their wares. The few coins he had would be needed the longer he stayed in the city. Ignore the stomach pangs, ignore the fear of uncertainty was what the voice in his head told him, but his stomach yearned for nourishment and his heart for courage. Handcarts trundled past him laden with firewood, others with bolts of cloth. Some carried heaped food, crops brought in from the surrounding countryside. Along each side street he turned into the beckoning call of stallholders and shopkeepers selling their wares rose above the jumbled voices of passers-by. Other than the tradesmen and labourers those who milled in the street were dressed differently than he had seen in France. The women seemed more beautiful and carefree, their heads without veils or hoods, hair tied and plaited; their gowns were as colourful as the hose and short jerkins of the men, who wore caps that seemed to balance precariously on their heads. Henry felt like a survivor washed up on a foreign shore. He was shouldered and barged, and some muttered insults and curses as he wandered lost among the crowds. How would he find his father and the men? His plan to enter the city had been accomplished but Milan was more vast than he could have imagined. With an increasingly sinking feeling he knew he should have thought through what he would do once he was here. He knew his father had travelled to the far side of the city and that meant going east, but it suddenly seemed a stupid idea to try and find him. What could he achieve? Love for his father and the friendship of the men who rode with him had spurred him to make a rash decision. It had not felt rash at the time but now the city overwhelmed him. He needed sanctuary and a place to escape the hubbub of the busy streets so he could think through his foolishness. He scoured the rooftops searching for the basilica's dome but the curved tiles of buildings' roofs around him simply rippled light and gave strutting pigeons the vantage point he needed. In desperation he approached a mendicant monk and asked directions. The old man's tonsure had not been shaved in days and his face was pockmarked with grime like the hands that grasped his begging bowl. The monk gazed at him longer than was comfortable. Perhaps Henry's Tuscan dialect identified him as an enemy of the Visconti; perhaps he had not been as diligent in his studies as he thought. The monk thrust forward his begging bowl.

'A coin and I will take you.'

The thought of sacrificing one of the few coins in his purse made Henry falter. He would not be able to deny himself food for much longer. He shook his head. The mendicant turned away. In panic Henry grabbed his arm and nodded his assent. He opened the purse stitched and embroidered years ago for his birthday by Countess de Harcourt in Normandy. It still bore her fine needlework and as his fingers touched the coin he remembered her giving him the gift. The memory tinged his thoughts with sadness but he quickly banished the past and dropped the offering into the bowl.

The mendicant turned on his heel and padded his way down a cobbled alley. Henry kept pace with the old man who moved quickly through the crowds. Perhaps, Henry thought, he was trying to lose him. He followed doggedly, ignoring the complaints of those that he now shouldered aside. And then as the passageway ended he stepped into the broad square and faced the basilica. The monk neither turned nor gestured and was quickly swallowed by another darkened alley.

Henry moved through the whisper-quiet nave of Sant'Ambrogio basilica towards the side cloisters. It was bitterly cold inside despite the many candles that threw shadows into the high wishbone ceiling whose ribs curved down onto ornately sculpted pillars. It felt as though he had been swallowed by Jonah's whale. He searched out a place in the shadows where he could think more clearly about what to do next. He kept a watchful eye on who was moving through the aisles as he skirted the walls. There had been no sign of anyone bearing the Visconti blazon when he had slipped into the basilica but his momentary sense of awe at the scale of the building had been quickly dissipated by the echo of a slamming door somewhere in the church. There were a few worshippers crossing the vast nave but only one or two glanced at the solitary boy who did not seem to belong among the well-dressed Milanese.

Henry found a corner in the cloisters and hunkered down for warmth. Lions, rams and horses – sculptured creatures on the pillars' capitals – glared down at him as if challenging an intruder's presence. Tortured with doubt, he felt the determination to fight at his father's side ebb away. It was not courage that he lacked but the means of achieving his goal. For a brief moment self-pity engulfed him. He was abandoned in a place of God, bereft of a murdered mother and sister and soon perhaps to be orphaned by his father's intent to avenge their deaths. It was as if fate had cast them all into this vipers' pit. Shadows squirmed as if confirming that even this holy place writhed with serpents.

He wiped the silent tears from his face and the self-pity from his thoughts. He got to his feet. He had already been banished to the classrooms of Florence, and there was no doubt his father would banish him again, but if he could at least find a way to save his father's life, years of study would be a small price to pay. He stepped around a pillar and did not see or sense the sudden movement of the shadow that struck him. The blow across the back of his head sent him sprawling, stunned, onto the stone floor. His head whirled; his ears rang. He tried to get onto his hands and knees but his strength seeped into the floor like spilled water. His final thought before darkness claimed him was that his mission to find his father was over. He had failed.

The cold stone floor pressed against his cheek and as he opened his eyes he saw the boots beneath the black cloak of the blurred figure who sat on a stone sill a few feet away. Henry groggily pulled himself up and sat with his back against the wall. The man opposite him was in almost complete shadow. The small knife in his hand sliced an apple and fed the pieces into his mouth. Henry's vision cleared and he gazed at Fra Foresti, who casually spat out the pips.

'You disobeyed me, boy, and your father. I am responsible for your safety. You deserve a thrashing and I've a mind to give it to you. Are you hurt?'

Henry's head throbbed, and the stone floor had grazed his forehead. He felt as though he had been kicked by his father's bastard horse. He shook his head.

'Liar,' said Foresti.

'I'm sorry, but I could not abandon my father.'

The Tau knight grunted. 'Well, you are under my care and I will not have you running off again. So, you give me your word or I will tie you like a dog and drag you to Florence.'

Foresti got to his feet, towering over the boy, who shakily stood, bracing himself against the wall until the strength returned to his legs. Henry lifted his chin defiantly. 'I cannot give you my word because I intend to find my father. So you will have to tie me like a dog.'

Fra Foresti sighed. 'You are your father's son and I half expected such wilful disobedience.' He gazed into the cavernous basilica. 'For a while we will be safe. The city is full of travellers, and my order of hospitallers is respected, so it would not be unusual for one such as myself to have escorted a pilgrim here, but it would only take one suspicious city watch commander to ask an awkward question and that might lead to difficulties. So, what are we to do, Master Henry?'

'Help me find my father.'

'For what reason?'

'So that I can be with him.'

'And why do you think your father wanted you to be taken to safety in Florence? Do you not see how foolish your action and desire is? If for any reason you are seized by the Visconti's men you will be used against your father. Your very presence jeopardizes his life.'

Henry's bravado faltered yet again. 'I had not intended to be captured and I didn't know how big the city was or how many people were on the streets, but there must be a way for me to find him,' he said hopefully, 'and with your help that's what I want to do, Fra Foresti.' He stared at the young Tau knight and then added: 'Even if you and my father give me a good beating.'

For a moment Foresti said nothing, as if mulling over the options that lay before him. 'We need a place of safety, and then we must find someone with influence who can discover where he is, or what has happened to him.' He deliberately left the statement unanswered and looked at Henry, whose mind raced quickly to the answer.

'The Princess,' he said.

CHAPTER SIXTY-TWO

A thousand pincers stung Blackstone's body. He opened his eyes not knowing whether he was in heaven or hell. If what seared his flesh was from Satan's imps, then he had descended into the underworld. His eyes adjusted to the near darkness and the shadows that flickered. Above him angels swirled, flying through clouds to heaven where a benevolent God waited with extended arms. He was lying flat on his back: he tried to move but couldn't. The last thing he remembered was hurling himself into the fray and being overwhelmed by a dozen blows as he cut down the Visconti's men. The screams of the dying and the bellowing rage that spurred on his men were now a memory. Except for his own breathing the eerie silence lay heavily. And then as he became more aware of his surroundings the soft spluttering of candles intruded into the near silence. He half raised his head. He was in a bow-roofed cellar or crypt whose brick ceiling's ribs curved this way and that. The plastered roof above him bore a painting of God and his angels and, like the Divine's crucified son, Blackstone's arms were outstretched and bound, as were his ankles. He was naked except for his braies and he could see that trickles of blood from a dozen wounds or more had dried on his torso. It was, he realized, the multiple cuts and cold air that stung his skin. He licked his dry lips, and felt the desperate need for water. There was no give in the bonds that held him and all he could see as he turned his head left and right were the walls of the cellar. There was no window to let in daylight or any sign of implements of torture. An iron-caged door was the only way in or out. Blackstone coughed congealed blood from his mouth and a moment later a light appeared on the other side of the door. A jailer raised a lantern and peered towards him. Then the man turned on his heel and took the light with him.

He had no memory of being brought to the ground during the fight. Killbere had been at his shoulder, so too John Jacob. It had been an act of defiance to attack such overwhelming odds, and he thought it likely that most of his men must have died in the street. There seemed to be no chance of escape from where he was being held so his only chance would be to try when they took him out for execution. Would they do that soon? he wondered. More likely, he reasoned, that they would not kill him publicly while the marriage was being celebrated. What he didn't know was how long he had been held captive. Judging by the wounds on his body it could only be a few hours. The thought comforted him. If that was the case it was likely he had a couple more days to live and in that time he would will the strength back into his body.

Time was swallowed by the candlelight and the nagging pain from his wounds but then as the flames began to falter and die he heard voices in the distance and the scuff of boots on stone followed by the jangle of keys. Two men emerged from the shadows. He twisted his head. Their dress identified them as noblemen. They stood over him: one a big man with a beard and the other a younger man with neatly trimmed facial hair and a slight but muscular body, who grinned. More of a wolf's snarl, thought Blackstone as the bigger of the two men held a burning torch over his body.

'Thomas Blackstone, you are mine now to cause hurt. I am Bernabò Visconti and the pain you have caused me in the past will be as nothing to what will be inflicted on you over many days until you beg for mercy and death.'

Blackstone said nothing. He wanted to sear the two men's features into his memory for when he escaped. The belief shone in his eyes. Bernabò laughed. 'Antonio, look at the beast. He's trapped and faces death and he still thinks he can reach our throats.'

Blackstone stared at the younger man. So this was the man behind the assassin and the killing.

449

'Turn your eyes away, Englishman. Or I will dig them out with my knife.' Antonio Lorenz prodded a bejewelled finger into a wound. Blackstone's body flinched involuntarily but he made no sound or complaint. Antonio's eyebrows rose. 'No?' he asked and then jabbed his finger deeper into the gash, turning it so the encrusted ring tore more flesh. Blood seeped. Antonio raised his hand and looked at the blood dribbling down his hand. 'The warrior's blood looks no different from any other man's. We thought you immortal. You're no god or demon, Blackstone, you bleed and hurt. That's good. We will have pleasure hurting you even more.'

Blackstone remained silent but he defiantly held the man's gaze.

'Look away!' Lorenz demanded and slapped Blackstone hard across his face. A ring caught his cheekbone and blood trickled. Bernabò placed a restraining hand on his son's impetus to strike again.

'You are alive because we ordered our men not to kill you, no matter what cost to them,' said Bernabò. 'The same with your men. Wounded and beaten, but alive. Torture offers more satisfaction than seeing bodies in the street. Anyone can die in the gutter but to be served up on the breaking wheel with hot irons and burning pitch is the measure of a man. We offer great sport for our people: they will be able to watch you die slowly. You do not come into the serpents' nest without being entwined, crushed and devoured, Blackstone.'

'I have a bill of safe passage from the Prince of Wales. Harm me further and you will answer to him,' said Blackstone. He knew his words, as an attempt to stave off more punishment, were futile, but they might buy him some time.

Bernabò leered and tugged out the parchment bearing the blood-red wax seal from his tunic. It was the pass Blackstone had given de Chauliac in a gamble that had failed. The seal had already been broken. Bernabò raised the pass towards the light and read the script.

'Know all that we, the Prince of Wales, have given leave and command safe passage, on the day of the date of this instrument, to Sir Thomas Blackstone, one of our trusted knights, to go to Milan as escort for the Princess Isabelle de Valois. In witness of this we have caused our seal to be placed on this bill. Given at Louviers 15th of May in the year of grace 1360.'

Bernabò raised his eyes above the document and looked at Blackstone. 'Such protection is worthless.'

He held the document in the flame and then waved it over Blackstone's body so the seal wax melted into his wounds. Blackstone flinched. 'The Frenchman betrayed you because he wished to gain favour with the Dauphin. The King's snivelling son is no warrior but he had enough cunning to bait a trap for you. And you could not resist the opportunity. When de Chauliac offered me this safe conduct he was sacrificing you for the cause of France. I ordered him to lead you to my men. I believe he knew I was sending him to his death.'

Blackstone spoke in barely a whisper, wanting them to lower their heads in order to hear him. 'Your vile corruption will stain the earth when I kill you. And when you die you will have my face close to yours.'

Within a heartbeat Bernabò's rage erupted. He grabbed Blackstone by the throat and throttled him. 'Whoreson! I'll break every bone in your body as you did with my son after he killed your bitch wife and daughter.'

The words penetrated Blackstone's mind as he gagged for breath. The assassin had been another of Bernabò Visconti's bastard sons. At least he had already inflicted some misery on the Lord of Milan.

Blackstone's body bucked as his windpipe was squeezed and his lungs denied air. Lorenz tried to pull his father off but he was violently cast aside. Bernabò's face was as purple with rage as was Blackstone's with lack of oxygen.

'My lord!' Lorenz cried. 'You'll kill him! And then there's no sport!'

Black spots exploded in front of Blackstone's eyes; his swollen tongue was forced between his parched lips. As Blackstone began to fall into unconsciousness Bernabò finally released his grip. He was sweating with rage and spittle flecked his beard but he deliberately stepped back a pace as if to stop himself inflicting more pain. He glared at the anxious-looking Antonio standing a few feet away. When Bernabò Visconti went into one of his rages no one dared confront him and that Antonio had done so meant it was possible his father would plunge a dagger into his own son's heart. However, Bernabò grunted acceptance of Antonio's admonishment. The Viper of Milan turned for the door, quickly followed by Antonio.

Blackstone lay in the dying light, forcing his mind to calm his rasping demand for air. He slowed his breathing and let the pain from his wounds envelop him, embracing it to spur his desire to survive and to find a way to strike back.

CHAPTER SIXTY-THREE

Galeazzo Visconti sat staring blankly at his advisers. His was a more formal court than his brother's, and matters of state and the running of his part of Milan were usually handled in the first instance by council officers among this retinue, but now his chancellor had delivered news that threatened the stability of his family's future. He had dismissed all those present except the chancellor. Galeazzo showed no sign of anger, nor muttered the vile curses that coursed through his mind. The celebrations were going well. The ambassadors and the noble families and wealthy merchants who had poured into the city were being entertained in the most lavish manner and they had no idea of the threat that had now crept into the heart of the Visconti family. What was important was that this threat be countered quickly and with the minimum of fuss, but with an end result that enhanced Galeazzo's side of the family in their pursuit of ultimate power. His heart beat quickly as he fingered the document that his chancellor had delivered.

'Can there be any doubt?' said Galeazzo.

'My lord,' his chancellor said with sufficient remorse in his voice, 'I fear not. The boy has a favoured relationship with the Princess and he was accompanied by a Knight of the Altopascio. The Princess confirms the story that she fell ill in Chambéry and that the woman who saved her has now been taken into your brother's palace. It appears that the woman who administered the poison has a daughter who serves in Antonio Lorenz's household.'

Lorenz. Merciful God. He was the one who had instructed the assassin to go against Blackstone and his family. That killer

453

had been their most efficient but still not good enough to escape Blackstone's wrath. Bernabò had chosen that lithe murderer because he was another of his illegitimate offspring. *Another.* The word stung because Bernabò's bastards were scattered across the whole of Lombardy. Damn! Lorenz and Bernabò, hand and glove. How would Bernabò not be implicated?

'The poisoner?'

'Dead. But the boy's story that an ambush was laid to kill Isabelle has been corroborated by the men we questioned who entered the city with Thomas Blackstone. My lord Bernabò is holding them in the cells beneath the city. They are all wounded, my lord, but Sir Thomas is not among them. One of them is an English knight, Sir Gilbert Killbere, and he gave a full account of what happened. The other men gave the name of the brigand who laid the ambush. He is known to Lord Bernabò, and the conclusion will be drawn that it was he who also made an attempt on her life.'

'Conclusions are not proof,' Galeazzo said, knowing there was a hollow ring to his words. It was likely that his brother had tried to halt the marriage by killing the child and in so doing preventing Galeazzo's closer links to European royalty. Galeazzo fingered the royal warrant from the English King that declared Sir Thomas Blackstone be granted safe conduct. The boy had approached the Princess and she had summoned Galeazzo's closest adviser to inform his master of what had happened. Bernabò had not only defied the English Crown but could be implicated in the attempt on Princess Isabelle's life. The indictment was the most damning since he and Bernabò had murdered their brother Matteo years before. And now the mad bastard Bernabò had thrown all caution to the wind and had moved against the family. But could Galeazzo prove it?

'My lord?' said the chancellor. 'What will you have me do?'

Galeazzo needed time to think. How to act against such a provocation? How to challenge the mad bastard? A direct confrontation with Bernabò could escalate into internecine war. His chancellor waited.

'Do nothing,' said Galeazzo. 'Yet,' he added.

Guards dragged Blackstone from where he was held. His hands were bound behind his back and they showed no concern as they shoved a shaft of wood behind his arms, forcing him to walk bent over and giving the dozen men who had been sent to escort a chance to subdue him should he try and escape despite his wounds and lack of clothes. They led him through a long underground passage lit by burning torches and then forced him painfully up stone steps into Bernabò's upper rooms. Bright daylight shone through the windows reflecting across the marble floors, causing Blackstone to squint. The guards kicked his legs away, forcing him down onto his knees, one of them keeping his hand firmly pressed against Blackstone's neck, so that all he saw was the veined marble. Blackstone heard a door open and the soft padding of bare feet approaching. A signal must have been given because the guard grabbed a handful of Blackstone's hair and yanked his head upwards so that he stared into the face of his captor, Bernabò Visconti. The big man was dressed in a loose silk gown and looked as though he had just crawled out of bed. He looked down at Blackstone and grinned.

'And so the sport begins,' he said and turned towards the broad terrace outside the room. The guards needed no orders to drag Blackstone to his feet and follow the Lord of Milan. Blackstone was held against the low parapet and for a moment he thought he might be flung to the yards below: the dog pens which he and his men had skirted before the fighting in the street. As one of the houndsmen made his way down the side of the yard the dogs sensed his presence and began to howl.

A servant offered a gold tray and goblet to his master and Bernabò took a mouthful of wine before turning to face his prisoner.

'When you fought de Chauliac, some of my dogs were released. Eleven were slaughtered; another eight needed to be killed because of their wounds. My men identified the one who smashed free the lock.' Bernabò's voice became more subdued, the pain of losing some of his beloved hunting dogs apparent. 'You will pay for my loss, Blackstone.'

Bernabò raised a hand to signal someone below that Blackstone couldn't see and then six of Visconti's soldiers dragged a bound Gaillard out. Even that great bear of a man could not fight those who held him. He was dressed in boots, hose and shirt, and his wrists and ankles were bound. He was forced to lie face down in the compound; guards held him at spear point while one of them cut his bonds. The guards quickly retreated out of the cage yard and slammed the gate closed behind them as Gaillard got to his feet.

Blackstone's stomach lurched. 'You vile bastard. Harm that man and I swear I'll slaughter your vermin offspring. I'll send you the head of your son Antonio Lorenz. I crushed to death your assassin who killed my family. He screamed and begged but I killed him slowly.'

Bernabò slapped him across the face, Blackstone spat blood back at him. ' Lorenz will know my blade across his throat. The whole of this city will hear *your* screams when I and my men destroy what you cherish.'

The threat made no impression on Bernabò. They were useless words from a condemned man. Bernabò nodded to the houndsman who made his way to the bolted kennel door.

'Gaillard!' Blackstone yelled. The man turned and looked up. There was no mistaking the look of fear on his face. Gaillard had been at Blackstone's side since the English archer was sixteen years old. Blackstone felt the tears sting his eyes and the words choking in his throat. 'I will avenge you, my friend. I swear it!'

'Vengeance has not served you well, Blackstone,' said Bernabò. 'Vengeance has brought you here, and look at you, hours away from your own death, and moments away from his. No, Blackstone, you will avenge no one for anything.'

Blackstone struggled against the guards in a vain attempt to lunge at the sneering Bernabò, but there were too many and they held him pressed against the parapet. His tears came and he summoned the strength to call down to the condemned man.

'Kill! Gaillard, use your strength and kill what this Visconti loves the most!'

His friend and companion raised his face to Blackstone again. 'Our time together is ended, Sir Thomas. I serve you still!' Gaillard reached down and tugged an undiscovered knife from his boot and brandished it up towards Blackstone and the man who stood at his side. It was too late for Bernabò to stop the gate being opened.

Bernabò cursed and flung aside the goblet. 'No!' he bellowed.

But the dogs were released and swarmed at Gaillard, who slashed left and right and then embraced one of them that leapt onto his chest. The animal squealed with pain as it died. The knife cut into others but the dogs clamped their bone-breaking jaws onto his legs. Gaillard went down. The pain- and rage-filled cries of a fighting man meeting his death echoed upwards. Suddenly it was over and his body disappeared from view as the snarling beasts tore into him. He had slain four of the hounds and mortally wounded three more before they ripped him apart.

Any look of pleasure had been wiped from Bernabò's face as he stared disbelievingly at the loss of more of his beloved dogs.

The crushing grip on Blackstone's heart lodged in his chest. 'Kill me now because as long as I am breathing I will find a way to come for you and the corrupted spawn that is your son.'

Bernabò's bulky frame moved quickly and Blackstone was unable to avoid the swinging clout across his head. He went down from the force of the blow to avoid further assault, and knew he was lucky that the barefooted tyrant could not kick him to death. Bernabò turned back inside the palace, leaving Blackstone face down. He pressed his face into the spilled wine and sucked its moisture before the guards hauled him to his feet. The pain in his body receded. His mind cleared. The memory of his wife and child and the cruel sacrifice of his friend forced strength into him. Death beckoned, but for now would be denied.

CHAPTER SIXTY-FOUR

The guards brought him food and water after they returned him to the vaulted cellar. They said it was to help him endure the punishing *quaresima*, the forty days' torture that awaited him. His wounds were festering and he could feel their poison beginning to claw at his strength. They no longer bound him and he paced the dank cellar using the weak light from the burning torch to search out any loose brick that might allow him to break through one of the walls. His grudging respect for the skill of the masons' work offered no comfort. A voice carried down the passageway and then a muffled argument, and after a few moments the sturdy gate was opened. Guards levelled their pikes to keep Blackstone at bay as two others came in and placed lanterns on the floor. The light reached up to the arched ceiling and the beckoning hand of God to his angels. As the men backed away Blackstone stared in disbelief at Aelis, who stepped into the warm glow.

'Are you sure, my lady?' asked one of the nervous guards.

Aelis turned. 'I told you, Lord Bernabò has sent me. Defy him at your peril. Now leave us.'

The guards looked uncertainly at each other and then obeyed her. Who were they to argue with their lord's woman?

Blackstone made no attempt to go to her. They stood facing each other. She was carrying her satchel and her concern for Blackstone was obvious. 'Thomas, you've more scars to bear.' She kept her distance, sensing his suspicion.

'Are you with the Princess?'

'No. I am with the Lord of Milan.'

'You whored yourself to him?'

'I did what was necessary. I am who I am.'

'And are you here to poison me?'

'I am here to treat your wounds,' she said and opened her satchel.

'He sent you?'

'He doesn't know I am here.' She sat on one of the two benches that had been laid out in the form of a cross and which had held Blackstone. 'There's not much time. Let me help you.'

The wrench of seeing Gaillard killed and now the shock of Aelis being in the same room and mistress to his enemy made him falter. The memory of her touch was too recent and he yearned for such tenderness again. Yearned for it but rejected it.

'I don't need your help, Aelis.'

'Our lives are still entwined, Thomas. You will need strength and those wounds weaken you. And your pride will stop you from fulfilling your destiny. Yield, Thomas, for once in your life.' She lowered her eyes. 'I beg you.'

He could not resist the gossamer spell she still cast over him. He sat next to her. She dabbed lotion on his wounds and he immediately felt the sting leave them as the cooling liquid soothed his torn flesh.

'These balms and lotions here,' she said, her fingers touching the bottles in the satchel, 'these are what will close the skin and heal.' After a few moments she began wiping the dried blood from his face. He saw her dark eyes were filled with tears. Her voice softened, as if with regret. 'I saw it all, Thomas, did I not?'

He nodded. 'The hand of friendship. Yes. De Chauliac betrayed me.' He studied her for a moment. 'As have you.'

She made no effort to deny his accusation. 'I knew where I would be at the end, Thomas. All of this is out of our hands,' she said as she cleaned and bound a deep wound on his arm whose split flesh was grimy with dirt and yellow pus already congealing. A knife wound had slashed the muscles in his thigh. She soaked and bound a strip of cloth around it. There were so many nicks and cuts on his body that she could not treat them all. But the most threatening had been attended to. She closed her satchel.

'It is not yet over.' She put her lips against his and he tasted her tears. 'You wear your wife's crucifix and the goddess of the silver wheel at your throat. Women protect you. Goodbye, Thomas, and thank you for my life.'

Before he could answer she got up and called for the guard. The gate opened and clanged closed behind her. Alone in the silence he suddenly felt bereft of all that he had held dear: wife, daughter, lover and friends. He gazed up at the beckoning Almighty. Blackstone almost went down on his knees to pray, but did not. He would live or die on his own terms. God would not help him now.

Galeazzo rode under escort to the cells beneath Bernabò's palace. He had sent no word of his impending visit to his brother, wanting instead to see Blackstone's captured men for himself and to hear from their mouths the bitter truth of what had been relayed to him. Fifty armed men flanked him as he demanded entrance and before any of Bernabò's guards could escape to warn their lord, Galeazzo's men blocked their way. Torches were lit and lanterns raised as he was taken along the pitch-black tunnel to their cell, which had been built more than a hundred years before. Water ran down the walls and rats scurried across the dirt floor at their approach. The stench of confined men told him that they were close. A jailer put an ancient key into a door lock and two of Galeazzo's men stepped inside holding aloft their burning torches. Galeazzo covered his nose with a perfumed handkerchief. Straw had been scattered across the floor; a bucket served as a latrine. He glanced at the bedraggled-looking men who shielded their eyes from the light. All seemed to be wounded. Some had torn their shirts for bandaging and bound their wounds. Four of Galeazzo's men crowded in behind him, swords in hand.

'Which of you is Sir Gilbert Killbere?' said Galeazzo. His eyes scanned the men and then one of them, using the wall for support, stood. His beard was matted with dried blood, and he nursed one arm. A torn strip of cloth was bound around his thigh.

'My lord?' said Killbere, respectfully acknowledging the finely clothed man. 'Have you come to throw me to the dogs?'

'What?' said Galeazzo.

'Your guards took one of us and threw him to the hounds.'

Galeazzo looked at these men as one by one they got to their feet. Despite their wounds they looked ready to fight. One of the guards behind Galeazzo took a pace forward but Galeazzo raised a hand and stopped him.

'I know nothing of your comrade. I am Galeazzo, Lord of Milan. You witnessed an attack on the Princess Isabelle. I want to hear about it from you.'

Another man, so tall he was obliged to stoop beneath the low ceiling, spoke up. His untidy black beard was matted and his thick hair tied back with a leather cord. 'Led by a man called Grimo. Before I cut his throat he offered me work with Lord Bernabò Visconti.'

'Three hundred men lay in wait for the French royal guard and the Princess. They would have slaughtered them all were it not for Sir Thomas Blackstone. Where is he? Have you killed him?' said Killbere.

'I have not,' said Galeazzo dismissively. 'Prove to me that these men were not waiting to ambush your sworn lord. He is our blood enemy.'

Killbere stepped closer so that the light fell clearly on his face. 'We dressed a boy as the Princess as bait and came up behind the routiers. They wanted her dead and we stopped them.'

'Three hundred men? You slew them all?'

'And hanged their bodies as warning,' said another of the prisoners, a stocky man with crow's feet scars on his head.

'Your son would be without a bride were it not for Sir Thomas,' said Killbere.

Galeazzo glanced at the men once more and then turned on his heel. Darkness fell as the door slammed closed with a final jangle of keys and the sound of the lock being turned.

Aelis lay across the silk sheets as Bernabò raised himself from her. He was sweating from his exertions as she reached for the carafe of wine. She poured two goblets and handed one to him. He looked at her warily.

'Only a trusted servant pours my wine,' he said.

'I am here to serve you, my lord.'

'You are here to obey me,' said Bernabò and pushed his goblet into her hand, taking hers in its place. 'Drink.'

Without hesitation Aelis drank a mouthful of wine.

'All of it,' said Bernabò.

She did as he demanded.

'All right,' he said and quaffed the wine back, spilling it down the side of his mouth into his beard. 'More. Pour more,' he commanded. She stepped closer and took his goblet, but he snatched her wrist. 'I will be done with you and then you can go back to the Princess, but while you are in my bed you are here for my pleasure, you do not defy me by visiting the Englishman. Did you think I wouldn't hear of it?'

Aelis winced with pain as his grip tightened. 'Forgive me, my lord, I went to put balm on his wounds because you said he would be tortured. If he was weak from them he would die quickly. I thought only to please you.'

'Liar. Did you open your legs for him on the way here?'

'I did not. I served only the Princess,' Aelis lied.

Bernabò grunted. 'Get the wine.'

She poured a full goblet and he swallowed half of what she offered. There was a knock on the bedchamber door. 'What?' Bernabò shouted.

The door opened and the chamberlain stood aside to reveal Galeazzo standing in the vast room that lay beyond. Bernabò's face creased.

'What drags you from the celebrations?' he said, wiping an arm across his mouth as he joined his brother. 'You'll drink?'

Galeazzo shook his head and kept his voice calm. 'I need to speak to you about the Englishman.'

'Now? I'm humping,' said Bernabò.

Galeazzo glanced at the woman who stood near the bed, her open gown revealing her breasts and her old scars. 'She's marked,' he said.

Bernabò shrugged. 'I don't care. She has good hips and tits and she enjoys me.' He grinned. 'You want her?'

'The Englishman,' said Galeazzo, ignoring the invitation. 'You took him.'

'He bleeds like the rest of us.'

'Let him go.'

Bernabò snorted. 'He's for the *quaresima*. I want to see how long he lasts when we break his bones. I want to hear him beg for mercy.'

Galeazzo pulled the King's safe conduct from his glove. 'He's protected.'

Bernabò ignored the proffered document and slumped into a chair. 'So what?' he said, choosing not to mention that he had already burnt Blackstone's other safe-conduct pass. He yawned and rubbed his eyes. The wine and the sex must be tiring him, he thought, as he looked blearily at his brother.

'The King of England gave him safe conduct. The Princess knows about this, and if she knows, others know. The King of England is important to me. To us. I do not wish to antagonize him. This pass must be honoured,' insisted Galeazzo.

'No. He's mine. I want the flesh taken from his bones. He came to kill Antonio.'

'Because Antonio sent the assassin to kill his family – which we were party to. Blackstone would kill us all given half the chance, but now that you have him you must appease the English King and give Blackstone the chance for revenge. Let Antonio face him. He's skilled enough to kill a wounded Blackstone.'

'No,' said Bernabò.

'Listen to me. To make certain our hands remain clean we must ambush and kill him only once he's outside the walls,' Galeazzo said, carefully withholding the fact that he knew Antonio had plotted to have the Princess murdered. There was no evidence that Bernabò was involved, but the thought nagged: how could he not be? 'Let him go and we can deal with Blackstone in our own way,' he said in a final appeal.

'He's beaten. He failed!' said Bernabò. His voice slurred. He shook his head to clear it and drained the wine. 'No. I won't send Antonio beyond these walls. Go back to your wedding celebrations, Galeazzo. There's nothing for you here.'

'Listen to me, Bernabò,' Galeazzo said evenly, restraining his impatience. His brother looked the worse for drink and danger would be lurking beneath the surface. The desire to tell Bernabò that he had witnesses who could testify that Bernabò's bastard son had tried to have the Princess murdered and that Bernabò's name was linked to mercenaries who had tried to ambush her was almost overwhelming, but he resisted it. Galeazzo's fifty men scattered between the room and the downstairs entrance would hold for a while but if Bernabò called for his soldiers then it would be a bloodbath. This moment when Galeazzo's family were strengthening their position by marriage could prove an ideal time for an enraged Bernabò to assassinate them all. He could wipe them out in one fell swoop. 'Release Blackstone,' Galeazzo repeated. 'Send him and his men beyond the walls. You have brigands enough in your pay. Then we rid ourselves of our enemy but cannot be accused of violating the English King's bill of safe conduct for him.'

Bernabò got to his feet. He staggered, and then steadied himself. 'I kill him here! And then I feed his remains to my dogs.'

Galeazzo knew he could not convince Antonio to venture beyond the safety of Milan without Bernabò's agreement. He would have to find another way. He was about to leave when Bernabò slumped to the floor. It looked as though he was in a drunken stupor. Galeazzo was about to beckon servants to take their master back to his bedchamber when he saw the woman, who had stayed sitting on the edge of the bed, slip onto the floor too. Uncertainty gripped him. Drunkenness was no stranger to this palace, which was infamous as a place of debauchery, but the explanation here might not be so simple. The woman was still conscious. Galeazzo went to her and bent down on one knee, ignoring her exposed breasts.

'Do you wish him dead?' she asked as if nothing were affecting her.

'What?' he asked foolishly as though he did not understand the question. Bernabò dead? He stepped away from her and looked at his brother's body. Bernabò dead gave him complete control over Milan. It removed a constant thorn in the Pope's side. It allowed Galeazzo to build his libraries, create places of learning. Bernabò dead gave Galeazzo everything. What it did not give him was a brother who led troops into battle, who fought and took cities, who ran Milan successfully, was feared by the Milanese but kept the city prosperous and the streets safe. Bernabò's death would point the finger of murder at Galeazzo. Unrest and uncertainty would sweep through the city like the plague.

'No,' he answered. 'I do not wish him dead.'

'Then release Thomas Blackstone and his men,' said Aelis, 'and do it quickly before I die or your brother will not receive the antidote.'

Galeazzo crossed himself. 'Merciful Christ in heaven, you have poisoned yourself as well.'

'If I hadn't he would not have drunk the wine. He'll soon be dead. Act quickly, my lord.'

Galeazzo half stumbled away. His brother lay unmoving but Galeazzo could see that he still breathed. Here was the opportunity to seize complete control but Galeazzo's wisdom denied him the temptation. Galeazzo was many things that others found to be cruel and calculating but one thing he was not was stupid.

The Viper of Milan regained his composure and like the lord he was barked out commands to soldier and servant alike. 'Fetch the Englishman. Clothe him and bring me his weapons. Release his men. Have their horses saddled and escort them to the Porta Tosa.'

Galeazzo looked back at the dying woman. She seemed to be in no pain. He turned and beckoned anxious-looking servants.

'Pick him up,' he said, pointing to Bernabò and then indicating an ornate, upholstered bench broad enough for a man to lie on. The servants struggled to lift the big unconscious figure onto the bench but once they had done so he gestured towards Aelis. 'Put her on the bed and cover her.'

The servants lifted Aelis onto the bed and draped the sheets over her. 'Raise me up,' she said, her voice weakening. 'So that I can see him when he comes.'

They half propped her on the pillows as Galeazzo strode back and forth in the larger room. His mind was working quickly. Bernabò needed to be saved and the Englishman released but there was still a benefit to be had from the situation. He beckoned the old chamberlain to him.

'Fetch Antonio Lorenz.'

'I don't know where he is, my lord.'

'If he is not in any of the palace rooms then he will be with his swordmaster. I want him here. Fetch him quickly or you will be beaten.'

Father Torellini's informant needed no further threat. He turned and scurried away.

Galeazzo stared at his dying brother and went to Aelis. 'How long before he dies?'

'Within the hour.'

'Where is the antidote?'

'In my satchel,' she said and looked to where the bag lay next to her discarded clothes. Galeazzo quickly took up the bag and opened it. An array of small bottles and containers nestled next to each other. 'Which one?' he said, unable to keep the urgency from his voice.

Aelis smiled. 'Only when Blackstone is freed.'

Galeazzo was about to threaten her with retribution for what she had done but knew it served no purpose. To do so might mean she refused to reveal which bottle contained the cure. He left her and called the captain of his guard. His mind raced. He had to plan ahead. Who knew the routes in and around Milan and could find them in darkness if necessary? 'Find the Tau knight who is with the Princess Isabelle. Have him wait at my palace. Treat him with respect. Tell him I have information that will benefit Sir Thomas Blackstone.' He waved the captain away.

He unconsciously reached for the carafe of wine to pour a drink, and then caught himself. A careless slip in the next few hours was all it would take for his plan to fail.

Blackstone was brought into the marbled room. He was dressed as he had first arrived in the city but his jupon was blood-splattered. Guards flanked him and his weapons were put on a table. Galeazzo stared at the tall, scar-faced knight. The Englishman looked bedraggled and the worse for wear. He limped from a bandaged wound on his leg, and dirt ingrained his skin. Galeazzo stared at the Visconti's enemy for a moment and then spoke brusquely. There was business to be done.

'A bargain has been struck. Your life for that of my brother.'

'How so?' asked Blackstone, glancing at Bernabò's outstretched body.

'Does a drowning man ask who throws him a rope?'

'I make no bargains with the Vipers of Milan.'

Galeazzo had kept his distance from Blackstone but his presence still sent a chill of fear into him. Face-to-face this man had the air of a relentless killer and it was not hard to imagine him leaping forward and striking him dead before the dozen guards could stop him. Galeazzo banished the fright from his mind. He took out the King's safe conduct. Blackstone suddenly realized that if the Visconti had that then they must also hold his son.

He kept the panic from his voice. 'Where did you get that?'

'It was given to the Princess Isabelle by a Knight of the Tau.'

Blackstone knew if Fra Foresti was in Milan then it meant that, for whatever reason, Henry might be with him. Yet Galeazzo had made no mention of him so perhaps the boy was not in the city or his presence was unknown to the Visconti. 'And what has happened to him?'

'Nothing. He is safe and will remain so.' Galeazzo handed the document to the captain of his guard and gestured that it be given to Blackstone. 'I honour your King's desire to see that no harm befall you. And I wish him to know it. What has happened here was not of my doing. You came here to seek vengeance. I offer you your freedom and I will give you the man you seek. It was Antonio Lorenz who sent the assassin to the heart of your home.'

'With your blessing,' said Blackstone.

Galeazzo hesitated. To deny it completely would be too obvious an untruth. 'No,' he lied. He glanced at the prostrate Bernabò. 'I did not consent. It was my brother and his bastard son. I will give you Antonio but you cannot have him,' he said, meaning Bernabò. 'You have already inflicted pain on the Lord of Milan by killing the assassin who was also his son. Now I give you the opportunity to settle your desire for revenge and cause him yet more grief. I will give you Antonio. It serves me as well as you. It weakens my brother if the bastard is killed. I cannot do it myself without causing a blood feud that would destroy us both. Milan is too important to be squandered in such a way. Strike the bargain, Sir Thomas, before it is too late, because if my brother dies then so do you. And then the matter is ended.'

'Lorenz tried to kill Isabelle.'

'So I have been told. Which is why I offer him up to you. He means nothing to me.'

'Your brother was involved.'

'There is no proof,' said Galeazzo.

'But you know it to be true,' said Blackstone.

Galeazzo ignored him. 'Make your decision and make it now.'

'My men?'

'Already at the entrance to the city.'

'Then give me Antonio Lorenz.'

Galeazzo turned and pointed to the bedchamber. 'Once you get me the antidote for the poison inflicted on my brother.'

Servants opened the great doors and Blackstone stepped uncertainly into the room. Then he saw Aelis lying propped on the bed. She seemed barely conscious but her eyes were half-open. He instantly realized that she had poisoned Bernabò to trade his life. He went quickly to her and eased his arms around her, holding her close. 'Aelis, it's Thomas.'

She nodded and raised her hand to touch his scarred face. 'This was the only way. I told you I knew how this would end. This is what I saw, Thomas. This.'

'Tell me where the antidote is and I'll give it to you.'

She shook her head. 'There is not enough. I took some before I drank the wine to make sure I would live long enough… but… but now… you must give it to him. You must,' she whispered. 'Otherwise my death means nothing.'

'I'll fight my way clear of this city. Take the antidote. I'll get us both out.'

'You cannot change what's meant to be, Thomas,' she said, her voice weakening.

'Mother of Christ, Aelis, you can live. Together we can free ourselves of this place.'

'No. Only you can do that. Thomas… I beg you … there's little time…'

He fought for words that wouldn't come. Nothing could be said to draw her back from the tide that would soon sweep her away from him.

They both knew there was nothing he could do to help her.

She smiled. 'Take the satchel and use what I showed you to heal your wounds… give the Visconti the dark blue bottle.' Her breath faltered. 'Hurry,' she said. 'Thomas… my debt is almost repaid.'

Blackstone held her hand to his lips and then leaned forward and kissed her.

Her eyes closed, her breath sighed and her features softened as death claimed her.

Blackstone held her a moment longer and then turned away.

He never looked back.

CHAPTER SIXTY-FIVE

The bastard horse had been too dangerous for the stable-boys to saddle and when Blackstone entered the stall it snorted and reared its head, baring its yellow teeth. Yet for some reason it did not attempt to bite or kick the injured Blackstone, as if sensing that its rider would be unable to tolerate its belligerence. Blackstone rode slowly through the city as shopkeepers closed their shutters and others ushered away chickens and pigs into safekeeping for the night. The evening streets were slowly clearing. The low sun cast deep shadows from the high walls that slithered with movement as men scurried to reach home before curfew. Galeazzo had sent six men as escort and they guided him towards the eastern gate of the city, the same he had entered through. As lamps were lit the city's eyes watched him leave. The soldiers remained silent and when they passed across the portal they returned Wolf Sword, his archer's knife and fighting axe. The massive gates closed behind him and as he urged his horse forward he saw in the distance a group of men waiting in the fading light. It was Killbere and those who had entered the city with him. As he got nearer he could see that they were all wounded and some were slumped in the saddle.

'They said you would be released,' said Killbere. 'If they hadn't done so we were going to ride to Will Longdon and bring the men and archers here to spoil their damned wedding tomorrow.'

'Is Henry or Foresti with you?'

'No. We've not seen them.'

'Then they're still in the city,' said Blackstone.

'Not Florence?' said John Jacob.

'No, for some reason they followed us. There's no knowing where they are now, but once this matter is settled we'll find them. I was told no harm would come to Foresti, so if Henry is with him then we can only pray they remain unscathed.'

'They threw Gaillard to the dogs,' said Perinne and spat in disgust. 'We were chained but we fought the guards. We had no chance against so many and we bear more wounds to prove it.'

'I saw him die,' Blackstone told them. The hurt of the brave man's death still burned. 'He had a knife hidden in his boot. He killed a few dogs before they took him.'

'He died unshriven,' said John Jacob. 'That's hard for men such as us.'

'The Almighty will forgive Gaillard's sins,' said Blackstone. 'The manner of his death will stand him in good stead with God and his angels.' He looked around at his determined men who made no complaint despite their wounds. He saw that one horse was being led without its rider. 'Where's Meulon?'

'He's stayed behind to avenge Gaillard. He said he'll escape on foot at dawn,' said Killbere.

Meulon's plan was only to be expected. The two stalwart Normans had served together before they accompanied Blackstone on his first fight against brigands in Normandy a lifetime ago. Those two bears of men had been at his side ever since. 'Aelis is also dead,' he told his injured followers. 'She gave her life so we could be given our freedom. We have safe passage and the man we want will be outside the walls tomorrow. We are to ride south where he'll be delivered to us and then we will finish this.'

'The bastards will ambush us, Thomas,' said Killbere. 'We won't have time to get help from Will and the others.'

'Galeazzo Visconti made a bargain,' Blackstone told them. 'He's more cunning than his brother and he wants Antonio Lorenz dead. But for all I know he could be offering us to him. If we die outside the walls then no blame can be laid at the Visconti's door.' Blackstone looked around him at the flat landscape. It offered little in the way of ambush sites but men riding hard could sweep down on their small band, and wounded men would not be able to ride hard for long in any effort to escape. There were no defensive positions to be seen. What Blackstone wanted was some rising ground, a vineyard perhaps, anything that would make a cavalry charge disadvantageous to the horsemen. They had seen woodlands on their flank when they rode into Milan, and if they were forced to defend themselves such a place would be preferable to being out in the open. He gazed at the sky. It would be a cold night and mist would rise from the rivers and blanket the land. 'We'll ride until we can no longer see the road. Another hour, perhaps, and then we camp. I have balm to help our wounds. A night's sleep and we'll be ready for whatever awaits us.'

'These are strange times we live in, Thomas,' said Killbere as the men urged on their horses. 'A man as rich as Croesus buys a child-bride from a French king for his son and strikes a bargain with his enemy to kill his brother's bastard. And our lives are saved by a woman we thought to be a witch.' He rode on a moment longer and glanced at Blackstone. 'I'll pay for a mass to be said for her. Providing we live long enough.'

Bernabò Visconti still lay unconscious despite the antidote being administered. The court physicians confirmed their belief that he would live and that by the following day they expected him to be conscious. He was a bull of a man. Perhaps, they thought, even to be well enough to attend the wedding ceremony.

Antonio Lorenz stood in the bedchamber and looked at his father, who was breathing slowly and deeply. He had not been told of the court physician's prognosis; instead Galeazzo stood in the dimly lit bedchamber with him, as if they were attending a dying man.

'It is not known whether he will survive the night,' Galeazzo lied. 'So you must ride out and kill Blackstone for the sake of our future. I was obliged to release him in an attempt to save your father.'

'Blackstone has a hundred men and archers south of the city,' said Antonio.

'No, they are out on the road to Florence. Blackstone cannot reach them in time. He is vulnerable now and you need to strike him.' Galeazzo put an arm around his shoulder and lowered his voice. 'Antonio, we must face the prospect that your father, my beloved brother, this great Lord of Milan, may be dead by morning. And if that is the case, then you must take his place.'

Antonio stepped back in shock at the suggestion that he would be granted such power in the city. 'You would give that to me?' he asked.

'I have already drawn up the document and the moment Bernabò dies then you will be honoured with his title and will control half the city as did he. His wealth must be divided between his wife and his legitimate children, but once you are in power then you will receive the taxes and the income. I am not being over-generous, Antonio; I need someone I can trust to govern. But we must rid ourselves of Blackstone once and for all. He will not rest until the day he sends an assassin in the night to kill you in your bed. Seize the moment, and ambush him. I know what road he takes. He has a dozen wounded men with him.'

'Then I shall do as you ask. I'll take my father's cavalry.'

Galeazzo hesitated. It was not part of his plan to have Antonio use the professional troops drawn from noble families who were loyal only to Bernabò. 'My brother has brigands outside the walls. Use them. We'll pay them well. Take two hundred with you, Antonio: you must be protected at all costs. The English are not the only scourge who ride beyond our walls. And when the English King hears that one of his favourite knights has fallen then the brigands will be blamed, not us. It is time for you to step forward from the shadows, Antonio.'

'Yes,' the young man said, his ambition expressed with little more than a sigh. 'And if my father lives?'

'Then you will be honoured by both of us for having killed Thomas Blackstone and ridding us of his threat.'

'I know where my father's men are. I'll leave tonight,' said Antonio. 'I'll bring Blackstone's head back on a pole.'

Galeazzo watched the young man's eyes peer into the half-light of the flickering candles at his father lying motionless. He licked his lips in anticipation. Galeazzo knew he would have to seal the room and post a strong guard to protect his brother because he sensed that Antonio Lorenz had already crowned himself Lord of Milan and his father's death was almost a formality.

As the night wore on servants came and went past the armed guards at Bernabò Visconti's bedchamber. As each approached to bathe their master's brow with wet cloths, a guard would stand next to him. Nothing was to pass the Lord of Milan's lips, not even the droplets from a wrung cloth. If any such attempt was made the soldiers had orders from Galeazzo to immediately kill the servant. And when the servant's duties were done, the doors were closed and Bernabò Visconti was left alone, caged in in his own private hell.

He was being dragged through the fires of the underworld. His body burned and his throat felt as though he had swallowed hot cinders. The stench of sulphur stung his nostrils and tears welled from his eyes. He choked and tried to turn his back to the screams of those consumed by the flames. An insistent voice beckoned him, shouting his name, demanding he awake. Breaking through the dream he opened his eyes. His head was thick as if from drink, his chest tight like a man drowning. He gulped air. Sometime in the night the screams became howls. Shadows soared like demons. Bernabò Visconti lunged from the bed, fell, gained his feet and stumbled for the terrace where a wall of cold air brought him half to his senses. Men were shouting and those howls of terror became louder. The clear night sky was a cauldron of flames. Bernabò pressed himself against the parapet, gulping the air, unable to grasp why smoke scratched the back of his throat. He shook his head and thought himself still in a dream as he gazed at the yard below where Blackstone's man had been thrown to the dogs. The kennels were ablaze. The pitiful sound of fifty or more of his beloved hunting dogs being burnt alive pushed a serrated blade into his chest.

He bellowed to the men below who were fighting a losing battle against the fire. They were pushed back as the flames seared across the yard. The wooden gates that secured the dogs were burning and some of the injured animals ran terrified through the flames, their coats ablaze, to die a terrible death as they tried to breach the iron gates. They writhed and howled as the fire consumed them. Bernabò Visconti clung to the parapet and vomited. His life's pleasures – violence, deception, stealing, intoxication and sex – were as nothing in that barren moment of witnessing their agonizing deaths.

From the high terrace he would not have seen the big man with his hair tied back moving quickly through the street's deep shadows. Beneath his cloak the jupon's blazon declared that those who bore it would remain *Défiant à la mort*.

CHAPTER SIXTY-SIX

Blackstone and his men had watched the distant fire glow in the night sky. The muted cries from behind the city walls soon fell silent and as the fire diminished the night's fog drew its veil over the city. They attended to each other's wounds and took satisfaction in believing that Meulon had inflicted misery on Bernabò Visconti. If luck was on their side they would add more grief to him the following day.

They broke camp as the grey dawn light touched the clinging mist that blanketed the flat plain. Like ghost riders they rode at walking pace through the damp air that speckled their cloaks and beards. As the sun rose higher in the sky and burned away the eerie covering a distant village church bell told them it was the third hour in the day. Now that they could see the road ahead they spurred their horses on. Antonio Lorenz had not laid an ambush as they thought he might. For someone who knew the lie of the land the misty dawn would have been the ideal time to attack. Perhaps, Blackstone thought, Antonio Lorenz was a lazy fighter, confident that he could destroy these few who had dared to challenge the Visconti, or it was as Galeazzo had promised and the assassin's master would be delivered to them.

It was early autumn and the small copse of trees they passed had already started to turn. In a few weeks winter would strike hard and the killing season would end. In the past it had made no difference to the English *condottieri*. Blackstone and his men had fought year round: it was what gave them the advantage over their enemies. But there was no denying that winter fighting and burying men in the frozen earth was a thankless task. Better to die and be put in the ground when summer blessed the land. But autumn's gentle escape to the year's end would still allow them to inter their dead because a part of Blackstone knew the day would not end without a fight.

He reined in the bastard horse. For a moment it fought the bit, but Blackstone tightened the reins and steadied it. 'Over there,' he said, pointing to a treeline that scuffed the horizon. Smoke curled from the houses of a nearby village.

'Two miles, then,' said John Jacob.

'Three more like,' said Blackstone, gauging the distance. 'And we can't see what's in those trees until we get there.'

'And that's where we are to wait?' said Killbere.

'That's where I'm going to kill him,' said Blackstone, and gave the impatient horse its head.

Men ploughed the fields planting winter wheat. The farmers were five hundred yards distant and barely raised their heads from their labours as they whipped their yoked oxen. Nothing seemed untoward. Blackstone realized that if he and his men were obliged to retreat across the open fields the torn ground would make heavy going. Their horses would be slowed and anyone in pursuit or loosing crossbow bolts would have them at their mercy. Did Galeazzo know that such a race for safety would be across ploughed fields? Had the cunning Lord of Milan placed Blackstone in the perfect place to be ambushed?

Blackstone drew the men to a halt a hundred paces from the treeline. All his instincts told him that men waited in the darkness of the forest. The horses' ears pricked and their muscles quivered as they too sensed other horses and riders. Blackstone and his men drew their swords and turned their backs to the stubbled cornfields that lay between them and the distant city. Their ragged line would be little defence should the woodland explode with a cavalry charge. If that happened it meant that Antonio Lorenz wanted the personal satisfaction of slaying Blackstone. He prayed that if this was an ambush then they would not bring him down with crossbow bolts before he killed the assassin's master. If his life was to have one final act it was to be the death of Antonio Lorenz.

The bastard horse whinnied, wanting its rider to ease the reins so that it could surge forward. Blackstone's skin crawled and he gripped Wolf Sword tightly. 'Be ready,' he told the men.

There was a rustling of undergrowth as the woodland darkness shimmered.

'We'll ride at them, Thomas. Take the fight into the trees. We'll stand a better chance,' said Killbere.

Blackstone was about to heel the horse when a black-cloaked figure stepped into the open, and a moment later Henry stood next to the Tau knight.

Milan's church bells peeled, as trumpets' and drums' cacophony reverberated around the city walls. Peacock-rich banners and flags curled in the morning breeze as the aroma of cooked meats and sweetbreads wafted through the air. Every edible fowl and beast had been prepared for the wedding feast. Swan, heron, goose, duck and songbirds, salted tongues, beef and eel pasties, lampreys, suckling pig, pullets, vegetables and beans. Spit-roasted oxen, boar and fat trout would soon grace the two long linen-covered tables, one for men, the other for women. The high table would seat the family and honoured guests. Course after course would satiate the guests until they were served cheeses and fruit.

Galeazzo Visconti gazed with affection across his city's skyline from his palace in the west of the city. The joyous pealing and fanfares of exultation proclaimed the Visconti's wealth and success. This day of October would be an historic one marking a new chapter in the fortunes of the Visconti family. They would be the talk of Europe. Milan was already renowned for its wealth and prosperity but this new era, beginning this very day, meant the house of Visconti would rise to the level of royalty. His diplomacy had paid off and the recent unpleasant situation with his brother and Blackstone would soon be resolved. Bernabò had survived the night, and the fire in the east of the city that had consumed part of the kennels and killed his brother's hunting dogs had been extinguished without loss of human life or damage to surrounding buildings. Bernabò had taken to his bed to drink himself back into a stupor until the agony of the night was subdued. But today was not about Bernabò; it was about Galeazzo's son and the future of the family. It would be the day when the Visconti flaunted their wealth so that ambassadors and guests would return to their countries and speak of the incredible fortune and power of the Visconti.

He patiently allowed his servant to fuss his lord's velvet and brocade tunic, richly studded with pearls and precious stones. Galeazzo would outshine the bride herself with his lace ruffs, gold and silver fringes and bejewelled belt. His hairdresser eased the weight of his hair into its net and settled it neatly onto his ermine-trimmed robe's collar, the brocaded viper's crest prominent on the scarlet and gold robe. His thoughts led his fingers to touch its depiction of the viper swallowing a child.

And so it was, he told himself. The house of Visconti had consumed friend and foe alike.

It was a good day for men to die.

By contrast to the finery being displayed in the city, Blackstone's men faced the open plain looking ragged and unkempt. They too could hear the distant sound of celebration. It mocked their pain and meagre food supply. Their bodies still ached from their wounds but they waited, mounted and ready, as the line of horsemen appeared from the wall of ground fog that extended across the plain a mile away. Antonio Lorenz had brought enough men to be certain that nothing went wrong.

The farmers felt the earth rumble as the approaching horsemen spurred on their horses. It gave them time to whip their oxen from the fields.

'Wait until they reach the ploughed ground,' Blackstone said, taking an extra turn of the reins in his left hand. He would not carry his shield: the wound in his arm was already weeping. He gripped the bastard horse with his legs, readying it to use its massive strength to surge forward. His leg wound protested but he ignored it. His horse snorted and ducked its head, yanking him forward in the saddle, but his own strength kept the beast in check.

The steady drumbeat thud of the attacking horses shuddered through the ground. At five hundred paces they saw that one man sat astride his horse in the middle of the line. Even from that distance they could see he wore the finest armour. Its shaped angles glinted in the sunlight; the war horse's chest muscles glistened. The men who rode with Antonio Lorenz were dressed no differently from Blackstone's. They wore jupons over mail, pieces of armour in strategic places on arm, shoulder and thigh. Open-faced bascinets exposed snarling faces.

At three hundred paces they began to shout – their blood was up and in their minds they had already spent the generous bounty promised by Lorenz – but then their horses' iron-shod hooves dug into the turned earth and the heavy soil slowed their charge. It made little difference to the brigands, who simply spurred the horses' flanks and raised their threatening voices further.

Blackstone lifted Wolf Sword and at his signal Will Longdon and Jack Halfpenny, with their archers, stepped clear of the forest and rammed their sheaves of arrows into the dirt in front of them. Those brigands who had seen how lethal English bowmen were yanked their reins, kicking their horses away. It made little difference. Killbere grinned as he heard Will Longdon call out his command: 'NOCK! DRAW! LOOSE!' followed by the whispering flight of the yard-long arrows.

'You're dead men, you whoresons!' Killbere laughed and spurred his horse.

The arrow storm fell in a perfect arc and the thud of bodkin heads punching bone and flesh turned the brigands' elation at imminent success into screams of terror. Horses foundered. Men fell into the ploughed dirt, some trapped beneath their mounts, others already struck through from the bone-shattering power of the arrows. Those who managed to clamber to their feet turned and ran. It was too late to halt the headlong advance of the surviving horses and Blackstone saw the look of horror on Lorenz's face. Despite their wounds Blackstone's front line urged on their own horses and, as the archers loosed a second flight, his men-at-arms who had been held in the forest steered their horses though the archers' ranks. Fra Foresti and Henry stood back in silent awe as the surprise attack struck the horsemen. Galeazzo Visconti had played the double cross with the ease of a magician casting a spell. *Ride to Blackstone's men on the road to Florence, ready them, and I will deliver Antonio Lorenz into Blackstone's hands*, he had instructed the Tau knight when he had been summoned to his palace. In one fell swoop the Lord of Milan had weakened his brother's influence and sacrificed his bastard son. No blame would fall on Galeazzo. The Tau knight could imagine the cunning man's explanation to Bernabò. How could he have stopped the headstrong and violent Antonio from going after the Englishman, determined to avenge what he thought to be his father's death?

The archers ran after the men-at-arms, ready to use their knives to despatch the fallen brigands. Foresti glanced down at Henry. Was the boy horrified by the slaughter? Henry Blackstone, mouth open, stared, mesmerized by the clash of horsemen as his father sought out Antonio Lorenz in the mêlée.

Blackstone swung Wolf Sword in great sweeping arcs, the power of his blows breaking a routier's arm. He gave the bastard horse its head which it used like a swinging war hammer. It bit and snorted and like the great stallion it was used its strength to barge into the opposing horses. Skinners were falling beneath his men's sword and axe blows. Perinne smashed down with his mace onto a brigand's helm. It caved in and then blood spurted down the dying man's face from a crushed skull. Killbere had forged through the attackers' ranks and leaned this way and that, cutting down the retreating men on foot.

Blackstone saw Renfred strike out at Lorenz but the Italian swordsman's skills were superior to that of the German. Renfred's helm took a huge blow and that saved his life as he fell unconscious into the mud. When Renfred tumbled from his horse a gap opened around Lorenz. Blackstone snatched the bastard horse's reins and, pressing his injured leg into its flank, kicked it around with the other.

Lorenz saw Blackstone strike out towards him. In that moment he realized that to have a chance of survival against the scar-faced knight he had to get clear of the swirling blades. His men were dying around him and Blackstone's fighters could soon overwhelm them. And then he would most likely be slaughtered like a sacrificial lamb.

Blackstone saw Lorenz wheel his horse as he shouted to the men closest to him. They looked at Blackstone and two of them spurred their horses towards the Englishman. They barged the bastard horse but its strength made them falter and they panicked, swerving away as Blackstone struck down the closest rider. The second man was fighting his horse and although he tried to bring the beast back on course to protect his paymaster's escape, its terror made it sway wide. Its rider gave a desperate sweep of his arm as it went past Blackstone and managed a glancing blow with his flanged mace. It struck Blackstone on the side of his head, rocking him back in the saddle. His vision blurred, almost causing him to fall, but he held on as the bastard horse's power carried him through the brigands' ranks. He spat blood as Lorenz spurred his horse in the direction of Milan. Was he running for home?

They were already half a mile from the fight and Blackstone knew that the Italian's horse could outrun his own. Like the armour on the man's back the horse beneath him was of the finest quality. Desperation began to claw at Blackstone as he saw his quarry slip away. The bastard horse lumbered on in pursuit and he knew that if nothing else the belligerent animal would never stop until its heart failed and it fell dead. He looked behind him and saw he was alone. The fight had snared his men in a killing spree. Blackstone's wounds had torn open and blood trickled down his arm. His lathered horse rumbled on and as its uneven stride settled into its own peculiar rhythm he felt the dizziness blur his vision once again. He knew in his heart he could never catch the man he sought so desperately to kill. Wolf Sword's blood knot bit into his wrist, its burn adding to the cuts that seared his body beneath his mail, rubbed raw by his sweat-soaked undershirt. He offered a prayer to the Celtic goddess at his neck and begged Christiana's spirit to help him. Anger at losing the chance to kill Antonio Lorenz spurred a fresh determination in him.

'Come on! Come on!' He urged the tireless horse because suddenly his prayer was answered and the assassin master's horse slowed. The Italian had looked over his shoulder and seen that Blackstone had momentarily slumped over the horse's withers.

Blackstone's vision blurred again; he shook it free. The man had turned! Lorenz was galloping towards him. The Italian raised the shield that bore the writhing viper, his sword arm ready to strike. His visor was down and the sunlight glinted off his burnished armour.

Blackstone put the reins into his sword hand and reached down for his shield strapped to the pommel. He ignored the animal-like bite that seared his muscles as he lifted its weight into place. Now the two men were less than two hundred strides from each other and Blackstone could see that Lorenz was an experienced tournament fighter because he had angled his body low in the saddle, leaving a smaller target for Blackstone to strike.

There was no time to think. It was all down to instinct now whether he would live or die. Blackstone had one advantage over Lorenz. He released the reins and felt the horse respond given its freedom. It nearly threw him from the saddle as it swerved and then straightened and within moments barged heavily into the other horse. There was a tremendous slap of muscle and the impact threw both men to the ground. Blackstone fell heavily on his back and felt the sharp pain thrust into his lungs. For a moment everything went dark and then instinct took over and he rolled clear, shield raised, Wolf Sword held low ready to strike upwards. But Lorenz was nowhere near him: he too was only just getting to his feet. His horse had been knocked down by Blackstone's but it raised itself and cantered away. The bastard horse stood still, head lowered, flanks heaving from the impact.

Both men staggered momentarily but then ran at each other. Antonio Lorenz was the lighter of the two and more agile. He clipped Blackstone's shield with his own, sidestepped and aimed a hefty blow towards Blackstone's neck. Blackstone raised the shield and the blade bit into its rim. He yanked hard before Lorenz could release his sword and the action threw the younger man off balance. As Lorenz stumbled his sword came free. He braced his legs and immediately attacked with a flurry of blows. He was muscular and had a tireless strength that Blackstone recognized in himself. Lorenz's determination and agility were in his favour, but his desperation to strike a crippling blow on the bigger and heavier man meant he concentrated on using the skills and technique taught him by the great swordmasters of Italy. He had never fought in a major battle where blood and spittle showered everything and where men killed with any weapon they had including their bare hands. Antonio Lorenz was a master swordsman and he would soon find a way through Blackstone's defence. But he did not know how to kill in a dirty fight.

Both men grunted, lungs heaving with exertion and muscles burning. Blackstone forced his shield into Lorenz's body, let Wolf Sword drop and dangle from its blood knot and with his sword hand now free gripped Lorenz's belt. Blackstone's momentum, size and weight did the rest and Bernabò Visconti's bastard son fell backwards, his sword arm smothered. His weapon had no blood knot and he was suddenly defenceless. Blackstone gripped his sword hilt again for the killing blow but Lorenz yanked his knife free and slashed. The blade caught Blackstone across his thigh where he had strapped a piece of armour to protect his old wound; as the blade caught the metal its momentum was halted and it slashed across the inside leg muscle. Blackstone fell. Inflicting the wound gave Lorenz a surge of strength. He rolled, pushed back his visor to suck in air and then threw his weight down on Blackstone, whose injured leg hampered his movement. All

Blackstone could do was raise his shield. It was the most natural reflex, but he knew that if he did Lorenz would simply smother it with his weight and strike low and fast with the knife.

Instead of doing what was expected he threw his shield arm wide and, as Lorenz dropped onto him, rammed his sword arm upwards, the heel of his gloved fist smashing into the rim of the man's helm. Lorenz's head snapped back with such force that he fell away, losing his grip on his knife.

This time he had no chance to roll clear because it was Blackstone who laid his weight across him. Lorenz bucked but could not shift him. Blackstone's arm was now free of its shield and his forearm pressed against the younger man's throat. Lorenz struggled for breath from the weight on his chest. He was being choked to death. His strength deserted him. Blackstone watched as the light faded from his eyes. He pulled off his gauntlets and freed Wolf Sword from the knot. 'Not yet,' he spat at the groggy man. 'You don't die this easily.'

Lorenz recovered and began to fight again. Blackstone almost lost his grip now his hands were bare on the blood-slicked armour. 'You sent the assassin who killed my wife and daughter and you thought I would never find you because you lived in the shadows. But I am here and I told you that when you die you would have my face close to yours,' Blackstone said, holding the wide-eyed man under him, pinning his struggling arms beneath his knees. His leg wound felt as though muscle was being torn from bone, but Blackstone welcomed the pain. It poured strength into his hands as he reached inside the man's helm and gripped his face and squeezed. Lorenz's heels kicked and he tried to buck. But Blackstone's hands were those of a stonemason and of a fighting man. He felt Lorenz's jaw break. The man screamed.

Antonio Lorenz half raised himself in agony, and gazed up in horror. The last thing the Lord of Milan's son saw in his life was the scar-faced Englishman sweeping Wolf Sword down onto his neck.

Like forsaken souls reluctant to leave their earth-bound world the shrouds of mist clung to the vast plain where Thomas

Blackstone stood over his vanquished enemy. Bernabò Visconti would soon have his son's head in a bloodied sack.

Blackstone let the tension drain from him. He offered a prayer that his murdered wife and child would now find peace. As he limped towards his waiting horse he thought he heard the laughter of angels, but it was only the lilting sound of music from a city in the far distance heralding a new beginning.

HISTORICAL NOTES

When Edward III invaded France in October 1359 he did so with a final determination to seize the French crown that he believed was rightfully his. The Second Treaty of London which he had secured from the French King had not been ratified by the interim French government. Three years earlier his son, Edward of Woodstock, Prince of Wales, had defeated the French King John II at Poitiers and taken him prisoner. It was a magnificent victory, one that overshadowed even that of Crécy in 1346. The English army, with Welsh longbowmen and Gascon men-at-arms, had once been the underdog of Europe but the defeat at Crécy of the greatest army in Christendom by this upstart English King shocked the whole of Europe. Edward's fortunes were in the ascendancy. He was an extremely able military leader who fought alongside his men (as did his son the Prince of Wales) and was complemented by loyal and experienced commanders. His army was well disciplined and fought with efficiency and skill. The French King was ransomed for a huge amount – an equivalent then of £600,000. After Poitiers the treaty was signed giving Edward all the territory he demanded but the French King's son, Charles, the sickly Prince Regent in Paris, doggedly refused to accept the terms and conditions, perhaps thinking ahead to the day when he would rule because when that day came it was unlikely he would wish to be monarch of a country so reduced in size that it would have appeared little more than a vassal of England.

Despite King John II's agreement to the treaty the Dauphin's refusal to implement it left Edward little choice other than to invade. The army that left England on that October day was already a month behind its proposed date of invasion. Shipping 10,000 men, horses and equipment was an enormous undertaking – and needed 1,000 carts and teams to be taken across the Channel in 1,100 ships. This vast, impressive undertaking was not paid for by the Treasury but by the King himself. King Edward set sail with all his sons. The Prince of Wales was already an experienced fighter and no doubt Edward wanted to have his other sons, Lionel, John and Edmund, win their spurs.

The invasion force landed at Calais on 28 October 1359 and on 4 November marched south in three divisions. The King led the main body of the army, the Prince of Wales shadowed him on a parallel course and the Duke of Lancaster took the middle route. Beset by supply problems from the start (even a thousand carts of supplies could not sustain an army longer than a couple of weeks), Edward had hoped to forage across the countryside but the Dauphin's plan of resistance was simple: abandon villages and farms, burn everything, deny the enemy any comfort. Walled towns were well defended and no French army appeared on the horizon. By December the English army had reached Rheims, the city where kings were traditionally crowned. If Edward hoped to seize the city and have himself crowned there he had not reckoned on its stalwart commander Gaucher de Châtillon, who was from one of the most prominent families in Champagne and a determined fighter. The English divisions attacked unsuccessfully, most progress being made by the Prince of Wales's men. But by January Edward had abandoned the siege.

Small towns did not fare as well. The Duke of Lancaster's men fought their way across defensive positions and with scaling ladders captured the town of Cernay. It was this operation that gave me the idea to have Thomas Blackstone seize the fictional town of Cormiers, but he needed a more important reason than merely securing food and drink. I had read that the Dauphin, safe behind the walls of Paris, struggled to fund troops beyond the city walls and it occurred to me that seizing gold coin fitted the bill, especially as the Constable of France was scouring the land for money to pay off independent captains whose routiers (mercenaries) plagued the countryside. So desperate were the French for money that the royal Lieutenant, Jean de Boucicaut, took over a local mint to pay his troops. Having Blackstone seize the gold for Edward gave me the perfect motive.

France was being devastated. Routiers and Englishmen roamed the land, stripping whatever the French themselves had not taken or destroyed. When Blackstone and his men set out for the fictional town of Balon to save the life of Killbere, the English army had already gone further south into the abundant landscape of Burgundy. For the large sum of 200,000 *moutons*, the duchy bought off the English with the promise of a three-year truce from Edward whose army could now fill their bellies.

The Picard nobleman Jean de Neuville had, in the meantime, led a small invasion force of a couple of thousand men to try and rescue King John. They landed on the English south coast and made their way to Winchelsea where they killed all those who had not had time to escape. English troops finally reached de Neuville's men and saw them off but Edward considered this assault as an act of betrayal against a signed treaty. I therefore used this attempt to rescue the French King as motivation to spur Edward on to besiege Paris. While the Pope's envoys were in conference with the English on Good Friday Edward launched an attack on the village of Orly, five miles from the conference centre. Half the population were massacred in the parish church. When Blackstone defies the Prince of Wales and refuses to attack civilians at the town of Arpajon he takes the more difficult choice of attacking the Benedictine priory that had been turned into a fortress by French troops. Records show that when some of the population sought refuge in the nearby church and decided to surrender to the English, French soldiers set fire to the church and nearly a thousand people died. As the survivors clambered down to the ground the English troops from the Prince of Wales's division killed them.

The English army burned and killed their way through the outer suburbs of Paris getting ever closer to the city walls. But the

Dauphin still refused to come out and face his enemy. Why should he? He was safe inside Paris and knew that even if the English breached the walls they would die in their thousands in the city streets. It was agreed that sixty French knights would fight thirty newly dubbed knights. One of them, Richard Baskerville, was unhorsed but saved and the thirty went on to defeat the French.

The English supply route failed and the weather – it was one of the worst winters for years: rain poured down for weeks on end, turning roads into quagmires – suddenly unleashed one of the most violent storms of the era as King Edward withdrew south from Paris and took the road to Chartres. A massive thunderstorm broke on Monday 13 April 1360. The English army was caught on the open plain without shelter. Enormous hailstones killed thousands of men and horses and this 'Black Monday' convinced Edward that his war had now offended God, and historical records suggest that it was the Duke of Lancaster's counsel that helped Edward decide to sue for peace.

I had used Simon Bucy, counsellor to King John before his capture, who was also adviser to the Dauphin, as a character in *Gate of the Dead*, and in *Viper's Blood* I decided to extend his influence in the negotiations between the Dauphin and the Visconti of Milan. They brokered a deal to raise the King's ransom money by selling the Dauphin's eleven-year-old sister, Princess Isabelle, in a marriage to Gian Galeazzo, the eight-year-old son of the despot of Milan, Galeazzo II Visconti.

When the Prince of Wales gave Blackstone a bill of safe passage I copied the Prince's words from 'the Jodrell Pass', which is the oldest surviving English army pass; it was given to an English archer, William Jaudrell, granting him leave from the Prince of Wales's army. The only elements I altered were the date and the name on the pass.

Historically Princess Isabelle was sent under escort from Paris to Milan via Chambéry, home of the transalpine prince, Count Amadeus VI of Savoy. At this time the plague had returned to Savoy and Lombardy and the Princess's journey faltered when she fell ill with a fever. For a time it was thought she had contracted the pestilence but fortunately she had not, and recovered sufficiently to travel over the Alps across the Mont Cenis route.

Count Amadeus VI was known as the Green Count from the days when he was knighted at the age of nineteen and had appeared at tournaments wearing green plumes and green silk over his armour. His sister, Bianca, had married Galeazzo Visconti so there was a connection between the two families. The Vipers of Milan were despots who ruled Milan (and surrounding towns and cities) by fear. The two brothers shared the rule of Milan although Galeazzo preferred to spend more time in his palace at Pavia, south of the city. He was responsible for great building projects, the founding of a university and a vast library. Galeazzo was the more diplomatically ambitious of the two. Bernabò Visconti was a complex man: educated, well read, but more volatile than his brother, his life was essentially consumed by debauchery and hunting. He was renowned for keeping five thousand hunting dogs in the city and woe betide anyone who caused suffering or neglect to these beasts. Both brothers have gone down in history as inventing the *quaresima* – forty days of torture inflicted on a victim. It began with a flogging, then a day's rest, another flogging, another rest, then limbs would gradually be removed – a hand, a foot, nose, ears, always a day's rest, until on the fortieth day, every limb having gone and most of the features, the victim was finally beheaded. I wonder, though, whether anyone could have survived for so long.

It was some years after the time of *Viper's Blood* when Bernabò attempted to kill his brother's son and limit that side of the family's influence, but this rivalry gave me the idea for Bernabò trying to thwart his brother's ambitions of marrying into the French royal family by killing Princess Isabelle.

When Thomas Blackstone and his men rode into Milan they entered through one of the eastern gates: the Porta Tosa. (This gateway was renamed Porta Vittoria but is now just a piazza.) The bas-relief of the medieval woman raising her skirts and about to trim her pubic hair with shears is from the twelfth century. It was removed from the *porta* by Cardinal Borromeo in the fifteenth century and is now in the city's Castello Sforzesco. Various legends exist about the image: one is that during a siege by Barbarossa (in the twelfth century) the vastly outnumbered Milanese thought their city would fall. A young woman climbed the ramparts and exposed herself to the attacking army and began to shave herself. The awestruck enemy dropped their weapons and retreated home. Another explanation is that when the Milanese asked Constantinople for financial assistance following Frederick Barbarossa's sack of Milan in 1162, their request was refused. The Milanese affixed the marble bas-relief to this eastern, Constantinople-facing *porta* as an insult to the Eastern Emperor.

The coded words used to introduce Blackstone to Father Torellini's informant: *Worldly fame is nothing but a breath of wind...* is a quote from the Italian poet Dante Alighieri's *Divine Comedy*: *Purgatory*, Canto XI, lines 100–2.

In avenging the death of his wife and daughter Blackstone was acting legally because of the Italian adherence to vendetta – although of course the Visconti were never going to give him a chance to exercise it. In law injuries to one member of a family were construed as injuries to all; they 'belonged' to the clan and could be avenged. *All of the family take up offensive weapons, for the injury done to one stains the whole house*, wrote one fourteenth-century lawyer. That obligation did not die with an injured party.

Whether Thomas Blackstone's act of revenge ended the vendetta remains to be seen.

I always welcome comments and can be contacted via my website: www.davidgilman.com; or on my author's Facebook page: https://www.facebook.com/davidgilman.author; and for those who are more fleet of foot: https://twitter.com/davidgilmanuk.

ACKNOWLEDGEMENTS

My thanks to Captain David Whitmore of the Shire Bowmen (Shire Bowmen, a free company of Roving Archers) and Patrick Hutchinson, readers of the *Master of War* series, both of whom are practising longbow archers and who spent time kindly answering my questions regarding the correct description for when bowmen are placed in enfilade.

So many of my readers contact me via my website or on social media about Thomas Blackstone's adventures, and their generous comments are welcome and appreciated, as are those who post reviews on sites such as Amazon and Goodreads.

I have the good fortune of being edited by Richenda Todd, who is as sharp as a bodkin point and, although she no longer puts me through the *quaresima*, takes no prisoners and always makes excellent suggestions that improve elements of my storytelling, as does my agent Isobel Dixon. My thanks to the team at Blake Friedmann Literary Agency who enthusiastically continue to sell Thomas Blackstone's adventures into other countries. Finally, my thanks and appreciation go to my publisher, Nic Cheetham and his team at Head of Zeus, whose unflagging passion for the *Master of War* series keeps the books' momentum going forward, rather like Thomas Blackstone on the field of battle.

David Gilman
Devonshire
2016

Turn the page for an exclusive preview of
the fifth book in the *Master of War* series

SCOURGE
— OF —
WOLVES

DAVID GILMAN

Coming in February 2018

After twenty-three years of fighting King Edward III has agreed a treaty and released the French monarch from captivity in England allowing him to return home. France is in chaos, flayed by mercenary bands, a situation which initially suits Edward as it keeps the French King from regaining control. But the vast tracts of territory gained by the English need to be claimed – by force if necessary. French cities and towns' loyalties cleave them to their own King but reluctantly one by one they succumb and agree to be ruled by the English. But not all towns are so easily convinced. Belligerent lords and self-serving mercenary captains refuse. Thomas Blackstone and the renowned knight and King's negotiator Sir John Chandos are tasked with bringing the recalcitrant defaulters under English control.

Outnumbered and still hunted by the French, Thomas Blackstone and his men face betrayal and a final suicidal mission.

PROLOGUE

Leicester, England
March 1361

King Edward III stood at the entrance to the room where Henry of Grosmont, Duke of Lancaster, the King's lifelong friend and adviser, lay dying. Lancaster raised his hand to stop the King from entering his bedchamber, fearing that the plague that had once again started its journey of death across Europe had now reached him.

Edward hesitated. He was blessed by God in victory and peace, should he challenge his own divine good fortune? He strode into the room and pulled the embroidered stool towards his friend's bed. The servants had been dismissed the moment the King mounted the stairs. What was going to be spoken between these two old warriors was as private as any confessional. No whispers were to filter down towards waiting servants.

'No, my lord. I beg you. I know not what ails me but it will take me. Step away.'

Edward reached out a hand and clasped his friend's. 'Age will bear us all away when it is good and ready, Henry. It is all in God's hands.'

The dying man wheezed. 'I am glad it takes me before you, sire. I would not bear the grief were it otherwise.'

Edward squeezed his friend's cold hand. 'So many battles, so many victories and so many of us leaving less than our own shadow on the land,' said Edward.

'You're wrong.'

'We are never wrong. We are the King,' said Edward, smiling.

'Ah, were it so, eh? No struggle with our own conscience or with those who would try to defeat us by fair means or foul.' Lancaster relented and reached out to grip the King's arm. 'You bless this realm with a burning sunlight that will cast your shadow across this great nation for lifetimes to come.'

Edward smiled compassionately at his ailing friend. How much time was there for any of them? The peace with France was barely delivered; more trials and contests would come their way. But those who had been at Edward's side since he seized the throne as a boy were becoming fewer and fewer in number.

'What is it we can do for you?'

Lancaster shook his head. 'Nothing for me, Edward. Everything for England.'

The King's gaze settled on the man who had been at his side since those early days. Lying on his deathbed the renowned duke's abiding thought was of the nation he had helped Edward build.

'A month past we saw the portents, the lights in the sky, the eclipse. They say the rain turned to blood in Boulogne. It heralds hard times again, Edward. The pestilence comes more quickly than the dawn. You must look to who can control the territories you have fought so hard for.'

'Our firstborn, Edward, will govern Aquitaine. Lionel will go to Ireland. The Scottish already give us their allegiance.'

'And your sons and those they command will serve you well, but our old fraternity is lost. Brave Northampton is dead; Thomas Holland, Reginald Cobham is ailing and many others are frail, taken one by one as night steals away the day. All gone. And I soon to follow. You have pursued your ambition, Edward. You have achieved greatness for this kingdom and such an inheritance must have its guardian. When the time comes who among the many leads by common consent? A man of loyalty who will speak his mind even at great risk to himself.'

Lancaster gave Edward a querying look. The King knew full well of whom he spoke.

'Blackstone,' said the King quietly.

Lancaster smiled. 'As you said, dear friend. You are never wrong.'

PART ONE

IN THE KING'S NAME

Limousin, France
November–December 1361

CHAPTER ONE

Thomas Blackstone's men rode to their death.

As they eased their horses through the town's narrow streets, Sir Gilbert Killbere saw the frightened faces of the townspeople who moments before had cheered their arrival. Some quickly turned away in panic, others scuttled behind pillars. Killbere knew immediately that they had been lured into a trap by the ill-named Breton lord, Bernard de Charité who commanded the citadel of St. Aubin la Fère. Before he could call out a warning crossbowmen appeared on the walls and the first bolts struck home. Horses reared, men fell. An animal-like cry soared up from the citizens as lust for the Englishmen's death twisted their features. Some dared to dash forward onto the bloodied ground and seize the fallen men's weapons. Soldiers appeared from the side streets and shop doorways and roughly pushed the townsmen aside and plunged sword and knife into Blackstone's wounded and dying men.

Killbere heeled his mount as his sword slashed two soldiers reaching up for him. Swinging the blade in swift practised arcs he slew three more as his warhorse kicked and turned. Killbere was no stranger to the melee of war. He had fought at Blackstone's side since the boy became a man and together they had taken part in every great battle and victory the English had secured in France and Italy. Now he knew he was going to die in a piss-stinking alleyway. Swordsmen jabbed low and thrust their blades deep into his horse's flanks and chest. Killbere cursed as he crashed down into the mud. He twisted his body desperately trying to parry the blows that assaulted him. His shield ripped free from its saddle ties as the wild-eyed horse bellowed in agony. He rammed his sword upwards into the groin of one of his attackers, the pain making him barge into the others. Killbere twisted and slithered, hauled the shield across his body and felt the heavy impact as a mace slammed into it. A blade jabbed at his side, he danced away, struck out at the man's ankles feeling the steel cut deeply through unprotected flesh. The man fell writhing, obstructing the attackers, his screams joining the cacophony of pain that echoed off the town's walls.

One of the attackers threw himself across Killbere's shield, smothering him with his weight as others grabbed his arms and yanked him upright. They had him now. Sweat and blood stung his eyes. He saw Blackstone's men going down from the overwhelming assault. Jack Halfpenny's archers had no chance to unsheath their war bows so the battle-hardened men, the backbone of King Edward's army, fought with archer's knife, sword and raw courage. An English archer's bow served little use in such a confined place. Crossbowmen were better suited for close quarter ambush and de Charité had used them well. Killbere saw the young ventenar jig left and right, crying out for the twenty archers he commanded to fall back, but most were already dead or dying and Halfpenny made one last desperate assault on the two men who cornered him. His archer's strength gave him the advantage and he smashed his left fist into one man's face, half turned on his heel, slashing the long archer's knife across the other's throat. Killbere struggled, brought up an elbow and felt bone break in his attacker's face. In that split second he saw Halfpenny take a stride towards him. The lad was already wounded in his side but seeing Killbere being held had urged him to come to his aide.

'No!' bellowed Killbere. 'Get Thomas!' The warning shout was barely made when those who held him clubbed him to the ground. The last thing Killbere saw before a sickening darkness engulfed him was Jack Halfpenny running for his life. If anyone had a chance to escape it was the lithe archer. That, at least, gave the old fighter a sense of satisfaction.

By nightfall the lifeless bodies of Thomas Blackstone's men hung from the gibbet in the town's square. Every man displayed evidence of the wounds received from the betrayal and ambush by the town's lord. Shadows danced in the torchlight as St Aubin's men and women, relieved from the usual curfew, were permitted to strike the dead with knives and staves, making the corpses sway from the assault and desecration. Nineteen more of Blackstone's fighters dangled outside of the high town walls as a warning from Bernard de Charité. Halfpenny had escaped the slaughter. A hue and cry had echoed around the walls. He clasped a hand over the wound in his side and forced himself to run hard and fast despite the pain. He had run through the labyrinthine alleys until he found a niche in a wall that he could just squeeze into. When darkness fell he concealed his bow in a narrow crevice between pillar and lintel. It had been his father's war bow and its heartwood that bent beneath father and son's hand was as precious to Jack Halfpenny as was the memory of the man who had taught him the skill to use it. Pushing aside his regret he made his way through the shadows until he reached the high walls. Once the night watch had turned their backs to cheer on the brutality being inflicted against the corpses in the square below, he skirted the parapet. Grasping the hemp rope that held the dangling body of one of his men on the outside wall he lowered himself down. Twenty feet down the man's body sagged as Halfpenny clutched at the corpse's clothing. Dried blood soiled the gaping mouth and swollen tongue, half severed by his teeth when the noose tightened. Halfpenny turned his face away from the man he had once commanded. He hoped his weight would not tear the man's head from his neck as he slithered down the corpse, using it to gain extra length before being obliged to release his grip and plunge into the dense briar patch thirty feet below. Praying that the scattered moonlight did not conceal rocks beneath the thick foliage he released his hold on the dead man and fell into the night.

The following day's weak sun failed to burn away the mist that clung to the frost-covered land. Ignoring the morning chill and the skin-splitting roughness of the stone they handled, Perinne and Meulon worked alongside their men as they hefted stone onto the defensive wall of a ruined building. The rising ground gave the derelict barn a commanding position over the surrounding countryside. They were twelve miles from where the ambush took place and, even though the shelter was temporary, Blackstone had demanded a low defensive wall be built. He and his men were tasked by the King's negotiator Sir John Chandos with securing towns ceded to King Edward in the peace treaty. At each village or town the burghers were called upon to give their allegiance to the English King. Some bemoaned what was asked of them, but eventually agreed when they gazed down from their walls at the battle-hardened men who made the demand. Others quickly saw the advantage of being under the protection of a strong warrior King while their own recently released monarch languished in Paris, bankrupt and sorely pressed to gain back control over what was left of his kingdom. France was soured by destroyed crops, poisoned wells and bitterness of defeat. Mercenaries who had fought on both sides of the war ravaged what little food and supplies remained. Towns were held to ransom and some French lords resisted until money was exchanged and then loyalties were switched with remarkable ease. Those who resisted the most were mercenaries who served the Breton lords. A civil war raged in Brittany and lands as far as the Limousin and Poitou were held by each of the warring factions. St Aubin la Fère was one such town. Payment had been agreed for the Breton lord to turn over the town and for the burghers to swear allegiance to the English Crown. Sir Gilbert Killbere had taken twenty archers and as many hobelars into the fortified town to deliver the payment and receive their signed agreement.

'There!' said Perinne, squinting into the morning sun, pointing to a lone figure emerging from the mist and stumbling across the open ground a half mile away. The men stopped work and watched the man stagger, raise an arm and fall. Caution made the men hesitate. The woodland that lay three hundred paces to the man's flank might conceal an enemy. Whoever it was that had fallen could be bait for a trap. A warhorse jumped the low wall, scattering the men. Its dappled black coat looked as though it had been singed by a fire's embers, part of the reason for its reputation of having been sired in hell.

'It's Jack!' cried Blackstone as he spurred the bastard horse on. Meulon and Perinne grabbed their weapons and ran after Blackstone. Perinne's eye caught the fluttering wings of the raptor that suddenly beat its way skywards from the forest. It made no sound until it found an up draught that spiralled it above Blackstone's race towards the fallen Halfpenny. Perinne's heart shuddered, not from exertion but from a long held belief that the screech of the buzzard beckoned death as it called for a man's soul. And now it circled above Blackstone.

As the men ran forward Will Longdon rallied the men behind the defensive wall. 'Stand ready!' Blackstone's centenar, Will Longdon ordered. Archers and men-at-arms swiftly readied themselves for any attack that might surge from the woodland.

Feet crunching on the hard frost, their breath billowing, Meulon and Perinne reached the fallen man at the same time as Blackstone's squire. John Jacob had caught up to them with one of the packhorses. Blackstone's belligerent mount would never allow another to be put onto its back and if Jack Halfpenny lived then he needed a horse to bring him into the protective wall of the old barn.

'He's alive,' cried Blackstone and picked up the unconscious man as if he were a child. John Jacob steadied the horse as Blackstone draped the wounded man over its withers. Meulon and Perinne had gone twenty paces beyond them, ready to guard against anyone who might have been in pursuit of their fallen comrade. If the buzzard's alarm was a portent of death for Thomas Blackstone then the forest might cloak the enemy.

Blackstone led his horse alongside John Jacob's slow moving mount which now carried Halfpenny. Once Perinne and Meulon were satisfied there was no ambush they raced to join the others. Perinne kept glancing skyward but the raptor had disappeared as quickly as it had appeared. As the five men made their way back to safety the squire glanced at Blackstone.

'If Jack has made it back what of Sir Gilbert?'

Blackstone looked around at the gentle undulating landscape. The countryside was plagued with routiers and it was easy to be caught in the open. 'Meulon, you and Perinne run ahead and take ten men back a couple of miles,' he said. 'Scout out the forester's tracks through the woods. If there's no sign of the others get back here quickly. And tell Will to ready a bed for Jack. He needs his wound attending to.'

The Norman spearman's hulking frame ran with Perinne at his side. The cold air from his breath freckled the big man's beard with frost.

Blackstone laid a hand on the unconscious man as the horse's gait swayed. 'They might have run into skinners,' he said. Some of the mercenary bands roamed in their hundreds and a small detachment of men such as that led by Killbere could have been overwhelmed. France was more dangerous now than when the English fought the French armies. Violence swept across the unprotected towns and villages and the slaughter would continue until King Edward claimed what was rightfully his, until the French King had reached an agreement with those who committed such violence without fear of retribution. Or were foolish enough to believe they could cause harm to any of Thomas Blackstone's men with impunity. 'But if those bastards at St Aubin have betrayed us I swear I'll burn it to the ground and kill every last one of them.'

CHAPTER TWO

Jack Halfpenny had quickly regained consciousness when nurtured with Will Longdon's broth and the young archer's gash in his side had been treated and bound. No longer did those who served with Blackstone pack their wounds with cow dung and grass because they had learnt better ways to treat their injuries from a woman who had once been thought a witch. She had been a herbalist and accompanied Blackstone when, a year before, he had gone into Milan to kill the man responsible for ordering the death of his wife and child. The so-called Witch of Balon had taught the men well and shown them how to gather plants and herbs, even in winter, and to dress wounds without bleeding the wounded. That she had died under her own hand to save Blackstone made the men honour her memory. Halfpenny had insisted on the slash in his side to be bound tightly and insisted riding with Blackstone despite his hurt. Once Halfpenny had recounted the betrayal anger swept through Blackstone's camp. Men seethed with vengeance. They wanted St Aubin razed to the ground. Blades were sharpened and talk was of the slaughter to come. They waited, alert and impatient, at the camp while Blackstone took his captains to reconnoitre the town's defences.

On the edge of a forest in the shade of its bare branches Blackstone and his men lay on the cold ground. They ignored their discomfort as they studied the walls of St Aubin. Their friends' bodies still hung there in a grotesque symbol of defiance against the English King. Halfpenny squatted next to his captain Will Longdon and Blackstone who had questioned him carefully about Killbere's fate but the archer could only recite what he saw. Killbere had been beaten into the dirt.

'We rode in through the east gate. Bernard de Charité stood on the gatehouse wall and welcomed us. Said he accepted the payment for the town and would sign the treaty himself.'

Will Longdon spat. 'Now the whore-son has taken the payment and killed my archers.'

'And the men-at-arms,' said Blackstone quietly without censure, keeping his attention on the high walls behind which half of his force had been betrayed and slaughtered.

'Aye, I wasn't forgetting them,' admitted Blackstone's centenar who despite his rank had had only sixty archers under his command, a number now reduced to forty. Those twenty dead men who could loose a dozen and more yard-long bodkin-tipped shafts in rapid succession were precious resources lost to any group of fighting men. The men-at-arms who laboured in hand-to-hand combat stank of sweat and piss as they took the fight to their enemy, but an archer, merciful Christ, Will Longdon crossed himself, an archer was worth his weight in gold and no other man's stench ever smelled sweeter. 'But our bowmen, Thomas, they can't be replaced as easily as a man-at-arms.'

Blackstone looked back at him. Longdon shrugged. The truth was the truth. 'A man like Sir Gilbert was worth ten men-at-arms, Will, let's not forget that,' said Blackstone and then crawled back deeper into the woodland as Perinne and Meulon's scouts reported back.

One of the captains, the German man-at-arms Renfred, shook his head. 'There is no way to scale those walls, Sir Thomas. Fifty feet high at least and over there...' he gestured to where he had just returned from his reconnaissance, 'they have cut the forest back even further. Open ground for at least four hundred yards. If they don't invite us in then I cannot see how we breach the walls. There's a lake that covers the other half of the town. No drawbridge. No postern gate to give access to the water.'

John Jacob studied the battlements and took the twig he was chewing to point out the irregular shape of the town's defences. 'And even if we got under their walls with ladders they would have us in enfilade. Their crossbowmen would cut us down as we assembled the ladders.'

'And we cannot get close enough to mine the walls,' said Meulon.

'This is why Chandos wanted it under the King's control. It's a stronghold worth depriving his enemies of,' said Blackstone. His stonemason's eye studied the walls. They were of recycled stone, a usual means of building up fortifications over the years. They didn't require the skill of a stonemason's cut, but that of sufficiently experienced men to lay the stone with mortar. The walls at St Aubin were well built. The skill of earlier stonemasons who once cut stone for another building nearby, probably a manor house or convent, benefited those who came later. Demolish the old and rebuild the new. Good walls but once Blackstone was inside them he knew how to bring them down, even though John Chandos and the King wanted the fortress to remain intact.

'Jack?' he said turning to the bandaged archer who sat propped against a tree, his hand pressing the wound that still seeped blood. 'What can you remember about the layout? How do we get to de Charité's keep?'

Halfpenny's brow furrowed. He shook his head. 'Like a whore's heart, Sir Thomas. Impossible to reach. A portcullis after the main gate, winding streets. Alleyways and small cloisters running along the street. Some of the merchants plied their wares under it. Stalls and suchlike. I remember them selling bread off the one. That smell of baked bread was the last thing I remember before the killing started.'

'Then they've enough grain and fuel for their ovens,' said Will Longdon. 'They'll have months' worth to withstand a siege.'

'No one's going to lay siege,' said Blackstone. 'I want to get inside the whore's heart and cut it out. Jack?'

Halfpenny nodded, knowing the more he could recall the better their chance would be of successfully storming the town. He knew from experience that his archer's eye always took in more than he realized at first. 'Houses are tightly packed on the one side of the street they took us down. That's where they ambushed us. We couldn't turn the horses. We had no chance and Sir Gilbert had men swarming over him. We fought as best we could but when I tried to reach him he commanded me to escape. I hid in a small overhang, that's where I left my bow,' he said glancing at Will Longdon. ' I don't want any barrel bow,' he insisted, his passion for his own war bow greater than any of the army's replacements, all painted white and packed in barrels. 'Mine belonged to my father and I want it back,' said Halfpenny.

Blackstone placed a hand on his shoulder. 'And you will, but we need to know more.' He turned back into the forest. 'Renfred, take me to the north walls. I want to see for myself.'

The men skirted St Aubin along foresters' tracks. What they saw convinced Blackstone that an assault would be impossible without a greater force prepared to suffer casualties. By the time they reached the edge of the lake it was obvious that the Lord of St Aubin had been blessed with a surrounding landscape that offered him maximum security. As Renfred had said the open ground was cleared back to the forest by four hundred yards and where the men now huddled in the dank gloom of the forest, the frozen lake stretched the same distance to the base of the sheer walls.

Halfpenny pointed towards the imposing walls. 'After I hid there were steps close by that took me up to the wallhead. They hanged the lands from the walkway behind the parapet. I looked over those walls when I escaped but knew I couldn't drop down into the lake. I'd have died under the ice. That's why I went over the south wall.' He turned to look at the walls and the bodies that still hung there. In the centre of the wall was a window forty feet up. 'That window, that's for a kitchen. It's a big place and on the other side is a walkway like a narrow bridge across the street below. It connects the kitchen to the main house. It leads through the pantry on this side and the buttery on the other. Once you're through that passage you're into the great hall.'

'How could you know that?' said John Jacob.

'I was lying in an alcove beneath that walkway. I could hear everything that was being said by the servants. I could smell the food and heard what was to be taken where. They were laughing, talking about how de Charité had fooled us. They were leaving their duties to go down into the square. They took ladles, kitchen knives, and cleavers. Sir Thomas, I saw what they did to the men they hanged. The lord of the town let the people mutilate and beat them. Two of my wounded men, Haskyn and Fowler were chased around the square until they were hacked to death. The crowd pissed on their bodies before they died. Those bastards in St Aubin hate the English.'

'And I will give them an even greater reason,' said Blackstone. 'But you didn't see Sir Gilbert's body?'

'No. I saw him struck down, but nothing more.'

'The King wants that town, Sir Thomas,' said Meulon. 'It's important to him. Him and Sir John.'

'Aye, well sometimes the King can't always have what he wants,' added Will Longdon. 'And Sir John Chandos might be a Knight of the Garter and the King's negotiator with these scum but he can kiss my arse if he thinks we've ladders long enough to clamber up any of them walls with their crossbowmen picking us off. And that ice wouldn't take the weight of a fairy's fart let alone men and ladders.'

'Your arse could be offered to them as a target while we assault the south walls. What say you, Sir Thomas?' said Meulon.

'Sir Gilbert kicked Will's backside often enough and I suspect he'd like to do it again. If he still lives. So we had better keep Will's arse in his breeches.' Blackstone and his captains eased back into the trees where the horses were tethered. 'We have to take the town and Sir John is due to join us tomorrow. We need his men.'

A coldness gripped his chest which had nothing to do with the chilled air. To picture his men butchered was a bitterness to be eased only by the desire to avenge them, but to think of Killbere being slain in such a fashion put steel into his heart. His mind's eye saw the French *Oriflamme*, the great war standard raised in battle against the English. He wished he had seized it when he struck out at the French King at Poitiers. He would raise it now. It signalled no quarter.

HOW TO GET YOUR FREE EBOOK

MASTER OF WAR

TO CLAIM YOUR FREE EBOOK OF
MASTER OF WAR

1. FIND THE CODE

This is the last word on page 350 of this book, preceded by
HOZ-, for example HOZ-code

2. GO TO HEADOFZEUS.COM/FREEBOOK

Enter your code when prompted

3. FOLLOW THE INSTRUCTIONS

Enjoy your free eBook of *MASTER OF WAR*